There was an undercurrent of menace in his voice.

Kate held her tongue. Her mind had at last begun to churn. She was lucid enough to stop herself before she revealed just how much she and Josh had discovered. Thrasher was stupid enough to underestimate her because she was a woman. Well, let him.

But for her own self-respect she couldn't leave without a parting salvo. He could do nothing further to her. "You're a little man in a big job, Mr. Thrasher. Someday soon someone's going to discover that."

His control shattered. "Get out of here, you bitch," he spat.

Kate's hand touched the doorknob as Thrasher rose.

"And I warn you that if you pursue this you'll wish you never had. You hear me? I'll have you fixed permanently! "

Kate slammed the door behind her. She found herself breathing hard and shaking slightly. Her legs were unsteady. Somehow she found her way to the elevator. Only when the paneled doors slid shut did the realization hit her that she was no longer employed. . . .

A WHISPER
OF
TREASON

Sandy London

FAWCETT GOLD MEDAL • NEW YORK

ACKNOWLEDGMENTS

Howie Solow, Shifu (master of kung fu)

Warren Koster, attorney-at-law

Ray Giannelli, an engineer of varied interests

Peter Lingard, freight forwarder of note

A Fawcett Gold Medal Book
Published by Ballantine Books
Copyright © 1991 by Sandy London

Library of Congress Catalog Card Number: 91-91814

ISBN 0-449-14694-4

Manufactured in the United States of America

First Edition: May 1991

Prologue

Kate left Colorado before the snows melted, before the birch and saplings leafed and the meadows turned shy spring green. There were no wildflowers below them as the plane took wing, only the stark cliffs of the mountains. And the memories, cold.

She stretched her hands out before her—long, tapered fingers, ringless. She should have kept the ring, she thought. But Kate had never been one to leave a chapter of her life unfinished. She wrote her epilogues and shut the door on the past. She had learned to do so with grace, her mother's daughter.

A succession of air bases around the world, a litany of good-byes. Stash what you could in a cardboard carton and leave the rest behind. Friendships lingered, sometimes for years, but it was easy to lock unbidden memories away when those who shared them disappeared from your life with regularity. She could tell herself that her childhood had been idyllic, a travelogue of exotic postings. The embarrassing moments of adolescence, first love, first drunk, first lustful fumbling in the darkness, faded easily. There was always another posting, a fresh start, a new and wiser Kate to begin again.

No one, nothing, had prepared her for loss, real loss. It had come with devastating suddenness. At the moment that love blooms like a flower and the petals unfold, releasing a natural sweetness that only lovers know, the winter snow had buried the blossom.

So Kate swallowed the ache and left the mountains, the deadly, haunting mountains.

Chapter

1

Ralph Payton's death was a mistake.

Those few who came to know the truth failed to see it as an omen of things to come. Officially it would always be supposed that the slim, graying little man died of a heart attack on that sultry night in mid-July.

He didn't.

Payton was the night watchman for a sprawling electronics plant on the west side of MacArthur Airport in rural Suffolk County, Long Island. The industrial park was a lonely stretch of territory after dark. Only the occasional approach or departure of aircraft disturbed the stillness.

Payton made a circuit of the factory every ten to twenty minutes, intentionally varying his pace. His professional unpredictability proved fatal. He always began in the front parking lot where the executives left their cars on weekdays. The night lights penetrated only a short distance into the darkness. He lost them as he rounded the corner and passed along the dim north side of the building.

At the rear of the factory were the loading docks. The great concrete bays sloped downward into darkness, large enough to accommodate three semis side by side. Beyond them was a ground-level entrance that Payton checked on each round. It was always locked. He would pause there on windless nights to smoke a cigarette. Camels, unfiltered, were his only vice. The arson squad said Payton's last cigarette ignited the fire.

A whisper of wind sprang up that night off the ocean to the south, but not enough to snuff a match. Payton paused at the rear entrance and lit up behind cupped hands. Out of habit he reached down and jiggled the door.

It opened. Payton froze. He almost dropped his smoke. He pushed the door in.

As the blow to his neck paralyzed him the cigarette did fall. Payton's body slumped inside the doorway. There was a smear of grease on the floor. Eager hands quickly found additional fuel for the flames. The fire hopscotched through the building, leaping higher and growing to a roar; consuming work stations and walls, desks and filing cabinets, cables and computers; scorching that which would not burn.

But the conflagration took some time. In those minutes the arsonists selected what they wanted and slipped away in the night.

In retrospect perhaps Payton's death should have set in motion the chain of events. As it was his murder became a footnote in the larger scheme of things.

But it was neither murder nor arson that lit the fuse. It was a simple piece of paper.

Chapter

2

Kate Fleming rose early that Monday morning, full of expectation, a presentiment she did not understand. Normally she was a lie-abed, burrowing under the blankets until the last possible moment, then scurrying around to dress for work and catch the subway downtown.

But on that particular morning, she would remember looking back, she was up by six-thirty and had time for a leisurely cup of coffee. Something inside told Kate it was to be the last leisurely morning she would have for a long time.

She was right.

George Dexter cursed himself for not having gotten an early start. Six-thirty in the morning and the highways into New York City were already clogged. He'd be late with his delivery to the Brooklyn docks.

Screw the Japs, he thought. Didn't they make enough of their own electronic gizmos anyway? What would they be wanting with what he was pulling behind him? Screw the traffic. And screw the blonde who'd soused him up on coffee at the diner the night before.

Special recipe, she'd said. Tasted funny. Went down smooth. Two cups and he'd thought it was wonderful. Four cups and he'd thought she was wonderful. Five and he'd found himself in bed with her.

Wonderful stuff.

In the morning she was gone. He'd expected his pockets to be emptied, but nothing had been touched.

He was just god-awful late and had a god-awful headache.

4

Swearing off coffee for life, he had nursed a quick cup of tea for breakfast. The rig was where he'd parked it, the seals intact.

BATT, Inc., read the inscription under the familiar logo of the flying rodent, its ears attuned to high frequency signals. Bahía Alert Transmission Technologies, Electronics for the Future. He'd checked the cab. Nothing taken. Satisfied, he'd hit the highway.

A conscientious trucker, Dexter constantly monitored the traffic on all sides, anticipating trouble in order to avoid it. There were few other rigs at that hour. His vision was unobscured. He looked patronizingly down on the passenger vehicles as they weaved in and out, jostling for supposed advantage in the daily scramble for Manhattan. The tan sedan behind him struck Dexter as odd, for it never wavered. The last place to be in heavy traffic was behind a truck, because a driver couldn't see what he might be getting into. Maybe the heavyset man behind the wheel was just timid.

Traffic inched forward at the tolled entrance to the George Washington Bridge. It took nearly twenty minutes to get through. With relief he revved up his diesel and plowed ahead. When he glanced up at the rearview mirror the tan sedan was still there. They headed across the bridge.

Suddenly Dexter heard a muffled explosion somewhere beneath him. A warning light on his control panel flashed, indicating a failure in his pneumatic system. He pulled the cord to warn other drivers, but the horn only bleated feebly and lapsed into silence. He slid his foot off the accelerator and flipped on his flashers, trying to get into the right-hand lane. He imagined the traffic copter pilots droning messages all morning about a truck stalled on the inbound GW, snarling rush hour.

The tan sedan shot past him, sliding through lane spaces left by cautious commuters who had seen the truck's warning lights. It continued across at an angle straight for a yellow school bus with CAMP WINNEPAUPACK emblazoned on the sides.

The startled bus driver saw the car coming and swerved to avoid it, only to careen into the path of the helpless semi.

Dexter slammed on his brakes. Nothing happened. Momentum still carried him forward.

The last thing he remembered was a file of panicked little faces looking up at him.

Kate curled into the corner of the bench, grateful she had a seat on the subway. At this early hour the day's stench had just begun to build and was still bearable. She flipped through the sections of the *Times* on her lap as the train lurched its way through the tunnels downtown. She could never read on the subway; it made her sick. But one headline in the "Metro" section caught her eye.

The BATT factory on Long Island had burned Saturday night. Extensive damage, one death.

"Jeez Louise," Kate muttered under her breath. Nothing like coming back from vacation to a crisis.

The dust was still settling on the acquisition. Only four months earlier the family owners of BATT, Inc., had sold out to LTS, Ltd., a larger, also private electronics conglomerate, conveniently headquartered in the same downtown high rise. Kate wondered how a management not yet stabilized would handle an emergency.

The train squealed to a halt. Kate stuffed the paper in her briefcase and shoved her way out. Moving with the crowd she climbed the narrow stairwell to the street. Bus motors, screeching brakes, newsboys hawking papers: the city symphony engulfed her. She pushed into the echoing lobby of her building and waited for the elevator.

She wasn't looking forward to her return to the office, Kate admitted. She mourned the preacquisition days when international operations had been independent of domestic, when export sales had accounted for nearly twenty percent of the company revenue, high for an American company.

LTS, with no previous overseas activity, had decided to form an international department under the vice president of sales and marketing to centralize the export of both the BATT and LTS product lines. Submerged in the acquisition, foreign shipments now accounted for barely ten percent of total sales. Maybe her family was right. Maybe it was time to move on.

The elevator opened. Kate stepped in and worked her way to the back.

She'd hoped that a vacation would help restore some of her enthusiasm, for BATT, for New York, for life in general. Combined with the Fourth of July holiday she'd been gone two and a half weeks, not nearly long enough.

She forced a bright smile as the elevator door opened at her floor, but the sense of foreboding that had awakened her early remained.

"Good morning. Boy, am I glad to see you." The expression

on Veronica Reese's coffee-with-cream face was more of relief than joy. Her black eyes were somber.

Kate knew her administrative assistant well enough to gauge her moods. Today the normally cool Veronica was tense.

"Good morning. I won't go so far as to say I'm happy to be back, but leisure can be boring."

Veronica smiled. "Sorry. How was your vacation?"

"Idyllic, the way we all oughta live instead of being cooped up in this squirrel cage. Most of the time I had the cabin to myself. No TV, no traffic, no BATT . . ."

"No Steve," Veronica finished for her with a laugh.

"No Steve." And she hadn't missed her lawyer friend all that much either, she had to admit. "So how are things on the home front?"

Veronica raised her eyebrows. "Interesting. Very interesting."

"Have you seen the headlines?" Kate asked as she flipped the paper onto her assistant's desk.

"Um-hmm. This place is a nest of rumors this morning. Latest seems to be that the fire was started by a disgruntled employee squeezed out after the acquisition."

"Paper says it was an accident."

"So it says," Veronica said dryly.

"Do we have any orders pending from that plant?"

"Nope. The last of them went out last week. Unfortunately."

"Unfortunately?"

"While you were gone we shipped seven million dollars worth of goods on unconfirmed letters of credit."

For a moment Kate just stared at her, open-mouthed. "You must be kidding," she said at last.

"Uh-uh," Veronica said with a shake of her head. "Do you remember that weird order we got from Hong Kong, the one with the unconfirmed letter of credit from a client we'd never heard of?"

"Yes."

"Well, we got three more orders and three more L/C's from three more countries almost exactly like it."

A tingle of alarm started up Kate's spine. "And?"

"Cosentino insisted I ship them."

"Seven million dollars worth in two weeks? Since when are they so efficient in Washington to get export licenses out that fast?"

"Not one item on any of those orders required a validated license. Believe me—I checked."

"But we don't carry that much inventory," Kate said.

"We don't make all the components the clients requested either. Somebody found some mighty obliging suppliers. And all seven million bucks worth went right out the door."

"Oh, my God." Kate sat down in the chair beside Veronica's desk. "Seven million dollars we may never see. I think I need a cup of coffee before I hear any more."

That amount of money uncollected would have been disastrous for BATT. Even for LTS it would cause serious disruption.

"Welcome back," Veronica said. "The papers are on your desk in a file marked 'Paul Strikes Again.' I'll get your coffee."

While Veronica was gone, Kate eased herself into the chair behind the desk and surveyed the documentary evidence of potential disaster. It was beginning to look as if her sixth sense were right. Her alarm grew as she read.

In any successful business transaction there are two sides to the equation, transferring legal title to the goods from seller to buyer and making sure the seller "collects" or gets paid. In international business, letters of credit, documents issued by banks, are often used to protect the interests of both parties. An "unconfirmed" L/C could tip the balance and jeopardize collection. Just as Veronica had said, all four of these L/C's were unconfirmed. None of the shipments should have been allowed to go out.

Kate's first instinct was to trace them. Her first recourse was the freight forwarder, the company that had booked space on a steamship for the cargo and handled outgoing customs formalities. Maybe she could catch the goods before they left the country.

Normally BATT chose the forwarder it worked with, but in this instance all four of the clients had named the freight agent to be used. And every one of them had specified Webb Overseas. Kate had never heard of them. The phone number was on their letterhead.

As she reached for her phone Paul Cosentino swept through the doorway.

"Good morning, beautiful. Welcome back."

"Thank you, I think."

Without waiting to be asked, Cosentino flopped sideways into one of the two guest chairs facing the desk. At thirty-nine he still had the boyish blond good looks that kept the single secretaries in the office sighing.

Formerly southeast regional sales manager for LTS, Cosentino had been called in to head up the new export department and spearhead the introduction of the LTS product lines abroad. He was a pleasant enough individual, friendly, funny. He had the reputation of being the best salesperson LTS had, but he didn't even know where Thailand was.

Kate waited for her new boss to open the conversation. She sat back in her chair, hands clasped.

Cosentino's eyes flashed briefly around her office. He coveted this space, she knew, with its pine-paneled walls and single window overlooking Battery Park and the mouth of the Hudson beyond. Not all BATT executives had been forced into cubbyholes, she thought.

She'd spent a good part of her life in this office since becoming manager five years before, gradually filling it with little corners of herself. Most of the books on the library shelves were her own, not the company's: finance, marketing, a full row of bilingual dictionaries on different topics, histories of the countries she visited. She had filled spare wall space with prints collected in the Orient. She imagined that he would replace them with his own framed awards for salesmanship.

"Well," he said finally. "Aren't you going to congratulate me?"

"On what?"

"On the biggest month of export shipments in the history of this organization."

"Not until we get paid," she replied.

His smiled dimmed. "What do you mean?"

"Didn't you notice anything odd about those orders?"

"Odd?" Cosentino sat up and swung his feet to the floor. His smile returned. "Come on now, Kate. You're just jealous. You've never turned over orders like that before. Your total sales last year were only ten million. We just came close to that with only four shipments."

"I've turned over bigger orders, Paul, but only when I knew BATT was going to get paid."

"What makes you think we're not?"

She leaned forward across the desk. "Didn't it strike you as strange that all four orders were essentially the same and specified the same forwarder for routing? Or that all four L/C's were advised by the same bank in New York but that none were confirmed? Or that none of the merchandise ordered required an export license?''

He shrugged. "No license meant we could ship right away."

"BATT sells defense and security products, Paul, not consumer goods like LTS. Someone who knew precisely what he was doing would have to pick and choose his way very carefully through the BATT catalog to avoid needing an export license on orders that large. Believe me. I've been here five years and that just doesn't happen. The U.S. government is very picky about controlling who we sell our technology to.''

"What are you saying?'' he demanded.

"That something funny is going on, that I'm afraid we might not get paid. We've never heard of any of these customers and, according to our reps, neither have they.''

"Maybe your people just don't know their markets as well as they're supposed to,'' Cosentino said as he rose. He plucked one of the papers off the pile in front of her. It was a copy of the L/C for the Panamanian shipment. He waved it in her face.

"This little piece of paper says the bank is going to pay me, not the customer. I don't give a diddly damn who the customer is.'' He smiled and laid the photocopy on her desk.

"Which bank?'' Kate asked softly.

"Huh?''

"I asked which bank is going to pay you.''

"Hong Kong and Shanghai Bank right here in New York.''

" 'Fraid not,'' she said. "They just advised us of the L/C, they didn't confirm it. That means they're under absolutely no obligation to pay us a sou.''

"Ah, but they will. Banks can be trusted.''

"But it doesn't work that way, Paul. The bank here never undertook any such obligation. It's the bank overseas that will pay us if anyone does. And there's another queer thing. . . .''

"I don't want to hear it. The orders are gone. We were lucky enough to get them out before the fire. That seven million dollars in cash flow will come in very handy. If I were you I wouldn't buck it. Bob Thrasher is pleased as punch. This is the impetus we need to really build this division.'' He stopped, as if he had gone too far.

"Don't mess with what's done,'' he advised. "Just enjoy the rewards.'' He rose to leave. "Welcome back.''

Kate stared after him, baffled. Cosentino really didn't understand what she was talking about. He didn't know the difference between a letter of credit and his own bank balance.

But he was her boss now, she reflected with resignation.

Her phone rang. It was Steve. She should have expected it. She imagined him leaned back in his heavy leather chair, heels propped amid the jumble of briefs on his desk. It was his non-chalant pose, a practiced show of casualness from a man who was never casual. Everything about Steve was practiced. After three months she'd known all his meticulously planned patterns of behavior.

"Welcome home. How was Vermont?"

"Maine. It was lovely." Whenever she needed tranquility she escaped to the mountains. Just not the Rockies. Never those mountains.

"Whatever did you do up there all alone?"

"Whatever I felt like. Some fishing, some hiking, some sailing. I wrote a lotta letters and read ancient *National Geographics*. . . ."

"Sounds a little barren."

"Actually it was delightful," Kate replied. Thinking about the cabin put her in a better frame of mind. "What have you been up to?"

"Sweltering. The air-conditioning went out in my apartment. Would you like to go to the Yankee game tomorrow night?" His firm had season tickets.

"No, thanks."

"I'll throw in dinner."

"At Rosas."

"How did you know?"

"Because you always go to Rosas before a Yankee game."

"Oh. Well, would you like to join me?"

"No, thanks," she repeated. "I have a lot to get caught up on at home."

Apparently he sensed the steadfast note in her voice. Decisiveness was something he respected.

"All right. But I reserve the right to call you this weekend."

"Okay. Have a good day." She tried to sound cheerful.

"Ciao."

Kate sighed. She had a soft spot in her heart for lawyers that didn't always serve her well. Steve had been a mistake. Veronica had warned her and as usual she'd been right.

The first time he'd taken her to Rosas and a baseball game she'd thought he was romantic. It took her three such evenings to figure out he was permanently programmed.

Spontaneity. That was the quality she missed most in Steve.

Clint had been capricious, spontaneous, uninhibited. He'd nurtured a wonderful quality of whimsy on top of his yuppy three-piece suits. . . .

Damn. She'd promised herself she wouldn't dwell on Clint anymore. Over a year since he'd slept his way out of her life and his memory still haunted her. It was a door she had trouble closing.

This just wouldn't do.

Resolutely she punched out the number for Webb Overseas. On the fourth ring a man's voice answered.

"Good morning," she said. "This is Kate Fleming, export sales manager for BATT, division of LTS. In the last couple of weeks you've handled four big orders for us."

"Yes, yes. I remember. Electronics stuff, wasn't it? Edgar Webb at your service. What can I do for you, little lady?"

Kate grimaced. "Well, first of all, we haven't received copies of the shipping documents." BATT should have received them days ago, she knew.

"All in good time. All in good time. My secretary's been on vacation."

"I see. Well, could you at least advise me the name of the vessel each of those orders sailed on and its ETA in the foreign port?"

"Well, hmm. Let me see here. Maybe I can find the files. BATT Manufacturing you said?"

"BATT, division of LTS." It still sounded odd to her.

"Uh-huh."

Kate fidgeted in her chair. "While you're looking, may I ask if you've handled other shipments for these customers?"

"Yep. Sure have."

"I see. Did you then consolidate any of our shipments?"

She was fishing. To consolidate a shipment meant combining the goods with other orders bound to the same destination for the same customer, saving both time and money. Strangely, however, all four of the L/C's in front of her had a provision against consolidation—and if the terms and conditions of an L/C were violated by the shipper, the bank could refuse to pay.

"Of course," Webb replied quickly. "All of them."

It sounded almost as if he'd combined all four orders into one delivery, she thought.

"Even though it was prohibited by the L/C's?" she queried.

There was a sharp intake of breath on the other end of the line. She'd caught him. Kate's hand tightened on the receiver.

"Mr. Webb?"

The forwarder recovered his composure. "Now don't you worry none, little lady. Don't you worry none at all. I called the bank to get clearance on the discrepancy. The bank said it'd be all right, seein' as how it'd save the customer freight costs."

She knew he was lying and scribbled the contents of the conversation furiously on the back of the Panamanian L/C.

"Which bank?" she demanded.

"The advising bank here in New York, of course."

"And they got cable confirmation from the opening banks overseas?"

"Well now, I guess so, or they wouldn't have told me so, would they, little lady?"

If he calls me "little lady" one more time I'll scream, she thought. She abandoned courtesy. The transplanted New Yorker in her came out.

"Mr. Webb, for shipping with discrepancies under an L/C without consulting with the shipper you should have your head examined."

"But I did get consent from you guys."

"From whom?"

"From a Mr. Paul Cosentino."

Kate groaned inwardly. Cosentino wouldn't have had the slightest idea of what he was doing. "In writing?"

"Well, no . . ."

"It should be in writing. From whom did you receive clearance at the bank?"

"I don't rightly remember just now."

I'll just bet you don't, she mused. "Mr. Webb, I'd like a copy of those cables, please, by messenger, along with copies of the documents for all four shipments."

"Well now . . ."

"This afternoon would be soon enough but this morning would be even better." It wasn't as if she were asking for anything out of the ordinary.

"Fine," he rasped, the irritation in his voice clear.

"Thank you." She slammed down the phone.

Veronica appeared and set a steaming cup of coffee in front of her boss, cream, no sugar.

"Any luck?"

"Not a lot. I spoke with Webb. He's lying. Paul dropped by. He has absolutely no idea what's going on."

"So what else is new?" Veronica asked.

"Do me a favor, will you? Call Peter at Morris Forwarding and see if he knows anything about Edgar Webb or Webb Overseas."

Veronica nodded.

Kate had one more phone call to make. All four L/C's listed a Mr. Chun Bok Tong as the administrating person at the Hong Kong and Shanghai Banking Corporation in New York. This also struck her as odd. Banks usually organized their export letter of credit sections geographically, even on a country by country basis, with one person specializing in, say, Italy or Kuwait. Mr. Chun was handling L/C's from Hong Kong, Panama, Mexico, and Switzerland simultaneously. But if anyone could defuse her concern now it would be the Korean bank official.

There was a number listed. She dialed it. Chun answered.

"Mr. Chun, this is Kate Fleming, export sales manager for BATT, division of LTS. Your bank recently advised us of four different L/C's." She gave him his reference numbers.

"Yes, Miss Fleming?" Chun said politely.

"I was wondering if I might have copies of the cables from the overseas banks confirming that those shipments could be consolidated?"

Chun sputtered. It sounded as if he had dropped the phone. When he came back on the line his voice had a new crispness to it.

"Excuse me. Summer cold. I am sorry, but those files are no longer on my desk."

"But surely they're accessible?"

"Of course," he said defensively.

"Very well. I would appreciate copies of those cables."

"I can assure you there is no problem, Miss Fleming."

"I didn't insinuate there was. I merely need copies to complete my files," Kate said evenly.

"You will get them, madam, as soon as I have time." Chun was now cold.

"Thank you," she replied with saccharine sweetness.

She hung up. Chun was lying, too. She knew it but she couldn't prove it, and until she had solid evidence of trouble and not just an educated hunch, she couldn't take the matter up with Cosentino again.

Veronica appeared at her door.

"Outside of Cosentino's little debacle it's been pretty quiet," she said with a nod at the piles on Kate's desk.

"Mmm," Kate agreed. "Come on in. I want to brainstorm with you and make sure I'm not missing anything."

Veronica glided into the room. For a woman of her height she moved with the grace of a cat. Raised in the Bronx, she was the first of her family to complete her education. The battle for dignity and independence had left her with a veneer of toughness. Somewhere along the way the tall, elegant black woman had acquired a polish that allowed her to slip easily in and out of any situation life could throw at her. But she retained "street smarts," that sixth sense that exposed phoniness and fraud. Kate valued her efficiency, her humor, and her common sense.

"What do you think?" Veronica asked. "Have we been hoodwinked?"

"I'm not sure. Why would anyone want to do that?"

Veronica shrugged. "Lotta people lookin' for a free ride in this world. Could be they thought LTS'd be easy pickings."

"Could be," Kate said. "But this is going to pretty great lengths for products of no particular technological value. It doesn't make sense."

"No, it doesn't," her assistant agreed.

"Have our people overseas turned up anything on the consignees?"

"A big fat zero. I'm beginning to wonder if they're real."

So was Kate. "What about the foreign banks? Have we contacted them?"

"Not directly," Veronica said.

"Let's send them telexes. I want copies of those cables confirming acceptance of consolidated shipments."

"Okay. I have the numbers of the containers in which the goods left our factory. I called the trucking company this morning. Both containers were delivered to the Webb warehouse in Queens."

"And after that we have no idea what happened to them."

Veronica shook her head.

"So we've lost control of title to the goods, we have no idea where they are, and we have no assurance we'll be paid."

"You know that and I know that, but nobody else around here seems to give a damn."

"Not yet," Kate said.

Peter at Morris Forwarding called late that afternoon. Kate had worked with him for several years. Peter was a Scot by birth.

The rolling cadence of his homeland added a lilt to his familiar voice.

"Hello, Katie girl. How was your vacation?"

"A welcome change of pace. How've you been, Pete?" She didn't mind him calling her "Katie girl." He rolled the *r* so beautifully.

"Slow. Summer always is. How'd you get mixed up with a shark like Webb?"

"Is that what he is? We were routed to him, of course. You know I throw all our business your way if I have anything to say about it."

"I know that, Katie girl. And yes, our friend Webb has something less than a sterling reputation. Thought he was out of business. But I did a wee bit of checking fer ye. He's back, has been for ten months or so. Office isn't much apparently, only him and one girl, but they're turnin' over inventory at that warehouse. And it seems he's drivin' a new car, a T-bird. Can't be doin' too badly."

"I guess not. Tell me something, Pete: Would he ship goods in violation of the terms of a letter of credit?"

The man paused. "He might. Did he do that to you?"

"He may have."

"Who's paying him?"

"Not us."

"Then you have no leverage on him."

"Nope."

"Katie girl, I'd say you may have a problem."

"That's what I was afraid of."

"Anything I can do?"

"Not right now, but thanks, Pete. I may be calling you."

"I'm here. If I find out anything else about Webb I'll let you know."

"Thanks. Good night, Pete."

"Have a happy."

Kate hung up thoughtfully. It was 5:15. No messenger had arrived from Webb. She picked up the phone and called. A machine answered.

As she left the building that evening and headed uptown, Kate's mind whirled. What if the orders were bogus? That was absurd. That would imply that someone had actually set LTS up. She preferred to attribute the dilemma to stupidity, not malice.

"So why should you care," she could almost hear Clint saying as she trudged up the steep stairs from the subway stop. "It's not your money. It's not even your company anymore. It's LTS, not BATT."

Clint had the marvelous ability to depersonalize professional activities. What he could control—fine. What he couldn't—well, he'd shrug his shoulders and say the heck with it. He didn't let himself worry about it.

When she'd first moved to New York to be with him she had admired that quality in him. That was before she learned that he could also program himself not to care about people.

I do care, Kate told herself. It might not be good for her stress level, but at least she could look at herself in the mirror in the morning. She might not have embroiled her merged corporate entity in this mess, but she would do her best to get it out of it.

Of one thing she was sure: She didn't need the headlines in the afternoon tabloids screeching the horror of George Dexter's spectacular accident on the GW to confirm that LTS was in trouble.

What she didn't know was that she was, too.

Chapter

3

Sitting on Kate's desk Tuesday morning was the first solid piece of evidence of impending doom. First Bank of Panama denied any knowledge of the L/C supposedly issued to cover the shipment to Panama City. They had never heard of Importaciones Tecnológicas Gómez, the supposed Panamanian client.

There was a chance, a slim chance, that the goods had not yet left the country. Webb had offered no proof to the contrary. Armed with evidence that the L/C was bogus and with help from customers, LTS just might be able to prevent exportation.

That was something Kate could not do on her own, however.

She closed her door for privacy, then sat down to commit what she knew and what she suspected to paper.

But first she called Webb. A female voice answered, low, accented with Spanish. Kate introduced herself.

"Ah, yes. Miss Fleming. It's about the papers?"

"Yes."

"They're in the mail."

"How nice. By the way, how was your vacation?"

"I beg your pardon?"

"Your vacation?"

"I have not yet taken my vacation."

"Oh, my mistake."

But it wasn't, Kate thought as she hung up. It was Webb's. One more lie.

She dated her notes of the conversation and jotted them on the back of the Panamanian L/C.

* * *

Kate did not like Bob Thrasher, the vice president of sales and marketing for LTS. Nor did she like leapfrogging over her boss in the company bureaucracy. Cosentino was out of the office, however, and time was critical. She made a one o'clock appointment to see Thrasher, copying Cosentino on the memo she would present to the executive VP.

At precisely one she presented herself to Thrasher's secretary, Dominique Attinger. As Kate anticipated, she was asked to wait. Thrasher always made people wait.

Kate sat down and proofed her memo once more.

"Would you like me to pass that along to Mr. Thrasher ahead of time?" Dominique asked coolly. The musky aura of her perfume hovered over the anteroom.

Dominique was a stately platinum blonde. With her air of superiority she was not popular with the other secretaries. "That chick could suck an ice cube all day and never melt it," Veronica had once observed. The hot topic in the lunchroom was why she remained with Thrasher, notorious for burning out secretaries in record time with demands outside of the job description, behavior that would not have been tolerated at BATT but apparently was at LTS.

"No, thanks," Kate replied.

"Suit yourself." Dominique returned to her typing.

At one-thirteen Thrasher condescended to see her. He did not come out from behind his desk to greet her.

Bob Thrasher was only five feet two. His desk concealed a hidden platform. He never stepped off it to greet anyone. It preserved his dignity.

He gestured to a chair and Kate sat. Her knees came up almost to eyebrow level and she realized that he had indeed had the legs on his guest chairs sawed off. Had she not been so preoccupied she might have giggled.

Thrasher picked up the memo she had laid before him, then threw it down again.

"I don't read memos. Brief me." He glanced at his watch.

Kate spoke calmly. "I received confirmation this morning that the letter of credit from Panama for the one point two million dollar order shipped last week doesn't exist. I think . . ."

"What do you mean it doesn't exist? I have a copy right here in my office."

"I have a copy, too, but I'm afraid it's a fraud."

"Come now, Miss Fleming. Do you really think I'm that naive?"

"No, sir. I just think no one read those L/C's very carefully."

"Isn't that your job?" he asked sharply.

"Yes, and I outlined my objections to the first L/C we received in a memo dated 27 June, prior to going on vacation," she said. She'd anticipated that responsibility for the fiasco would fall on her department. Fair was fair. If Cosentino wanted credit for the seven million dollars in shipments he would have to shoulder the blame if the invoices went unpaid.

"What are you suggesting, Miss Fleming?"

"I am suggesting that we may be out seven million dollars."

"And what do you suggest we do about it?" His tone revealed no concern at all. Somehow she had to make him understand.

"Everything we can do to prevent those orders from leaving the country."

Thrasher rose to his full aided height and leaned his hands on the desk. His voice boomed. "Young lady, when I need your advice on how to run this company, I'll ask for it."

Kate swallowed.

"Do you have any idea what these four orders mean for the future of this company?" he thundered. "Do you know how many strings I had to pull to get them shipped on time, how many chips I had to call in to get our suppliers to ship components fast enough? They had to shortchange other clients. I had to sign forty-five day notes to get them to commit so much to us short term. And you say stop those orders?"

Lord, Kate thought. When did the invoices from the suppliers come due?

Thrasher rumbled on, carried by the momentum of his own oratory. He brushed his dye-black hair back with one stubby hand. "Do you have any idea what's happened to this company in the past four days? Not only did the BATT factory in Suffolk burn, cutting our production capacity for God knows how long, but yesterday a BATT driver rammed a school bus on the GW. The liability suits on that one aren't even filed yet.

"I warned Phil not to acquire BATT, but he wouldn't listen, and now see where it's gotten us."

He sat down again, winded slightly.

"Miss Fleming, we're not going to call those shipments back. We need that seven million dollars. May I suggest that you go back to your typewriter."

Kate stood. She could feel her cheeks burning. Stunned, she could think of nothing further to say.

"Thank you for your time," she stammered.

She pivoted and left, leaving her carefully documented memo behind.

"I see the steam," Veronica observed when Kate returned to her office.

Kate rolled her eyes and took a deep breath. "He wouldn't even listen to me and we're committed to paying for the non-proprietary components in those shipments in forty-five days."

"No shit?"

"No shit. Do me a favor, will you? Figure up how much of that seven million we owe somebody else."

"You've got it. What are you going to do now?"

"I'm going to see our prevaricating little friend Chun at Hong Kong and Shanghai."

Kate went into her office and shut the door behind her. She was short of breath. How she hated confrontation. She didn't think well on her feet. Unfortunately, confrontation seemed to be the LTS management style.

She sat down and willed herself to breathe slowly, deeply. "Why should you worry," she heard Clint saying again in his calm matter-of-fact way. "It's not your money."

Oh, shut up, she thought. This is my job and my department and like it or not we're going to be held accountable.

She scooped up all the "dead letter" files. On impulse she made photocopies of everything, including her notes. Thus armed she left the originals in the top drawer of her desk and grabbed her briefcase.

"Don't wait up for me," she told Veronica.

The New York offices of the Hong Kong and Shanghai Banking Corporation had the plush, carpeted hush of a library. Kate had been there before. She went directly to the third floor where the export letters of credit were handled. After a query or two she found her way to Mr. Chun. He sat busily behind a walnut desk, a clone of all the other desks around his, pushing paper from one pile to another.

"Mr. Chun Bok Tong?"

"Yes?" He looked up, startled but smiling.

"I'm Kate Fleming."

The smile faded.

"I thought I'd stop by on my way home for the copies of those cables."

"I'm sorry. I haven't had time to find them."

"That's all right. I'll wait," Kate said cheerfully. She sat in the chair beside his desk and removed the files from her briefcase. She began to leaf through them, the manila folders open just enough for him to see. His eyes widened.

"I don't think you understand," he said in a low voice, his fingers curling and uncurling around the telephone cord. "I do not have time to find them right now."

"Then perhaps you could ask your secretary to get them."

"I do not have a secretary." He stood. "And if you will excuse me I am late for a meeting. I will copy the cables for you tomorrow." He gestured her to the door. "Will that be sufficient?"

If she objected, Kate saw, it would cause a scene. One per day was enough.

"I'll make my request in writing tomorrow." She smiled sweetly.

She left him fidgeting nervously with his tie. In the lobby on the way out she paused to call Veronica.

"The plot thickens," she said. "Mr. Chun couldn't wait to get rid of me. I don't know what he's hiding, but I suspect it isn't legal."

"That's heartening," Veronica said. "Want some more good news?"

"What?"

"LTS owes different suppliers a total of three point two million dollars, most of it to Omer Electronics. Near as I can figure, the payables all come due between August 15 and 25."

"Jeez Louise. Have you got that documented?"

"Uh-huh."

"Terrific."

"What are you going to do with it?"

"I don't know," Kate said honestly. When she hung up the pay phone she felt very alone.

It was a lovely summer evening. The skyline of Manhattan shone clearly against a ceiling of faint stars. A light breeze ruffled the humidity and kept the smog at bay. Lovers strolled in pairs, their arms about each other.

Chun Bok Tong was too anxious to notice. His heels clicked the sidewalk impatiently, his short legs thrusting forward in long unnatural strides. Every few blocks he would dart into a doorway and wait. Breathing in gasps, he would peer out to see if anyone followed. He was not trained in surveillance, he thought frantically. How was he supposed to know if anyone was tailing him? Still, he had been warned to come alone. So he tried.

Brooklyn Bridge, eleven o'clock, his contact had said. Bring the papers. Chun had. He had felt a great relief just removing them from the locked drawer of his desk.

At great risk (and for a high price) he had agreed to prepare the formal notices advising LTS of the letters of credit on Hong Kong and Shanghai documentary letterhead and fake copies of the cabled L/C's themselves. Yesterday he had been ordered to fabricate more cables, another risky undertaking. And today this . . . this woman had come storming into his office flashing photocopies of the incriminating papers.

Now no one at the bank would ever know. He could deny everything.

At five to eleven he started slowly across the East River. A pale moon pierced the darkness and reflected off the sluggish water below. Traffic was light.

From the Brooklyn side a figure approached. And passed. Chun sighed. Too early. He paused in the middle of the span and leaned his arms on the railing. The bustle of the city seemed gloriously distant. Perhaps he should get away for a while, he thought, go home to Korea to visit his mother. Chonju would be lovely this time of year. His wife had been pining for home. For once he had the money, more than enough. Perhaps that nest egg had been worth all the tension, he mused.

There were no footsteps. There was only a shadow suddenly beside him.

"Koguryo, Paeche," a soft voice said, chanting the names of two of the three ancient kingdoms of Korea.

"Silla," he replied with the name of the third.

Satisfied, the contact asked, "Did you bring the papers?" Chun smiled. She was lovely. "Yes."

"May I have them please?" Crisp she was, efficient.

He handed her the bulky gray envelope.

The contact opened it.

"Is this all?"

"Yes."

"And the cables?"

"In the white envelope. I did them late this afternoon. No one noticed."

"You kept no copies?"

He shook his head.

"Good."

She tucked the white envelope in her pocketbook. Then she began to shred the papers, letting the pieces flutter away into the darkness to death in the river below. When she had finished she held out her hand to him. He took it.

An alarm rang through his body. His vision clouded. His throat was paralyzed. No sound came.

"And now for you, Chun," she said.

Chapter

4

Edgar Webb went fishing Wednesday morning.

Whistling through cigar-stained teeth he pulled the battered little motor launch off his Jeep as the edge of the eastern horizon glowed orange. Not a lot of people were about at this hour. The parking lot was empty save for a tan sedan that pulled in a few moments after Webb and parked some fifty feet away. The driver, the lone occupant, didn't move. His features were obscured.

Webb decided the car was beyond hailing distance. Besides, he liked his solitude in the morning. For him that was part of fishing. His stubby body cast no shadows as he slipped the boat into the gently rocking water of Jamaica Bay. He stowed his pole and tackle box, his thermos of coffee warmed with whiskey, a slimy bucket full of fresh bait, two sandwiches from the corner deli, and a Ziploc bag of fresh cigars. Then he shoved off.

Seabirds wheeled above him and the waves lapped at the gunwales. A warm breeze blew in from the Atlantic. Webb clipped and lit his first cigar of the day.

Next year, he thought, he'd buy a bigger boat, seagoing with an inboard motor. He had more time for fishing now. His business was regular and predictable. Webb knew it wasn't entirely legal, but forwarding was fiercely competitive. He'd never liked drumming up customers. He hadn't the charm for it. Having a regular client who routed to him assured a steady flow of goods through his warehouse—and hefty fees. The office his client provided gave Webb Overseas a veneer of respectability. He knew better than to ask questions. For the first time in his life he had both money and security. As he saw it, he deserved them.

Nobody had ever given Edgar Webb a fair shake. He'd always been squat and fat. He'd balded early. Women had never found him attractive. School had not been to his liking so he'd quit. He'd run a newspaper kiosk for a while, though he'd found running numbers more lucrative than peddling dailies. But that had tied him to a grubby little street corner in Brooklyn and he'd wanted more than that.

Always good with figures, he'd gone to work for a forwarder in Queens. In a month he was hooked. He'd pecked out documents sending goods to exotic ports all over the world: Goa, Dubai, Rio de Janeiro. So what if he only pushed papers? Forwarding also offered much opportunity for side activities, for a little personal wheeling and dealing.

Not drugs. Webb would never touch those. But he would do favors for clients: repack goods in deceptive packaging, slip extra goods out on benign invoices, that sort of thing. And keep his mouth shut.

So if someone were willing to set him up in business and hand him a steady income in return for a little unethical cooperation, he'd take it.

Until now the operation had gone smooth as glass. Until now. He'd told them those L/C's were trouble.

He cut the motor, flipped his line into the water, watched it run out of the reel. The plug bobbed on the surface of the bay.

LTS had been mighty pushy about those papers, much more than expected. Made him nervous. He'd told his client as much.

"They could make real trouble for us," he'd warned.

"How so?" his contact had asked.

"They keep asking questions."

"So? You're clean. You complied with your client's wishes; you cleared the consolidation with the banks."

"I don't have written confirmation of that."

"You will have," his client had affirmed.

"I still say LTS could make trouble for us. They could go to the authorities."

"With what?" The last had been said with a smile and Webb had understood. "Everything is under control, believe me. Why don't you take tomorrow off?"

So Webb went fishing. After all, he'd earned it.

The man in the tan sedan watched until Webb was well off shore. The end of the freshly lit cigar glowed red against water still dark with night. The launch bounced gently with the tide. The driver backed out and drove away.

* * *

The Swiss Bank of Zurich disavowed knowledge of the second letter of credit. With typical Swiss thoroughness they also confirmed that the Tsholl Trading Company of Vienna, Austria, for whom they had supposedly opened the L/C, was listed neither in the Vienna telephone book nor in the commercial registry. They advised Kate to check her records.

Kate had no records to check. What she did have were two and possibly four dead letters of credit.

And no files.

She and Veronica had turned the office upside down. The four suspect order files were missing. Veronica insisted that she had locked the office the night before. Kate believed her.

"I'd say somebody was listening to you yesterday," her assistant observed.

"Either that or somebody wants to cover his tracks," Kate replied.

"Paul's here today. You want me to tell him about the files?" Veronica offered.

Kate smiled. "Thanks, but no. I'll handle it." Somehow, she thought.

The phone rang and she left Veronica to answer it. She was beginning to feel trapped and hesitated to mention, even to her assistant, that she had copies of everything in all four files in her briefcase. Discouraged, she sat down at her desk to think.

Cosentino and Thrasher considered themselves heroes, clapping each other on the back like trainmen who've just topped a mountain after a steep climb—and were steaming merrily toward the valley below, not realizing that a few miles down the track a bridge was out.

Did they know something she didn't? Maybe she should go with her instincts and resign, she reflected. But quitting wouldn't solve anything—and it would definitely make it easier for them to blame the whole mess on her when the shit hit the fan.

Veronica buzzed her on the intercom.

"Yes?"

"We just got a call from the corporate controller. He wants to see you right away."

Kate sighed. Maybe it already had.

The body was found shortly after nine A.M. by a jogger. Floating only a short distance from the Brooklyn Bridge, it had been beached by avid, greedy hands sometime after midnight and stripped. Gone were the Bally shoes and the new Rolex watch. Gone too was the tailored jacket, but the trousers remained to testify to the exclusiveness of the label. There was no ID left to find. The body entered the Manhattan morgue at Bellevue Hospital as an Asian John Doe, cause of death unknown, a suspected homicide.

BATT, now a division of LTS, continued to occupy two floors of the lower Manhattan building. LTS dominated five. Formality demanded more space. No attempt had been made to harmonize the cheerful, efficient office layout of BATT with the dark wood partitions, deep carpeting, and closed doors of the new parent company.

Kate did not yet know her way around the executive floor. She felt as if she were treading enemy territory. At LTS unknown faces were escorted. Kate was an unknown face, but since she looked as if she knew where she was going no one challenged her.

She found finance in the southwest corner. The office of the controller was guarded by his secretary's desk, a mirror of Thrasher's suite on the opposite side of the building. But Josh Garrett's secretary was not in place and his door was open. She knocked.

Garrett was younger than she expected. The dark brown of his hair appeared natural and framed a tanned, outdoors face, smooth shaven. Crow's-feet crinkled the corners of his eyes. A deep crease split his forehead. No, it was not a crease, she decided, but a scar. It gave his countenance needed texture.

He smiled slightly. "Miss Fleming?"

"Yes."

"I'm Josh Garrett. Please come in." He rose to meet her and shake her hand.

Kate's sense of apprehension dissipated. He motioned her to a chair and she sat. His office furniture was of normal height.

"You're probably wondering what this is all about," he said.

"I think I know," she said quietly.

He reached across the desk to hand her a piece of paper. "A memo of yours was accidentally clipped to some documents I received from Bob Thrasher's office this morning."

She took the paper from him but she didn't have to read it. She knew what it was.

"Now then," he said, "if I understand you correctly, Miss Fleming, you believe we're about to lose seven million dollars."

She nodded.

"With an assertion like that you have my attention. Why isn't Bob Thrasher breaking down my door?"

"I'm not sure he understands the situation," she said carefully. Or wants to, she thought to herself.

Garrett sat back in his chair. "I'm not sure I do either. Why don't you explain it to me?"

Kate paused, re-forming her presentation. Begin with the headlines and work down, no equivocation, she thought. "We've just shipped seven million dollars worth of goods on unconfirmed and possibly nonexistent letters of credit."

"Which means what?"

"Which means we might not get paid."

"Can you elaborate on that a little bit?"

"Do you know how an export letter of credit works?" she asked hesitantly.

Garrett shook his head. "I suppose I studied it somewhere, but we've never done any overseas business—as I'm sure you know."

"Yes, I know," Kate said. "It's really not that complicated. Money's transferred between governments and private parties in different countries all the time. The Japanese buy oil from Indonesia and sell Toyotas to us. We sell computers to France and buy wine from them. The banks facilitate the flow of payments between countries. One of the most common methods and one that potentially provides the most protection to us as the exporter is a letter of credit."

"Go on," he prompted.

Garrett's blue eyes were intense, as if he were collecting as much information through sight as sound. Kate was suddenly aware of a run in her stocking.

"An L/C," she explained, "is a document representing a line of credit that our customer overseas has opened with his bank. It's a unique line of credit in that it's solely in our favor for the shipment of the goods the customer has ordered. In other words, we can't draw on it unless we present proof that we've shipped the goods. That's the bank's collateral."

"Fair enough," Garrett said.

"Now, the foreign bank doesn't deal with us directly," Kate went on. "Rather, it sends the L/C to its correspondent bank here in New York, say Bank of America. B of A in turn advises us that the L/C has been opened in our favor and what the terms and conditions are.''

"Terms and conditions like what?" Garrett queried. He was following her explanation intently, digesting details. She knew now he would hear her out and relaxed.

"Well, usually an L/C specifies the maximum value of the credit, the date on which its validity expires, how and where the goods are to be shipped, and the documents to be submitted to the bank.''

"And if we comply with their terms and conditions and submit the proper documentation, the bank, not the client, will pay us?''

"Right," she said. "But foreign banks can be sneaky. They can set any off-the-wall conditions they feel like. That's why we try to specify terms of our own in the pro forma invoice.''

"Such as?''

"Such as stating that the L/C must be confirmed.''

"What does that mean?''

"That as long as we comply with the terms of the L/C we'll be paid directly by the bank here in New York, not by the bank overseas.''

"Highly preferable," Garrett agreed. "So essentially what happens is that upon presentation of documents proving that we've shipped the goods specified in the client's order, we get paid by the U.S. bank.''

"Right," Kate nodded.

"It's a little confusing," Garrett said.

"Not really. Just think of it as a chain reaction. There's no direct financial relationship between us and the client in Panama. We're linked together by the banks.''

Garrett sat forward and leaned his forearms on the desk. "So what went wrong with these four L/C's?''

A lot of things, Kate thought, a lot of things that shouldn't have happened.

Garrett sensed her hesitation. "I realize this puts you on the spot, Miss Fleming, but I came to you, you didn't come to me.''

She nodded, emboldened. "Well, first of all, none of them were confirmed. That in itself makes them unacceptable. An amendment should have been demanded.''

"Is that possible?''

"Sure.''

"Why wasn't it?''

"Because the matter was taken out of my hands.''

"I see. Go on." Garrett's expression had hardened.

"There were a number of oddities about the orders," she said. "I've outlined them in the memo. And all four of them were shipped with a discrepancy, which means they didn't comply with the terms and conditions of the L/C's."

"In what respect?"

"All of the L/C's specified that consolidation was not permitted. All four shipments were consolidated anyway. Neither the forwarder nor the advising bank here in New York seems able to provide proof that the opening banks overseas agreed to the discrepancy."

"Which means?"

"That technically the overseas banks are not obligated to pay us anything."

Garrett's eyebrows rose and a low whistle squeezed through his teeth.

"In the long run I don't think that matters," Kate continued in a soft voice, "because I don't think those four letters of credit exist at all."

She placed her telex correspondence with the banks in Zurich and Panama before him.

"I haven't heard from Mexico or Hong Kong yet, but I'm willing to bet their responses will be the same."

"Is this possible?" he asked, a bit of skepticism in his tone.

"Yes. I've never seen it before, but I've heard about it. Nigeria is famous for L/C's drawn on nonexistent banks. In this case the banks are real. The L/C's aren't."

"And all of these orders have been shipped?" Garrett asked.

"Yes."

"On whose authority?"

"Paul Cosentino's."

"Where were you?"

"On vacation."

"Does anyone else know about this?"

"I've tried talking to Paul and to Bob Thrasher."

"And?"

"They told me to mind my own business." Actually, they'd put it in stronger terms, she reflected, but she wasn't sure how Garrett lined up politically with Thrasher. If they were in the same camp she was already in over her head. "I guess they think that as long as they have an L/C it's as good as cash—only it's not."

Garrett grunted. "Seven million dollars worth of shipments

makes them both heroes, especially under current circumstances.'' He looked up and she felt as if he were reading her thoughts. ''And they can't imagine not collecting. What do you think our chances are?''

''Mr. Garrett . . .''

''Josh.''

''Josh. My sources haven't been able to verify that those clients even exist.''

''Holy shit.'' Garrett leaned back in his chair and stared at the ceiling.

''That's not all,'' Kate told him. She was in this deep. Garrett might as well know the rest. ''Thrasher signed forty-five day notes to our suppliers in order to secure the needed components in a hurry. We're obligated to pay next month.''

''He what?'' Garrett snapped to attention, a menacing glint in his eye.

The sudden shattering of his composure silenced Kate. For the first time she saw the controller as something other than a pleasant number cruncher who was willing to listen to her. There was a restrained power in the man.

''He doesn't have the authority to do that, not on his own,'' he said in an icy voice.

''Well, he did. And we have three point two million dollars worth of short-term liabilities coming due next month.''

For a moment Garrett withdrew inside himself, his mind grappling with the ramifications of the dead letters. Then he seemed to return to the immediacy of her presence.

''Miss Fleming . . .''

''Kate.''

''Kate, would you like to go to lunch? I think we'd better talk to Phil about this as soon as possible, but I want to get my thoughts straight first.''

Phil Petersen was the president of LTS. She'd met him only once. In an organization such as LTS managers didn't deal with presidents.

''Yes, thank you,'' she said.

They bought sandwiches and soda at a deli and wandered into Battery Park to eat. Pigeons flocked to beg from noontime visitors, and tourists flowed to and from the ferry berths. Garrett spotted an empty bench.

The park was crowded but offered less opportunity for eavesdroppers than the neighborhood watering holes. They spread their lunch between them. Kate divided the napkins.

She had practical fingers, he noted, nails trimmed, short and rounded, unpainted, an artist's hands. Everything about Kate Fleming seemed practical: the spare touch of makeup on a face that needed little, the blond hair cut simply and falling to her shoulders, the skirt suit that stated professionalism above femininity.

"So what do you propose we do?" he asked as he unwrapped the salami hero.

"Prevent the goods from leaving the country, if we can," she replied.

"And barring that?"

"Try to find out where they're going."

"And if they're not going anywhere?"

"What do you mean?"

Garrett swallowed a mouthful of his sandwich. "I'm not sure." He shrugged.

"You don't think they were ordered simply to provoke a financial crisis at LTS?" Kate stared at him, her brown eyes wide with bewilderment.

"It's a possibility," he said, but even to him it seemed farfetched.

"I hadn't thought of that." She nibbled at her tuna.

"What did you think?"

"That somebody wanted to make a quick buck. I don't know. None of this makes much sense."

Not yet, Garrett reflected, stretching his legs, scattering the greedy pigeons.

"There is one more thing you should know," she said. "My office file copies of those orders disappeared last night."

"Disappeared?"

"From my office, from my locked desk drawer."

"Could anyone have borrowed them?"

"Everyone who could have an interest in them denies it. The microfilm records in the order processing department have also been conveniently wiped out."

"By accident?"

"Not likely."

For the first time Garrett felt genuine alarm. Until now he'd thought the situation somehow retrievable, a product of ignorance and coincidence, not deliberate malice. No longer.

Kate swallowed the last of her diet cola. "Between you and me," she confided, "I have duplicates. I thought I might need them at the bank yesterday afternoon."

He did not question her intuition. "Let's keep that our little secret for a while, shall we?" he said.

Kate eyed him shrewdly. "You think there's a possibility that Thrasher's behind this, don't you?"

If he were a corporate animal, Garrett reflected, he would hasten to assure her of the contrary. One never shared the confidences or conflicts of the upper echelon with middle management. But he had not forgotten his days of camaraderie on the soccer field. Besides, Kate was no fool.

"He's an ambitious man, but I find it hard to believe he'd jeopardize the whole company," he replied.

It's either that or he's stupid, Kate fancied, which was an uncharitable thought to harbor about your boss's superior. "What does he want?" she asked.

"The presidency."

Of course, she thought. What else. "He was against the BATT acquisition, wasn't he?"

"Uh-huh. So were a minority of the board members."

"And you?" she asked.

"I thought the diversification would be good for us, good for future growth."

"Does Thrasher have support on the board?"

"Yep."

"Anyone who can legally tie up credit?"

"The treasurer."

"No wonder you popped a cork," Kate acknowledged. "He superseded your authority."

"He did." She saw through to the core of a matter, no female wavering to left or right. He almost smiled despite the situation, despite his own reticence.

Strangely, Kate laughed. Starting as a rumble deep in her throat, the sound emerged heartily. "That's refreshingly candid," she said. "How did you end up crunching numbers in the midst of this snake pit?" To marketing people accountants were number crunchers.

"That sounds rather like 'what's a nice girl like you doing in a place like this.' "

She grinned. "Sorry. But every other LTS exec I've met is an empire builder in a stuffed shirt."

Garrett laughed then, for it was an apt description of some of his colleagues. He knew that whatever he shared with Kate Fleming would go no further.

He shrugged. "I wanted to do something useful with my life after soccer."

"So you went to work for LTS?" She said it as if she thought his logic were faulty.

"Not immediately," he admitted, turning to stretch his legs again, rubbing the left knee. "My soccer career ended prematurely. That was in the days before arthroscopic surgery and other modern refinements. I didn't know what I wanted to do with myself. I knew I didn't want to accept any sweetheart offers and end up being a figurehead for some insurance company—all form and no substance. And I wanted to come back to the States."

"What about endorsements?"

"In those days American soccer players didn't count for much here at home," he said wryly. "Italians and Brazilians maybe, but not Ivy Leaguers from Connecticut. However, I did have an undergraduate degree in accounting and a sizeable stash of liquidity. So, I went back for an MBA in finance, worked for a few years for one of the big firms, earned my CPA accreditation, and here I am." He smiled. "Now you've heard my life's story, it's almost one, and we still haven't decided what to recommend to the president."

He rose and offered her a hand up.

"I'd like to have a little face-to-face talk with Mr. Edgar Webb," she said. "He for one must have some idea what's going on."

At quarter to twelve Mrs. Chun Bok Tong called her husband's desk. He had not come home the night before, and he had not made his customary midmorning phone call to her. She was worried. When he did not answer his extension, she asked for Hugh McFee, his supervisor.

McFee questioned the frightened woman carefully. Had the employee in question been almost anyone save Chun, he might have written the disappearance off to an overly indulgent night with the boys or perhaps a bit of philandering. But Chun was a stolid, conscientious man, an exemplary employee. McFee had met Mrs. Chun at bank functions. She was not given to hysterics. It seemed her husband had left for a business appointment around ten-thirty the night before and never returned. McFee knew it couldn't be bank business. He checked with his staff. No one had heard from Chun.

He called the police.

* * *

Phillip Petersen collected miniature liquor bottles. So Kate had learned during the formal rounds of introductions after the acquisition. Petersen had chatted pleasantly with the surviving managers as he was escorted through BATT headquarters. In his brief exchange with Kate he had mentioned his hobby and asked if she traveled to exotic places. She did, regularly. On her next trip she'd picked up half a dozen tiny bottles of Asian liqueurs. He remembered.

"Miss Fleming. A pleasure to see you again. I stopped by your office to deliver my thanks in person but they told me you were on vacation. How was it?"

Stocky and gray, he came forward to shake hands with her.

"Very relaxing, thank you, sir." Kate smiled shyly.

She was not normally awed by position, but she found herself nervous in this office. Nine stories higher than her own and abundantly windowed on two sides, it commanded a sweeping view of New York Bay. Sunlight poured through polarized glass, expanding the dimensions of the room. Kate felt her heels sink into the deep burgundy carpet.

But it was Petersen himself who subdued her. The mystique of the presidency clung to him, adding height to his average frame, dignity to his bearing. His hazel eyes were penetrating, even when he smiled.

"I gather you two are not here on a social call," he said, motioning them to a sofa in one corner of the office. Selecting a chair for himself, he unrolled a fresh cigar and tossed the wrapper in a huge crystal ashtray. "Shoot."

Garrett moved like an athlete and sat like one, Kate observed. Even when his body appeared relaxed, as it did now, he seemed to have a controlled sense of where every part of him was.

"Phil, we may be facing a crisis even more serious than the Suffolk fire. I'd like Kate to explain it to you and I'd like you to hear her out."

Petersen's eyebrows rose. "All right."

Once again Kate explained the dead letters, step by step: how foreign transactions were routed through the banks and why, the peculiarities of the four orders, the danger of discrepancies on L/C's, her inability to communicate her fears to her boss and his. She was really in the soup now, she thought.

While she spoke the president doctored his cigar and lit it. Then he watched their faces, his gaze flicking from one to the other. He absorbed everything she had to say without a word.

When Kate had finished, Petersen puffed quietly for a moment. They waited. Until then she hadn't noticed how foul the odor of the cigar was. She sat back from the blue haze of smoke.

"I don't believe in coincidences," Petersen said at last. "The question is do I believe in stupidity, in this case Thrasher's." He fixed his eyes on Garrett. "Do you think he's behind this?"

"He's ambitious enough," the controller replied.

"Mm. Ambitious enough to cook up this scheme and initiate those letters of credit or ambitious enough to believe in them?"

"I don't know. Who else might be gunning for us?"

"No one that comes to mind," Petersen said, tapping ash off the tip of his cigar against a sloping side of crystal. "I don't have many enemies and neither does LTS. Do we have enough to cover the three point two million when it comes due?"

"Not without a serious drain on our working capital. Acquiring BATT left us short. Suspension of production on Long Island won't help our cash flow either."

"And if we don't collect on those four orders, our name will be mud in financial circles."

"That would please Thrasher no end," Garrett said dryly.

"And push me out rather quickly."

"Surely not when Thrasher's responsible," Kate said.

"As far as the board of directors is concerned, my dear, that may be immaterial," the president said. "The buck—or lack of it—still stops here."

Kate studied her lap.

"What options do we have?" Petersen asked. "At this point we have no actual proof of wrongdoing, just assumptions."

"I think we should press the bank officials," Garrett replied. "We still have copies of the advices on the L/C's on Hong Kong and Shanghai letterhead, signed by an official Kate met yesterday. I think they'll find them most embarrassing."

"We should also pay a visit to the forwarder," Kate ventured. "He's the only one we can get to who knows what happened to the merchandise—and what he did with the original L/C's after he received them from us."

"All right," Petersen agreed. "I'll leave that to the two of you. I'm going to consult a lawyer friend of mine." He rose, a signal to Kate that the interview was at an end. "Please keep me informed—and for the time being I shall trust both of you to keep this to yourselves. If someone inside the company is implicated I don't want him to know what we're doing. And I certainly don't want word leaked to the press."

Kate breathed a silent sigh of relief. She couldn't believe the abrupt change in her fortune. She had allies, powerful allies. Maybe she wouldn't lose her job—and maybe it wasn't too late to stop those shipments. Her heart felt lighter.

Garrett stood up. "Have we implemented new security procedures at our other facilities yet?"

"We're in the process of doing so," Petersen said. "You'll be briefed shortly."

He chuckled as he led them to the door. "You'd think we were developing the super megabyte chip. Industrial espionage is not something we've ever had to worry about."

"Do we now?" Garrett queried.

Petersen shook his head. "How much will our insurance cover for the fire?" he asked.

"We don't know yet," Garrett told him. "The inventory was just completed yesterday."

"Anything missing?"

"Yeah. A number of triwall cardboard packing crates."

"Missing? Weren't they burned?"

Garrett shook his head. "Nope. Fire never got that far. Either the BATT inventory was off or someone lifted them."

"Does the fire department still think it was an accident?" Kate queried.

"Yes. Why?" Garrett responded.

Petersen closed the door he had only partially opened.

"That is strange, isn't it?" Humor had faded from his face. "What percent of the goods in those orders came out of the Suffolk factory?" he asked Kate.

"All of them," Kate replied. "They were either produced there or assembled there from purchased components."

"You don't really think there was a connection, do you?" Garrett asked.

"I don't know," Petersen said. "But it's beginning to look like somebody wants to put us out of business."

That thought rattled around in Kate's head all afternoon.

Shortly after two o'clock Hugh McFee identified the body of Chun Bok Tong, known to his American friends as "B.T." Initially the autopsy was to say that he had drowned, though no one could explain how he had slipped or fallen into the East River. No evidence of alcohol or illicit substances was found in the bloodstream. Suicide was suggested, but McFee objected. Chun, he insisted, had not been suicidal.

The body was released to his wife while the official investigation continued.

Kate's apartment was tucked away from the street and faced the courtyard of an old brownstone off Columbus on the West Side of Manhattan. The original house had been carved up strangely. Her apartment occupied part of two upper floors, a one-bedroom flat cut into two small blocks. The lower floor consisted of a small sitting room and an even smaller kitchen. The bedroom and the bath occupied the second, which also had a small veranda. Kate often ate there on summer evenings. The place was small, but comfortable, full of light for her forest of plants and unexpected storage crannies. It had character.

And it had no traces of Clint. He had never been here. Even in the midst of the nightmare of his betrayal her common sense had surfaced. The less she associated him with her daily existence the better off she would be. So she'd moved.

Usually she found her home a haven from outside pressures. Not tonight. She couldn't get the conversation with Petersen out of her mind.

Kate fed Misha, her Siamese cat, and lingered over her dinner preparations until the national news was over. Then she sat down on the veranda with her meal to read the tabloid she'd picked up on the way home.

She found the article on page five. The reporter wrote with more passion than objectivity, speculating on whether Chun Bok Tong might have been the victim of suicide or murder. He had apparently interviewed the widow, who contended that the drowned man had been an excellent swimmer.

Until that moment Kate had not known what it meant for one's blood to grow cold. A chill spread out from her spine, fingers of cold fear clamping the muscles of her jaw and quickening her heartbeat.

When she could finally move, she unwound her crossed legs and stumbled down to the kitchen. She had to call someone.

Only hours after having spoken with her the Korean banker had died, a silent, stealthy death. Someone had killed Chun, someone had stolen her files, someone had wiped out the microfilm records. Someone had arranged for the dead letters of credit.

These things all touched her—and they frightened her. But whom could she call? She couldn't prove anything of what she felt she knew, except that no one else seemed to have records of the mysterious L/C's either. She was certain Chun's desk and the bank's files would be found empty.

Josh Garrett! She should warn him, she thought. At least he would listen, wouldn't think she was overreacting. He lived on Long Island, she remembered.

She had a Nassau County phone book, but there was no Josh or Joshua Garrett listed. She didn't know what town he lived in, she realized. Information would be useless. She didn't know whom else to call. There was nothing she could do until morning.

Then she remembered the papers.

She'd left her briefcase on the coffee table. Flipping it open she retrieved the dead-letter files. She didn't dare carry them around anymore, but she wasn't sure where to stash them.

"What do you think, Misha?" she asked the disinterested Siamese. "The desk is out. What about the freezer?"

She really should make extra copies of them, she decided, but not in the office. No telling who might be glancing over her shoulder. She shuddered. No. She would copy them over the weekend, but in the meantime . . .

It was time to clean the cat box, she reflected. Recovering a semblance of serenity, she tucked the papers into a large plastic freezer bag and sealed it. It fit snuggly in the bottom of the cat box. She covered it with fresh litter.

No one, she thought, would look in a dirty cat box.

She was wrong.

Chapter

5

Kate Fleming arrived in his office before his morning coffee had cooled. She wore her composure like a pale mask. Beneath the thin veneer Josh saw fear.

"Kate, are you all right?"

"I have to talk with you," she replied, fingering the tabloid in her hands.

"Sure." He strode to the door and asked his secretary to bring in a second cup of coffee. "Come in and sit down," he told Kate. He took her by the elbow and led her to a chair.

Circles deepened the inset of her eyes. Her hands were cold when he took them in his own. It seemed a normal gesture, for all they had just met the day before. She didn't pull away.

"Chun's dead," she said without preamble. "I think he was murdered." She handed him the paper.

"Are you sure this is the same man?" Josh asked when he had finished the article.

"Yes. The picture was taken when he was younger, but it's the same man."

"Police say he drowned."

"And his wife says he was an excellent swimmer."

Someone knocked. Kate jumped.

"Relax," he said kindly. "It's the coffee. A little caffeine is just what you need."

She managed a weak smile.

Josh's secretary, Irene Warren, ferried a tray in and set it on his desk. She was a matronly woman, a lady of the old school, inconspicuous, efficient, discreet.

"Will there by anything else?" she asked.

41

"No. Thank you very much."

Irene nodded and left.

"How do you like your coffee?"

"Cream, no sugar," Kate said.

She could well be right about the banker, he reflected as he stirred the coffee. But that was not to say the murder necessarily had to do with the dead L/C's. If so, however, that would put a whole new complexion on the affair. It would mean that someone was willing to kill for . . . for whatever.

"Why didn't you call me last night?" he asked.

"I tried. I couldn't find you listed." She seemed calmer. Her hands were steady when she accepted the cup. Her blond hair was pulled back in a ponytail, as if she hadn't had the time or patience to arrange it that morning.

He grinned. "I'm listed, but not under Josh."

"Then what?"

"Joseph H., Junior, actually. They called me Josh to differentiate me from my father and the name stuck."

"You don't look like a Joe."

"Thanks. Did it occur to you that even if Chun were murdered it might not have anything to do with our problems? Might have been a mugger. Maybe he ran up debts to a loan shark. Or maybe he was involved in something shady and crossed his partners."

"I think he was involved in something shady, all right. He knew about those letters of credit. You should have seen his face when he saw my copies." The self-assurance he had come to associate with Kate crept back into her voice.

"He may have been the only one at Hong Kong and Shanghai in that case," Josh said, stretching his legs out.

"How do you know?"

"I have a college friend who works there. She checked out their records for me yesterday. Nothing."

Kate took a thoughtful swallow of coffee. "Could he do this?" she asked quietly.

"Thrasher?"

"Uh-huh."

"I don't know," he replied. "I don't think so."

Could he? Josh wondered. Could the man's bravado and lust for power have escalated into violence? He wanted to dismiss the idea, but there was enough arrogance in Thrasher to give him pause.

"Should we call the police?" Kate asked.

"With what? Hunches? We're getting in over our heads, Kate. And we have an awfully weak case for persuading anyone else. The threads connecting the letters and Thrasher and Chun are very fragile and may be entirely in our minds."

"And the fire?"

"It was an accident."

Kate's silence betrayed her doubts. He chose to ignore them, but the possibility of arson would not melt away.

"We're missing something, Kate. We're missing the motive, the underlying connection between all this, and until we find it nobody's gonna buy our theory that it all relates."

"You're probably right," she admitted.

"If we went to the police now they'd accuse us of having overactive imaginations," he said more quietly. "At this point there's an alternative explanation for everything that's happened."

"What about the L/C's themselves? They're no figment of anybody's imagination."

"Do we have the originals?"

"No. The originals all went to the forwarder, then, supposedly, to the bank with the other documents."

"Then they're all copies, Kate. The bank could contend that we just doctored previous documents."

"But we didn't! I saw the original of the first one before I went on vacation."

"I don't doubt you. I'm just saying that at this point we can't prove anything."

Kate sighed. "You're right." She raised her brown eyes to his. "Then I guess we have to find the connection, don't we?"

"Mm-hmm. How good a detective are you?"

She looked startled.

"I think it's time we paid a visit to Mr. Webb. While I distract him maybe you can do a little snooping."

"You can't be serious."

He grinned. "I have this roguish streak, rarely exercised. Besides, Webb sure as hell isn't gonna volunteer any information. He may not have all the answers, but we may be able to find out where he sent the goods."

Kate brightened. "We'll have to wait until that secretary of his has gone for the day. She's a sharp cookie."

"Webb isn't?"

"He doesn't think as well on his feet."

"Around five then—and we'll hope to catch him in."

"Okay." Kate smiled. "I'll feel better just doing something instead of waiting for the next ax to fall."

"Keep a low profile in the meantime," he advised as he escorted her to the door. "Just go back to your office and act normal."

And I'm going to ask the president to consider the possibility of sabotage on the GW Bridge accident, he thought. And now who's getting paranoid?

The morning was routine until the mail arrived.

Through her open door, Kate could hear the firm rip as Veronica opened the envelopes, the crinkle of paper unfolded, the solid thump of the date stamp. Suddenly the metal opener clattered on the desk. A few moments later Veronica was in her doorway. She held a manila folder.

"You ain't gonna believe what I found," she said.

Kate looked up from her expense report. Receipts were scattered across her desk. She was two months behind as usual. "Pray tell."

"Copies of cables to the Hong Kong and Shanghai Bank here in New York."

"Agreeing to the consolidation of those orders?"

"Yep. The weird thing is they were mailed in a plain white envelope. And from an uptown zip code, not downtown where the bank is."

"What?"

Her assistant laid the papers before her. Kate studied the envelope, the faded copies of the four cables from the banks overseas, confirming that consolidation of the shipments was acceptable.

"They aren't real," Veronica said.

"How do you know?"

"They were never transmitted, just typed up on a telex machine and a hard copy printed out on the same machine. Banks usually use some sort of code between themselves to authenticate this sort of exchange. None of these have been authenticated. Chun must have done them himself and figured we wouldn't know the difference."

Kate checked the postmark on the envelope. A chill spread down her spine.

"He may have," she said. "But he didn't send them."

"What makes you say that?"

"They were mailed yesterday morning. By that time Chun was dead."

Kate called Webb Overseas from a phone booth before they left Manhattan. She claimed to be the secretary for a customs official and made an appointment for a Mr. Evans at 4:45. Webb would be there.

Josh stood beside her for moral support. It seemed so natural to accept him in that role. She'd known him a day and they were off together on an adventure that required implicit trust between them. And she never wavered.

"That wasn't as hard as I thought it would be," she confided as they climbed back into Josh's blue BMW. "I think I actually enjoyed deceiving that worm."

"You're a natural," he grinned. He eased the car into traffic and turned on the air-conditioning.

Kate settled her briefcase modestly on her lap, keenly aware of his masculine presence. Her heart felt free. For the first time in months she was with a man and didn't wish he were Clint. Steady girl, she cautioned herself. Business before pleasure and never mix the two.

She glanced at her watch. It was nearly four. They should make it. Just.

She had used her lunch hour to rush home, dig up the files in the cat box, and make an extra set. One she planned to mail to her sister in Sacramento with a note to save the papers for her. The second she carried with her now. She had already decided that if she did find something in Webb's files there would be no time to read it. She would have to take it. The files couldn't be left empty. Perhaps the related documents she had in her briefcase would delay the discovery of her pilferage.

"What's Kate short for?" Josh asked.

"Pardon?" she said. Such an odd question.

"Kate. What's it short for?"

"It's not," she replied, grateful for the diversion. She was not looking forward to confronting Webb.

"Just Kate?"

"My mother says I kicked a lot during my gestation. So she wanted a name short and snappy to fit my personality. Katherine sounded too formal, so she called me Kate Elizabeth, Elizabeth for my grandmother, Kate just for me."

"Catchy."

"Well, at least people can find me in the phone book."

"Touché."

"Have you ever done anything like this before?"

"Like what?"

"Play spy."

Josh shook his head. "Nope. I leave that to my brother. He's a police detective."

"Here in New York?"

"Phoenix. He likes warm weather."

Kate thought quickly. "Would he be willing to do a little snooping for us?"

Josh chuckled. "I doubt it. He hates New York."

"Not here. By mail." She told him what the mail had brought that morning. "I want the cables and the envelopes dusted for fingerprints and compared with something we know Thrasher has touched."

He turned to look at her, his eyes twinkling. "You really are getting into the spirit of this thing, aren't you?"

It was nearly five by the time they found the place. Josh went in first. Kate waited in the car. They had to be sure the secretary was gone for the day before she entered.

The forwarder's office was a crumbling one-story affair adjacent to the warehouse. The windows of both structures were barred. The strip of dusty ground before them was littered with broken glass, tufts of sun-dead grass, and scraps of cardboard. A chain link fence surrounded the property. Across the street was a garage that specialized in body work, its future projects strewn haphazardly on the lot and at the curb. Josh's BMW was out of place. Kate was glad it was daylight.

Without the air-conditioning the compartment steamed quickly. She wondered how Webb organized his files; by country, by shipper's name, by a code number? She would not have long to figure it out.

At last the door to the office opened and a tall, dark woman dressed in black stepped out. She was quite thin, a feature accented by the tight skirt she wore. Her head and bust line seemed out of proportion with the rest of her body. Her makeup was severe, an attempt to cover what looked like acne scars.

She slammed the door shut, then paused, as if debating. At last she tossed black hair from her face and teetered away on high heels.

The harsh buzz of the car phone startled Kate. It was the signal from Josh. She picked up the receiver.

"Hello, darling," Josh said cheerfully. "Just wanted to let you know I'll be a little late for dinner."

Kate laughed. "Does he have a separate office?"

"Yep."

"Just keep him in there as long as you can, honey."

She waited until the secretary drove off in a vintage Chevy. Then she locked the BMW and crossed the street, briefcase in hand. Her skirt billowed up in the humid breeze.

Webb's door was ajar. Josh must have opened it for her. She went in.

The building was as dingy inside as out. She could hear a murmur of masculine voices behind a closed door.

The outer office was furnished with a battered gray metal desk, military surplus, and a row of equally dilapidated file cabinets. Both were littered with piles of papers that spilled out of bins. But every pile was orderly and held in place with a paperweight. The typewriter and calculator were shrouded with plastic covers and the ashtray had been emptied. Kate didn't see a speck of dust. There was a name tag on the desk. Juana Medrona. Well, she thought, Juana Medrona was certainly organized.

The file drawers were neatly labeled—by number. There had to be a log somewhere, Kate reasoned. Failing that she would start with the most recent files and work backward.

Stealthily she sat at the desk. A logbook should be within easy reach, she figured. Her eyes swept the desk top. Stashed between a Spanish-English dictionary and a secretarial handbook was a three-ring binder. The sections were neatly indexed: correspondence, telexes, invoices—shipments. She flipped to the last section. It told her everything she needed to know.

"I don't appreciate your coming here under false pretenses," Webb said. His gray eyes peered owlishly from behind thick glasses. A dead cigar drooped from one corner of his mouth. When he spoke he revealed stained teeth.

"Would you have seen me if I'd told you the truth?" Josh countered. He'd carried the farce through the pleasantries with the secretary. Now she was gone. Placating her had not been easy. Josh wondered who really ran the office.

"Why not?" the forwarder said, but he did not meet Josh's challenging glare.

He had not been asked to sit, but Josh moved a pile of girlie magazines to the floor and sat anyway, planting himself between Webb and the door.

"Mr. Webb, where are the goods we sent to your warehouse?"

"On their way overseas, of course."

"Consolidated."

"Yeah."

"With what?"

"Can't tell ya off hand. They were all different and we handle a lotta shipments, ya know," the little man whined.

"Uh-huh. You've handled shipments for these four customers before?"

"Well, I guess so."

"You ever have payment problems with any of them?"

"Nope."

Josh paused. They'd agreed not to reveal to Webb that the overseas banks had denied any knowledge of the L/C's. He tried another tack.

"Well, Mr. Webb, as you probably know, this whole business is new to LTS. We'd never exported before we acquired BATT."

"Uh-huh," Webb said shrewdly.

"This whole matter just seemed a little strange to us, what with the customers never responding to telexes and . . ."

"Mr. Garrett, you have to remember that a lotta people in the world take longer vacations than we do here in this country. Four, five, even six weeks. I haven't been able to contact 'em by telex either. I wouldn't worry about that if I was you."

"Just seems a little strange that they would run off on vacation without ever sending us delivery instructions. We don't even have addresses."

"Sure you do, Mr. Garrett."

"No, sir. Just post office boxes. We have no idea where those goods are going. Now, am I wrong or can a customer in Singapore or Panama buy something and then have it delivered somewhere else—say Indonesia—or maybe Cuba."

It was a shot in the dark, but the cigar fell from Webb's mouth. His round owl eyes dilated.

"Now, hold it just a fucking minute, Garrett. Are you accusing . . ."

"I'm not accusing anyone of anything. I just want to know what the hell happened to seven million dollars worth of our production." Josh kept his voice low and reasonable. He glanced at his watch. Only five minutes had passed. He smiled disarmingly. "Like I said, Mr. Webb, we're new at this. The whole process is sorta like a mystery, ya know. So, when things didn't go down by the book . . ."

"What didn't go down by the book?" Webb asked.

"Oh, little things. Pushing the orders out the door so fast, getting them consolidated when the banks had all instructed us not to do so . . ."

"I cleared that with you people."

"I never heard about it. Then not knowing where the stuff was going. In our business we have to be careful, Mr. Webb. A lot of what we produce needs an export license and . . ."

"Like I said, it's on its way overseas, to Hong Kong and Panama and whatever. And none of it needed no export license. I'm sorry you ain't received your copies of the documentation yet, but my secretary's been on vacation."

"She was here today."

"And she had other things to do."

"Then why don't we make a copy now?"

"I'm not a file clerk, Mr. Garrett. I have other people to do that sort of thing and when they get to it, they get to it. Now, if you'll excuse me I'm late for a poker game. And I'll be happy to advise my clients not to deal with LTS again if this is too much for you to handle."

"I'll extend the same courtesy, Mr. Webb," Josh told him. "We're well connected in the business community. We can damage your reputation a helluva lot faster than you can damage ours."

"From what I hear yours don't need a lotta help about now," Webb huffed. He rose with startling quickness and trotted to the door. There was no time to warn Kate. "After you," he said.

Kate stood at the clerk's desk, shutting her briefcase.

"Who the hell are you?" Webb demanded.

"Kate Fleming," she said. "Pleased to make your acquaintance. It got a little warm out in the car."

"Ah, the smart one. Brought in the heavy artillery, did ya now, girlie? Well, sorry you didn't find our service up to snuff, but . . ."

"Yours is supposed to be a service business, Mr. Webb."

"So it is, and I've done mine. Now get out—both of you."

Josh glanced at Kate. She winked.

"Good day, Mr. Webb." He took Kate's arm and guided her out of the building. They didn't speak until they were in the car.

"Did I give you enough time?" Josh asked.

Kate's face was slightly flushed. She broke into a wide grin. "It was a snap. Juana is a neatnik. Everything is exactly where it's supposed to be."

"And?"

"I don't know yet. I'm afraid to look."

"You mean you just took them?" He closed his door with a slam.

"Well, I didn't have time to read them. Don't worry," she assured him. "I cleaned out the contents of the files, but I stuffed copies of some of our in their place. I even remembered to wipe my fingerprints."

"Very professional," he said dryly. He gunned the motor. "Well, tuck them away for now. We're not finished here yet."

Kate raised her eyebrows. "You're going back in there?"

"Nope. I want to get into that warehouse."

"Why?"

"Because I got a most strange reaction when I mentioned Cuba."

They cruised the neighborhood until Webb had left. He took his time about it. The shadows lengthened. At last he passed them in a shiny white Thunderbird. He was in a hurry.

Josh parked a block from the forwarder's office.

"Stay in the car," he told Kate.

"Why?"

"Because there's a fence around the place. Somehow I can't see you climbing it in nylons and heels. Besides, I may need a fast getaway."

Kate sighed. "You're right. What do I tell the police should they pass by and see a man in a dress shirt and tie invading the property?"

"The truth, I suppose." He grinned and slipped off his jacket. "The distance between respectability and petty crime isn't that great, is it?"

"No, I suppose not," she admitted ruefully.

"Lock the doors. There may be other petty criminals in the area."

It was not yet dark, but already the neighborhood was deserted. There were no streetlights.

He was halfway up the fence before the dogs detected him.

There were two of them, Dobermans. His eyes focused on the gnashing teeth as they hurled themselves at the steel mesh.

Josh dropped to the ground. Adrenaline pounded through his system. He glanced up at the top of the chain link. It was at least ten feet high. They probably couldn't jump it, but he didn't want to tempt them.

Kate roared up in the car.

Josh pulled open the passenger door and reached for the glove compartment.

"Get in, for Christ's sake," Kate cried.

"Just a minute. They can't get out." He found his binoculars and straightened up. "Keep the motor running," he added.

Dusk was falling fast. It was almost too dark to see. The dogs continued their barking frenzy.

"Aim the headlights between the buildings," he called to Kate.

She backed the car into the street and angled it at the fence. The pitch of the Dobermans' chorus rose.

Josh stepped as close as he dared to the barrier and focused on the scraps of cardboard. The dogs impeded his view. He climbed up on the hood of the BMW, placing his feet carefully. Height improved his perspective.

When he'd seen enough he jumped down and scrambled into the car.

"Go!" he said.

Kate backed away from the fence and put the car in gear.

"What was that all about?"

"Drive. I'll explain later, under quieter circumstances."

Webb was livid, angry enough to address his client without the usual deference.

"I don't give a flying fuck what your source said about LTS. They may well be babes in the woods, but this dame Fleming ain't and somebody's listenin' to her. She had the fuckin' controller here this afternoon!"

"What did you tell them?" demanded the crisp voice on the other end of the line.

"Nothin'. What the fuck did you think I'd tell 'em? But you can bet your sweet balls they suspect somethin'."

"How so?"

"Askin' where the goods got shipped and if I'd ever had collection problems with the clients, probin' around about shipments to Cuba . . ."

"He was fishing."

"The hell you say. You shoulda heard 'im pressin' for documents."

"So make up dummy documents and send them copies."

"Dummy docs! Eventually they gotta find out. You'll blow my whole deal here."

"Relax. They won't find out until it's too late, We'll just make sure both Fleming and the controller lose their jobs in the midst of the turmoil. No big deal. The documents will disappear, case is closed, and you can go back to your routine shipments."

Webb paused. Seemed to him there were a lot of ends dangling.

"Look" his contact said. "You call LTS first thing in the morning. I'll tell you just who to talk to."

They debriefed in Kate's apartment over paper cartons of Szechuan beef and moo shu pork from the Chinese takeout on the corner. Kate opened a bottle of Chablis and set the table sparingly, leaving space for the piles of papers she had pilfered from Webb.

"It's warm," she said. "Would you like an ice cube?"

"Sure," Josh replied. He sat on the sofa, scratching the cat behind the ears. His eyes swept the tidy little sitting room. Kate had furnished it with antiques, small pieces built for another time when lives were confined to smaller spaces. A drop-leaf table fit snugly against the wall just outside the opening to the kitchen. Leaves down, it would just accommodate two. Only the proportions of the sofa on which he sat, his back to the window, dwarfed the room. To his left, stairs led to the second story.

"Are you always so organized?" he asked.

"Only on the first floor," Kate called from the kitchen. "I never make my bed." She reappeared with two glasses of wine, ice clinking against crystal. "Misha doesn't usually take to strangers," she added, handing him a glass. "She's shy."

"Thanks. She knows her friends. I have a Siamese, too."

"You do?" She sounded surprised.

"Mmm. One of the few things I salvaged in my divorce settlement. Cheers."

"Cheers," she echoed. They toasted. "I didn't know you were divorced."

"You mustn't read the society columns."

"Not usually."

"Just as well." He raised his glass. "Not bad."

"Normally I have a bottle in the refrigerator," she began.

"So we'll rough it." He grinned. "Beggars can't be choosers. After all, the least I could do after luring you into a life of crime is treat you to dinner, however humble.''

Kate laughed. ''Tell me about your cat.''

''Fred? He's an independent little buzzard, a chocolate point with highly discriminating tastes. If he likes you he'll post himself on your lap, whether you sneeze or not. The dull he ignores. And if he really takes an aversion to someone, he bites.''

''That must make life exciting.''

''He and I usually see eye to eye, but Fred used to drive Diana crazy. Toward the end he began staging sneak attacks and biting her heels. Ran innumerable pairs of stockings.'' There was a stronger note of grim satisfaction than humor in his voice, he noted. He smiled at Kate. ''Sorry,'' he added, gulping the rest of his wine. ''Diana left a bad taste in my mouth.''

Her smile was warm. ''Safer to share it than save it,'' she told him. ''Would you like some more wine?''

''Yeah. I think my pulse is just returning to normal. I was sure those damn Dobermans were coming over the fence.''

''So was I,'' she said with a shudder. ''Whatever were you after?''

Josh sat back and stretched his legs out under the coffee table. ''I think I found the packing crates that were missing from the BATT factory out in Suffolk.''

Kate's mouth dropped open. ''But whatever would Webb want with them? And how can you be sure? He did receive two container loads of our goods.''

''The crates I saw in that yard had never been put together. They were new, flat, knocked down. Besides, a used crate would have marks on it, wouldn't it? The name and address of the customer, identifying numbers, that sort of thing?''

''Yes, but . . .''

''Well, these were clean, nothing on them but the logo stamped on them at the factory.''

''That still doesn't explain why he took them,'' Kate said. She sat down beside him.

''Did you have time to study anything else in that office?'' he asked.

''Well, I flipped through his order log.''

''And?''

''Most of the shipments seemed to be going either to Hong Kong or Austria, some to Malta. There didn't seem to be a lot of activity, actually, and most of it was pretty recent.''

''What other U.S. shippers are using Webb Overseas?''

"Looked like mostly electronics companies."

"Uh-huh. Ya know what I think our friend Webb is doing? I think he's a front for exporting restricted material—without licenses."

"To whom? Not a lot's restricted now, not since the Wall came down."

"But aren't there still countries American companies can't do business with?"

"Yes. Cuba, Vietnam, North Korea, Libya."

"And there are still destinations and commodities for which licenses are needed—right?"

"Oh, sure. Most of the former Eastern Bloc. The difference now is that it's a formality. Sales of high technology are no longer prohibited in most cases, just carefully monitored."

"And does the Department of Commerce ever refuse a license?"

"Sure, if the buyer's not authorized," Kate said carefully.

"And what would constitute an unauthorized buyer?"

"I guess it depends on what you want to export." She was puzzled about where his questions were headed. "They're obviously not going to license nuclear technology for Pakistan or military hardware for private groups in Colombia—or anything for the countries off limits."

"Well, you should have seen his eyes today when I mentioned the possibility of shipping to Cuba," Josh said. "He almost came across the desk at me."

Kate caught her breath. "Josh, that's not funny. Remember Chun? If this is true, Webb's a criminal, a real one. He could be a very dangerous man." Her face was so solemn he had to smile.

"Probably so," he agreed. "Maybe I just have an overactive imagination. Shall we eat or take a look at those papers?"

"You've dampened my enthusiasm," she admitted. "Let's eat."

The food was still warm, the wine now a bit more chilled. Josh watched Kate spoon pork into the flour pancake and wrap it thoughtfully like a limp taco. Strands of hair had escaped from the ponytail. She swept them aside before tackling the dripping pancake.

"Don't look so worried," he told her. "There's probably an innocent explanation for all of this. The banks just misplaced the L/C's, Chun drowned, Webb's just careless."

She chewed hurriedly and swallowed.

"And you don't believe a word of that, do you?"

Josh sighed. "No." He didn't know what to believe. He was touching something alien, something malignant. Corruption, white-collar crime, those he had dealt with. He'd seen money passed to throw soccer games or coax a reluctant customs official. As controller he was the guardian of company funds, ever watchful for bureaucratic abuses. Those were money crimes, clean crimes. But there was something dirty about the matter of the dead letters. Dirty and deadly.

"I'd like you to let the matter drop," he told Kate gently. "Whatever we find in those papers, I'll handle it from here."

She paused to look at him. "I appreciate your concern," she said, "but I always finish what I start."

"You've done your part. Consider it finished."

"Josh, part of my job is to make sure we get paid."

"It's gone way beyond that, Kate."

"I know that."

"It's a criminal matter now, something for the FBI, Customs, maybe the National Security Agency."

She studied him intently over her wineglass.

"And the only hard evidence we may have of illegal activity we stole," she said. "I don't think your brother would approve."

Josh sat back in his chair. "Probably not."

Kate rose and crossed the room to her briefcase. She removed the papers from Webb's office and returned to the table. "So, let's see what we have." She began sifting through the pile.

First she separated four official-looking documents printed on pink, patterned paper with cablegrams attached. "The original L/C's," she said. "If this operation were legit they should've been sent along to the bank." On top of them she laid two bulky invoices typed on LTS forms. Kate flipped through the several pages. "Looks like Webb consolidated the four shipments all right. I wonder who furnished him blank LTS invoices."

"Where did he ship?" Josh asked.

"Part of it went to Hong Kong, part went to Vienna."

"Everything?"

"Looks like it. But the volume of goods shipped mysteriously doubled. What we sent to him in two twenty-foot containers required four to ship overseas." She looked up. "You may be right, Josh. They may be exporting illegally."

"Lot of money for our friend Webb in kickbacks from an operation like that," Josh said.

"Enough to kill for?"

"Maybe."

Kate thumbed through more of the papers. "Well, isn't this interesting." She laid a piece of LTS letterhead before him.

"What's this?"

"A note from Paul Cosentino supposedly authorizing Webb to consolidate the orders in violation of the L/C's—except that it isn't Paul's signature."

"Looks like Webb is trying to cover all his bases."

"Yes, doesn't it." She paused. "Oh, my God, Josh. These are my file copies, the ones that were stolen from my office."

The shock in her voice made the hair stand up on the nape of his neck.

"Are you sure?"

"These are my notes, dated Monday and Tuesday, in ink." She stared up at him. "Webb *is* working with someone inside LTS," she whispered.

Kate met crises differently than Diana did, Josh reflected a short while later as he watched the woman organize their leftovers and dirty dishes in her tiny kitchen. Her movements were sharp, her face pinched in thought; mind and body worked independently. Hands snapped off the plastic wrap in sure, even squares. Her thoughts were distant. He could imagine their course, seeing a connecting thread between Webb and Thrasher, between the dead letters and the dead night guard.

But Kate was thinking. Diana never bothered.

He poured her a fresh glass of wine and rose from the table.

"Why don't you come on into the living room?" he suggested. "Dishes'll wait."

Kate glanced up from the sink. "You're right," she said with an apologetic smile. "My mind just doesn't work well when my hands are idle."

"So I've noticed."

She laughed and followed him to the sofa.

"I suggest we put Webb and company out of our minds for the rest of the evening," Josh said, resting his stockinged feet on the coffee table. "There's nothing we can do about it tonight anyway."

"A murder may have been committed, your employer is on

the brink of disaster, and you're going to put it out of your mind?"

"Only till tomorrow."

"You compartmentalize your life that easily?" She settled herself beside him.

"Preserves my sanity." He sipped his wine. "I'll speak to Phil first thing in the morning, then talk to Customs. I think I've seen enough for them to start an investigation."

"And that'll be the end of it?"

"No, the beginning." He looked squarely into her brown eyes for the first time. No, not the first time, he thought, but the first time he had really studied them. They were dark for a blond, smooth circles of smoky crystal, rimmed in gold just before the whites began. "But the end of our involvement," he said.

He realized suddenly that it was important to him for Kate to be estranged from the dead letters and whatever they portended.

"Meaning mine," Kate said. "What do you want me to do with the files?"

"Give them to me. I'll put them in my safe at home."

"And the papers for your brother to examine?"

"Put them in a plastic bag and I'll mail them tomorrow. Promise."

She smiled over the rim of her wineglass. "I'm not accustomed to business associates taking a personal interest in my welfare."

He broke contact with her eyes. He didn't usually take a personal interest in business associates, especially women. He made a conscious effort not to. "Normally there's nothing threatening about merely making a shipment and collecting on it," he said.

"Would you be so chivalrous about this if I were Paul Cosentino?"

"I don't like Paul Cosentino," he admitted, raising his glance to meet hers again, finding a hint of merriment there. "And the BATT export sales manager doesn't much concern me either. But I like Kate Fleming."

"You compartmentalize that well?"

"Not usually. I have a rule about dating people I work with."

"So do I."

He listened for any coolness in her voice, any distance, but heard none. He reached out a hand to stroke her hair, pull her to him for a kiss.

Their first embrace had familiarity, a joining of two people somehow not strangers. Kate's slim body felt warm against his, vulnerable. He set their wineglasses aside and took her in his arms. She tasted faintly of Chablis and soy sauce.

They both drew back. He saw the same surprise in her eyes that must be reflected in his own. And perhaps some fear.

"I'm sorry," he said softly, not for what he had done but for what he would do if he stayed. "I won't hurt you, Kate." Someone had, he saw. Someday he would know who. Someday he would know everything about her.

"I think we broke the rules," she said shyly.

"Do you mind?"

"No. As long as you don't."

"I don't, but I think we've both had a long day." Josh smiled as he stood up, pulling her up beside him. "Will you see me again, outside of office hours?"

"Is that an invitation for more snooping?"

"No, for more conventional courting rituals like dinner and picnics in the park."

Kate paused.

"Please?"

"I'd love to," she said.

Garrett did not return home until after eleven. That left six hours of his time unaccounted for. Regrettable, but surveillance had to begin somewhere. His instructions had been explicit: pick up the mark as soon as possible. That just happened to be 11:24 P.M.

He retreated through the shadows of the garden to his car and radioed in that contact had been established.

Kate Fleming turned out her lights just before midnight. A watchful pair of eyes made note of the time. In his log he failed to record that Garrett had left the building ninety minutes before. He had not yet seen Garrett's photo. There had not been time.

Chapter

6

Every neighborhood has its characters. Kate's favorite was the retarded delivery boy who breakfasted outside the bakery on the corner every morning. His name was Gary and he wasn't exactly a boy. She put his age somewhere between forty and fifty. But he was a boy in mind and in his simple belief in the goodness of his fellow human beings. Neither was he permanently employed. But merchants in the neighborhood who ran out of change or who wanted to send out for lunch had come to hang a red handkerchief in the window. Gary would be there, the bell on his ancient bicycle with the wire basket cheerfully tinkling. He was everyone's friend.

And every morning he posted himself outside the bakery. Kate for one bought him a cake donut with chocolate frosting. He had other regular customers, too, she knew.

He would always say, "Thank you, Katie. Best donut of the morning." Then he would give her the weather report: "Gonna be a nice day, Katie," or "Gonna rain cats and dogs and crocodiles. You better go back and get your galoshes, Katie."

Gary was a cheerful note in her daily waking process.

But this Friday morning he wasn't there.

It was the first sour note in a day when she had awakened singing. Misha had stared at her askance. Kate was not a morning person. Hair, makeup, and clothes were about all she could manage, and that by remote control. But not this morning. Her body had awakened alive, her mind alert. She had bounced down the stairs to the street.

"Where's Gary?" she asked Joe the baker.

Joe looked like a frosted piece of pastry himself. He had a

pale pink face, quite round and topped with a frizz of white. He had not balded with age, but every hair on his head, eyebrows and mustache included, had bleached out like icing on a wedding cake.

"Mugged," Joe said morosely.

"What! Gary? When?"

"This mornin'. Right down the street there. Near your buildin' actually."

"You're kidding! Who would mug Gary?"

"Dunno. Little man with a brown shirt, they said. Been standin' there a long time, I guess, an' you know ol' Gary. He can't let nobody stay a stranger fer long. So he goes over to say hi and the guy clobbers him an' runs off. Better not show his face 'round here again, all I can say." He handed her a chocolate eclair.

"Thanks. Will he be all right?"

"Yeah. He has a hard head. Come here afterwards. He knows I always get in early. Sometimes he helps with the bakin'. Cryin' shame, that's what it is."

"Thanks, Joe. Let me know how he's doing, will you?"

"Sure thing."

Kate left the bakery with dampened zest for the day and plodded for the subway. Since Monday she had been constantly reminded of the venal side of humankind. She was weary of it.

Except for Josh. The thought of him made her smile again.

Commuters less awake than she jostled and squeezed their way down the staircase. Far below she could hear the screech of brakes as a train pulled in. The crowd surged forward, conditioned to cram themselves into the cars at all costs. To have to wait for the next train was to lose the game. In New York no one liked to lose.

Kate resisted the tide, hanging back against a wall to eat the eclair. Not having stopped to speak with Gary, she was ahead of schedule.

Another figure from the crowd did the same, sliding around to the far side of a pillar. It was a small man in a brown shirt.

Kate wouldn't have noticed him save for Joe's description and an odd furtiveness about the man himself. She tried not to seek him out as the station filled with another wave of commuters, but her spine tingled.

She did not see him again until the next train pulled out. He remained standing on the platform, staring at her through the grimy windows. His eyes were a cold gray.

* * *

"How could you have been so stupid!" the Cuban screamed.

"I wasn't stupid," Webb said defiantly. "You were here when he arrived. Why didn't you know who it was if you're so smart? Huh? You just went off and left me here with 'em."

"Them?" Juana queried.

"Yeah. That Fleming dame was with 'im."

"When did she come in?"

"While we was talking."

"In your office?"

"Yeah."

"And she was out here alone?" Juana's questions were getting sharper.

"Yeah. What of it?"

"How long?"

"How long what?"

"How long was she out here alone, for Christ's sake?" She was screaming again. Juana always screamed when she was angry.

Webb drew himself up to his full height. "Look, girlie, I don't have to answer to you. I already talked to the Viper first thing last night an' I know just how to handle it. I'll make the phone call this morning and fix 'er ass." He was careful to keep the whine out of his voice. Part of the agreement he had with his client in return for their financing of his business was that he hire Juana as his secretary. Webb was under no illusions. He knew she was there to spy on him. But, by God, he didn't have to answer to her.

Juana quieted, but her black eyes were slits. "How long was she in here?"

"I dunno."

"You mean the door was closed?"

He nodded. "I always close the door when I have a conference."

The Cuban rolled her eyes. Her voice was a hoarse whisper, a lethal hiss somehow more menacing than her screech. "Did it ever occur to you that she might have been snooping, that she might have seen or taken something?"

Webb paled. No, it hadn't.

"You go make your fuckin' phone call," she told him. "I'll make sure we're still in business."

Webb made his phone call. As promised the man was easily reached.

"Look, Mr. Thrasher, I'm just doin' my job and keepin' my part of the bargain an' I really don't appreciate some broad tellin' me how to do it."

There was a brief silence at the other end. "I'm not sure I know what you mean," Thrasher said at last.

"Fleming."

"What about her?"

"She was here yesterday with the goddamned controller askin' me what I did with yer precious goods and why haven't they got the papers and why wasn't I doin' things by the book. An' you don't wanna know what he insinuated about my operation. Can't you control your people?"

"I'm sorry," Thrasher responded, a sincere note of apology in his voice. "I assure you I was not aware of this. She was told to mind her own business the day after she came back from vacation. I'll take care of her."

"See that you do."

"You won't have any more problems."

"Good. That means that we won't, if you catch my drift."

"Yes. Thank you."

"Good day."

Webb hung up and sat back in his chair with satisfaction. The conversation had gone just like the Viper had said it would. He had no idea who the Viper was. Webb had no name and no face to go with the code name. But the Viper always knew how to handle things.

Juana appeared at the doorway, a manila file folder in her hand, a thundercloud on her face.

"That bitch broke into our files."

Webb sat up straight. "Are you sure?" He tried to remember the scene in the front office the day before, the woman standing beside Juana's desk, closing her briefcase.

"These aren't my papers," the Cuban said accusingly. "Not all of them anyway."

God, if she had the files . . . He didn't want to think about it, but he forced himself. What could be gleaned from those papers? Nothing, he concluded, as long as no one found the damn L/C's. There was nothing illegal about a shipment to Hong Kong or Vienna, and the goods were gone now. Customs hadn't opened one box. Only the L/C's could be incriminating. Why had the Viper insisted they be kept?

"What do you mean?" he demanded. "What's missing?"

"Those dead L/C's for one thing."

Webb paused. The Fleming woman must have them then, he thought. Well, he'd just have to get them back. He wasn't going to let a bitch like that ruin his whole setup. He'd worked too long and too hard.

"I took those," he said.

"What! When?" Juana was skeptical.

"When that dame started callin'. Couldn't have 'em lyin' around, could we? I told the Viper from the beginning those L/C's were bad news."

"What did you do with them?"

"Never you mind."

"What about the invoices for the actual shipments?"

"What about 'em?"

"They're gone," Juana said.

"Don't know anything about it."

"I still think she was in my files."

Webb met her suspicious black eyes with a glare of his own. "Then you let me handle it. Understand?"

Juana wheeled and returned to her desk.

"Close the door," he barked. It was his business and he was going to save it and how he did it was none of hers.

"Bad form," Josh told himself as he picked up the phone, strictly against his code of separating the business and personal aspects of his life.

But he couldn't resist calling Kate. The tone of her voice would tell him if the passion of the evening before had cooled. Somehow it was important for him to know that it had not.

He found her name in the company directory. As he dialed someone knocked on his door. He jumped like a boy caught with his hand in the cookie jar. The receiver clonked on the desk and fell to the floor.

"Come in," he called out, sheepishly picking up the phone. The receiver rattled oddly.

"Good morning," Irene said, poking her gray head in the door. "Would you like coffee?"

"Good morning," he said. "Yes, please."

When she had gone he examined the phone, feeling somewhat silly. The receiver still rattled. He unscrewed the mouthpiece. A small metal disk fell out in his hand.

Josh stared at the glinting object for a long minute. He knew what it was but he couldn't quite believe it.

It was fortunate he hadn't reached Kate, he thought. He had

been going to tell her that the files were safe and that he had mailed the cables to his brother—along with a memo that he'd had Thrasher sign.

Shortly after nine her phone rang.

Kate paused before answering. Perhaps it was Josh. Should she tell him about the man in the brown shirt? she wondered.

It wasn't Josh. It was Dominique Attinger. Her voice was as cool over the phone as was her demeanor in person.

"Mr. Thrasher would like to see you," she said.

"Fine? When?"

"Now."

Somewhere in Kate's head an alarm went off. "Did he say why?"

"No, he did not, but I suggest you come up immediately."

The woman hung up, leaving Kate holding an empty receiver.

Josh bulled his way into Petersen's office without preamble.

"I knew you wanted these reports right away so I thought I'd deliver them myself," he said rather more loudly than necessary.

Petersen looked up, startled.

Josh plopped a file on the desk. On top was a printed note that said, "I found a bug in my phone. Let's check yours."

The president's eyes widened, but he recovered quickly.

"Why, thank you, Josh. I appreciate it. Have you had coffee yet?"

"No, sir." Josh reached for the phone and carefully removed the cover of the mouthpiece. The disk was attached to the inside, chilling in its simplicity and implication.

Petersen swallowed and nodded. "Well then, why don't we wander down to the coffee shop in the basement? I have a craving for one of those obnoxious sticky buns my wife says I'm not supposed to have."

Josh smiled, admiring the man's poised self-command. "Thank you, sir. I'd like that."

Kate composed herself in the elevator. She took slow, deep breaths. Instinct told her why she had been summoned. Webb had called Thrasher. She should have expected it, she reflected. Someone at LTS had stolen her files and given them to Webb. Now she knew who. But why? Perhaps he had only wanted her notes. Perhaps he wanted all trace of the shipments obliterated.

She had no time to puzzle it out. The elevator opened and she was on the executive floor.

Her face was known now. No one seemed to notice Kate as she swished by. The thick carpet swallowed even the clicking of heels, but her muffled footsteps seemed somehow loud. It was as if the entire floor held its breath.

Dominique was not at her desk. The door to Thrasher's office was open. She knocked on the frame.

"Come in." He sat behind his desk, chair tilted back, doing press-ups with his fingers, one hand against the other. He reminded Kate of a spider poised at the edge of its web. "Close the door."

She obeyed. Vapors from Dominique's sultry perfume lingered in the office.

"Sit down." He did not ask, he commanded.

Kate sank into one of the low chairs, determined to meet the man with defiance.

"I received a call from a Mr. Webb this morning," Thrasher said, still working his fingers. "He told me you're harassing him."

"I've been trying to get him to do his job," Kate told him.

"And I told you to mind your own business, did I not?"

Kate was silent.

Thrasher snapped his chair forward. "Ms. Fleming, you may believe me when I tell you that LTS will be paid for those orders, but you won't be here to see it. I've had it with your meddling. You're fired."

Kate was stunned.

"You have until noon to clean out your desk. I'll instruct the payroll department to cut your last check."

Kate felt glued to the chair. Her limbs were temporarily paralyzed. She realized that her mouth had fallen open and closed it.

"You may go," Thrasher said.

She stood. Movement restored her voice. "You realize, of course that you're wrong. And the president knows . . ."

"I have a few years on you, my dear. Now, who's Petersen going to believe: me or a young woman who has obviously been promoted beyond her abilities?"

"I have proof," she said stubbornly.

"Your briefcase will be searched before you leave the building." He smiled. "And if I were you I wouldn't pursue it."

There was an undercurrent of menace in his voice.

Kate held her tongue. Her mind had at last begun to churn. She was lucid enough to stop herself before she revealed just how much she and Josh had discovered. Thrasher was stupid enough to underestimate her because she was a woman. Well, let him.

But for her own self-respect she couldn't leave without a parting salvo. He could do nothing further to her. "You're a little man in a big job, Mr. Thrasher. Someday soon someone's going to discover that."

His control shattered. "Get out of here, you bitch," he spat. Kate's hand touched the doorknob as Thrasher rose.

"And I warn you that if you pursue this you'll wish you never had. You hear me? I'll have you fixed permanently!"

Kate slammed the door behind her. She found herself breathing hard and shaking slightly. Her legs were unsteady. Somehow she found her way to the elevator. Only when the paneled doors slid shut did the realization hit her that she was no longer employed.

Josh made a detour through his own office. Kate needed to know about the electronic surveillance as soon as possible. He certainly couldn't call to tell her. He sat at his desk and hastily scribbled a note.

"Our phones are bugged," he wrote. "Assume someone may be listening and watch what you say. I'll call you at home tonight. Burn this." He hesitated to sign it and wondered if she would recognize his script. He added, "Careful compartmentalization necessary."

As he stuffed the note in an intracompany envelope his phone rang. He almost ignored it and let Irene take a message, but on second thought he picked it up.

"Josh, this is Kate. Thrasher just fired me."

He gasped involuntarily, but the bug tempered his response.

"Gee, I'm sorry to hear that, Miss Fleming. Did he give you any notice?"

Kate paused, obviously bewildered by his neutral tone. "No," she said at last, deflated. "He told me to be out of the building by noon." He could hear the hurt in her voice.

"That's too bad. Well, Thrasher must have his reasons. Sometimes these corporate adjustments are difficult. Would a reference help?"

"Yes, thank you," she said coldly.

"I'll have my secretary type one up and deliver it. Chin up,

Miss Fleming. This could be the best thing that ever happened to you.''

She was quiet.

''Good luck, Miss Fleming,'' he said.

She hung up.

Josh replaced the receiver slowly. Please understand, he thought. Lord, Thrasher must be getting nervous.

He opened the envelope and removed the note. ''We won't be breaking any rules now,'' he jotted on the bottom. He asked Irene to deliver it. He couldn't entrust it to interoffice mail.

''My, he does compartmentalize well,'' Kate said bitterly. Then she caught herself.

The man with whom she had just spoken was not the same person who had embraced her the night before. He had been impassive, objective. There must have been someone in his office, she realized. Maybe even Thrasher. She shuddered.

Veronica appeared in the doorway.

''Are you all right?'' she asked.

Kate swallowed. ''I've just been fired.''

''Holy shit! By whom?'' Veronica came in and sat down as if her legs could no longer support her.

''Thrasher.''

''That mother! He can't do that.'' Her cheeks were reddening.

''He has.''

''Effective when?''

''Now.''

''Kate, Kate, what are you gonna do?'' Veronica's voice was urgent, her black eyes filling. In all the years they'd worked together Kate had never seen her cry.

''I don't know.'' She remembered now the threat implicit in the man's voice when he'd warned her not to pursue the matter. She remembered Payton the guard and Chun the bank clerk and realized he meant what he said. She looked up at Veronica.

''I'm going to go home and watch a soap opera and put my thoughts together,'' she said.

''But what are we going to do without you?''

''Just pretend I'm on a trip and hold down the fort. It won't end here, Veronica. I promise. But for now we just have to pretend that it will.'' She leaned across the desk. ''Do you trust me?''

''Yes.''

"Then don't make waves. Be honest about your feelings and don't kiss up to anybody, but don't jeopardize your own job."

"I don't kiss ass for nobody."

"I know." Kate smiled.

"Who do you think I'll have to report to?"

"Probably Paul, but I don't think Thrasher's thought that far ahead."

"What'd he go and fire you for?"

"Insubordination. I went to see Webb yesterday. Webb didn't like it."

"Well, screw him! That bastard's an unethical worm."

"Yes, he is," Kate agreed. "But promise me you'll stay out of that affair, Veronica."

"Dead L/C's, stolen papers . . ."

"Dead people," Kate added quietly, but for some reason she knew that statement had to be retracted. "I've lost my job over it. I don't want you to lose yours."

"You're taking the fall for him?" her assistant demanded.

Kate shook her head. "The shit hasn't hit the fan yet," she assured Veronica, "and when it does, it's gonna fly all over him."

"I'll buy Thrasher working with Webb," Petersen said. "I'll even buy that they're illegally shipping restricted technology. There's still money to be made in that. Cuba, Khadaffi, cocaine barons, plenty of buyers. But why in God's name would anyone have an interest in bankrupting LTS?" He kept his voice low. The clanking of the dishes and chatter at the counter kept his words from carrying beyond their booth.

"I don't know," Josh admitted. "Maybe there's no link at all."

Petersen sipped his coffee. "No, I think there's probably a link all right. Someone professional set Ralph Payton up."

"To get the shipping crates?"

"Maybe."

"How do you know?"

"Because his medical records were faked. The medical examiner attributed his death to a heart attack. He pointed to the records of Payton's physical when he joined the company which showed evidence of coronary heart disease. The records of the doctor who did the exam back then confirmed it. But you know and I know that Payton wouldn't have been hired for that position with a history of heart disease. And his wife was as surprised as we were. Payton had never mentioned any heart problems to her.''

"Can we press for a second autopsy?''

Petersen shook his head. "Payton was cremated Wednesday. A 'mistake' the funeral home called it. They were supposed to cremate some guy the county was burying, a drifter. They 'accidentally' cremated Payton instead.''

"Jesus.'' Josh let his coffee grow cold.

"Fortunately the truck involved in the GW Bridge accident was impounded by the police, however,'' the president went on. "They found evidence of sabotage. The brakes didn't fail. The compressor was destroyed by some kind of explosion.''

Josh's jaw tightened. "But why?''

"The cops think we have some nut on our hands with a grudge against LTS. They're even willing to concede that the fire might have been arson.''

"What about the letters of credit?''

"I mentioned them. No one knew what I was talking about. They saw it as a financial problem, not a criminal problem.''

"Did you mention Chun?''

"No.''

"Just as well,'' Josh said. "They wouldn't have jurisdiction.''

"Who would?''

"The feds, I think. Both bank fraud and illegal export come under federal jurisdiction.''

"Then I guess we'd better talk to them,'' Petersen observed. He seemed older somehow, Josh noted, his face a shade grayer.

"It won't save LTS, but it'll put Thrasher where he belongs,'' Josh said quietly.

Petersen was subdued. "I kept hoping it was just our imagination, Josh. But the police report and your findings yesterday . . . well, it's real.''

Josh felt a stab of pity for the older man. Petersen had spent the better part of his adult life building LTS.

"Do you know anyone who can make a sweep of our offices—privately?''

"Yes, I suppose so. The BATT Division manufactures that kind of equipment.''

"Great—as long as no one else in the company knows about the sweep.''

"Yes.'' Petersen sighed. He squared his shoulders. "Business as usual in the office. I don't want that bastard to suspect anything until they come for him with handcuffs.''

"He fired Kate this morning," Josh said.

"He what!"

"He fired Kate. She just called."

Petersen's face softened. "Poor kid. That lady knows her business. But we can't interfere, Josh. You know that. Thrasher would be suspicious."

Josh sighed. "I know. I'll explain it to her."

"Tell her that as soon as this is over she's welcome back and I'll personally promote her and double her salary."

Josh restrained a smile.

"You handle the lady and I'll make an appointment with the FBI," Petersen told him. "I want you to come with me. I'll call you for 'lunch.' Be ready."

She kept expecting Cosentino to come in and gloat. Now he would inherit her office, she thought mournfully. But it was Dominique Attinger who came in to supervise her packing.

"We just want to make sure you don't take anything that's not yours," she said with a cool smile.

Kate could have smacked her. She thought she would choke on the woman's perfume.

Veronica brought boxes from the mail room. Kate dismantled her office and began to pack her books and prints, wondering how she was going to get it all home. She supposed she'd have to call a cab.

Both Irene and the interoffice mail arrived at ten-thirty, and with them Josh's note.

Kate sat down and cried. Her world began to come together again.

The call didn't surprise him. Thrasher had to cover all his bases. Read "cover his ass," Josh thought.

He sat for a while, organizing his thoughts. The less he said the better, Josh reflected. Above all the VP could not be spooked. If he were to sense just how much of the plot was known, he might bolt. The conspiracy might dissolve before it could be unraveled and the odds on LTS surviving would diminish. No, until he and Petersen turned the case over to the FBI, he would have to play it as though his only concern were recovering the seven million dollars.

Josh stretched his legs and stood. He paused beside Irene's desk.

"I've been offered an audience with Thrasher," he said. "I won't be long."

The vice president's door was closed and his secretary was nowhere to be seen. Josh was pleased. He had an aversion to the tall, cool blonde. She reminded him of his ex-wife.

He rapped on Thrasher's door. From within he heard a startled scuffling.

"Just a minute," Thrasher called.

Josh waited.

A few moments later the door opened and Dominique stepped out, composed and icy.

"Mr. Thrasher will see you now," she said.

He glanced past her. Thrasher was behind his desk as usual, standing on his ridiculous little platform. As Josh moved closer, he could see the blush in the man's cheeks. His tie was slightly askew. Josh wondered fleetingly what it would be like to screw a woman eight inches taller than he was.

"Come in, come in," the VP said heartily. "Have a seat."

Josh eyed the low-slung chairs warily. "I'd rather not. What do you want?"

A look of chagrin passed over Thrasher's face, as if he were unaccustomed to his subjects refusing to be treated as such. He flashed a strained smile.

"Would you prefer the sofa then?"

"Yes," Josh replied. He knew it would pry the little man off his pedestal.

Reluctantly Thrasher joined him.

"What do you want to see me about?" Josh asked.

"Well now, I think there's the danger of a misunderstanding between us and I just want to get it cleared up, that's all."

"Really. What?"

"Well now, I understand that you visited Webb Overseas yesterday afternoon with Miss Fleming of my department." His voice underlined the "my department."

"Yes, I did."

"Well, I can understand you're being worried about getting payment from those L/C's, but Miss Fleming's panicking unnecessarily and Mr. Webb was righteously upset."

Josh glared at him. "I am also concerned that you superseded your authority in compromising the credit of this corporation."

"I had the approval of the corporate treasurer," Thrasher said with an edge in his voice. He caught himself and smiled again. "You were out of town and time was of the essence. Besides, the credit extended is backed by those L/C's."

"I can't believe our suppliers accepted unconfirmed L/C's as collateral."

"They accepted my word," Thrasher said, his tone hardening once again. "How much experience do you have with international shipments and payments, Josh?"

"Not a lot," Josh admitted.

"Precisely. Let me assure you that I do—and that I consulted with a friend of mine who is a specialist in the field before I made the move. We will receive the payments on time. Let me also advise you that Miss Fleming has a history of responding to crisis with typical female hysterics rather than calm objectivity. It's in her personnel file. BATT may have tolerated that. I won't. I dismissed her this morning and plan to replace her with Paul Cosentino."

So they'd altered Kate's personnel file, too. He resisted the urge to tell Thrasher exactly what he thought of his ethics.

"So, there you have it. The little lady was crying wolf and threatened to panic half the organization with her."

Josh swallowed. "Well, I'm certainly glad to hear that everything is under control. Phil and I have been quite worried about that seven million dollars."

"I can well understand why. I'm writing a memo to explain everything to Phil, but I felt you should hear it from me personally."

Josh rose to leave. "Thanks, Bob. I appreciate it."

"You're quite welcome."

Thrasher held out his hand. Josh took it. It was damp.

"Let's work together on these things in the future," Thrasher said as he walked Josh to the door. "After all, we're both on the same team."

Josh forced a smile. We're not even working for the same country, you son of a bitch, he thought. But he was relieved to find that Thrasher seemed not to suspect that anyone knew that.

The taxi found a space at the curb in front of her building. Wearily Kate climbed out as the driver began unloading her boxes from the trunk.

A mournful wail greeted her. A Siamese cat sat huddled in the entrance to the brownstone. With a start Kate recognized Misha.

"Misha! Misha, what are you doing here?"

The cat never left the apartment. Exposed to the street for the first time, she was terrified. Her claws clung to Kate and she tried to bury her face in the crook of her mistress's arm.

"Misha, poor little kitty, how did you get out?"

With alarm Kate realized that the only way for Misha to have gotten out was for someone else to have gotten in.

"You need some help, Katie?" asked a slow voice.

It was Gary, a white bandage around his balding head, but smiling.

"Yes, Gary. Thank you," she said, breathless. "Those boxes there? They're mine. Could you help me bring them up to the apartment?"

"Yes, ma'am." He grinned amiably.

"Are you all right, Gary? I heard about this morning . . ."

"Oh, I'm just fine. Joe says I have a hard head."

"Yes, I suppose so. I'm glad. I'll see you upstairs."

Clutching Misha with one hand, she ran up the stairs. The door to her apartment was ajar. She stopped, listening. The apartment was silent.

With trepidation, she pushed open the door. The first thing she saw was kitty litter all over the floor. She couldn't bear to go in, not alone.

Gary puffed up the stairs behind her.

"This yer apartment, Katie?"

"Yes," she whispered.

"Boy, yer cat sure does make a mess."

"Yes. Gary, would you please go down to the bakery and ask Joe to call the police? Someone's been in my house."

Petersen's explanation was terse. "Some big drug bust or something has all their people in the field," he said in a hurried conversation in the elevator. "We can't get an appointment until Monday. I'll see you then."

He left Josh in the lobby of the building, bewildered.

Josh returned to his office and jotted down the number of the FBI. He made the call from payroll—after checking the receiver.

No appointment was necessary to talk with the FBI.

He found that less disturbing than Petersen's state of mind during that elevator ride down to the lobby. The man had not just been agitated. He'd been scared.

* * *

Kate didn't know whom to call. Everyone she knew was at work. And Josh's phone was bugged. She was afraid to stay in her apartment, she was afraid to leave.

The police had been kind, but not helpful. They said that whoever had entered had been professional. Her locks had been picked. There was no damage to the door. She could find nothing missing to file in their report, but she was positive she knew what the intruder had been after. It was in Josh's safe. She couldn't tell the police that.

Josh. She ached to warn him, but she was afraid to call LTS. She did check her own phone and could find nothing. She spent the afternoon behind her chained door straightening her ransacked apartment and calming her frightened cat.

At five she began calling Josh's house, praying that perhaps he would leave work early. She reached him at seven-fifteen.

"Kate. I'm sorry I haven't called. I got caught in a traffic jam on the LIE."

She was so relieved to hear his voice that she almost began to cry again. "Josh, is your house all right?"

"I think so. Why?" he asked in a puzzled voice.

"My apartment was broken into."

"When?"

"Sometime this morning."

"My Lord. Are you all right? Was anything taken?"

"There was nothing for them to take, Josh," she said in a quiet voice. "You have it all."

"Shit. They must know we took the papers."

"Someone was watching the building, Josh. He waited for me to leave."

"You know who it was?"

"No, but I think I know what he looks like. Josh, I'm scared."

"I'll be there as soon as I can," he said gently.

"But your house . . ."

"I have an alarm system and a cop for a neighbor. Just stay put. I'm on my way."

He first saw the blue Chevy as he turned onto Route 107 and headed south for the Long Island Expressway. It was an older model, traffic worn and rusted. Josh would not have noticed save for two things: a car in such condition was out of place in his neighborhood and he himself was driving substantially over the speed limit. The Chevy kept pace.

As he zigzagged around slower traffic on the four-lane road, he saw the Chevy spurt out of the crowd and fall in behind him, two cars back.

Josh would not have given it a second thought except for the fact that he had already found his office phone bugged that day and Kate's apartment had been invaded.

He kept his eye on the two men in the blue car as he veered unexpectedly and went up the entrance ramp to the LIE. They followed, nearly running a Cadillac off the road in the process. He held his breath and cut across to the left-hand lane. The Chevy did not attempt to overtake him.

He felt strangely exposed. Though he tried to concentrate on his driving, his eyes continually wandered to the rearview mirror.

The evening was sticky; there were thunderheads on the horizon. The AM band on his radio crackled. Josh rolled up his windows and turned on the air-conditioning.

The Chevy dogged him, no longer blatant about its moves, but always present. It was never more than two cars behind him, keeping to the middle lane, from which vantage point it could observe him clearly and move left or right as necessary.

Josh had never been tailed before, at least not to his knowledge. He dared not lead them to Kate's, nor return home to face them alone. He glanced at his gas gauge. It was half-full.

The exits ticked by. It was also getting dark. His pursuers had the advantage now. With the twilight, deepened by the advancing thunderclouds, the highway behind him was reduced to a melange of headlights. The outline of his vehicle, however, with its identifiable taillights, could still be distinguished by a following party. He darted in and out of traffic, trying to draw the twin beams of the other car, seeing nothing. But he knew that somewhere in the glare behind him lurked the drab blue Chevy.

He exited at the Cross Island Parkway, deep in Queens. He needed stoplights, cross streets, anything to make pursuit more difficult. He opted for the airport. La Guardia should be nicely crowded this time of night.

As he zipped along the Cross Island, fed into the Whitestone Expressway, and picked up the Grand Central Parkway, he had no way to confirm that he was still being tailed, but he had to assume that he was. He pulled off at Ninety-fourth Street, the exit for the airport. Several cars fell in behind him.

At the entrance to the garage he would have to stop and pick up a ticket. Everyone would. He followed the signs for arriving flights, staying to the left. If he could spot them, if he were far enough ahead of them, he could actually park, slip into the terminal, and take a cab to Manhattan.

But eventually he would have to return to the car.

Traffic edging up to the terminal ground to a halt for a light. He made sure his doors were locked, glanced in the rearview mirror. They were behind him all right, five cars back in the next lane, a slower moving lane, signaling left.

"Please, nobody be polite and let them in," he prayed.

The light changed and he spurted ahead. The blue Chevy was still signaling.

The storm hit as he pulled into the line for the garage. The air shivered with a great clap of thunder and huge drops splotched his windshield. The prelude ended abruptly in torrents of water that obscured his rear view. Josh flipped on the wipers, front and back. Between swipes he glimpsed what he thought was the Chevy, far behind him, muscling its way through the crowd.

He inched forward toward the machines that dispensed the parking tickets. Snatching the soggy piece of paper, he accelerated up the ramp.

The ground floor was full and closed to traffic; so were the second and third. The ramp spiraled upward. There was no one immediately behind him. The fourth floor was also blocked, but the sawhorse that served as a barricade had been placed haphazardly.

Josh braked quickly. There was just enough room to squeeze the BMW by. Killing the lights he sped into the dim recesses of the garage, slipped between two rows of cars, and took his foot off the brake. Through a slot between a Toyota and an Escort he could see the ramp.

He waited. Thunder exploded and the building seemed to quake. Flashes of lightning cast abrupt shadows. The rain fell with a roar. He half expected a dark figure to come up behind him with a gun.

At last the Chevy whisked by, its tires squealing as it careened up the ramp. Two other cars followed, enough to assure that the Chevy would not be coming back down, not in time to follow him.

Josh flicked on his lights and gunned for the exit.

"Why did he go to the police?" he demanded.

She smiled and ran her fingers across his cheek, down his smooth chest.

He grabbed her hand. "Stop playing. There's time enough for that later. Why did Petersen see the police yesterday?"

She leaned back against the headboard and reached for the cigarettes on the night table. She selected one, long and elegant like her fingers.

"They came to see him," she replied. The lighter sprang to life in her hands, casting brief dancing shadows around the room, revealing the essential orderliness of its occupant. With a snap darkness returned. Only the tip of the cigarette glowed. There had been no time for him to study her face.

"I know that. Why?"

"Because the BATT truck was sabotaged."

"Is that all?"

"As far as I know, yes."

"What do you mean, as far as you know? You're supposed to know." His tone was harsh, harsher than he had meant it to be.

"One of the bugs in Petersen's office apparently malfunctioned."

"Or was found?"

Her hair rustled against the pillow as she shook her head. "No, it was bad. It's been replaced."

"You're sure?"

"Yes."

He sighed. "So what else did they cover in that meeting?"

"I don't know."

"I don't like it. He met with Garrett in a public café this morning. Our man couldn't get close enough to overhear. This afternoon Petersen called the FBI. This smells."

"The FBI?" For the first time she sounded disturbed.

"Yes. And we can't afford that now."

She laid her cigarette in an ashtray and slipped her arms around his neck. "But we're so close, darling. It's nearly time for you to make your move."

"I know." He ran his hand up and down her flanks, so smooth, so perfect. He was lucky to have her, he thought, to work with her, to sleep with her . . . But that, of course, was precisely what she wanted him to think. Her career was on the line, too.

"Petersen we can handle," he said as she began to nuzzle him. "The Fleming woman we took care of today, no sweat. Now we have to come up with a way to neutralize Garrett."

"Trouble from an unexpected quarter. Methinks you underestimated him, my dear,'' she murmured. ''Everyone's followed true to form except our intrepid controller—who's showing a bit more imagination and initiative than we bargained for.''

''He swallowed the Fleming woman's tales.''

''And tail. And then sold the president on the package.''

''We won't have to worry about Petersen any longer, believe me. Or Webb, that fat fool.''

''And Garrett? Why don't you let me handle him?''

''Not on your sweet life, my dear. I don't want to share you with anyone.''

He rolled her beneath him, possessing her with his bulk. Her lips parted to receive his eager, thrusting tongue. His hands grasped her breasts and savaged the nipples until she cried out in protest. He shifted his weight just enough that her slender fingers could gently stroke his genitals, his balls so full and heavy, his penis, short and massive. He did not enter a woman, he split her, filling her cavity tightly if not deeply. She called him the bull.

He fingered her inner labia and toyed briefly with her clitoris. A woman had to be well lubricated to receive him. She was ready.

He plunged into her and strangled her cry with his tongue, pressing thoughts of the tall, handsome controller out of her mind.

She felt so safe in his arms, a sense of security she had not known since Clint walked out of her life. Josh offered solidity and assurance in the face of her increasing vulnerability to an evil she did not understand. Somehow she had stumbled upon something craven and corrupt—and deadly. The familiar had become alien. The unthinkable had become her waking reality. She walked on trembling ground until he pulled her to safety.

''We'll start the ball rolling Monday,'' he told her. ''These people, whoever they are, are careless. I think they were counting on our naive complicity in this conspiracy, whatever it is, and we caught them by surprise. We can give the FBI a lot to work with. You'll be back at work before you know it.''

''Do you really believe that or are you just trying to make me feel better?'' Kate asked.

''Both.''

''But what do I do in the meantime, Josh? I'm scared.''

He wrapped his arms around her. ''Come home with me. We'll spend the weekend behind my burglar alarms.''

Kate laughed. "Is that a modern version of 'come up and see my etchings?'"

"I do have ulterior motives," he said. His hands stroked her body, longing to probe more intimately. He wanted her with an intensity that verged on physical insistence. But he never felt her hesitate. She yielded as he undressed her. Her slender fingers deftly unfastened the buttons on his shirt to expose the thick dark curls on his chest. She lifted the elastic of his shorts over the bulge in his crotch.

Josh lowered himself gently, pausing to cover her throat with kisses and swallow her breasts briefly with his hands, teasing the nipples to erection. Then he entered.

Kate's hips rose to meet him. He wondered fleetingly why he felt none of the awkwardness of a first encounter, none of the tentative exploration that usually accompanied a casual one-night stand.

There was nothing casual in his loving of Kate Fleming. Body and soul he submerged himself in her.

Neither of them spoke for a long time afterward. He was replete and hoped she was, too. Kate lay in the crook of his arm and ran her fingers through the hair on his chest.

"This isn't the only reason I want to take you home with me," he said at last, stroking her cheek.

"No?"

"No. I want to get to know Kate Fleming. I want to know everything about her."

"That might take longer than forty-eight hours."

"I hope so."

He kissed her, a long languid kiss that melted her tensions. His hands began to caress her body, to untangle her from the sheet.

"Can you drive after sex?" she whispered as she felt his hardness against her thigh.

"No. We'll have to drive out in the morning."

It would be light then—but he didn't mention that.

Chapter
7

The missing L/C's still worried him, but Webb wouldn't let them ruin his Saturday morning fishing junket. Besides, how could the broad prove he'd ever had the fucking documents? What was she going to do? Admit she'd stolen them from his files?

So he'd packed his lunch and headed for the boat ramp.

He shivered as he launched his little outboard, but the chill came more from the dark than the temperature. It would be another scorcher. The sun was just peeking over the horizon when he pushed off, the whine of his motor carrying far over the quiet bay.

Out of the corner of his eye he saw headlights pull in beside his truck and hesitated. The driver had trouble getting his lights off. They flickered once or twice. Webb turned to get a good look. It was the tan sedan. He remembered it from Wednesday morning, but didn't give it a second thought. Some people just liked to watch the sun come up.

Webb forgot about the tan sedan as he approached his favorite fishing spot. He killed the motor and slung a small anchor over the side so he wouldn't drift so easily with the current. Then he set about preparing his tackle and baiting his hook.

The seabirds greeted the morning with their squawks. Far away across the water he could hear the sounds of sleepy civilization, dogs barking, a car horn. A plane flew in low overhead, heading for Kennedy Airport. As the sun revealed itself, Webb could pick out other boats, here and there. He supposed he could hail them if he had a mind to. He didn't. He relaxed and lit his first cigar.

Suddenly he heard a splash behind him, a strange sound that could not have come from the slap of the waves against the boat. He turned. As he watched a hand gripped the gunwale.

"What the . . ." he began.

There was another splash to his right. A diver encased in black rubber surfaced and grabbed for him.

Webb dropped his pole and struck at the man with his net, but a third set of hands restrained his arm.

Before he could cry out he was flipped over the side into the water. His first sensation was of cold. Then he realized he was being dragged under and opened his mouth to scream for help.

It was a fatal mistake. Seawater rushed in, choking him, blinding him. The hands would not let him go.

He kicked and scratched, but his ears told him he was being dragged deeper.

Mercifully he blacked out before death took him.

Chapter

8

The Dobermans knew him. They came sniffing and whining up to the fence, anxious for the liver biscuits with which he had always rewarded them. They had no objections to his scaling the barrier to join them.

He walked carefully across the open ground on rubber-soled shoes, stepping on tufts of grass or bits of cardboard where he could. It would not do to leave footprints, even if the water jets would later erase them.

The keys fit the locks just as the Viper had said they would. He scratched each of the dogs behind the ears and softly shut the door on them.

He selected the north wall, away from the adjoining building. By the time the flames reached the south side they would be a roaring inferno, more likely to leapfrog the intervening ground and swallow the warehouse, too.

Moonlight spilled in the windows. Good. He wouldn't need a light. With deft strokes of the hacksaw he cut out a chunk of the Sheetrock. He found the bundle of wiring, just as the blueprints read. He set the small charge and gave himself ten minutes to complete his task.

Following instructions he cleaned out the second and third drawers of the middle filing cabinet, the files that might raise eyebrows were Customs to inspect them carefully, and piled them on the floor beneath the ruptured Sheetrock. Then he left the office, locking the door behind him.

The dogs gamboled at his side as he made sure the fire could find a path to the warehouse. Just in case the wind was wrong, he piled the discarded packing boxes and hunks of wooden crates in a bridge between the two buildings.

The Dobermans would be all right, he thought. They knew enough to stay out of the fire. They would also be a welcome diversion when the fire company came, giving the flames more time to do their work.

Faulty wiring. That's what the police would say. Nobody could have gotten past the Dobermans to set a fire.

Four minutes later there was a puff of smoke inside the north wall of the office and the wiring began to sizzle.

Phil Petersen always rose early, even on weekends. On Sundays his wife, Virginia, slept in. Petersen prepared Sunday brunch and collected the *Times*. It was a tradition from the earliest days of their marriage and had survived four children, numerous corporate moves, and, of late, the first admitted signs of aging.

True, they had both grayed in their forties. But it was only now, when arthritis kept Virginia off her beloved tennis court much of the time and Petersen's doctor ordered a low-cholesterol diet, that they saw more years behind them than ahead.

On summer Sundays they brunched beside the pool. Bacon was now excluded from the menu, but Petersen insisted on his omelette once a week. After all, he had been perfecting the art for over thirty-five years and he didn't want to fall out of practice.

This July morning was no exception. Petersen was up at six-thirty, padding around in the first shafts of sunlight, dazzling with a clarity the day's haze would soon dim. Before their children had left the nest this had been his only moment of peace in the household, he remembered.

He sat down in the middle of the soft green carpet of the living room to do his exercises. The skylighted room was the least confining area of the house for his exertions. He almost felt he could breathe better there. But only on Sundays. Any other day the maid might stumble across him, a stout man in Jockey shorts who could not quite reach his toes anymore.

He finished and went on to the kitchen. The blue tile counters were neat and orderly as usual. Cynthia, their cook, never went home until everything was in its place.

Petersen set the teapot to boil and wandered to the refrigerator to choose coffee beans to grind for the first pot of the day.

The doorbell rang.

Petersen started. Neighbors didn't come calling at seven in the morning. It was too early for the *Times*.

The terror of the previous Friday afternoon resurfaced: the voice on the other end of the phone, so clipped, so precise, rattling off his address, listing the number of azaleas and junipers in his front garden, the names of the flowers blooming in the beds around his pool. Then, most horrifying of all, the voice had said, "Your wife is wearing a white pantsuit today, trimmed in black and yellow, and I'd get home early, Mr. Petersen, if you want to see her again. And do us both a favor—don't call the police."

He hadn't. He had come straight home and checked his alarm system. Virginia had met him at the door—wearing a blue sundress. He had begun to hope it was all a hoax.

And now his doorbell was ringing. The sound echoed in the empty house.

Virginia had awakened. Gray hair tousled, she stood uncertainly in the archway leading to their bedroom.

"Who on earth, Phil?"

He shrugged. "Maybe we forget to pay the *Times*," he said as he strode to the door.

He glanced through the peephole and sighed with relief. A man in a gray suit stood on the doorstep, flanked by two officers in blue.

"It's the police," he called to his wife. He wrapped his robe around him and tied the sash.

"The police? But what . . ."

Petersen opened the door.

"Mr. Phillip Petersen?" asked the man in gray.

"Yes, officer. May I . . ."

"Mr. Petersen, you're under arrest."

Shock numbed the corporate president as he stood in the doorway of his house in his Jockey shorts and robe, frozen in place. His hand still grasped the doorknob. The sash of his robe loosened and hung idly.

"Under arrest? F-for what?" he stammered.

"For conspiracy to commit arson and for murder in the second degree."

Josh Garrett's home was not what Kate had been anticipating, precisely because it was a home. But then Josh himself was full of surprises.

She had half expected him to have a roommate, though

whether Josh would be the Felix or Oscar end of the duo she didn't know.

He was neither. And both.

His den was a sanctuary of sport, homage to his days on the soccer field. A younger Josh, face unlined, usually bearded, stared out at her from team pictures and group shots, his arm around some celebrity or another, few of whom she recognized. There were plaques and cups arranged on shelves, clippings framed on the wall, only some of which she could read. Many were in German.

But the mementos were confined to the den, the past carefully compartmentalized from the present.

The present Josh liked bright, airy rooms and comfortable, gracious furnishings. She wondered if he had had a decorator and decided that he probably had—and had then added his own personal embellishments. How else could one explain a living room sculpted in a Chinese motif, down to the the figurines on the mantelpiece, and then a big, ugly, roomy recliner, right in front of the inlaid armoire that housed the TV? A decorator's nightmare.

The kitchen was neat but unorganized. A stray frying pan shared a cupboard with the stoneware and a can of cleanser had found its way to the pantry amid the tomato sauce.

But Josh could cook.

"Had to," he admitted. "Diana never learned and I got tired of eating out all the time."

"However did you manage to keep the house?" she asked.

"Didn't. This is all mine. Bought it the day the divorce was final. She got the co-op in Manhattan and she's welcome to it. I don't need that rat race anymore."

He had moved far from it, she noted. The house sat well back on a three-acre lot, shielded from neighbors and passersby by groves of trees and bushes of mountain laurel. A little stream bisected the property before flowing on into a neighbor's yard. Someone long ago had crisscrossed the rivulet with a series of bridges, some covered, creating the illusion of a miniature world of horses and buggies. The brick and lumber were covered with moss now; myrtle and ivy had grown in thick along the stream. The garden had a sense of isolated timelessness about it.

Decks, a more recent addition, extended from the master suite and living room. The two joined at a staircase leading down to the pool. Built with wedges of granite, the pool was suited to the garden setting as a modern structure of blue painted cement would not have been.

Josh had been right about spending the weekend behind his burglar alarms. There was safety here, and seclusion.

Kate lay beside the pool, listening to birds chirp and the murmur of the stream. The sunlight was warm upon her back and she could smell bacon frying. The city, LTS, and Bob Thrasher were miles removed.

And what am I doing here, Kate asked herself. I've only known this man for three days.

Three days. Time enough to know that there was something basically decent and honest about him—and that he cared for her. Asking her to visit Petersen and the escapade at Webb's, that had been business. Asking her to spend the weekend with him was not. And something inside told her Josh issued such invitations as rarely as she tumbled into bed on the first date.

Only once before, she thought, before she shoved Clint out of her mind. He went with surprising ease. Had she felt this way with Clint? She tried to remember, but only Josh came to mind. Her heart skipped a beat at the thought of him and she was full of the sense that nothing more wonderful in the world had ever happened to her.

Here she was, unemployed, caught up in God knew what criminal mischief, and she was happy.

Happy? She was floating.

And that, my dear, she told herself, is a good old-fashioned schoolgirl crush. Perhaps it wasn't real, perhaps it wouldn't last, but the hold Clint had had on her had melted as if a spell had broken.

Perhaps that was what the fairy tales were really about, she thought. The evil witch is a love affair gone sour and the spell she casts is the hurt it leaves behind, and only someone extraordinary can wake the sleeping princess.

She felt more alive than she had in a year. Lying there dreaming by the pool she wanted to sing.

"Would you like some coffee?" Josh asked suddenly.

She could see his bare toes hanging over the edge of the deck above her. The rest of him was lost in glare.

"Yes, thanks." Kate sat up.

"What were you so deep in thought about?" He stepped into shadow and came into focus as he came down the steps. He was wearing a pair of light blue tennis shorts and a gray T-shirt.

Kate smiled. She couldn't tell him, not yet. What had she

been thinking about before her reverie about witches and spells? Oh, yes.

"I was thinking about how your home reminds me of my folks' place in Wyoming and how far apart they really are. My mom has to drive twenty-five miles to a grocery store and you're within twenty-five miles of midtown."

She accepted the steaming cup from him and they sat together in the shade of the picnic umbrella.

"Is that where you grew up, in Wyoming?" he asked.

"Not really. My folks are from Cheyenne, but my father was a lifer in the air force. We lived all over."

"So that's how you became an internationalist. It's not normal, you know."

Kate shrugged. "I guess I just never considered a career that would tie me to the same four walls every day."

"Or the same country."

"Yes." She smiled.

"Most people aren't like that. They're comfortable only on their own little familiar piece of turf. God forbid you transplant them." He spoke matter-of-factly.

"I guess I was never in one place long enough to think of myself as a New Yorker or Bostonian or whatever," Kate said.

"An internationalist by training."

"Not really. I have an older brother and sister. She raises kids and pedigreed collies in Sacramento and he's a dentist in Boulder. Neither of them even have passports now."

"But you never gave yours up."

Kate shook her head. "It wasn't that easy," she said, studying her coffee.

He was silent for a moment, studying her. Then he said softly, "Safer to share it than to save it."

She looked up, recognizing the echo of her own words.

"I told you I wanted to know all about you, Kate. I meant it." He waited.

She shrugged. "I didn't start out to be an internationalist," she said at last. "I started out to be an educated housewife, like Barbara."

"The sister who lives in Sacramento."

"Yes." Colorado seemed so far away now. She'd run as far from it as she could, but the hurt never died.

"So why didn't you?"

"Why didn't I what?"

"Become a housewife."

"Because he died." She steadied herself with a gulp of coffee. It was hot. "His name was John. He was a law student. He was going to get his degree and start a small practice in Denver, I was going to raise the kids and the horses." They had had such nice dreams together, she thought.

"I'm sorry," Josh whispered. His blue eyes were focused on her, on her soul. His fingers tightened on hers. "Do you want to tell me about it?"

Kate took a long breath before she began. "One day he went skiing. It was spring. Spring skiing in the Rockies is the best. We have real mountains out West, not the foothills you call mountains in the East. They went skiing for a lark, he and a friend, on a Thursday. Cut classes. Probably the only time in his life he cut classes. There was an avalanche. They both disappeared." She paused to take a deep breath.

"They found him in May." When the flowers start to come out on the high ridges. Five weeks they had waited hoping, but he was gone, and with him all their dreams. She took another swallow of coffee, cooler now.

"And you?" Josh asked.

"I graduated and left Colorado. I stayed for a while with my sister. She's older, more stable than my parents were then. They were in the process of another transfer from one continent to another. Barb is my anchor, she and Bret and the kids."

"So you went to her to heal?"

"And to settle," she admitted. "But Barb wouldn't let me. 'You have to fly,' she said. 'You have to be all the things I might have been if I were half a generation younger.' " Kate laughed half-heartedly, her courage returning. "I was the family afterthought. She says I've always been the most independent of the three of us."

"And are you?"

"I suppose. She convinced my brother the dentist to help put me through graduate school. 'A woman needs all the credentials she can get.' she said. And she was right."

"And she was right about you."

Yes, Kate realized, she was. God bless Barbara. She smiled.

"So how'd you end up in New York?" he asked.

She wouldn't tell him about Clint, she decided. Clint intimidated other men as John could not. They assumed her bitterness would carry over. But no one who had known John could harbor bitterness for all men.

"This is where the jobs were for a service brat with a master's in international business and an undergraduate degree in history and languages.''

"And so you came to BATT.''

"With a few odd jobs in between.''

"And no man in your life since John.''

"None that mattered.'' Clint didn't matter anymore. Kate shook her head. "The rest of my family thinks I'm crazy to live in New York though.''

"I can think of places I'd rather live, too,'' Josh admitted, "like Colorado or some little hamlet in the Alps. So why'd you choose business? Why not the diplomatic corps?''

Kate laughed. "Because diplomacy requires tact.''

Josh smiled and the scar across his forehead disappeared in a good-natured collusion of creases.

"How about you? How did you become a traveler?'' she asked. She didn't want to talk about closed chapters of her life anymore. Josh seemed to understand.

"Soccer. We had an Italian foreign exchange student stay a year with us when I was fourteen. He could do amazing things with a soccer ball. I was hooked.'' His nose wrinkled. "Oh, jeez. I'll bet the bacon is burning.''

He bounded up the stairs and disappeared in the house. Kate followed.

The bacon was indeed blackened and burning. The kitchen reeked of smoke. Flamelets danced around little spatters of grease on the stove, sizzling.

Josh clicked the burner off and fumbled for a pot holder.

"Why don't you take it outside on the grass?'' Kate suggested, punching the button to start the exhaust fan. "Where do you keep the baking soda?''

"Second shelf in the pantry on the left.'' Josh stumbled outside with the frying pan as the phone rang.

Kate plucked the receiver from the wall. "Hello,'' she said, reaching for the soda with her free hand. The smoke stung her eyes.

"Hi. Josh there?'' It was a man's voice.

"Sure. Just a moment please.'' Covering the mouthpiece she handed the phone to Josh and sprinkled soda liberally across the stove top. The sizzling abated. Fine white dust joined the smoke in the air, causing them both to cough. She tried not to laugh.

"Hello.''—cough—"this is Josh.'' He gave her a thumbs up sign as the flames died, then strode over to open the window. "Oh, hi, Troy. How's life in Phoenix?''

Kate's ears perked up. Troy was Josh's brother, the detective.

"Really? That was fast. Find anything?" Josh's face frowned in concentration. "Huh. Maybe. I'm not sure. . . . It's a long story, Troy. . . . No, I'm not in trouble. I think my company may be. . . . Sure. Thanks a lot. Call you Monday night." He hung up.

"The fingerprints?" Kate asked.

"Yes," Josh said thoughtfully.

"How did he get them so fast?"

"Federal Express."

"And?"

"He got them yesterday afternoon. Should have an answer for us tomorrow."

"Great. More evidence on Thrasher," she said enthusiastically.

"You're confident of that, aren't you?"

"Uh-huh. If we can tie him to the cables I think we can tie him to Chun—and to Webb."

Josh took her out of the smoky kitchen and led her to the clear air of the deck. "And we promised each other we wouldn't think about LTS this weekend," he said, dropping a kiss on her forehead. "Phil and I are going to the FBI tomorrow. You and I are through playing cloak and dagger games. All right?"

"Yes." She did want the deadly game to end. She wanted to forget fingerprints and dead letters and dead men.

"There is one redeeming factor in all this," he said.

"What?"

"I found you." He hugged her in the sunshine. "We have twenty-one hours left before the bell rings and I have to return to corporate life. Let's make the most of it."

Chapter

9

Traffic pressed in on them, negotiating bottlenecks as it converged on the access routes to Manhattan. Josh relaxed, empty of the aggressiveness that normally compelled him to fight for every car-length of progress. Kate was beside him and he felt no compulsion to hurry.

"I'll meet you for dinner at seven and give you the lowdown on our visit with the FBI," he said as they queued up for the Midtown Tunnel. "I don't trust phones at this point. You realize, of course, that they'll want to speak with you, too?"

"I look forward to it," Kate replied grimly.

"Might not be a bad idea if you hotfooted it out of town afterward."

"Why?"

Josh shrugged. "Just a precaution. I don't think Thrasher and his merry band will take too kindly to being formally investigated."

"I hadn't thought about that," she admitted. "I guess I just assumed that when the FBI came in we were out."

"Almost," Josh said. "I'll make it clear when I talk with them that we've both been followed, bugged, broken into, and otherwise harassed. They can arrange for protection."

"Yeah, I guess so," Kate began.

A passing headline on the news caught Josh's attention.

"Shh," he said.

". . . was arrested at his home yesterday morning by detectives of both the NYPD and Nassau and Suffolk counties on a warrant issued by the New York County Criminal Court," the radio report continued. "Petersen was fingered by an informant who confessed to his role in the factory fire. The man has been granted immunity in return for his testimony against the LTS president. Petersen is also implicated in the sabotage of a company truck last week. It struck a school bus on the New York side of the George Washington Bridge last Monday morning. The driver was killed and several children critically injured.

"Police theorize that Petersen hoped to get insurance payments to help cover a recent decline in his company's working capital. He is being held at the Criminal Court Building in Manhattan pending arraignment on the charges related to the truck sabotage.

"Summer suntans look great, but can leave your skin dry and chapped. . . ."

Josh turned the radio off.

"Jesus H. Christ," he swore. He braked as a Cadillac limo cut in on him.

"I don't believe it," Kate said flatly.

"Neither do I. Informant my ass."

"What are we going to do now?" Kate asked.

"I don't know."

He remembered the fear on Petersen's face the previous Friday afternoon as he had hurried off with limp explanations. Someone was pulling strings, stage-managing. Toward some specific end, or to protect something?

"I don't know," he repeated softly.

The executive floor was humming. Rumors hadn't had time to gel, but accounts of news reports expanded with each telling.

Josh called a staff meeting at 9:15. He told them what he knew about the arrest. It wasn't much. "When more facts become available you will receive confirmation from me. In the meantime I don't want anyone in this department to indulge in any fanciful speculation. Gossip we don't need now. If you are approached by the press, refer them to the PR department. Period."

Much the same instructions were given at an executive meeting convened in the board room at ten. The only difference was the announcement by the chairman of the board that Thrasher had been named acting president. The applause was limp.

Josh clapped mechanically, his mind racing. It was all too neat and tidy. Petersen discredited, Thrasher in the driver's seat. His eyes wandered to the new acting president of LTS.

Thrasher sat to the right of the chairman, for once deprived of his platform. The chairman was bullshitting about how he was sure Phil would be exonerated, but in the meantime he was confident they would all support Bob.

Bob, Josh thought. Almost no one called him that.

The diminutive executive beamed triumphantly.

He was a poor choice, Garrett thought, but he had seniority—and the support of a vocal minority on the board. Petersen's supporters had apparently been cowed by the turn of events.

Josh resolved to keep a low profile as he pushed his chair back and prepared to follow his colleagues out of the room.

It was not to be.

He felt a heavy hand on his shoulder and turned to find Thrasher.

"Why don't you stop by my office?" he suggested. But it was not a suggestion, it was an order. They were no longer on equal footing and Thrasher wanted him to know it.

"When?" Josh asked.

"On the way back to your office. We'll be working more closely together from now on."

"At least for the foreseeable future," Josh smiled.

"Well, uh, yes," Thrasher faltered.

Josh followed the man back to his office. He wondered idly if Thrasher would be moving into Petersen's suite. To make that move too soon would be brash even for the acting president, however.

"Congratulations, Mr. Thrasher," Dominique said with near enthusiasm as they passed her desk.

"Thank you, my dear," he said.

How could the news have leaked so quickly, Josh mused.

Thrasher closed the door, gestured him to the sofa.

"I just want you to know that I don't intend to make any startling changes around here, Josh," he said as he sat down. "Phil put together a pretty good team and we're going to have to work together now. These are tough times."

"You can count on me," Josh said, hoping his voice conveyed a note of sincerity he didn't feel.

"I do. And I need your expertise. You know, of course, that this scandal will just make our credit situation more difficult. We're going to have to come up with other ways to improve our finances. The first thing we have to do is review the budget, tighten our belts. We can't count on that insurance money now. It'll be tied up in the courts for years."

"I can have a complete budget review on your desk by the end of the week."

"That's fine. Thank you." Thrasher smiled. "I'm sure things will work out."

Josh rose. "I'm sure they will."

The new acting president stood. "There is one more thing."

"Yes?" Josh turned, his hand on the doorknob.

"I understand you've been seeing the Fleming woman."

A warning went off in Josh's brain. "And how would you know that?" he asked, though he thought he already knew.

Briefly Thrasher's mouth gaped open; then he seemed to recover. "You've been seen," he said lamely. "And if I were you I'd put an end to it."

Josh faced the man square on. For a long moment he simply stared, searching his face. Was Thrasher alarmed about what he and Kate might know or merely humiliated because Kate had caught him with his financial pants down? Josh decided it was the latter. He kept his voice low when he spoke.

"Let's get one thing straight, Thrasher. My private life is none of your business. And since you've fired Kate, the time I spend with her is definitely private."

But even as he said it he knew it wasn't true. Unseen informants followed their every move.

He pivoted and left, feeling the man's eyes on his back.

Virginia Petersen was frightened, confused. Still, she trusted Josh. She had given him the lawyer's number. Petersen's defense attorney, pressed by his client to accept Josh's request, had arranged the meeting.

Petersen had been arraigned that morning and remanded to custody on Riker's Island, the sprawling prison complex in the middle of the East River behind La Guardia Airport. Since he would have to take a bus beyond the first checkpoint anyway, Josh took a cab out to Queens from the office. He was searched, screened, and escorted aboard the dilapidated old school bus along with other visitors. After passing muster at another checkpoint he was transported, again by bus, to Petersen's cell block and led to the large open room that served as the visitors' area.

The room was dingy. Once pale green, the paint was now aged and peeling. A musty odor hung in the air, a tang of stale dust and cobwebs long undisturbed.

Petersen slouched into the room dressed in gray prison garb. His feet shuffled when he entered, escorted by a guard. A shudder seemed to pass through him when the metal door clanged shut somewhere behind him.

Josh rose to meet him, alarmed by the pallor in his boss's face. The president managed a wan smile and recovered his dignity. He held out his hand.

"Thank you for coming," he said.

Josh smiled and shook the hand warmly. They sat across from one another at the aging metal table. It was bolted to the floor.

"This was planned," Peterson began.

"It's a damned frame-up," Josh agreed.

"But planned, Josh, from the beginning." He wrung his fingers together before he caught himself and stilled them. "No way could they have known we intended to see the FBI today. I'm charged in connection with the Suffolk fire. I'm convinced that plant was burned for the express purpose of getting me out of Thrasher's way."

"Well, it certainly did that. The board named him acting president this morning."

Petersen pursed his lips. "I'm not surprised."

"Have you told the police anything yet?" Josh asked.

Petersen shook his head. "I'm afraid to. First of all, they think they have an open and shut case. They have the arsonist— at least they think they do. Apparently he's tied me to the truck sabotage, too. I'm not sure the police would be willing to invest in any further investigation at this point. Secondly, Josh, whoever these people are they're professional. If they even suspected how much we've already figured out they might come after you and Kate, too."

Josh recalled Thrasher's admonition about dating Kate and saw it in a new light.

"So what do you propose we do?"

"We need someone more subtle than the police, someone more in the same league with Thrasher and his cronies."

"Like who?"

"Like the FBI. But you can't see them personally. You're being watched. You took a chance just coming here this afternoon and I appreciate it, believe me, but if anything were to happen to you or Kate both LTS and I are finished."

"Then what do you suggest?"

"You have to get the information to them anonymously."

"Anonymously?" Josh was bewildered.

"Yes. Don't you see? If these people can frame me they can frame you. God knows there's enough crime to go around. Then where would we be? Thrasher fired Kate, for example. That would make it easy to undermine her credibility. No, we can't afford to alarm them any further. And you and Kate must keep very low profiles.''

Josh stared across the table at the president. Petersen was quite serious and had obviously given a lot of thought to the matter. And he was right. The downfall of LTS and the rise of Bob Thrasher had been meticulously planned. Any threat to the conspiracy would be handled with brutal efficiency, already had been.

"We'll put everything on paper," he said, "everything we know, everything we suspect, everything we've seen, all the pieces of the puzzle. Then I'll get Kate out of town for a while.''

"Good idea. Aren't you due for a vacation yourself?''

"I could be,'' Josh said slowly, "but it'd be sticky to leave just now.''

"On the other hand Thrasher may welcome the opportunity to get rid of you. Find someone totally above suspicion to deliver the package. Then quietly disappear.''

"But there must be something more we can do,'' Josh insisted. "At this point I'm not sure what we have will convince anyone but ourselves that a conspiracy exists.''

"We have to have faith, Josh.''

The controller paused. "Phil, why did you run out last Friday?''

Petersen sighed. Then he lowered his voice and related the story of the menacing phone call.

"Do you still think they don't know we've spoken with the FBI?'' Josh asked.

"I don't know. I do know that as long as I'm in here I'm safe. I'm not going to post bail. And as long as you and Kate get out of this now you'll be safe, too.''

That wasn't enough, Josh thought as the cab fought its way downtown an hour later. You don't open a tiger's cage, then just build a wall around it and pretend the neighborhood was safe. You find the tiger and put him back in his cage. Tigers could leap fences.

On the way back to the office he asked the cabbie to pull over and wait while he called his brother, then Kate. Troy's report was intriguing; Kate wasn't home. That worried him.

Traffic was sluggish. For once he didn't mind, for it gave him time to think. He wanted desperately to have something more substantial to turn over to the authorities, but he had no idea how to go about getting it. They had only two links to the conspiracy, Webb and Thrasher.

And the arsonist, he reflected, but someone had to be paying him to keep his mouth shut and the police hadn't released his name.

Webb was obviously the weak link. They had enough documentary evidence on him to at least prompt a Customs investigation and they had a logical and legitimate complaint against him. The forwarder had acted unethically. That's where they would begin, he decided.

When he returned to LTS he found a note from Dominique on his desk. Thrasher wanted to see him. He picked up the phone and tapped out the acting president's extension.

Dominique answered. "I'm sorry. Mr. Thrasher is gone for the day," she said in her usual cool manner.

"Do you know what he wanted to see me about?" Josh asked.

"No, I don't."

"Great. Tell him I'll be in tomorrow."

"I shall."

Josh hung up, faintly relieved. At least he still had a job. Could Thrasher already know about his visit with Petersen? Yes, he reflected, he could.

The afternoon had left him jittery. The sooner he and Kate left New York the better.

"Just how soon are you planning to take care of our friend Garrett?"

The woman's eyes were shrewd, her tone sharp, revealing an inner coil of tension, a capacity for the sudden, unexpected strike. She came by her code name naturally. Viper. The ice in her martini clinked as she set it down in favor of a cigarette. He always made her brush her teeth before they went to bed.

"Soon," he said. He drank only mineral water and never smoked. He was not fastidious. He merely did not want to engage in a habit of which he might someday be deprived.

"It can't be soon enough. Garrett went to see Petersen today."

"Do tell."

"Mmm. And tonight he's with the Fleming woman. I don't like it."

"Jealous?" he asked.

"Be serious, darling. We don't know what they might have discovered at Webb's."

She smiled quickly as the waiter appeared at his elbow.

"Ready to order, sir?" So proper, so polite.

"Not just yet. Would you like another martini?" They made her so compliant in bed. Always gin, British, imported, expensive. Never vodka. Vodka called up ugly memories.

"Please," she said.

The man nodded and left.

Their table was tucked in a corner, from which vantage point they could observe the entire dining room between them. The restaurant did not rely on crowds for survival. It allowed decent, genteel intervals between tables. The menu testified to quality over quantity. He'd grown accustomed to such refinements, he realized. He would miss them if he were recalled. Or worse.

"There was nothing in the girl's apartment," he observed.

"So? She might have given it all to Garrett. More's the reason to get rid of him."

He sighed. "I agree. He's a dangerous link. They might not go beyond the Webb operation, the sidetrack we intended, but we can't risk our main objective. The stakes are too high. Petersen has been neutralized, the girl put out to pasture, but Garrett could conceivably still hurt us and I'm not sure Thrasher can control him."

She snorted. "I think not. Can we do it without drawing suspicion?"

"I've already made the arrangements."

"I should have known." She smiled and saluted him with her martini.

Josh arrived at Kate's apartment with the *Times* still tucked under his arm, folded to the article about the burning of Webb Overseas. He recognized the knot in the pit of his stomach. He had felt it before taking the field for particularly crucial games. It was fear.

There was a new lock on Kate's door.

"It's fake," she said proudly. "There's no tongue. But if you play with it an alarm goes off. I'd show you, but I've already awakened the whole neighborhood once this afternoon."

She welcomed him with a warm hug.

"Do you like Mexican food? I hope so, 'cause that's what we're having."

"It's fine," he said.

"So tell me what happened," she prompted. "Did you see Petersen? Thrasher? Can we still go to the FBI?"

He took her hands. So much had happened this day, this afternoon. And he had to tell her all of it. He had to convince her to go away.

"Pour some wine and I'll tell you everything," he said, trying not to sound despondent.

"All right." Her good spirits faded. She kissed his forehead as if to relieve the tension she saw there. She took the bottle he offered and carried it into the kitchen.

"Don't try to open the windows until I show you how," she called. "We took a cue from you. Misha and I are now wired."

Josh smiled and settled into the couch, joined by the cat. What were they going to do with the cats, he wondered idly.

Kate reappeared with two glasses.

"Cheers," she said, no cheer in her voice. "Now what happened?"

Josh sipped his wine, then pulled the notes on his conversation with Troy from his pocket.

"One thing at a time, I guess," he said. "I spoke with my brother this afternoon."

"And?"

"He was able to match the fingerprints on the copies of the cables that were postmarked in Queens and the memo from Thrasher all right. Eliminating your prints and Veronica's, based on the samples we sent him, there's one set of matching prints left over."

"That ties him to Chun," Kate said triumphantly.

"Not so fast. The interesting part is that Troy says that whoever it is has very slender fingers—probably a woman."

"A woman?" Kate leaned back against the sofa, pondering the unexpected development. "It stands to reason that Dominique may have handled the memo. But the cables? They were delivered straight to our office unopened. How could she . . ." She stared at him.

"It may still be Thrasher," he said.

"He has stubby little fingers."

"How about Cosentino?"

Kate paused. "Yes, he does have slender hands, but . . . Josh, whoever sent those cables had to have gotten them from Chun, at least I think so. Which means that whoever dumped them in the mail may have killed Chun, or at least set him up."

He smiled. "Now we are leaping to conclusions."

"You can't deny it's all connected."

"No. But can you see Paul killing anyone? Or Dominique?"

Their eyes met.

"Do you remember when she was hired?" Kate asked. "I do. It was a month after the BATT acquisition."

"She moved in like she owned the place," Josh recalled. Like Diana.

"And do you remember what happened to the previous secretary?"

Josh laughed. "He had several."

"But if office scuttlebutt is right the one just before Dominique had lasted quite some time, hadn't she?"

"For Thrasher, yes."

"And what happened to her?"

"An automobile accident, I think."

"Uh-huh."

"Oh, come on, Kate. This is preposterous." But it wasn't, he knew. It made sense. Bob Thrasher wasn't smart enough to have put the whole conspiracy together himself. That had nagged him from the beginning.

"I don't know. A week ago I came home from vacation in Maine expecting to find life status quo and this afternoon I installed burglar alarms." Her voice trembled.

He took her in his arms. "I know, I know." Josh sighed. "Kate, it may not be enough."

"Why? What do you mean?" She pulled away so she could see him.

He told her about his conversation with Petersen. "He thinks we're in danger, Kate, and I agree with him."

"Can't the police protect us?" Her eyes were wide and frightened.

"I don't know." He paused. "Webb Overseas burned to the ground early Sunday morning. The police say it was an accident, an electrical failure. You and I know that's not true. A Customs investigation of Webb was the one tack we might have taken that we could back up and that might have blown the whole conspiracy wide open."

"What about Webb?"

"He's disappeared."

"Good Lord." Kate leaned against him, small and vulnerable.

"Is there someplace you can go?" he asked. "Someplace remote?"

"My parents . . ."

"You could be followed there."

She shuddered. "Josh, for how long?"

"I don't know. As long as it takes the FBI to take us seriously, I guess."

"I have an uncle in Maine," she ventured. "He's not a blood relative, just a close family friend."

"Perfect. Now we just have to figure out how to get you up there." His mind began to tackle the problem of spiriting Kate out of New York unnoticed. He was an amateur at this game of cat and mouse and he had very little time to learn. Perhaps Troy could help.

"But, Josh, what about you?" She touched his cheek.

"One thing at a time, darling. For the short term Thrasher needs me and he knows it."

"Is that enough to keep you safe?"

"I hope so." He spoke more confidently than he felt. "After dinner why don't we try putting together those briefings?"

"All right." She was hesitant.

Josh smiled. "We're still in control, Kate. They don't know how much we have on them."

"That's what worries me," she said.

Chapter
10

He almost took the Jaguar out the back entrance to his property that morning, just to elude the tail he knew would pick him up en route to the expressway. No, Josh decided. They didn't know he had a Jaguar, at least he didn't think they did, and the less they knew about him the better. The Jag was one of the few possessions Diana's lawyers had left him. He kept it in the garage behind the house.

Driving the familiar BMW, he headed north for Route 25A, however, instead of south for the expressway. He watched with amusement as a gray sedan scrambled to make a U-turn. He was growing tired of the game and wondered vaguely what the men behind him were thinking. Did they believe he did not see them every morning or did they no longer care? What orders had been given them? By whom?

He had lain awake the night before, studying what to do. Long past midnight he'd called Troy, only to discover that his brother was on duty. Still, Josh had resolved to get professional advice.

Thrasher called him before his morning coffee arrived. That didn't bode well for the day, Josh reflected. He squared his jaw and strolled over to the acting president's office.

Dominique was in place as usual. She seemed surprised to see him, and none too pleased.

"I believe he's busy," she said.

"He just called to invite me in for coffee," Josh replied. "I like it black."

He knocked on the door.

102

"Come in," Thrasher called. He was enthroned at his desk. "Thank you for coming, Josh. Shut the door."

He seemed agitated, Josh thought. The man's words were clipped and precise, posture stiff.

He closed the door. "What can I do for you?"

"Did you read yesterday's *Times*?" Thrasher queried. A newspaper was spread before him on the desk. He did not invite his guest to sit.

"Yes. Why?"

"You read what happened to Webb?"

"I read what happened to Webb Overseas."

Thrasher stabbed at the article with one stubby finger. "Disappeared, they say. Just like that."

Josh glanced up from the newsprint, not knowing what to expect in Thrasher's face, unprepared for what he found.

Thrasher was scared.

"What does this do to us?" the acting president demanded.

"I don't know what you mean," Josh said.

"The payments, the letters of credit, the seven million dollars. What does this do to them?" His voice rose, but any further outburst was stilled by a knock on the door.

Without waiting for a reply Dominique entered bearing two white plastic cups of coffee. The bright red of her long nails stood out in contrast. Inspiration flickered in Josh's mind. He accepted the cup by the rim.

"Thank you."

"You're welcome." She handed the second coffee to her boss. "May I be of assistance, Mr. Thrasher?"

"No, thank you. We have some private matters to discuss, my dear. I'll go over today's schedule with you in a few minutes."

"Very well."

The woman left, but her musky scent lingered.

"Well?" Thrasher commanded.

Josh set his coffee on the desk untouched.

"I guess I hadn't thought about it," he said. He stepped to the window, his back turned so he could think in private.

Was Thrasher playing a game, attempting to trap him into admitting what he knew about the dead letters? Or did he really not understand what was going on? Under normal circumstances the L/C's would already have been negotiated by the bank. The subsequent fate of the forwarder would have nothing to do with whether or not an exporter collected. But this case was different, and for some reason Thrasher thought—or wanted him to think—that the collection was somehow tied up with Webb.

Josh decided to play the script as it should have been written, as if the transactions were legitimate.

"Why would Webb have anything to do with collecting on the L/C's?" he asked, turning to face Thrasher again. "The matter was out of his hands the moment the shipment was made."

Thrasher looked surprised, suspicious. "Then why were you and that Fleming dame so hot to chase him down last week?"

"Because he shipped with discrepancies. Kate explained that all to you. But there's not a damn thing we can do about it now. What's done is done."

"And we'll still get our money."

"I didn't say that," Josh replied. "The shipments were botched. But you assured me last week that this specialist friend of yours said that the payments will still come through, so I can only assume that they will—unless Webb is your specialist. Is he?" He watched Thrasher's eyes.

"No, no. Of course not," the little man said hastily. His eyes were not evasive.

"Then what's the problem?"

"I . . . I just wanted to be sure, that's all."

"It's your deal, Thrasher," Josh said grimly. "You're the expert. I just hope for the company's sake that we get the seven million."

"Of course we will." The acting president was visibly shaken, his tone unconvincing. "Just because our export people mismanaged . . ."

"Don't try to hang this on Kate," Josh warned him. "She cautioned you about those L/C's from the beginning, in writing."

Thrasher's face hardened. Josh caught himself before he said too much, before his words could be construed as a threat.

"The Webb fire doesn't change anything," he went on, "not as far as the L/C's are concerned."

The other man seemed to relax a little. He almost smiled. "Fine. I just wanted confirmation of that."

"You have it." No, Josh thought, as far as the L/C's were concerned the fire changed nothing. As far as his future was concerned it had changed everything. "Will that be all?"

"Yes, thanks. Send Dominique in on your way out."

Tense and confused, Josh left. He took the white plastic coffee cup with him. It had Dominique's fingerprints on it.

They had Kate's escape route planned. It had seemed melodramatic at first to call it an escape route instead of an itinerary. They no longer thought so.

Wednesday morning she would catch an 8:30 flight on Precision Airlines, a small commuter operation, from La Guardia to Boston. Only it was a connecting flight through Rutland, Vermont, and Kate would deplane there. She would pay in cash and travel under an assumed name. In America no one asked for ID if you paid in cash.

A friend would meet her in Rutland, rent a car in his name, and drive her south to Springfield where he would leave her. He would drive the car for the rest of the week, putting on mileage. He could claim to have dropped her off far from Springfield, Boston even.

Kate would don a dark wig and take a bus north to Maine, again using an assumed name. The friend would know nothing of this part of the plan.

He had run the scheme past Troy and his brother had admitted that it would take a concentrated effort to catch up with her. He had also wanted to know what she had done. Troy was beginning to be mighty suspicious. Josh did his best to deflect his brother's questions. It wasn't a comfortable phone call.

With Kate's route settled, Josh returned home for a change of clothes. It would be their last night together for perhaps some time and he planned to spend it all with her.

He knew there was something amiss when he entered the driveway, though he could not put his finger on just what it was. The gray sedan had left him at the corner as usual. He wondered whose eyes followed him the rest of the way home.

Senses alert, he stepped out of the BMW and glanced around the property. Then he knew.

It was dusk. The porch light should have come on automatically. It hadn't. There were no lights around the pool either. Other houses on the block were lighted. If his electricity were off, so was his alarm system.

Cautiously Josh circled his home. He checked the back door first. It was locked. So were the glass doors that led out to the deck. He returned to the front porch to enter as he always did—only he didn't need his key.

Common sense said he should cross the street and ask his

neighbor the policeman for help. But the intruder would surely have heard the car in the drive.

Gently Josh pushed open the front door. It creaked on its hinges. He had never noticed it do that before.

Fred did not come yowling to greet him, as he should have done. Josh was late and so was Fred's dinner. There was an odd odor in the house, but he did not recognize it just then.

He froze in the shadows of the living room and listened. Nothing. On tiptoe he searched the living room and den. Everything was intact, including the safe. His stereo equipment had not been touched, nor his trophies. The house seemed to hold its breath. The only sound he heard clearly was the beating of his own heart.

The bedroom was as he had left it, the bed unmade, sweat-clothes draped across a chair. But something nudged at him. His eyes swept the room once more. There was a blank spot over the bureau, the place where he hung a pair of tsumutao, butterfly knives, the long sculpted blades used by practitioners of kung fu. He had studied for several years, though it had been some time since he had participated. Still, he kept the knives. Now they were gone. Odd booty for a thief.

He tried the light in the bathroom, small enough not to alert the prowler if he were still in the house. The light was dead.

He thought he heard something in the living room, the brush of a careless footstep on the carpet. He moved quickly enough to see a shadow slip out the sliding glass door.

"I called the police from my car, you asshole!" he yelled as he bounded after the fleeing figure. He wished he had.

He found himself on his deck faced with a slim, cruel-looking man brandishing his butterfly knives. From the way he handled them, it was obvious the intruder knew what he was doing.

Shit, Josh thought.

"You give me the pleasure of completing the job myself," the man said in accented English. "This way we'll know when the house blows that you were in it." He lunged.

Josh sprang backward. His heel brushed against the wooden picnic bench to the right of the doorway. He grabbed for it.

Grasping the clumsy bench by the legs, he raised it over his head just as the assassin sliced downward with both knives. The blades thudded into the seat as one, sending wood chips flying.

The man swung the knife in his right hand over his head and whipped it down toward Josh's left side, but Josh blocked the blow, then drove the bench into his foe's belly. Delivered with sufficient force, a bench, too, was a weapon. The movement felt awkward. It shouldn't have. But kung fu like other arts grew rusty when unused, he thought grimly. He regretted that now.

The intruder sidestepped, then chopped at Josh's neck. Josh ducked, spinning himself as he did so, the bench extended at arm's length to sweep the other man's feet from under him.

Roll with it, flow with it, he told himself. Don't fight the natural momentum.

The man eluded the move but was left unbalanced.

Seizing the advantage Josh flipped the bench so that he now held it by either side of the seat and slammed downward at an exposed foot with one of the wooden legs. His opponent swiped at his legs with the targeted foot.

Flowing with his own downward movement, Josh planted the bench firmly on the deck and lightly turned a cartwheel over it. The maneuver left him momentarily out of reach.

The man leaped after him, both knives slashing. Josh blocked the blow from the right, then the left. The gashes whittled into the bench multiplied. The man feinted right again, but came in from the left, delivering a glancing blow to Josh's left side. He felt the knife split his flesh, felt it collide with his ribs. He retreated a step, his breath coming in short gasps.

Seizing the moment, the assassin drove both blades at his quarry's abdomen. He was overconfident. Josh's arms fell, the bench striking both weapons down. Summoning all the strength he had, he brought one corner of the bench up at the other man's chin and caught him square on the jaw.

Josh followed the direction of movement he had established and cracked his opponent's head with the other end of the bench. The man dropped like a log and lay still. The knives clattered to the wooden deck. One of them was bloodied.

Josh knelt beside the intruder. The jaw was purple and already swelling. Blood seeped from a long indentation in the left side of the scalp. The man was not going anywhere for a long while.

Josh remembered his own wound. He acknowledged the pain now and it sickened him. Holding his side with one hand he stumbled into the house. His phone was dead. In the bathroom he had gauze, he thought. He had to stop the bleeding.

There was no light, which was just as well. The sight of his own blood always made him a little shaky. He was already feeling light-headed.

He eased out of his shirt. There was a long slash in the one side and the light blue cloth dripped darkly. He almost blacked out then and slumped on the toilet. No one's going to come and get you out of this, he reminded himself. In a moment his head cleared. He stood and rummaged through the medicine cabinet for the gauze and a roll of athletic tape he kept there.

The gash was about five inches long as far as he could see. The blood seeped through the gauze almost immediately. He added a dry washcloth on top and began to wind the tape around his body. The cut was deep, the nerve endings in the flesh severed, but his ribs had begun to throb.

It was dark when he finished. It was then he smelled the gas.

"This way we'll know when the house blows that you were in it," the man had said.

Jesus Christ.

Josh staggered back into the bedroom and slipped a sweatshirt on over the crude bandage. He might not have much time, he thought. He would take only what was essential.

His athletic bag was on the floor. He emptied the dead tennis balls and stale socks. From the bathroom he grabbed a few toiletries, the gauze, and the athletic tape; from the bureau some underwear, T-shirts, and a pair of jeans. Then he made his way into the living room. The safe was behind the portrait of his parents over the sofa. In the dark it was difficult to see the combination. The smell of gas was stronger.

The safe contained his passport, some family jewelry, and the BATT papers. He stuffed them all into the bag and ran for the front door. As he cleared the porch there was a tremendous explosion.

The impact flung him to the ground. The rumble of his disintegrating house rolled over him in waves. The air was choked with dust. Something solid and sharp struck his head. Debris fell all around him. He shielded his face with his arms and waited for the violence to pass.

When it did, he lifted himself carefully, finding strength from the adrenaline coursing through his body. Blood dripped into his eye.

His home was gone. Orange flames licked greedily at the remains. A chunk of concrete had landed square on the BMW's windshield. It could have landed on him, he reflected.

What was left of the deck was burning. His nose identified the odor of burning flesh. He shuddered.

He sat down in the rubble heap that had once been his garden and tried to clear his head. He could hear neighbors shouting and the distant wail of fire trucks.

They can't find me here, he thought. They have to think I'm dead. No one would doubt the identity of the body on the deck. Unless they checked dental records. There would be no cause to do that. His car was in the driveway.

Car. He had to take the Jaguar. Now. Before the neighbors came.

He grabbed the athletic bag and stood up, blinking his eyes to adjust to the night. Then he tottered to the unattached garage. It was battered but still stood. The Jag was untouched.

Keys. He needed keys. There should be a spare set under the weed killer.

There was.

He climbed wearily into the driver's seat and turned on the compartment light. In the rearview mirror he could see the gash that creased the hairline on the left side of his head. He couldn't drive with blood in his eyes, he thought vaguely.

Josh fished in his bag for a square of gauze and a length of athletic tape. He found a tube sock. It should be long enough to tie around his head. His fingers trembled slightly, but he managed.

He turned off the light and started the engine. The Jag purred as usual. Slowly he backed out of the garage. The fire trucks were closing in. He could see their flashing lights.

In the darkness he crawled out the back entrance to the property. There was a tan sedan there, hidden amid the shrubbery, deserted; it must have been the intruder's car, he thought. The street was empty.

He flipped on his lights and took off, glancing back to see if anyone followed. There were headlights. Had they pulled out behind him or had they been there before?

The road was narrow and winding. Josh stepped on the gas. The Jag took the curves easily, putting distance between him and the car behind.

There was no waiting for tomorrow. He had to get Kate out tonight.

"Kate?"

"Josh?" she asked hesitantly. The voice was Josh's but somehow distant. At least this time the caller spoke to her, did not just breathe and hang up.

"Yeah," he answered.

"You sound so far away. Where are you?" She had been trying his phone for hours. It had been out of order, leaving her frightened and alone.

"Here in Manhattan, just a few blocks away."

He sounded detached, impassive.

"Are you all right? Where have you been? I tried . . ."

"We have to get out tonight, Kate."

"Why? What's happened?" She was alarmed now. The dreamy quality in Josh's voice was not in the line. Perhaps someone was imitating him, she thought, luring her into a trap.

"They just blew up my house. They think they blew me up with it. Can you be ready to go in ten minutes?"

"Yes," she said slowly. "Josh, are you all right?"

"I'm a little worse for wear, but I'll recover. I'll meet you downstairs in ten minutes."

"In the BMW?"

"No, the Jag."

"What color is it?"

He paused. "It's dark green. You've seen it."

Yes, she knew, the car was green. My God, his house . . . if this were Josh.

"Josh?"

"Ten minutes. Kate."

Suddenly she was terribly afraid. What if this were not him? What if this were . . . were one of them? That would mean Josh was already dead. She was paralyzed, not knowing what to believe or where to turn. My God, if they could blow up his house . . . And whoever it was was coming.

"Kate, did you hear me? Ten minutes."

She swallowed. "Josh, what happened to Fred?"

"What?" The voice was incredulous.

"What happened to Fred?"

"I don't know. I don't think he was in the house. I hope he was out in the woods someplace. Why? There's nothing we can do. Bring Misha. We have to get out of here."

She began to sob. "I just had to know this was really you. Josh, there've been other calls."

His tone softened. "It's me. Pack. I'm on my way."

She hung up, silent tears falling. Her heart beat wildly. Ten minutes. She ran upstairs to her bedroom.

Misha's travel box was on the floor of the closet. She flung it out along with her overnight bag. Just the essentials, she thought. Traveling frequently, she always had a spare toiletry kit packed and ready. She threw it into the suitcase and emptied half her underwear drawer. Jeans, a couple of blouses, travel documents. She tossed her purse into the case, too. It fit.

She carried everything downstairs. What else could she not leave behind? Jewelry. She ran back upstairs to get it. In the kitchen she had a box of dry cat food. She couldn't think of anything else.

"Here, Misha." The cat came running. "Into the box, Misha." She picked the cat up and stuffed her in the travel carrier. There was no time to be gentle.

She grabbed a light jacket from the closet and took a last look around her little home. She could spare no moments for sentimentality. She lugged everything into the hall and shut the door.

"Need some help?" asked a man's voice. He was short and dark. Kate did not recognize him.

"No, thanks," she said as she turned the locks.

"Here, let me help you." He reached for her suitcase.

Kate drew herself up. "I said no thank you. I can manage." He smiled, a slit between thin lips.

"What's your hurry? No time to let a guy be a gentleman anymore?" He spoke with an accent, Slavic maybe.

"Sorry, no."

She tried to push past him but he seized her arm. He wore gloves.

"Won't do ya no good to run." He spoke as if he knew something she didn't.

"Who are you? How did you get in here?" She wrenched away from him and dashed for the stairs. On stealthy rubber-soled shoes he was after her.

Kate stepped aside at the top of the staircase and flattened herself against the wall. The abrupt move caught her assailant off guard. He stumbled. Kate shoved him with her foot. With a howl he plunged headlong downward, bouncing and bumping against walls and steps. He crumpled in a heap at the bottom and lay still.

Misha was screeching in her carrier. Kate tightened her grip on both her burdens and hurried down, stepping gingerly around the man. She wondered if he were still alive.

The night was sultry and smelled of rotting garbage and stale exhaust fumes. The door had not closed behind her when a green Jaguar squealed to a halt in the street. Josh flung the door open for her. Kate tossed the overnight bag in the back and scrambled in with the cat. The door slammed shut as Josh floored the gas.

He shot through a yellow light, then accelerated up to Broadway and turned left. As long as the lights were green he did not say a word. The car bolted and braked as he weaved through traffic.

He looked like a pirate with the sock wound about his head. Only when they finally hit a red light and he turned to look at her did she notice that the sock was bloody. His face was drawn and pale.

"Josh, you're hurt."

"We'll worry about it after we get out of here," he said.

He needed dispassion to stay in control, she saw. She laid a hand on his thigh. She would tell him about the man later.

"What do you mean she got away!" he exploded. "We had her under twenty-four–hour surveillance."

It was nearly midnight. The Viper cupped her hand around the mouthpiece of the receiver.

"Shh. It's Russo. He says she's gone."

Enraged, he grabbed the phone from her. The room reeked of sex. To be disturbed in the middle of the night heightened his anger.

"You idiot! Do you want them to know we're together?" she hissed. She pulled the phone back. "You idiot! How did she get away?" she demanded of the caller. "Very brave of you. Have you checked her apartment?" Pause. "Did you see anyone? Wonderful. Go home. Go to bed." She slammed down the receiver.

When she turned to face him her features were furious, violently beautiful in the moonlight.

"He says the Fleming woman up and left."

"How? With whom?"

"He doesn't know."

"What do you mean he doesn't know?"

"He fell asleep."

"Then how the hell does he know she's gone?" he demanded.

"She is," the woman said firmly.

His mind began to spin. She couldn't have learned about Garrett. The explosion had hit the late news broadcasts, but his identity had been withheld. Her departure must have been preplanned.

"She doesn't have anything on us," he said. "We took that place apart."

"Perhaps," the Viper said.

"He's dead and whatever he had went up in smoke. What the hell can she expect to do without him?"

The woman observed him coldly. "I'd still feel better if we knew where she was." She didn't move, yet he could feel her draw distant from him in the bed. "Are we sure Garrett is dead?"

"According to our people at the scene, the police found his body in the fire."

"And we've not yet heard from Muller," she reminded him.

There was no margin for error. She did not have to remind him of that.

"There'll be an autopsy," he said.

"Yes. What with Petersen in jail and questions of sabotage and arson already raised, I'm sure there will be."

"That may hurt us."

"A little late to think about that now, isn't it? Besides, Muller knows his business. Did anyone question the fire at Webb's?"

"No."

"So. I'll arrange for the girl to be found."

"See that she is."

She lay down again and turned her back on him. He did not like the Viper when her professionalism interfered with her sexuality.

They were not being followed. Josh was sure of that. Like a bat he would prefer to end his wandering before dawn, to be safely hidden when the sun came up.

But he was weakening. The adrenaline in his system had dissipated. Now there was only pain and a great weariness. And he was cold, his hands frozen on the wheel.

"I think we should stop," Kate said. "I can drive."

He turned to glance at her. Her expression was as firm as her voice.

"You're right," he agreed. A sign announced food, gas, and lodging three miles ahead. "We'll stop there," he suggested.

She nodded.

The gas station was self-serve-only at night. The attendant sat behind bullet-proof glass.

Josh pulled to a halt and pushed the door open with his right hand. If he moved his left too far away from his body his ribs complained bitterly and the edges of the gash cracked. He planted his feet on the ground and stood up.

The world began to spin. Then he was on the pavement and Kate was beside him, cradling his head.

"Josh, Josh. Why didn't you tell me?" She turned to the attendant in the glass cage. "Please help. Can't you see he's hurt?"

The man was unresponsive.

Josh's head was beginning to clear. He must have lost more blood than he'd realized, he thought.

"Josh, can you get in the car?"

"I think so," he mumbled.

She opened the back door of the Jaguar and helped him crawl in. He was too heavy for her to lift. He heard one door close, then another. The distant hum of traffic on the thruway faded. They were shut in the car again. He felt dainty points of pressure on his legs. It was the cat, come to investigate. The car lurched as Kate found first gear.

"Where are we going?"

"To a hospital," she replied.

"We can't," he protested, pulling himself to a sitting position. The sock around his head had come loose. The air felt cool against his forehead. "They'd have to report us to the police. We could be traced."

She braked and turned to face him.

"A motel then. You need rest, Josh."

He was too tired to argue.

Chapter
11

When Josh awoke Kate was gone. There was only the cat at the foot of the bed. He recalled vague images of what had happened the night before after the gas station, Kate's anxious face bending over his, the pain as she had worked to clean and close the wound in his side with little butterfly bandages, the carton of milk that had come from somewhere to pave the way for two codeine tablets.

That was the last he remembered. Now it was morning and Kate was nowhere to be seen.

Gingerly he eased himself off the bed and stumbled into the bathroom. Bloodied gauze and terry cloth from the night before filled the sink. No wonder his head was reeling. He dumped the refuse on the floor. They couldn't leave it to be found, he realized.

Josh splashed his face with cold, fog-clearing water. He could only use one hand. To move his left arm was excruciating, a deep ache of bruised bone overlaid with the sharper pain of the slash.

He retraced his steps and sank wearily onto the bed next to the phone. His mind was working now. He glanced at his watch. It was six-thirty in the morning in Phoenix. He called collect. Troy answered. Josh scarcely recognized his brother's voice.

"Is this some kind of joke?" Troy demanded.

"No, Troy, it's real," Josh blurted before the operator cut in.

"Will you accept the charges, sir?"

"Yes," Troy said faintly.

"Go ahead," said the operator.

"Troy, I know what you've heard, but it's not true. I'm alive."

115

He could hear his brother's ragged breathing and realized he must be crying. "I'm sorry. There was no way I could warn you, no way I could have gotten to you earlier."

"You bum," his brother sobbed. "Are you all right?"

"Yes."

"Oh, thank God. Where are you? What happened? It has something to do with the fingerprints, doesn't it?"

"Yes, it does."

"What the hell have you gotten yourself messed up in?"

"I'm not sure yet," Josh said.

"The house wasn't an accident, was it?" his brother asked.

"No. No, they meant to kill me. They damn near did."

"Who did they kill?"

"I don't know. He broke into the house, sabotaged the gas line, I think. I smelled gas just before the explosion."

"How'd you get out?"

"I was lucky."

"They think the body was yours."

"Good," Josh said emphatically. "I want the people who think they killed me to go on thinking that for as long as possible."

"Who are they?" Troy demanded. He had recovered his composure. His detective instincts were surfacing.

Josh paused. "I don't know," he said at last. "But whoever they are they're willing to kill to protect an operation that I think is slipping controlled technology out of this country illegally."

His brother whistled. "That's a very lucrative, very risky business."

"Apparently so. You have to identify my body, Troy. Recognize a necklace, the set of my jaw, a scar on my knee, anything that's left."

"All right," Troy said slowly. "I'll verify you're dead. What do I tell the folks?"

Josh felt a pang of regret. "Oh, Lord. I can't do this to them. They'll have to know the truth. But can you keep the services private? Keep Mom and Dad secluded? I don't want anybody to have any reason to approach them."

"That won't be easy with the press. Your face is plastered all over the papers. In death you're still a public figure, even more so than in your glory days."

"I haven't been a 'public figure' for years."

"Well, you are now. You have to admit it was a rather spectacular way to go."

"I guess," Josh said.

"Well, the press thinks so. Your career is being revived. Your tearful ex-teammates are being interviewed by satellite, along with film at eleven of your heroic days on the soccer field in Europe, taking it to the Frenchies and Brits on their own turf. . . ."

Troy's laughter was jittery, interspersed with sobs. Relief was wiping away the pain of the last few hours, unleashing the tension. Josh softened his voice.

"You have to try to protect Mom and Dad, Troy."

"I'll do it." A long sigh came over the waves from Phoenix. "I'm so glad you're alive, I think I can handle anything. What about Diana?"

"What about her?"

"Should I tell her?"

"Not on your life—or mine."

"And your girlfriend?"

"Kate's with me."

"Mmm. All right. Where are you now?"

"I'm not sure. Even if I were I wouldn't tell you. The less you know the better."

"Very noble of you, big brother, but not very practical."

Josh smiled. "We're gonna lie low for a few days. You'll be at the folks in Connecticut?"

"Yes."

"Good. I'll call you there."

"Josh?" His brother's voice was quietly insistent. "You are hurt, aren't you?"

"Yeah. Nothing serious."

"Get help, Josh. Go to the authorities."

"I will, as soon as the dust settles a little bit."

"Be careful," Troy added.

"Always."

Josh hung up reluctantly. Just to hear Troy's voice restored sanity. He turned to find Kate staring at him, her eyes wide.

"How long have you been there?" he asked.

"Long enough," she whispered. "Who was the man?"

"I told Troy the truth. I don't know."

"But he tried to kill you?"

"Yes."

"And that's how you were really hurt?"

He nodded.

Kate swallowed. Leaving her package on the night table she

sat down beside him. "Somehow it seems so much more sinister. A bomb is impersonal, but an assassin . . ."

He slipped his good arm around her, grateful for the warmth of her closeness.

"Josh, they really want you dead." Her voice shook as if the reality of their flight the night before was just dawning on her.

"I didn't tell you last night, but there was a man in my building, on my floor. He tried to stop me. . . ."

"My God, Kate!" He took her by the shoulders. "Why didn't you tell me? How did you get away?" The realization that he might have lost her drained him further.

"He fell down the stairs. I just ran. You came just in time."

Had the man seen the car? Josh wondered. He remembered seeing no one besides Kate come out of the building, but he hadn't been in the best of shape at the time.

"Oh, Josh, I just want to hide."

"I know." He embraced her and rested his cheek against hers. Don't panic on me now, he thought. I need you. A great weariness was coming over him.

Kate swept the hair off his forehead and kissed him gently. Her arms supported him.

"Lie down, sweetheart. We'll think about it all when we get to Uncle Dimitri's." Her sudden shift from quaking vulnerability to warm, rational concern alarmed him vaguely.

"I'm all right," he insisted.

"I know. You're just a little feverish and if I mother you I keep my sanity. Humor me. Lie down."

He did feel the tightness in his head he associated with fever. He leaned back on the pillows. Kate brought his feet up on the bed. The diminished blood supply in his veins returned slowly to his brain, bringing a greater awareness with it. He noticed the circles under her eyes for the first time, the firm set of her mouth. Kate wouldn't panic on him. She was tense, worried, but she wouldn't permit fear to distract her from handling immediate concerns.

"I love you," he said.

"I love you, too." She hugged him tightly. His lips brushed her hair.

"Do you feel like eating a little something?" she asked.

"Not really."

She sat up. "Well, drink this anyway."

She pulled a carton of milk from the paper sack. As he sipped it she produced two plastic prescription bottles from her cos-

metics case. One of them contained the white codeine-laced
Tylenol tablets, the other pink capsules.

"What's that?"

"Penicillin. Are you allergic to it?"

"No."

"Good."

"You're a walking pharmacy," he observed.

"World travelers have to be." Kate smiled. The life returned
to her eyes. "I'm also your doctor."

"I can't drive if I take the codeine."

"You're not driving."

She handed him the medication. He took it.

The Viper was late. Her associate sipped his Perrier and surveyed the restaurant entrance with rising irritation. He did not
like tardiness any more than he liked loose ends. This operation
was supposed to have been run with punctuality and precision.
He should have been inside by now. Instead there had been an
unacceptable level of unforeseen obstacles. A simple miscal-
culation and the whole project was sidetracked.

The Fleming woman should have had an accident while on
vacation.

Time was getting short. He would have to regain control.

The Viper appeared. Platinum wisps had blown loose from
sprayed, clipped restraint, softening her appearance. But her
mouth was pinched into a severe line.

"Please accept my apologies," she said as he rose to greet
her. "The office is distraught. Thrasher is terrified. It's all I can
do to coax him into acting presidential."

"That's all we need," he said with disgust. "What's his problem? He's right where he wanted to be."

"With scandal and potential bankruptcy falling down around
his ears?"

"He needs a knight on a white horse."

"Not yet. We don't need any suspicious coincidences."

"Mmm. Perhaps." But he would not let the woman make
that decision for him.

"Have you heard anything about the autopsy on Garrett?"
she asked.

Her contact shook his head. "They have no official ID on the
body yet. The parents couldn't face it. His ex-wife went into
hysterics at the morgue. The coroner is waiting for a brother to
come in from Arizona."

Belatedly a waitress appeared, pad at the ready. They ordered chef salads.

"And Muller is still missing?" The Viper resumed when the woman had gone.

"Yes."

"What about his car?"

"No one's seen it."

"What were his orders after torching the house?"

"To call in, confirm the kill."

She stared across the table at him, eyes devoid of expression. "Has anyone looked for spare body parts?"

A shudder crept down his spine. The thought had occurred to him, too, that perhaps Muller had at last fallen victim to his own creativity. After all, his was a deadly speciality. Good saboteurs, men of Muller's talent, were hard to come by, and more often than not their lives ended abruptly. He accepted that. But to hear such speculation from the Viper's lips was somehow chilling, for she dehumanized the man and his death with her cold objectivity.

"We have one body, one death. Garrett was home. His car was in the driveway," he said.

"What about the Fleming woman?"

"No one has seen her. We've made discreet inquiries of her friends and family. Nothing. Garrett's death is all over the papers. Maybe she'll turn up for his funeral."

"Frankly," she said, "I'm more concerned about what she knows than where she is."

"There's one way to find out," he mused.

"How?"

"Talk to Petersen."

She smiled. The effect was not warming.

The presidency was not what he had expected. Thrasher found himself in the midst of a maelstrom, spiraling downward.

He had always envisioned mapping grand strategies for expanding LTS operations, foreign and domestic; cleaning house of deadwood; returning home each night with a deep sense of satisfaction for having accomplished great corporate deeds.

Scandal, lawsuits, and charges of possible malfeasance had not been part of his scenario. He had not been prepared for the press attention lavished upon LTS and focused on his office.

With Garrett alive the situation had still been manageable. The controller had had a good grasp not only of the financial realities, but of how to manipulate the LTS bureaucracy. Thrasher hadn't realized until it was too late that he lacked perspective on just how departments outside of his own were coordinated, especially since the BATT acquisition.

But Garrett was dead.

Thrasher's imagination was beginning to run away with him.

When he had started down this road his direction had seemed so clear. Seven million dollars in export orders was icing on the cake, an unforeseen windfall of revenues, coup enough to win him increasing support from the board. By coincidence the Suffolk fire had made the shipments vital, made him a hero. After all, he'd pulled the strings to get the orders out of the house in record time, had gotten the receivables on the books before the fire closed the factory. Those had been heady days.

But he did not yet have the seven million dollars and he was beginning to doubt he ever would. Then how long could he expect to hold the presidency?

His phone rang. He waited for Dominique to pick it up. Apparently she was still out to lunch. He did not want to speak with the press again. Who would have put a call through on his private line? Didn't the switchboard know better? It must be an internal call, he comforted himself. He lifted the receiver distastefully.

"Thrasher," he said gruffly.

"Bob, Ken Bailey, Keiser Electronics," said a jovial voice.

Bailey was president of one of LTS's strongest competitors, or at least they had been until the BATT acquisition. No wonder he was so cheerful.

"Hi, Ken. What can I do for you?"

"Oh, I think maybe the question is what can I do for you," Bailey replied.

"Really?"

"How would you like to meet me for lunch tomorrow?"

"I'm a bit pressed for time just now, Ken."

"I can imagine," the Keiser president said dryly. "But what I have to say may just save your skin—not to mention your career."

"That's a pretty provocative statement."

"It was meant to be."

Thrasher paused to think. How much did Bailey know? he wondered. The headlines only hinted at the turmoil inside LTS. No word of the export deal had leaked. Or had it? Could his

rival have sources that had revealed to what extent the company
was strapped financially as well as legally?

No, he thought. He knew why Bailey was calling. The man
wanted the home security division. Keiser Electronics had made
an offer to Phil Petersen once before.

But he had to be sure.

"What time?" Thrasher asked.

The passenger seat was deeply reclined and Josh slept. Occasionally Kate would reach back to stroke his face. It was hot.
She hoped her prescription of penicillin lasted long enough to
fight the infection.

Summer traffic clogged the highway north into New England.
Dozens of cars and campers huddled together for miles in the
same window of relative speed. Hovering between fifty-five and
sixty-five, they would leapfrog one another over the hills and
down the valleys, a seething, unorganized caravan.

Kate dared not call attention to the green Jaguar by traveling
faster or slower than the norm. Yet in the familiar crowd of
vacationers she could not determine if they were being followed.
It was unnerving.

She turned off the interstate to find a gas station. As far as
she could tell no one followed.

There was not much left of the body.

Troy Garrett had steeled himself for the moment. The coroner
had been kind, preparing him for the ordeal of seeing what fire
could do to a human being. It was not pretty. The lower half
was charred, not identifiable as human. The stench of death and
seared flesh was overpowering.

The charring dissolved into blistered and puckered flesh. The
man had been alive when he burned. The face had melted.

Troy turned away, his stomach churning. Thank God it's not
Josh, he reminded himself. It's not Josh.

But it had to be identified as Josh.

He took a deep breath and turned back. Dental records. He
had to avoid dental records.

He forced himself not to look at the head. The man's hands
were strangely unscarred, as if he had thrust them out in front
of him, desperately trying to claw his way to safety before the
flames had swallowed him.

There was a ring on the right hand, a gold ring with a large

sapphire and an event commemorated in German. How convenient.

"This is my brother," he said softly. "He was given that ring when he played soccer in Europe. He never took it off."

"I'm sorry," the pathologist said.

"So am I," Troy said. He turned to go.

"Would you like the ring, sir?" the man asked.

The ring. "Yes, thank you." He couldn't watch as the ring was removed from the dead, roasted finger.

Now he had two clues to Josh's problem. He had the fingerprints of a woman and the ring of the man who had tried to kill his brother.

"Mr. Garrett, sir. Excuse me, but what would you like done . . ."

"I've made arrangements for cremation," Troy said.

He'd made them before leaving Phoenix that morning, before grabbing a ten A.M. flight that put him into New York early enough to identify the body before anyone attempted to check dental records.

Cremation. The job may as well be finished.

Chapter

12

It was pitch-black when he awoke. Josh waited for his eyes to adjust to the darkness. They didn't.

He groped about his surroundings with his right hand. He lay on a narrow bed, his body covered with quilts, his rib cage bound with bandages. He was otherwise naked. The floor beside him was cold and felt as if it were cement. The air was vaguely musty.

His eyes sought light, however faint. There was none. He could hear nothing besides his own breathing and the distant whir of a fan. He had no recollection of where he was or how he had gotten there. The unknown was suddenly frightening.

"Kate!" he called into the darkness. The nightmare memories of explosion and flight were real. The bandages confirmed that. They had escaped together. He remembered that, remembered the drive through the night woods. She'd been there. "Kate."

Something stirred in the darkness, beyond his sense of sight. He shrank from it. A match scraped a harsh surface, flared. It reminded him of the explosion.

"I'm here, Josh," Kate's voice said. The tiny flame dissolved into the soft glow of a kerosene lamp. Slowly she came into focus. Her hair was tangled from sleep. She wore only a T-shirt. She knelt beside him. "Hello there. How are you feeling?"

"I'm not sure. Where am I?" His throat felt cottony, unused.

"In Uncle Dimitri's basement."

"I don't remember getting here."

"You passed out when you stood up. We carried you down

124

together," she explained. "He thought it would be best for us to be hidden down here, at least for a few days."

"You told him?"

She nodded. "Everything. He had to know he was harboring fugitives. Are you hungry? Can I get you anything?"

"I'm not sure. What time is it?"

Kate glanced at her watch. "Just past six."

"Morning or evening?"

She smiled and kissed him. "Morning. And I think your fever's gone. You must be going to live."

"That's comforting. What time did we arrive last night?"

"About ten."

"What did you do with the Jag?"

Kate laughed. "We hid it in the barn. Uncle Dimitri rearranged his haystack. The bales are piled around the car like a wall. He's very good at hiding things—including people."

Josh glanced around the low-ceilinged room. It was furnished with two cots, a table and chairs, and several multigallon jars of water. "Does he have frequent guests?"

"Not anymore," Kate said cryptically. "Would you like some breakfast?"

"Isn't it a bit early?"

"Not for Uncle Dimitri. He's always up at dawn."

"Then yes, please."

Kate mussed his hair, then reached for her jeans. "Comin' right up," she said cheerfully.

She padded barefoot to the far corner of the room and pulled on a dangling rope. A short, narrow staircase came down. She disappeared.

Uncle Dimitri's cabin was comfortingly familiar. The broad, windowed sitting room that dominated the ground floor still smelled of its cedar paneling. The weathered green sofa she remembered from childhood was still there, though more weathered. So was the pair of lamps with glass bead shades. Only the contents of the bookcase changed with time as Dimitri Oberman updated his collections of history and biography.

Older people should never change their furnishings, Kate thought nostalgically. There should always be someplace to go where immutability could be relied upon. Her parents had never been in one place long enough to develop that kind of security. Until Wyoming. But by that time she was out of the nest. Her parents' retirement home had never been hers.

Uncle Dimitri's cabin took the place of what a grandmother's house would have been to her—if she had had grandparents. He had retired early to this quiet corner of Maine and the children of his old friend Colonel Fleming had always been welcome.

Even as a child Kate had fallen in love with the solitude of the retreat. She remembered feeding the chickens in the morning, collecting their brown eggs and locking them securely in their pen for the night, for one never knew when the foxes might come calling. She and her brother had built forts in the barn and gone on long twilight walks to watch the deer come down to feed. They had also hidden in the cellar, pretending they were rescuing groups of people fleeing the Nazis—or the Russians, just as Uncle Dimitri had done.

Everyone knew he had been in the OSS and had worked with the German and French undergrounds. In the aftermath of the war he had smuggled refugees out of Eastern Europe. No one knew precisely what he had done for the thirty years after that, though it was said that he had retired from intelligence and pursued a career as an economic advisor. It was during this time, when Kate's father was stationed in Iran, that the two men had become fast friends.

In 1978 Oberman had been injured in an accident and permanently retired to Maine. Since then he had walked with a slight limp.

Now she was back in his house, in his cellar, hiding. Only it was not a game.

She went in search of her uncle.

Two dogs, monstrous Great Danes, came bounding up to her, whining recognition. As a child she had ridden their predecessors.

"Good morning, Goliath; good morning, David," she greeted them. They accepted a hearty pat in the shoulders before they galloped off on some important investigation of their domain. It was fortunate that Misha was an indoor cat, Kate reflected.

She found her uncle behind the barn, freeing the chickens from their nightly captivity. Tall, slender, hair a distinguished gray, he did not appear to have aged in fifteen years. Kate had always thought of him as handsome and imagined that in his youth he must have been even more so. She wondered that he had never married. Perhaps he had. Uncle Dimitri was a secretive man, easy to weave romances around.

"Good morning," she called. "Can I help?"

He looked up and smiled. "Hello. Are you sure you should be about?"

Kate hadn't thought about that. Uncle Dimitri's seemed so safe, so remote.

"I guess maybe not," she said. "Hiding is rather new to me."

"I can imagine. Why don't you take these eggs and go back in the house? I'll be along in a minute." He handed her a wicker basket. "Is your friend all right?" he asked in a lower voice.

"Yes. He's better."

"Good. Just go in the back door. Okay?"

Kate took the eggs from him. They were brown.

It was early for Virginia to visit, Petersen thought. His wife came every day, in a limo arranged by his lawyer. She had never been a driver. Usually she arrived after lunch. It was not yet ten o'clock.

He combed his thinning hair before he followed the guard down the echoing hallway.

To his surprise and puzzlement Virginia was not his visitor. It was Bob Thrasher's secretary. Petersen approached with caution. He put a disarming smile on his face.

"Good morning, Dominique," he said.

She wore gloves and did not offer her hand.

"Good morning, Mr. Petersen. I must say it's a relief to see you looking so well." She smiled pleasantly, but she was lying. He had seen his reflection in the metal mirror that morning.

"Thank you," he said. "Please sit down."

She did. So did he. Then he waited. He would not give her the opening of asking why she had come.

"I suppose you're wondering why I'm here," she said at last.

"I assumed that Bob had sent you."

"No, no. I'm afraid it's more confidential than that." She leaned across the table and lowered her voice. "Actually, I'm here for Josh Garrett."

Petersen stared at her stonily. Garrett was dead and with him Petersen's hopes for redemption. The news had greatly saddened him. Issues aside, he had liked the controller. His death was a waste.

When the president did not respond, Dominique plowed on. Her voice was pleading, but there was something about her eyes. . . .

"You see, he confided in me, Mr. Petersen. He told me that

you and he and Kate had discovered something, something about the big export shipments early this month. He was real worried about it. And scared.''

They were cold, he decided, calculating. That was it. Her eyes did not concur with the warm insistence of her words.

''He said it might be dangerous for me to know, but that if anything ever happened to him I was to come to you. And now, well, it has.'' Her voice trembled a bit.

''What for?'' he demanded.

''I beg your pardon?''

''What were you to come to me for?''

''Well, I . . . I guess to help you,'' she said, pitching the words with sincerity. ''After all, you're here in jail and we all know it must be a frame-up and poor Josh is dead.''

''Where's Kate?'' he demanded suspiciously.

''I don't know. Bob . . . Mr. Thrasher fired her, you know, and no one's seen her since.''

Petersen sat back and studied her. He might be a ruined man, but he still had his wits about him. What did this woman want? What did Thrasher want?

''I don't know what you're talking about,'' he said.

She feigned surprise. ''But Josh said you'd been about to go to the FBI with the information,'' she said. ''He said it was very important. Please, Mr. Petersen, won't you let me help you?''

She reached out and took one of his hands in hers. The gloves were faintly damp. He pulled his hand away.

So they had known of his plans to see the FBI, he thought. He observed the woman with new eyes. He would not have suspected her of complicity, he mused. Virginia had always told him he had a tendency to underestimate women. Perhaps she was right. He smiled.

''It's nothing for you to worry your pretty little head over, my dear,'' he told her. But she was worried. He could see that. The conspiracy must be desperate to know just how much he and Josh had learned. That must mean that Kate Fleming was still a threat to them. A threat to them, a ray of hope for him. There must be a way to get word to her that Dominique was in on it, he thought.

''But Josh told me I could help,'' she insisted. ''Just the afternoon before he died he came to my office and left some papers. He said you would know what to do with them.''

Petersen didn't believe her for a minute. ''I'm afraid I don't know what you're talking about. Perhaps you should show them to Mr. Thrasher. After all, he's the acting president.''

"But Josh was quite specific. . . ."

"I'm sorry." He rose to leave.

She reached out and shook his hand fiercely with both her own. The gloves felt sticky.

"Believe me, Mr. Petersen, I really want to help."

"I'm sure you do, my dear, and you can best do that by standing by Bob now. Whatever Josh knew died with him."

He called for the guard to let him out and left her standing alone. The grim expression on her face was a strange combination of disappointment—and triumph. It left him disquieted.

In the cab Dominique removed the gloves, careful not to touch the outer layer of felt. They were lined with latex. She dropped both in a plastic bag, which she deposited in a trash bin before she returned to her desk.

"Wouldn't be the first time a perfectly legal export shipment was used to cover the movement of pilfered technology,'' Oberman acknowledged. "Heck, back in the forties the Israelis acquired a whole surplus munitions factory, broke it down into pieces like a giant jigsaw puzzle, shipped it out as something perfectly innocuous—dairy equipment I think it was—and put it back together in Palestine. Worked too. Heck of a coup. Nothin' topped it since.

"Still happens." He shrugged. "Remember the Iraqis and that big gun of theirs a few years ago?"

"Well, we think that's what's going on with LTS," Kate said. "What we shipped to them in two twenty-foot containers required four by the time it left the country."

"But what makes you think it's going to Eastern Europe?"

"Because one of the shipments went to Austria."

Oberman mulled that over for a moment, then nodded. "We do still have capabilities that reasonable men—and women—wouldn't want to fall into . . . undesirable hands. The illegal trade of technology to unfriendlies is still a serious problem. Thing is, it's gotten a lot harder to control since Eastern Europe opened up, not easier.

"Take Long Island for instance, where Josh lives. Two counties there, Nassau, snuggled up next to the city, and Suffolk, out farther east. Both of them bristling with defense contractors and telecommunications companies, high-tech stuff. Time was when, legally, that superabundance of 'innocent' Soviet citizens working at the UN, hundreds of 'em, weren't even supposed to set foot in Suffolk County. It was restricted on their visas, just like Silicon Valley. So what do they do? They buy an estate on the north shore of Nassau County—and the dishes on the roof weren't for watching cable TV. And now Moscow and Nassau County are 'sister cities,' a nice cozy relationship designed to promote trade. Nassau County sure as hell ain't gonna ship 'em string beans and tomatoes.

"No, thing is the Soviets can pretty much get their hands on anything they want now without playing games. And even if they couldn't, it doesn't explain why anyone would kill to get their hands on LTS."

"Get their hands on it?" Josh snorted. "They're trying to drive us out of business."

"I wouldn't be so sure of that," the older man said.

Sunlight spilled into the sitting room. The open windows formed a breezeway to dispel the summer heat. Josh lay stretched out on the green sofa. Kate sat at his feet, Misha on her lap.

"I'm not sure what you mean," said Josh.

"Well now, supposin' I was to covet that Jag of yours," Oberman explained, his Carolina childhood evident in soft inflections. "An' suppose when you take it outa that haystack there was an oil leak. An' no sooner do you get that patched up when the brakes fail, an' then the transmission. Pretty soon you've put a heap of money in that car and it's lost a little value in your eyes. An' then what if I was to come along and make a fair offer to take it off your hands?"

"I might sell," Josh said. "But I still can't figure why anyone would want LTS that badly."

"You know yer business. I don't," Oberman admitted. "I'm just speculatin' on a motive for murder."

"Three murders," Kate said from her corner of the couch.

"Three?" Josh asked.

"Payton, Chun, and you," she replied.

He swallowed. He'd forgotten that he was supposed to be dead. Oberman had no television and the day's paper had not yet been delivered.

"I should call my brother," he said. "If he couldn't identify the body I may not be 'dead' very long."

Oberman nodded. "In the meantime if I was you I'd plan on turnin' in whatever information I had to the authorities. I don't see that you have any alternative at this point."

"We're just not sure how to do that without exposing ourselves," Kate said. "They've already tried to kill Josh once."

"Maybe I can help," her uncle told them. "But let's see whatcha got first."

Thrasher was not looking forward to lunch. At least Bailey had selected a discreet rendezvous, Alfredo, a quiet restaurant on Central Park South, far from the office. Thrasher did not even tell Dominique where he was going.

Ken Bailey was waiting for him, seated in a dimly lit booth, sipping what looked like a gin and tonic.

"Glad you could make it," he said, offering his hand.

Thrasher shook it and sat down.

"What'll you have?" the Keiser president asked.

"Scotch on the rocks."

"Done." Bailey signaled a waitress. "Scotch on the rocks and another Perrier with a twist, please."

Thrasher appraised the man again. He was suspicious of those who did not imbibe. Bailey was a little younger than he, an adolescent athlete gone to fat around the middle. The cheeks were too thin to match. Face-lift, he thought reprovingly, an image chaser. He disliked the type. Perfect white teeth, manicured nails, styled hair, Ivy League business school. None of them had ever had to work their way up, had ever worn out shoe leather pounding pavement.

"What do you want to talk about?" he asked.

"Oh, I think you know," Bailey replied.

Josh spoke with his parents first, when his voice was strongest. His mother cried. His normally stoic father was euphoric.

"We don't understand this, Josh, but your brother says it's on the level. You want us to pretend you're dead, we'll do it. Just as long as it's not a dress rehearsal for the real thing. It isn't, is it, son?"

"No, Dad, I promise. I'll explain everything to you when I can."

"Well then, you can count on us. You know your mother gave up the stage to marry me. She'll give a bravura performance at the funeral tomorrow. You want tears?"

"In moderation."

"You got 'em. I hope you don't expect them from me."

"Not on stage, Dad."

"Well then. Take care of yourself. Here's your brother."

The phone changed hands. Troy came on the line.

"Josh? You okay?"

"Yeah, I'm fine." Josh leaned back on the pillows. His blood supply had not yet caught up with the energy demands he was putting on his body.

"I went out to your property this morning. Guess who I found."

"Fred?"

"The same."

A surge of joy filled him, the first in days. "Hot damn! That's great. Is he all right?" He covered the mouthpiece and whispered to Kate, "Troy found Fred."

"Yep. He's a little worse for wear, but his appetite is healthy enough. Listen, Josh, I found something else, too. A car, hidden in the brush. Did you know about it?"

"I saw it as I left the property that night. It was still there?"

"Uh-huh. I think it belonged to your friend in the morgue."

If Troy had found it, Josh mused, other people must have missed it.

"Could be," he said. "Eventually his friends are going to come looking for it. What did you do with it?"

"Searched it, dusted it for prints, and had the police pick it up."

"The police!"

"Josh, relax. It's an abandoned rental car. Two will get you five whoever signed for it did so with false ID and a false credit card. Chances are this will mean it will take these people longer to find it."

Josh sighed. "I guess you're right."

Dimitri had left them alone. Only Kate was with him, wrapped in an old army jacket as the evening shadows crept across the floor.

"Where's the body?" he asked.

"In an urn," Troy replied wryly.

"What?"

"I had it cremated."

"But, Troy . . ."

"We'll be able to identify him," his brother assured him. "I had an imprint made of the teeth. Privately. I also have the ring."

"Is that how you supposedly identified me?"

"Uh-huh. So I have a few little pieces of the puzzle."

"You'll have another one. I sent another package to be dusted and it should match the first two."

"Terrific. Now are you going to tell me what the hell this is all about?"

Josh paused. "You have to promise me something first."

"What?"

"Not to act, not to get involved. These people are murderers, Troy. I could never live with myself if they got you, too."

"All right. I promise."

Josh told him. It took him nearly an hour. The room darkened as he spoke. Kate got up and lit the lamps. Dimitri returned from the evening chores as Josh's voice droned on.

When he had spilled the whole story his brother was quiet for a long minute.

"Troy?"

"I'm here. I'm thinking. Josh, you gotta come in." He interpreted Josh's silence as resistance. "Look, you've got plenty for the authorities to go on. You can tie this woman, whoever she is, to the dead letters and possibly with the dead banker. Most importantly, you can prove that someone tried to kill you. We have a line on who the murderer is, how he got to your place. It's all connected, you know that. Let the police prove it."

Josh felt a burden sliding from his shoulders. "You're right. I'll talk it over with Kate."

"Great."

"We'll have to figure out a way to come in safely."

"I'll help."

"No! I want you out of this. You promised," Josh said urgently. "Even this phone call may be dangerous. We'll figure out a way."

"All right," Troy agreed. "What's your number? I may have to reach you."

"I don't think . . ."

"I'll charge the call to a third party. They won't be able to trace it."

Josh told him.

"Terrific," Troy said. "Now, about your funeral . . ."

"Carry on. I'll pay for it later."

Thrasher always thought better aloud. With an audience.

He screened his secretaries for this among other purposes. Not only must they be enthralled by his reasoning power, but they must be discreet. He would float trial balloons. If his con-

fidences were kept, he knew he had a sounding board as well as
. . . as well as other qualities more easily evaluated.

He had never doubted Dominique's confidentiality, but he
was beginning to doubt her sincerity or her reverence for him.
Lately he had begun to sense that somehow she was directing
him instead of the other way around. He didn't like it. She was
as compliant, responsive, and efficient as ever. Yet there was
something in her manner, in the way he would catch her looking
at him, that was vaguely disquieting.

He took his ruminations instead to Paul Cosentino, his pro-
tégé. He invited him for a beer after work.

Dominique had been frantic when he returned from lunch, a
rare state of mind for the woman. Her comments had all been
reasonable ("We really should be able to contact you at all times
now, you know; we have to be careful whom we speak with."),
but they all boiled down to one theme: you didn't tell me where
you were going and with whom. He had almost told her it was
none of her business, but that would only serve to intensify the
woman's curiosity.

Thrasher wanted to avoid a replay of the scene.

He asked Cosentino to meet him at a local watering hole.
That way they left the building separately. No explanations necessary. To anyone.

The bar was crowded as he had known it would be. Cosentino
had saved him a spot in a corner. The younger man looked
harried as he gulped a beer, his eyes darting from side to side.

"Rough day?" Thrasher asked as he sat. He liked bar stools.
They made him tall.

"Sort of." The newly promoted export manager smiled
crookedly.

"Me, too." He ordered a scotch on the rocks. "Have things
settled down in your department?"

"I guess," Cosentino replied. "It'll take awhile to get a grip
on everything, mesh the two systems."

"Uh-huh."

Thrasher was not really interested. Cosentino sensed it.
"Have you spoken with Petersen?" he asked.

Thrasher shook his head. "Our lawyers advised me against
it."

"Do you think he's guilty?"

The acting president paused. Based on available evidence,
the legal authorities had reached a logical conclusion. Except
for one thing: Phil Petersen was no crook.

"I think the wolves are beginning to circle," he said. "I met with one of them for lunch today."

"I don't understand," Cosentino said, bewilderment written all over his face.

"Think, Paul. Isn't it a funny coincidence that the Suffolk fire, the Webb fire, the truck accident, even those big, mysterious, tempting overseas orders all happened at about the same time?"

"What? Coincidence? No. Petersen planned 'em. And the orders—you're not saying they were fakes, are you?" He took a fortifying swig of beer. It left foam on his carefully trimmed mustache.

"I'm not sure," Thrasher admitted.

"But your consultant said there'd be no problem."

"That's true."

"And now?"

"I'm just suggesting that perhaps there is a connection, that somebody wants to get their hands on LTS—or at least part of it."

Cosentino's mouth dropped open.

"I had lunch with Ken Bailey today," Thrasher said, observing with satisfaction the effect of his theorizing.

"President of Keiser Electronics?"

"Uh-huh."

"What did he want?"

"The home security division."

Cosentino drew into himself, eyebrows knitting. "You think he faked those orders?" he asked in amazement.

"I think someone did, someone who had something to gain from a weakening of LTS."

"Keiser?"

"Maybe." Thrasher shrugged, effecting a casual pose.

"What did he offer?"

"He wasn't talking money, he was talking opportunity."

"For whom?" the younger man asked sharply.

"Very shrewd," Thrasher acknowledged. "Bailey wants the home security division and he wants someone to run it. They don't know anything about that market."

"You?"

"Uh-huh. His line was that LTS is going down and why should I go down with it."

"Are we going down?" Cosentino queried.

"We are if we sell off the home security division."

"I can't believe Bailey wants it that badly. He has an avaricious reputation but . . . but murder?" He looked up. "What are you going to do?"

"I'm not going to sell out to Keiser."

"If I were you I'd fire your consultant," Cosentino added before he drained his beer. "He may be in on it."

Thrasher glanced at him sharply. Did he know who . . . ? No, he couldn't. But it was very possible that he was correct. After all, the chronology was right.

For the first time he felt truly betrayed.

"What are you thinking about?" he asked.

"The Fleming woman," Dominique said between the hairpins clenched in her teeth.

She was getting dressed to go out again and he was jealous. By the nature of their relationship they could not operate together in public. He regretted that, but then, it was part of the reason they were such a successful team. There were still times when he would have liked to appear with her on his arm.

"I wish you would let that go," he said. She had become obsessed with the missing woman.

"Have you?"

"Of course not. We'll find her." He still lay naked in their bed and saw no reason to get up. Dominique would dominate the entire bed and bath until she swept out the door.

Dressed only in her stockings and slip she sat beside him. "But have you really put yourself in her head? Asked yourself what you would do if you were she?"

"Have you?"

"Yes," she said intently. "First of all, we know the girl is frightened. She ran. That must mean she knows enough to fear for her life. Secondly, she's not stupid. That means she and Garrett probably collected documentation to support whatever they knew or thought they knew. Juana's positive they got into the Webb files." She did not mention that Petersen had revealed nothing about what that might be. She did not like being reminded of her failures. "Third, she's a civilian. Like most Americans she probably has a naive amount of faith in the due process of law. She'll go to the authorities."

"Probably the FBI," he concluded for her. "Because that's where Petersen was going. And we should put out a net to pick her up when she comes in. We already have."

She smiled. "How nice. Have you also gone through the

same process with Garrett?'' she asked as she rose and glided back to the mirror.

''Garrett's dead.''

''Mmm. But what did he do when he was alive? Were you aware that he has a brother and that that brother is a detective?''

''No. Where?'' He did not like the unexpected. Even in death Garrett seemed to be a disagreeable source of surprises.

''Arizona. They were talking about it at lunch today. He identified the body from a ring, by the way. A German ring. It was in the paper.''

Their eyes locked. Muller had worn a sapphire ring with a German inscription.

''Perhaps we should send a man to Arizona,'' he said.

''Perhaps so.''

Petersen did not move when the guard brought him his dinner tray. That was fine. Maybe the old guy was just tired, the guard thought. But when the tray was still untouched an hour later, Artie Simmons became suspicious.

He called the prisoner's name. No response.

Then he called for assistance. One should never enter a cell alone. But he did not need reinforcements.

Petersen was dead.

Chapter

13

There was no coffin. The remains fit easily in the ornate urn that Troy carried under one arm. With the other he supported his mother.

The small huddle of invited guests gathered in the sunshine beside the open wound of freshly dug earth in the Garrett family plot. Ashes or no, "Josh" would be buried beside his ancestors. Someone had forgotten to advise the grave diggers that there was no corporal body. The hole loomed large.

The press hovered at the edge of the cemetery, jostling one another for camera angles.

Troy did not recognize many of the mourners. A few close friends of his parents, his ex-sister-in-law yes, but not the faces from his brother's professional life. They had lived too far apart. Josh's secretary, Irene Warren, was there, and the chairman of the board and a tall cool blonde who was officially representing the president. He suffered their presence. He had turned others away. This intrusion on their privacy was enough.

Troy hesitated when the moment came to place the remains of the murderer in his brother's grave. It seemed blasphemous to defile his family's last resting place. His father took the urn from him, knelt, and placed it on the ground. His mother wept with dignity, her gray curls hidden by a black veil. Behind him he could hear more anguished sniffling. Probably Diana, he thought. She had insisted upon coming.

The minister closed the simple service and stepped over to speak with the elder Garretts as they moved slowly away.

Diana fell into step with her ex-brother-in-law. She was dressed in black, but that was as far as her solemnity went.

138

Diamonds dripped from her ears and adorned her throat and fingers. They caught the sun and dazzled in the light.

"I'm sorry," she said, sweeping a lock of calculated blond hair away from her face. Her makeup was waterproof, he noted. "I really am, Troy. I know the two of you were close."

"Yes, we were," he said.

"I never stopped loving him, you know."

She had never loved him, Troy reflected, only his money, his media exposure during the heyday of his career and the endorsements it had brought him. She had left Josh as soon as he had bowed out of the limelight and settled on a more traditional career. He said nothing.

"It's true," Diana insisted. "He was such a dear, sweet person. I've often asked him for a reconciliation, you know."

"You never asked him for a reconciliation," Troy told her—quietly, for they were approaching the press gauntlet. "You only asked him for more money."

"Well, he owed it to me," she said ruefully.

"Why? What did you ever do to earn it? What did you ever do for him?" He stopped and kept his voice low. He could now see where this conversation was leading. "You took everything after the divorce, Diana. Whatever my brother leaves now he earned on his own account, afterward. And no, in case you're interested, you're not mentioned in the will."

She gasped and grabbed his arm. Real tears fell from her blue eyes. "You can't mean that. Josh loved me, I know he did. I'll go to court. I'll fight it."

He pulled away. "Go ahead, try it. As an ex you haven't a leg to stand on. I'm the executor of the will and I'll make sure his wishes are carried out to the letter."

She turned placating, pleading. "But surely there's something I can have to remember him by, something that no one else would want?"

"Like what?"

"The Jaguar . . ."

"Forget it. That car was the one thing he salvaged out of marriage to you and that only because you can't drive a stick shift. You'd be the last person he'd leave it to."

"But I've been out there, Troy, and the car is gone. Where is it?"

Troy almost responded that he didn't know, but caught himself. "He loaned it to a friend."

"To that office girl he's been seeing?"

"It's none of your business."

She sighed dramatically. The reporters were descending. "I'll see you in court," she huffed.

Troy ignored her.

"Mr. Garrett, Anita Rodríguez of the *Post*. I know this is a bad moment, but you're a hard man to track down." The woman was tall and slender. Though her face was pockmarked, she was dressed attractively in a light blue skirt suit and carried herself well.

"There's a reason for it," Troy said. "I have no statement to make."

"But, Mr. Garrett, our readers share your grief and they want to know the story behind it. They have a right to know. . . ."

"They have a right to know nothing. Excuse me."

"But, Mr. Garrett, just one question, about the ring. What did the inscription say? Where did he get it? What will you do with it?"

Troy observed her coldly, then pushed through the gathering swarm to be with his parents as they climbed back into the black limo.

Anita Rodríguez pounced instead on Diana.

"Mrs. Garrett?"

"I really don't feel like talking just now."

"But I just overheard you speaking with Troy Garrett about a car, a Jaguar I believe."

"Yes," Diana sniffed. Publicity couldn't hurt her case, she reflected. "Josh left it to me in his will—his original will. Now Troy won't let me have it."

"Why wasn't the car found on the property after the fire?"

"I don't know. It may have been there. The garage is still there. I think maybe they took it so I couldn't find it." She blew into her sodden handkerchief.

"What about the ring, Mrs. Garrett?" Rodríguez prodded.

"What?"

"The ring, the one found on his finger that led to the identification of . . . of the body?"

"I don't remember a sapphire ring. I don't remember Josh wearing flashy jewelry. It wasn't his style."

"Thank you, Mrs. Garrett. I know this has been painful for you, but it will make good copy." The reporter smiled. Her face was almost pretty.

"You're welcome. When will it be in?"

Rodríguez glanced at her watch. "Little late for this afternoon's edition. Try tomorrow."

"Thank you."

"Thank you, Mrs. Garrett."

Diana strode majestically, tragically to her own car, a Mercedes, and got in. She had not been invited to join the family.

The reporter watched her go, rechecked her notes. Diana had been more helpful than she knew.

Thrasher did not like funerals. He was pleased when Dominique offered to go in his stead. Her absence meant also that he could hold private conferences without her hovering. He did not want her to know he was getting anxious about the L/C's for the export orders. She had been so confident they would be honored. She called the bank every other day to check and assured him that the wired funds were expected momentarily. She had even connected him with an official at the Hong Kong and Shanghai Banking Corporation who had given him the same assurances.

But the first and largest payment he had promised to a supplier involved in the deal fell due in less than three weeks and Thrasher was nervous.

Omer Electronics was not a big company. They had worked overtime shifts and extended delivery times to other customers to meet his demands—demands that he had coupled with the threat to find an alternate supplier if they did not come through. A late payment would cripple their ability to conduct business as usual. They needed the money to pay their employees, their own suppliers. They had already asked once if Thrasher could speed payment of their invoices. He had promised to look into it.

He took advantage of the absence of Dominique's curious probing to pay a casual visit to the financial department to see how their cash flow stood. It did not look good. He was glum as he trudged back to his office.

A familiar face came toward him. The man seemed tall to him, but Thrasher supposed that he was only of medium height. Brown hair, gray eyes, a merry grin. Staff people he passed called out greetings, and he responded.

"Hi, Judson." "Good to see ya, Rosie." What brings ya home, Jud?"

Thrasher remembered then. Judson Rosen had been part of the BATT research and development team, another casualty of the acquisition. An electrical engineer, he was rare for the breed, personable and outgoing. He had served as unofficial liaison between the eggheads in R&D and the solid business types that ran the company. Thrasher thought that Petersen had made a mistake in letting him go and had said so at the time.

"Hello, Judson," he greeted the man.

"Hi, Bob. How are you?" Judson grinned amiably and offered his hand. "Congratulations, by the way."

"Congratulations?"

"On being named president."

"Well, thank you. But I'm only acting president," he said, aware that other people were listening.

"Do you really imagine it will stay that way long?" Rosen asked.

"We'd like to think so," Thrasher said quietly.

"Oh. Uh, yes. Well, I guess so. Sorry . . ."

"That's quite all right. What are you doing these days?"

The smile returned to Rosen's face. "I'm in the consulting business. My firm specializes in mergers, liquidations, acquisitions."

"Isn't that a bit removed from electronics research?"

"Not if you're specializing in the industry."

"True enough," Thrasher admitted. He heard his name on the unobtrusive office page and moved to escape.

"As a matter of fact I came to talk to Mathers in credit about one of your suppliers," Rosen said.

"Oh, really. Who?"

"Omer Electronics."

Thrasher froze. "Why?"

"I have a client who's interested in acquiring them."

That meant someone would be snooping through Omer's books, realize that their financial well-being depended on a note from LTS, a note secured only by his signature.

"I know Omer pretty well," he said cautiously. "I brought them on board as a supplier eight years ago."

"Maybe you're the man I should be talking with then."

"Maybe."

"Do you have a moment?"

Thrasher hesitated. Better the information come from him, he thought. That way he could control it.

"Sure. Come on back to my office."

The page was insistent now. He reached across the nearest

desk and picked up the phone, stabbing the button for the switchboard.

"This is Thrasher. Who's calling?"

"Cole Yaeger, Mr. Petersen's attorney."

"Tell him I'm on the way back to my office, then put him through there."

"Yes, sir."

Thrasher turned to Rosen. "I'll just be a minute. Do you mind waiting outside my office for a few moments?"

Rosen shrugged. "No problem."

Thrasher led the way back to his office and closed the door. His phone was ringing.

"Thrasher here. What is it, Cole?"

"I'm afraid I have bad news," the attorney said in a lugubrious voice.

"Yes?" He was impatient to confront the problem posed by Rosen.

"Phil died last night."

"What?"

"In his cell. Looks like natural causes, but an autopsy is pending. They kept it out of the papers until this afternoon so all the family could be notified. I thought LTS should have advance warning, too."

"Thanks, Cole. I'm very sorry about this, I really am. Phil and I may have had our differences, but he was a good man and he was no crook. I hope you still plan to clear him?"

"Yes. We won't let this die."

"I'm glad to hear it. Please tell Virginia how sorry I am, will you?"

"Yes."

"Thanks—and thanks for calling."

He hung up, wondering if Petersen's death would diminish or intensify the press scrutiny of LTS. Then he remembered Rosen.

"Come on in, Judson," he called.

The engineer turned consultant came in, still smiling, then saw Thrasher's face and sobered.

"Are you all right?" he asked. "You look pale."

"I'm fine," the acting president responded. There was no reason to tell Rosen. He would know soon enough. Besides, it would sidetrack their conversation. "Please have a seat."

Rosen seemed more average-sized to Thrasher as he looked

down from his desk. His guest sank into one of the chairs facing the platform.

"What do you need to know about Omer?" Thrasher asked.

"Oh, the reputation they have in the industry for quality, reliability, delivery, staying on top of technology. Why over fifty percent of their receivables are due from LTS." He slipped the last question in almost casually.

Thrasher eyed him shrewdly. "I imagine you're most interested in the latter."

"I'm interested in when the receivables are going to be paid." Rosen was still pleasant, but he spoke with quiet firmness, menacing in its simplicity.

"It will be paid when it's due."

"Two point one million dollars?"

Thrasher nodded. "That's right. You can check our credit rating. LTS always pays on time."

"As a businessman do you think it's wise to run up such a large percentage of receivables to one customer?"

"I don't run Omer. I run LTS."

"Do you always secure purchases with unconfirmed letters of credit?"

Unconfirmed, unconfirmed. The Fleming girl had explained what that meant. What had she said? He couldn't remember.

"Omer has my personal note and a long history with LTS. Go ahead. Take a look at our credit record."

"I have. I've also been reading the papers and your cash flow must be a bit weak right now."

"Our cash flow is just fine."

"Not according to my sources. I know that Phil wanted to go public so that LTS would have the capital it needed for further expansion. I also know that a public offering is out of the question now. I think LTS is in trouble, Bob, more trouble than the press reports indicate."

"Nothing we can't handle."

Rosen smiled again. The cunning left his face. "I'm sure. But let me give you something to think about. My client is big, very big. LTS is basically a sound company, well managed, good reputation. My client might be interested in acquiring you both—together. Then it wouldn't matter who owed whom, would it?"

Thrasher laughed.

"I can understand your reluctance," Rosen said. "Here you are, president at last. Lord only knows what a merger would do to that. But my firm could use a good marketing man, Bob, someone with experience in the electronics industry.''

"I'm flattered. That's creative, Judson, but I don't think the board would be interested.''

"They might be if they knew about the two point one million dollars.''

Thrasher's eyes narrowed. "They do. And they also know we're going to pay on time.''

"I'm glad. I always liked this company, was looking forward to being a part of it when you acquired BATT.'' He rose. "Let me leave you my card, just in case you change your mind.''

"Thanks, Judson. And good luck to you.''

"I'm not the one who needs it,'' Rosen said. He turned and left.

Rosen always had been one for flying by the seat of his pants, Thrasher thought. Brash ideas, innovation. Too much so for Phil Petersen.

The invoices would be paid. He put Rosen out of his mind.

The first of the phone calls arrived asking for his reaction to the president's death.

"You were laid to rest with great dignity,'' Troy reported.

"Lots of press?'' Josh asked.

"Yeah, and more mourners than we expected. You were a popular guy.''

Josh laughed. "Must have been a slow news day if they had to dredge up a long-retired soccer player.''

"Who died in a blaze of glory under mysterious circumstances and has a socialite ex-wife. . . . Diana will be terribly disappointed to discover that you're still alive,'' he added.

"What did she want?''

"Your Jag.''

"That figures.''

"Mm. I told her where to get off. I've wanted to do that for years.''

"I wish I could have been there.''

"So do I. Josh, there is one other thing you should know. It hit the papers this afternoon. Phil Petersen died last night.''

Josh was stunned. He sat frozen with the phone at his ear.

"Police say natural causes, Josh.''

"My ass! Find out who he was caged with, who visited him yesterday.''

"His attorney already did. He had two visitors yesterday, his wife and a Dominique Attinger."

"Shit," Josh swore.

"Someone I should know?"

"No. Don't worry about it."

"I'm sorry, Josh. I understand he was a nice man."

"He was," Josh said grimly.

"I hope this doesn't change your plans to come in."

Josh sighed. "No. We'll come in. We may end up still in hiding for a few months, but we'll come in."

"Good."

"When are you heading back for Arizona?"

"Monday. I'll spend the weekend with the folks, help make arrangements to protect your estate."

"Thanks. I appreciate it."

"Anything for a dead brother."

They laughed together.

"Call me," Troy said.

"Promise," said Josh.

When he'd hung up he turned to Kate.

"They killed Phil," he told her.

Now they were alone, he thought. It was their word against the conspiracy.

The police arrived at five. Thrasher was not surprised. He had expected the investigation to land on his doorstep sooner or later.

Dominique was gone for the day. They marched in unannounced, two of them, both detectives in plain clothes. The elder of the two, Jensen, was a graying fifty, still slim, distinguished looking in his blue suit. Thrasher wondered abstractly where he got the money. Timothy, the younger cop, was a yuppie type with a receding hairline and slight paunch.

Retaining his throne, Thrasher invited them to sit. He kept his hands in his lap, lest he nervously twist his fingers, and concentrated on making eye contact with his inquisitors.

"We realize this must be a difficult time for you," Jensen began, removing a small spiral notebook from his vest pocket. "Did you know Petersen well?"

"We worked together for over fifteen years," Thrasher replied. Keep it short, direct, the corporate lawyer had said.

"Were you aware of any lingering health problem he might have had?"

"No."

"Any personal financial problems?"

Thrasher shook his head.

"What about personal interests on the side that might have . . . drained his resources?" Timothy asked.

"I'm not sure what . . ."

"Women, gambling, that sort of thing."

The suggestion that Phil Petersen might have had a mistress did surprise him. For a moment he wondered if . . . No, he thought. Petersen was under investigation, not him.

"Not to my knowledge," he said, scarcely missing a beat. "That just wasn't like Phil."

"Was it like Phil to commit insurance fraud?" Jensen was asking the questions again.

"No. I don't know who your witness is that claims Phil paid him to commit arson, but I'm willing to bet he was lying. Phil Petersen built this company. He would never do anything to jeopardize it." Thrasher was confident that he sounded suitably forceful.

"You do realize what you're saying?" the older cop said. "If Petersen wasn't behind the Suffolk fire and the truck sabotage then someone must have set him up. Do you have any idea who might have done that?"

"No."

"If there were such a conspiracy it would almost have to involve people both inside the company and out," Timothy went on. "Think. Who might have had something to gain or a score to settle?"

They were right, Thrasher realized. The thought chilled him despite the fact that the room was slowly warming. The computers that controlled the artificial environment were cutting back on the air-conditioning. It was after office hours.

"Come now, Mr. Thrasher," Jensen chided. "LTS has just completed a merger with BATT, Inc., a merger that according to press reports was not entirely bloodless. Do you expect us to believe that there were no hard feelings?"

A light went on in Thrasher's head. There might be no way to recoup the seven million dollars, but perhaps he wouldn't have to take the rap for it. He gazed straight into Jensen's brown eyes.

"There were definitely some disgruntled people at BATT," he said, "people who either lost their jobs or found them diminished. I fired one of them for incompetence just last week."

"And what's his name?"

"Her name is Kate Fleming."

Dominique paced the length of their living room, her silk robe flowing behind her. "So," she said, "Fleming didn't come to the funeral, Muller's disappeared, Garrett's Jaguar is missing, and his ex-wife never saw him wear a sapphire ring. Where does that leave us?

"I'll tell you where that leaves us," she went on before he could respond. "Garrett is alive and they're in hiding—somewhere. We have every available agent on the East Coast searching for two civilians and no one can find them."

She flopped down on the opposite end of the sofa and fumbled for a cigarette. He waited for the storm to pass.

"I don't think the picture is as black as you paint it," he told her.

"No? My friend, this operation could blow up in our faces and our careers with it."

"Over a couple of amateurs who may suspect we're shipping classified technology out of the country? And make no mistake about it, my dear, that's precisely what they think. To protect such an operation is a motive for murder. To take over a company is not, even in America. They kill each other corporately, but not literally.

"The decision was made before we began to sacrifice the Webb operation. It was time to close him out and install a replacement anyway. Customs was beginning to be suspicious of him. Besides, if Garrett and the girl send the authorities off scurrying for stolen goods, so much the better. The buy-out of LTS will all be perfectly legal. The project will go forward and my placement remains safe. They'll run around chasing rainbows."

She sighed, exhaling lungsful of smoke.

"You're right, of course. It's my German blood. I like things neat and tidy."

"I know." He smiled.

"So perhaps it is time you saw Mr. Thrasher."

"I already have."

The quiet statement hit Dominique like a surge from a stun gun.

"You what! But we didn't agree to that. We decided it wasn't time."

"You decided. I decided it was the perfect time."

"I wondered what he was doing for lunch yesterday," she mused.

He looked at her quizzically.

"But he said nothing," the woman added.

He paused. That was puzzling. Thrasher had certainly had the opportunity.

"Perhaps you've been a bit too aggressive with him, my dear. Perhaps he feels he can reassert control by keeping his own counsel."

"Perhaps," she admitted. "What did he say? How did he react?"

"He hasn't taken the bait yet, but he will," he said confidently.

She snuffed out her cigarette and slid over to him. "Well, at least Petersen is out of the way," she purred.

His turn to be startled. "You did that?"

"Yes, of course. Chemically, untraceable, like Chun. I was afraid he would talk." She tickled his ear with her tongue.

"You should have asked me first."

"We all have our little secrets, darling." Her slender fingers sought the buttons of his shirt. "What do you think we should do with Garrett's brother?"

"Leave him alone," he said as he submerged himself in her perfume. "We don't need another investigation on the periphery."

Her hand slipped under his waistband to his crotch, seized him. He put business aside.

"First of all I think you'd better stay dead, son." Oberman was tossing the salad before joining them at the table.

"But that means Kate has to go in alone," Josh objected.

"Yer not up to travel and I sure as hell wouldn't want to see you in public until you grow in that beard. Right now you don't have enough fuzz to fool anybody and you still get dizzy every time you stand up."

He was right. Josh was silent.

"But I can't just go waltzing into the FBI with the package under my arm either," Kate said.

"Nope," Oberman agreed. He sat down. "You don't take the papers with you and you go prepared to run if you have to."

Kate glanced forlornly at Josh.

Her uncle went on, attacking both his dinner and the subject at hand with equal relish. "We'll stash the documentary information and your full statements in a safe-deposit box. You give the key to the FBI.''

"But won't they need my signature to open the box?" Kate asked.

"Nope. The authorization can be done with numbers instead.''

He put down his fork and took Kate's hands in his own. "And you, my dear, will make a very credible witness.''

"Why on earth should they believe me?" Kate asked.

"Because you're you—and because you'll present them irrefutable evidence that the late lamented Josh is alive.''

She swallowed.

Oberman smiled. "Relax and eat your dinner. We'll run you in with a wig on." His eyes sparkled.

"It just might work," Josh said. "By God, it just might work.''

"We'll drive down to New York Sunday," Oberman said, "borrow an out-of-state license plate along the way, probably in Massachusetts, so that anyone who does see my Buick won't be able to trace it. We'll spend the night in Jersey, then on Monday I'll drive Kate into Manhattan.''

"Why New York? That's where they're most likely to be waiting," Josh objected.

Oberman nodded. "It's also the city in which Kate has the best chance of escaping on her own if something goes wrong. She knows the subway system. And if it becomes known that she's turned up somewhere farther north they may zero in on us here. That's the last thing we need.''

Chapter
14

They never made it to New York.

Kate and Oberman had spent Sunday night in a motel just across the river in Fort Lee, New Jersey. Spare, serviceable, it catered mostly to traveling salesmen who didn't want to pay Manhattan room rates. She'd waited in her uncle's nondescript blue Buick with its "borrowed" plates while Oberman paid for their accommodations in cash.

"You're registered as Amanda Sullivan," he had told her when he'd returned to the car.

"And who are you?" she'd replied.

"Frank O'Brien. Always thought my parents should have given me a more American-sounding name."

He could still make her smile.

The room smelled faintly of mildew and cigarettes, but it was clean. The last tenant had left a copy of the *Times* behind, Saturday's edition. Kate had tossed it aside. She didn't like being reminded that some stranger had slept in the same bed the night before, on the same pillow, as a succession of strangers had done before him.

She'd slept poorly and was up before the sun. To fill the empty hour before dawn she skimmed through the discarded newspaper, hungry for news after nearly a week of isolation:

There was an article on page ten with a lead describing Josh's funeral. The bylined reporter then summarized the other recent tragedies that had befallen LTS.

The last paragraph stunned her:

Sought for questioning about a possible connection between these events is Kate Fleming, 31, a former employee of BATT, Inc., the recently acquired division of LTS, who was allegedly dismissed for mishandling several large export shipments. Fleming is reported to have befriended Garrett shortly before his death and disappeared immediately afterward. A warrant has been issued for her arrest on suspicion of conspiracy.

Kate laid the paper beside her on the bed. Her hands were shaking, her heart pounding, demanding more oxygen. When she could finally move she picked up the phone and called Oberman's room. She forgot to apologize for waking him.

"Uncle Dimitri, they think I killed Josh!" The lie was so monstrous she wanted to scream.

"What makes you say that?" he asked.

"It's in the paper in black and white. There's a warrant out for my arrest."

"Lower your voice. Lie down and take long, deep breaths. I'll be right there."

She couldn't lie down. She paced until he knocked on her door. Though she was expecting it, the sudden rapping made her jump. She flung the door open. Oberman wore only jeans and a T-shirt. He was barefoot.

"It's there, on the bed," she said, pointing to the newspaper as if it were a loathsome creature to be disposed of. "Page ten, column left."

Oberman closed the door, then sat down to read the article. When he'd finished he said, "Get dressed and pack. We're leaving, now." He paused to drop a kiss on her forehead. "They say conspiracy, not conspiracy to commit murder. You'll be fine. We'll just turn around and go home."

"But I can prove Josh is alive. We have the note in his handwriting, the photos." The morning before they'd snapped Polaroids of Josh holding up a sign with the date on it, just like hostages in Lebanon sometimes did.

"True. But you can no longer go to them discreetly. Your appearance would be public. The papers would jump at the story. We can't take that chance."

"Wouldn't the authorities protect me?"

"Did they protect Petersen?"

No, Kate realized. They hadn't. She felt more hunted than before.

* * *

"Good morning, Bob," said the cheerful voice. It was Ken Bailey.

Thrasher sighed. "Good morning," he said. "What can I do for you?"

"Just calling with my condolences," the president of Keiser Electronics replied. "I was very sorry to hear about Phil."

"We all were."

"I can imagine. Listen, under the circumstances I can understand that you'll have your hands full, at least for a while. My offer still holds, mind you, including a spot for you, but I'm certainly not going to push it now. When you're ready to give me an answer, just call. I'm confident this deal would be good for everybody, good for us, good for you, and I'm willing to wait."

Nice, Thrasher thought, especially since he had no intention of accepting it. "That's kind of you," he said dryly.

"I mean it, Bob. You have my number."

"Thanks, Ken."

"No thanks necessary. When are the services?"

"This afternoon at three, in Syosset."

"I'll be there."

"Thank you. I know he would have appreciated it." His tone softened. The outpouring of regret over Phil Petersen's death had surprised him.

"I'll see you," Bailey said.

"Fine. Good-bye."

Thrasher hung up thoughtfully. In the viciously competitive world of business, the sincerity of sentiment expressed for the dead LTS president surprised him. Commercial rivalry was forgotten, basic human decency rose to the surface. He realized suddenly that Petersen would not have been surprised by it. Petersen had never sacrificed integrity for commercial advantage. It had been his greatest strength as a businessman—and his greatest weakness.

The realization hardened Thrasher's conviction that Petersen had been framed.

Why?

He always came back to that question. The only answer that made sense to him was that someone was terribly anxious to get their hands on LTS—or part of it. He had two candidates: Ken Bailey and Judson Rosen.

* * *

The church was packed. Highly respected in life, Phil Petersen was mourned widely in death. His widow huddled in the front pew, guarded by her sons, oblivious to the murmuring and movement behind her as her husband's colleagues, friends, and peers filled the chamber and lined the walls.

Thrasher found a place with an oddly assorted collection of LTS people, secretaries, accountants, and salesmen. They greeted him awkwardly. It occurred to him that he should have dismissed them all for the afternoon. Most of them were probably using their sick leave to be here, to pay a last homage. Phil would have done that, he reflected. Until that moment he hadn't realized that he, Bob Thrasher, now would have to earn the respect and loyalty of these people. They would not come with the title.

He smiled in what he hoped was a reassuring fashion. A few smiled back.

The service was simple and dignified. The widow and her children were led through a door in the front of the church. Only family would accompany Petersen to his last resting place.

The casket was wheeled back down the aisle. The rest of the mourners filed out of the building, back into the gray summer drizzle.

Thrasher noticed Dominique for the first time. She was alone, dressed in subdued black. It was too late to return with her to the office, he thought with regret. The black against her pale complexion and flaxen hair gave her an air of fragility, most arousing. Perhaps she would come with him to his condo further out on the island.

She seemed to sense his eyes on her, for she turned. She broke into a warm smile. Someone stepped out of the crowd to greet her, to take her hand, kiss her cheek in a strangely familiar way.

It was Ken Bailey.

Phoenix was a furnace. Heat waves shimmered up from the concrete slabs of the freeway, a suggestion of hell. The wheezing air conditioner failed to keep the occupants of the car comfortable. The sun beat down on Troy Garrett's lap.

"I should have stayed back East," he confided in his partner, Vinnie Duluth.

"It's been brutal," Duluth agreed. "Water in my pool is so warm you can poach an egg in it." He was a big man, heavier than Garrett, and he sweated buckets in the Arizona summer. They always carried a large thermos of ice tea in the car.

"Supposed to break any time soon?" Garrett asked.

"Nope."

"Terrific." Easterners always said that Arizona heat wasn't so bad because it was dry. In Phoenix you perspired your own humidity, he reflected.

Duluth dropped him off in the driveway of his sprawling adobe ranch house.

"Much obliged, Vinnie."

"My pleasure. Tomorrow morning at seven?"

"See ya then."

Garrett waved good-bye, then picked up his suitcase and trudged up the front walk. His garden needed watering, he noticed. Skip two days in this sun and the grass toasted brown. He turned the spigot to flood the lawn. A sprinkle evaporated before it did any good. In Phoenix you soaked instead.

He fished in his pocket for his house keys, turning the lock in the knob before the dead bolt. The door opened. A tingle of alarm went down his spine.

Cautiously he swung the door open. The air in the house was stale, hot. He'd left the thermostat up at eighty, he remembered.

He carried no weapon. The airlines objected.

Garrett stepped quietly into his home. His visitors had not been subtle. Nothing remained untouched. Furniture was upside down, drawers emptied, carpet peeled back from the walls. The intruders had been thorough.

Strangely they had not found the automatic behind the canned beans in the pantry. Or perhaps they had not been interested. He checked the magazine. It was full.

The electricity had been shut off, but the phone was still functional. He called 911 for assistance. Then he dialed Josh, twice, charging the call to a blind number the police department used. The first time he broke the connection after two rings. The second time he waited for his brother to pick up.

"They've been here," he said.

"You just get home?" Josh asked.

"Uh-huh. Place has been turned upside down."

"Get out," Josh said.

"I have a call in to 911."

"I don't care. Get out! Please."

"I doubt they found it, Josh."

"If they didn't find anything they'll try to get it out of you. Please, run!"

"Five minutes," Troy began. He felt a breeze on the back of his neck. He turned. In the living room there were shadows.

"Oh shit," he breathed.

"Troy?" Josh's voice was anxious.

"I have company." He drew his gun.

"Troy, please, back out."

Softly Troy Garrett put down the phone.

Troy's voice was gone. Josh clenched the receiver, straining to catch sounds from the kitchen twenty-five hundred miles away. For a long moment there was only silence. Then a flurry of sharp reports rattled in his ear, echoing like firecrackers in a confined space.

"Troy!" He found himself screaming. "Troy, for Christ's sake answer!"

But the phone was silent again.

He was panting. He was a witness to murder, but helpless to act. Please let it not be Troy. He waited for someone to pick up the phone, but there was only emptiness.

The house was dark as they approached. The dogs came bounding out to greet them.

"You go on in and see how the patient is doing," Oberman said. "I'm gonna check on the chickens."

Kate nodded. She was tired. Disappointment and the shock that she was a fugitive from the law as well as from the conspiracy had drained her. She accepted the house keys from him and let herself into the front room. The house was quiet. Misha came to her, yowling. She was hungry.

It was only just past nine. She had half expected Josh to be waiting for them.

"Josh?"

No answer.

She searched the ground floor first. There was no sign of him, no sign that he had eaten. That was strange.

She climbed down into the darkened basement, turned on the dim bulb at the steps.

He was sitting on the cot, his head in his hands.

"Josh?" she said softly.

He looked up at her then, his face a mask of grief.

"They came after Troy," he whispered.

"Oh no."

He nodded mutely. He seemed so remote, so rigid.

She knelt beside him.

"They were waiting for him when he got home. I was on the phone with him when it happened. I heard the gunfire, but I couldn't do anything." His voice was a monotone, expressionless. "For a while I thought they'd killed him. Then the cops came. I heard them, too. They think it was a robbery. It was, but it was them. The last package we sent Troy, the one with the cup with Dominique's fingerprints on it, is missing."

"Is Troy all right?" she asked.

He nodded. "I shouldn't have told him anything," he said bitterly. "I shouldn't have gotten him involved."

Kate took his hands in hers. "It wasn't your fault. Maybe they were just robbers."

"No." Josh bounded up, his face set in hard lines, the scar on his forehead creased even more deeply. "Damn them! My whole family's in danger. They'd have killed Troy if he hadn't been armed." He stopped pacing and turned to her. "What about you? Were you able to speak with the FBI?"

Kate shook her head and told him what had happened.

"Well, this changes things, doesn't it?" he said when she'd finished. "Phil warned me. 'There's more than enough crime to go around,' he said. I guess he was right. We can't go to the police now. Dominique and Thrasher are just waiting for us to surface. They know we're alive." He stood very still, mystified. "They anticipate our every move."

Chapter
15

Wednesday was a clear bright morning in New York. The storms of the night before had washed the air clean of smog and humidity. It was a day for the beach, not the office.

For Veronica Reese it was to be her day of liberation. She intended to submit her resignation.

LTS was alive with rumors, none hopeful. Rumors Veronica could ignore; facts she could not.

On the day she was fired, Kate Fleming had let slip that the dead letters of credit were somehow linked to dead people. Of those who had had some knowledge of those perverted documents, three were dead: Petersen, Garrett, and the banker Chun. Two, Kate and Webb, the forwarder, were missing. Veronica feared the worst. Bob Thrasher, under whose direction the questionable shipments had been made, was now the acting president of the company.

The police might not see a pattern emerging, but Veronica did. She did not know what was going on, but she wanted no part of it.

Cosentino had taken to coming in early since his promotion. She found him in his office, puzzling through the morning's influx of faxes. She knocked.

"Come in, Veronica," he greeted her. "Maybe you can decipher what the hell the Saudis are asking for."

Veronica laid a simple sheaf of paper on his desk.

"What's this?"

"My resignation," she responded, "effective two weeks from today."

Cosentino's jaw dropped. "You can't mean this."

"I do." She turned to leave.

"But . . . but why?" He sprang after her and shut the door. "Why don't we sit down and talk about this? I'm sure we can work something out."

Veronica knew they could not. She also saw that he was flustered. She sat down.

"Now then," he said in a calmer voice, "why is it you want to leave?"

"It's in the letter," she replied.

"I see." He examined the formal resignation for the first time. " 'Dissatisfaction with management changes.' " He looked up sharply. "Meaning me?"

He was the perfect alibi, she reflected.

"No offense, Mr. Cosentino, but you don't know the first thing about international business. You're not running this organization, I am. You just can't wait to go running around the world on the company's money. Meanwhile, I'm making the quotations, answering the correspondence, managing the staff, settling service problems, and shipping the goods. I do the work, you get the glory—and the salary, I might add. What would you do?"

"Well now, I might try communicating my dissatisfaction to management and try to work something out. After all, part of what you say is true and, frankly, Veronica, I need you. I need time to learn this business."

"And I get to teach you so you can be my boss and tell me what to do."

She had not intended to be unkind to Cosentino. He wasn't a bad guy, just more political than competent.

"I think we could do better than that," he said.

"I doubt it. I'm the wrong color and the wrong sex for this organization."

"Are you accusing me . . ."

"I'm not accusing anybody of anything. I'm leaving, like it says, two weeks from today."

She rose, expecting him to dismiss her summarily. It was the LTS management style. But he watched her go in silence. Later, she thought, after he'd gone running to Thrasher.

She felt confident, however, that no one would suspect the truth of her leaving.

She fervently hoped not.

* * *

Josh slept fitfully until nearly ten. Kate wondered if sleep were his shield from pain, both physical and emotional.

The previous day was a blur to her. It was as if the terrifying reality of their predicament had struck them both at once. Josh had reacted with anger, a deep anger that isolated him from her, but the guilt was in his eyes. Kate had only wanted to hide.

She lay now beside him while he slept. His beard was passing the scruffy stage and the gash on his forehead had closed. His hair begged a trim.

She loved him, she realized—not the urgent bloom of first crush, but a deep, pervasive commitment. She'd never expected to feel that way again.

Staring at the cedar planking in the ceiling of her uncle's guest room, Kate conjured up John's face, his merry grin and his tousled blond curls. She'd known John for months before she'd realized that she loved him and it had happened just this way, waking up beside him in a cabin in the mountains.

For years she'd locked the memories away. Why were they slipping out now? She felt warm tears trickle down her cheeks toward her ears. John's image blurred.

I do want to remember, she thought. I want to remember a time when I was warm and safe. I want to go back to Colorado and forget about New York and BATT and the dead letters. . . .

A hand touched her cheek.

"It's only me," Josh said gently when she started.

He gathered her up in his arms and let her cry. The memories flowed out: John riding horseback across a meadow; John dressed in waders, a fishing pole on his shoulder; John stalking the living room of their apartment, rehearsing his closing remarks for a moot-court jury, dressed for the part in a three-piece suit. John's face, stark and white, frozen in death.

She cried until she was empty. Clint had only made her cry in anger, never in despair. Only loving bred despair.

Josh rocked her until she subsided into stuttering sobs. Then he swept the hair and the last tears from her face.

"Was that for me or for John?" he asked.

She didn't know how to answer him.

He kissed her cheek. "That was then and this is now, Kate."

His fingers played with her hair. He had a dancer's hands, she thought, tapered and expressive.

"Diana wasn't my first love, you know," he told her. "She caught me on the rebound. The real love of my life wouldn't have me. She wanted a prince, a real one. I only played soccer."

His voice was calm and soothing. He'd long ago exorcised his demons. "Diana loved me, in her way, as long as I played soccer, as long as I was a public persona. Thank God the people who count don't judge me by the company I keep. First divorce in the history of the family. I think Mom and Pop Garrett have given up on having grandkids. I'm divorced and Troy just never bothered to get married." He shrugged. "Course, he's only thirty, so there's still hope."

He smiled at her, a warm smile. "So you see, I have my memories, too. And, no, you don't remind me of her, if that's what you're thinking. What we have together is separate and new. I leave my memories where they belong, in the past."

She reached up to touch his cheek. "I know how dangerous rebounding can be," she said, the recollection of her early return from Japan to find Clint in bed with someone else frozen like a staggered progression of photographs in her mind. She banished them. "You're not a rebound."

"Thank you, I think," he said with a twinkle in his eye. "And now that we've got that settled come and help me take a shower."

She slipped her arms around his neck and loved him.

"I've been through his files, I've been through his desk. No address book. Either Garrett was an intensely private man or he had no friends."

Dominique had come home for lunch to report her findings on the clearing of Josh Garrett's office.

"Nothing?" he asked.

She shook her head. "No address book, no personal letters, nothing. That leaves the girl's apartment, but we've been through that."

"Yes, looking for the papers that might have disappeared from Webb's files. I still wish we'd questioned him about those L/C's before he went to the bottom."

She ignored the oblique criticism. "Well then, hit the place again," she said. "They can't have just run away. They had to be running to something—or someone."

He nodded. "Someone professional," he added as an afterthought.

Dominique at last ceased pacing and sat down. "Why do you say that?"

"Because she's covered her tracks so well. Hell, even the

police can't find her, and they can approach her friends and family openly—thanks to our buddy Thrasher.''

She winced. Damn Thrasher. If he hadn't suggested to the police that the girl was worth questioning she probably would have come out in the open.

"What about the girl's father?" she asked.

"Colonel Fleming, retired? He's at home in Wyoming entertaining his elder daughter and grandchildren from Sacramento.''

"Dead end.''

"Uh-huh.''

She sighed.

"But the apartment may not have been,'' he added.

"Oh?''

"We found her address book.''

"Why in heaven's name didn't you tell me?''

"At the time it wasn't important.''

Time was running out. Thrasher peeled back the leaves of his desk calendar with increasing trepidation.

Omer Electronics had called again, asking if he could accelerate payment. Mathers from the accounts receivable department had called to ask for details on the export letters of credit for the involved shipments. Couldn't hurt to have someone besides Dominique following up, Thrasher decided.

He searched the files for his copies of the L/C's. He found nothing. The folders were no longer in his desk where he'd left them, nor in his secretary's. When it came to the larger filing cabinets he had no idea where to start. He couldn't figure out how the contents of the drawers were organized.

He did not want to ask Dominique.

Instead he called Paul Cosentino.

"Hullo,'' his subordinate responded. "I was just coming to see you.''

"Oh? Problem?''

"Well, uh, yeah.''

"Come on up. And bring those files on the shipments the Fleming woman questioned, will you?''

"Sure. Anything the matter?''

"No,'' Thrasher lied. "I just can't find my copies.''

The intercom buzzed as he was hanging up.

"Ken Bailey to speak with you,'' Dominique's disembodied voice announced.

"I'll take it." He stabbed the flashing button on his phone. "Thrasher here."

"Bob, greetings. How goes it?"

"Quite well, thank you."

"Not according to my sources. I had lunch with Mel Zim of Omer Electronics the other day." Bailey left the rest of the statement unsaid.

"And?" Thrasher prompted.

"I don't think I have to add more, Bob. You're in trouble. I can get you out."

Thrasher set his jaw. "Really?" he said with sarcasm.

"Think about it. Proceeds from the sale of the home security division would cure your cash flow problems. You could stay with LTS. Or you could come to work with me. Sit where you are and you go down with LTS. Some of your people are already talking Chapter XI reorganization as a defense against the lawsuits."

"And how would you know about that?"

"I have sources."

It was true, Thrasher reflected. And he was willing to wager he knew who the source was. Somehow he had to get rid of her. The problem was she knew too much. What if she went to the press?

"I wouldn't spread rumors I couldn't substantiate if I were you," he said coldly. "And learn one thing, Bailey: I don't respond to intimidation."

He slammed the phone down.

Deepening shadows blurred the union of water and sand. He could hear the ripple of waves lapping softly at the beach, but no longer see them. Across the lake a muddle of lights defined the little settlement that catered to the needs of the summer visitors: beer, crackers, and rental canoes. Kate walked beside him. Somewhere in the woods the Danes prowled.

Oberman had decreed that at dusk they could escape the confines of the house. Josh seized the opportunity. With physical strength returning, he suffered from a severe case of cabin fever, aggravated by the despair of being forced to comfort his loved ones from a secretive distance and share his frustration with near strangers.

No, he reflected. That wasn't fair to Kate. She was no longer a stranger. Still, he yearned to be with his family, not cooped up here.

As did Kate, he knew. They couldn't risk her calling her folks, however, not even her sister Barbara. So Troy had called Kate's family, assuring them that she was safe, asking them not to mention the phone call to anyone. They were bewildered but they'd agreed.

Josh and Troy figured that there was safety in numbers, so Troy had asked for and received a leave of absence to stay with his parents. They hadn't been told about the attempt on their younger son's life. He had explained instead that together they could all better carry off the ruse that Josh was dead.

Troy had advised that one of the intruders in his house had escaped. The package Josh had sent containing the cup with Dominique Attinger's fingerprints had been delivered, UPS records showed, but Troy never found it. Nor was there any trace of the documents he had first received.

"Damn!" Josh swore aloud, shattering the stillness of the evening. "Everywhere we turn they've been there first. Every avenue we have for establishing credibility they anticipate."

"It would be easier if we knew what they were trying to protect," Kate said.

"True. And we won't find out what it is sitting on our butts in Maine."

"Then what do you suggest?"

Josh stopped and faced her, trying to discern her features in the growing darkness.

"Something completely unexpected," he said. "The one thing they'd never expect us to do."

"What?"

"Trace the shipments."

"But we have . . ."

"No, I mean follow them."

"Overseas?" Kate was startled.

"You see?" he said. "It wouldn't have occurred to you either, but what's the last link we have left with the conspiracy? The two shipments themselves. Besides, we'd be a helluva lot safer over there than we are here, smack dab in the middle of their operation with the police searching for you and the conspiracy looking for both of us."

Her voice came out of the dark, shaken. "But Josh, why not just let it die before someone else is killed? After all that's happened, do you really care what happens to LTS?"

"No. But they damn near killed Troy, blew up my house, and have you running like a fugitive. Somebody's going to pay."

A chill breeze came off the lake. Kate shivered. "What would we do if we found one of those shipments?"

"Go to the authorities at the embassy and show them the evidence we have that they're illegal. No one will be expecting that, not in Vienna or Hong Kong, not like they'd be waiting for us in New York."

"And if they won't help us?"

"I'm going to find the man who ordered my brother's murder," he told her.

"And yours," Kate reminded him. She took his arm. "Maybe Uncle Dimitri can help us," she said.

"I can't," Oberman said quietly.

"Can't or won't?" Josh demanded.

Oberman rose and poured himself a fresh glass of bourbon.

"Can't," he repeated. He stirred the drink idly with his finger.

"But I thought you had . . . well . . . connections," Kate ventured.

"I did, once upon a time." He spoke curtly, forestalling questions. The dogs glanced up from their naps, ears tilted forward at the unaccustomed tone.

Josh waited. Oberman was debating within himself whether to share something unpleasant, something buried. He didn't speak for a long time.

"I'd like to help you," he said. "You must believe that. But my name and my presence would do you more harm than good." He sat down and stretched the damaged leg out in front of him, as Josh often did with his injured knee.

"The men I knew in the Company are retired now, most of them," the older man began. "Or dead. Even if I knew anyone they would turn away at the sound of my name. I was discredited years ago."

Josh watched the disbelief spread across Kate's face. For years the man had been the object of her childhood fantasies. She couldn't accept that Uncle Dimitri had ever done anything against his country.

"They stopped short of accusing me of being a double agent. They canned me on the basis of stupidity. The Soviets were never sure what I was, whether I was on their side or not." There was no bitterness in his voice, only a bleak acceptance.

"What did happen?" Kate asked.

Oberman took a sip of his drink. "I fell in love, something

not recommended for a man in my position. Caring about anyone can make you vulnerable.''

"And they fired you?''

"Exiled me, barred me from setting foot in Washington or any restricted military area, or leaving the country, or having any contact with Soviet types.''

"Sort of like a South African banning,'' Josh said with distaste.

"Sort of.''

"You mean . . . all these years . . . you've been trapped here?'' Kate's eyes widened with horror.

Oberman smiled. "It's restful. Sometimes they send me 'guests' to entertain, defectors and the like. I still speak Russian well.''

"But that's monstrous! This is America. And they banned you for falling in love?''

"Sonya was not an ordinary woman. She was KGB.''

"And you knew that?'' Kate asked.

"Yes. I turned her cover. I used her. She led me to some very interesting contacts. She was also a decent, beautiful human being.''

"Did she know who you were?'' Josh asked.

"Not at first. But love demands honesty. I knew that if I didn't tell her, her superiors eventually would. They're always checking up on their own people and those with whom they associate. I also knew that if she could accept me as I had accepted her that we had a chance.

"She did,'' he said wistfully. "She came over. I retired—or tried to. We lived together for five years. She bore me a son. And then someone tired of the game. Neither side was profiting from our relationship so they decided to end it. Sonya was ordered back to Moscow.''

He stared into his drink. "Humanity has no place in the scramble for power. And that's all it is, this endless battle for geography, the arms race, the brushfires. Little men in uniforms, navy blue or gray pinstripe, who put ambition ahead of anybody's best interests and call it patriotism. It sucks.

"We thought we could turn our backs on it. We tried to escape. But Washington put out an APB on me and held us until the KGB caught up. They took my wife and son and left me for dead. When the Company scorned me, however, the KGB actually made me an offer. But it didn't include Sonya or Sergei. I think they killed her.''

He finished his drink in a gulp. "So you see, I am quite content to be here, not to have to deal with a world I realize I can't change. All you can affect is your immediate environment, the people you can reach out and touch. The power to change is ultimately in the hands of a few sons of bitches who don't give a shit about the hungry, the homeless, and the health of the family unit. Power doesn't care about people."

Kate stared at him.

Maine was not Oberman's retreat, Josh realized. It was a cage in which he was permitted to live by both sides. He had put himself in jeopardy with the foray to New York. No wonder he had been so careful to switch license plates.

Josh wondered how old the boy Sergei was now, if he were still alive. He understood loss better than he would have three days before. He'd almost lost Troy. He ached for Oberman.

"We still need you," Josh said.

Oberman looked up wryly. "I do provide a good place to hide."

"That's not what I meant. Kate and I can play detective, but we need your brains or we'll trip over our own feet."

The older man paused.

"It's true, Uncle Dimitri," Kate affirmed.

"It might be possible," Oberman said slowly. "I'd be the station chief and you two would do the legwork."

He got up to pour himself another drink, thought better of the idea, and splashed soda over the tired ice instead.

"What do you have that could identify the goods to begin with?" he asked.

"The container numbers and copies of the bills of lading," Kate replied.

"What does that mean?" Josh queried.

"The ID numbers on the containers in which the goods were packed when they were sent overseas. That information was in the documents we stole from Webb."

"Do they know you have them?" Oberman asked.

"I don't know," Kate told him. "Webb's office burned down. We have no way of knowing what they discovered before it did."

"Mmm. Josh is probably right though. They won't be expecting you to use that information to trace the shipments themselves."

"They," Kate repeated. "Uncle Dimitri, who are 'they'? The KGB?"

Oberman paused. "I don't think so," he said slowly. "They'd

probably know about any operation shipping goods to the East. At least they would have in the past. Things have changed so since the Bloc disintegrated. Now the Soviets can get their hands on damn near anything they please. I can't see them being so desperate to protect a smuggling operation. Why?''

''Just wondering,'' Kate said. ''Because whoever it is has resources behind them.''

''An organization,'' Oberman agreed. ''But it doesn't smell like the KGB.'' He sounded so confident, Kate thought.

''How do we use the container numbers?'' Josh asked. Who did not interest him so much at that moment as how.

''Given that and the bills of lading, the customs officials overseas will be able to tell you if they've already cleared the shipment,'' Oberman explained. ''If they have, the jig is up. If not, you have a chance. You don't have the original documents required to take title, but you have the copies. So your asking about the goods shouldn't raise eyebrows, at least as far as the customs people are concerned.''

Josh smiled grimly. ''So we go.''

''Not so fast. You'll need clothes, cover, passports. . . .''

''Passports we have,'' Kate said.

''But they're your own,'' Oberman said.

Chapter
16

Kate clipped the labels from their new clothes. Oberman had not been able to purchase all they would need for the journey. There were garments they would have to try on. But at least they had alternatives to the few changes they had managed to bring with them.

"Are you as handy with a needle as you are with scissors?" Josh asked.

"Not really. Why?"

"Because men's suits always come with a hem in the trousers and we can't afford to wait around for a fitting."

"Oh." She looked up slyly. "Whatever do you do when you lose a button?"

"I take it to the laundry and have it sewn back on."

Kate laughed. "Then don't ask me again if I would like to stay here with Uncle Dimitri."

He had half-heartedly tried to persuade her. But Kate's French was fluent and his German was rusty from long disuse. Besides, she understood the fine points of international shipping better than he did. He needed her.

Oberman was arranging passports for them as husband and wife. They did not ask him how. He had snapped pictures of them the day before.

"I think we should head for Austria first," he said.

"It may be too late," Kate said, repeating her argument of last night. "Shipping time to Vienna is three weeks max."

"There are other things in or near Vienna," he replied.

"Like what?"

"Like money. I don't want to have to borrow any more from

Dimitri and we can't use credit cards. They can be traced. Traveling is expensive if you're not on an expense account. We can't charge this to LTS, you know.''

"I've thought of that," she said. "What does Vienna have to do with it?"

"I have a bank account in Switzerland, right next door, a remnant from my days on the soccer field." He paused. "Sometimes I did listen to Troy. He was right about Diana. There were some assets I protected from her.''

Kate smiled gently. "I can see one small problem," she told him.

"Oh?"

"How are you going to withdraw money from your account carrying a fake passport with someone else's name?"

"For that I'll use my own passport. The Swiss bank won't know I'm supposed to be dead.''

"They might. You made headlines in New York. European papers may have picked it up, too.''

"It's a chance we'll have to take. Swiss banks are very discreet, as long as they get their interest.''

Kate threw the last shirt down. "Let's go for a walk. I need some exercise.''

He took her hand. "We can't go outside yet, my dear, it's daylight. But I have a better idea.''

She smiled.

"There is one other advantage to Vienna," he said as he led her into the bedroom.

"Oh? What?"

"I had a friend who lived there when I played in Europe. I think he works for the CIA.''

Thrasher waited until noon to call Dominique into his office. Most people went out to lunch on Fridays. The office would be quiet.

Dominique had been almost subdued of late, no hovering, no coaxing him into telling her of his latest triumphs. Thrasher was suspicious.

She slunk in and sat down, steno pad at the ready.

"I'd like the files on the seven million dollar export shipments, please," he said.

"Is that all?" she asked with surprise. He frequently wanted something more on the lunch hour.

"Yes."

"Well, I think I sent them back to Paul Cosentino. . . ."

"He doesn't have them."

"But surely his secretary . . ."

"She doesn't. I want them, Dominique. I want them now."

She smiled. "Of course. It's been a week since we've talked to the bank, hasn't it?"

"Yes."

"Would you like me to call?"

"No, thank you. Just the files, please."

"Yes, sir." She left compliantly.

He knew she would not find them. He and Cosentino had turned the office upside down the night before. No trace of the four orders was to be found. But he wanted Dominique to discover that for herself.

It was a lovely day to play hooky. Patrick Freeman took his secretary out on his boat. He had long promised to do so and this seemed the perfect opportunity. Both his wife and his boss at the brokerage company thought he was attending a seminar in New Brunswick. Ellen had merely called in sick.

She wore short shorts and a halter top. Her chestnut hair rippled in the wind as Freeman headed the cabin cruiser for open water. She was not at all put off by the thought of baiting hooks and riding waves as was Rita, his wife. She laughed, rejoicing in the sea as much as he did. Freeman laughed, too.

They anchored distant from other boats and Ellen took off her top. She obviously sunbathed nude, just as he had imagined. He approached her from behind and caressed her breasts.

"Not yet, Pat," she said. "Let's get the lines in the water first. You don't want the boat to look deserted, do you?"

She was right. They baited and cast the lines, secured the poles in their stands. Then they went below. It was just as he had fantasized.

Two hours later when he emerged one of the poles was bobbing and a substantial amount of line had run out, was still unreeling.

"Ellen, I think you have something," he called.

She appeared, still naked, and grabbed the pole.

"Pull back gently," he advised. "Then take up the slack in the line."

She settled herself in a deck chair and obeyed. The line came in steadily.

"How does it feel?" he asked.

"It's big, but it's not running out on me," she said.

She played with the catch for nearly fifteen minutes, pulling it in slowly, evenly.

At last Freeman, peering over the side, saw a dark shadow.

"Thar she blows," he cried with excitement. "It's a big mother."

"What is it?"

"Can't tell yet."

He grabbed a gaff and waited for the fish to surface.

But it was not a fish.

He didn't recognize it at first. The legs had been gnawed off to stumps, the arms were completely gone. The widened eyes staring out of the battered, bloated face were not human. Only the shrunken, uneaten genitals identified the thing as what had once been a man.

Freeman vomited all over the new paint job of the cabin cruiser.

"I tell you he's suspicious," Dominique said.

"But he can't fire you, my dear. You could ruin him and he knows it."

"So what if he really starts snooping? I can't keep him distracted any longer, not even by blowing him. We just can't eliminate him like the others."

"No, that's true. We can't afford another near disaster like Garrett."

They had not intended for Troy Garrett to walk in on the job. The cleanup of that mess had been expensive. Two local hoods had been garroted and items burgled from the Garrett house had been planted on the bodies. The police considered the crime solved.

"But if you will recall, my dear," he went on, "we have another carrot for our friend Thrasher."

"And we have the stick that his ambition landed LTS in the soup to begin with," she added.

"Mm-hmm. Don't worry. When the time comes we'll replace you. Until then we need you in that office."

She came and sat on his lap. The silk of her nightgown was smooth and soft against his skin. He teased a nipple until it rose, then took it in his lips.

"There is someone else in the game, you know," she said, arching her back slightly.

"Who?" he mumbled.

"I don't know. Thrasher is being rather closemouthed. I heard through the grapevine that someone else is making an offer for LTS."

His head jerked up. "Are you serious?"

"I don't joke." Her fingers fluttered down his naked back, a tantalizing sensation. She opened her legs, wrapped them around his torso. "I'll find out more on Monday," she promised. "Come fuck."

He lifted her buttocks slightly and drew her down on his swollen cock. She moaned. His penetrations were always somewhat painful, but he suspected that she relished that. The muscles inside her rippled, caressing him without a single outward movement. She smiled knowingly. He began to pant.

The phone rang.

"Shit," he muttered.

Dominique never took social calls at this number. She eased off him and reached for the receiver. He leaned back, still stiff, hoping the message was routine. Apparently it wasn't.

"What?" Dominique exclaimed. "That's wonderful! Get a team up there. Now! Yes, and keep me posted."

She slammed down the receiver in triumph.

"We have them," she said, springing to her feet, her nightgown clinging to her skin.

"Who?"

"Garrett and the girl. Guess who was listed in her address book."

"Who?"

"Dimitri Oberman."

"That doesn't ring a bell."

"Apparently it was all very hush-hush. We ran everyone in that book through the computer files. They all came out squeaky clean. Except Oberman. He came out very dirty. He lives in Maine."

Kate made the call. She wasn't happy about it. She didn't want to involve Veronica in what had proven to be a very deadly gambit.

But Josh was right. They needed a contact inside LTS. The company was their only other link to the conspiracy. What happened at LTS might very well have an effect on their actions overseas, might give them a clue as to what the conspiracy was after.

"And it might lead us to the SOB who went after my brother," Josh had added.

Josh would never stop until he learned who was responsible, she knew. It did not seem to matter to him that Veronica's life might be endangered. For Josh there were no longer noncombatants. There were only people who could be useful and those who could not—and those who must be stopped.

So she called. Her former assistant was home.

"Veronica, this is Kate."

"Lordy, girl. Where are you? Police've been lookin' all over for you."

Kate swallowed. "Veronica, I need your help."

"How so?"

Kate took a deep breath. "I'm working with some people who are trying to solve this thing, but we need to know what's going on inside LTS and there isn't anyone else we can trust."

"Ain't it the truth."

"We're not asking you to do anything overt, just to keep your eyes and ears open. You won't have to get in touch with us. We'll call you."

There was no answer.

"Veronica, you don't have to do this if you don't want to. These people, whoever they are, are very dangerous."

"Tell me about it. They just drug up Webb's body this afternoon. Least they think it's Webb."

Kate gasped.

"There's another thing you should know, too," Veronica said. "I resigned."

Kate's heart sank.

"Course now, Cosentino hasn't accepted it yet. He's still hopin' I'll change my mind. If I let 'im 'persuade' me to stay they won't have much cause to be suspicious of me, will they?"

Kate wished she could hug her. "Bless you," she said. "We need you, Veronica."

"Everybody needs me these days," Veronica said dryly.

"Could I ask you something?"

"Sure."

"Why are you doing this?"

"Because these people got my hackles up, girl, and I wanna see 'em swing."

"We'll do our best," Kate vowed.

"You do yours and I'll do mine."

"Thanks, Veronica."

"Bye now."

Kate put down the phone with a mixture of relief and a lump in her throat. "She's on our team," she said.

"Terrific," Josh said. "Two more days and we're outa here."

"There's something else, Josh: they found Webb's body."

The grin faded from his face. "Jesus. Phil, Chun, Webb, probably the night guard . . ."

"You," Kate added, "at least in theory."

"How big an operation are these people trying to protect?"

"And how large an organization are we dealing with?" Kate echoed.

"I think the sooner we get out of this country the safer we'll be," Josh said.

Chapter

17

"There's a dark sedan under the trees at the turnoff," Josh said. It was dusk. He couldn't make out the color.

"Mm-hmm," Oberman said, taking his foot off the gas for a moment. "Both of you duck." He spoke calmly.

Kate and Josh obeyed.

Oberman drove past the entrance to his property, neither slowing nor picking up speed.

"Just stay down for a while," he told them. "They may have other lookouts posted."

Josh's heart had begun to pound. He wished he could reach out and take Kate's hand, but she was in the backseat. Why now, he thought in frustration. Twenty-four hours more and they would have been gone. In the trunk were the other purchases they would need for the journey, luggage and shoes, cosmetics and underwear. In his pocket was enough cash to get them started. Damn! How had the conspiracy found them?

"Kate, are you all right?" he called.

"Yes," she whispered back.

"Hold on," Oberman advised. "There's a dirt track to the back of the property. I doubt they've found it."

The road surface changed. The smooth whir of the tires on asphalt became a symphony of sand and rock pummeling the underside of the car as they jounced from one pothole to the next. Josh steadied himself against the dashboard.

"Nope," Oberman said. "Nobody's been this way." He sounded satisfied.

They bounced along for several minutes.

"You can come up now," their benefactor said at last.

Josh sat up. They were running without lights, but enough daylight remained for Oberman to follow the narrow, rutted path.

"I'm taking you to a clearing in the woods about a hundred yards uphill from the lake," he said. "I want you to get down to the water and wait for me. If you go straight down to the lake, to your right will be a little shed. There's a canoe inside. Take it out and put it in the water underneath the big pine tree. You'll see what I mean. Get in and be ready to move. Take everything in the trunk with you.

"I'll arrive whistling 'Michael, Row the Boat Ashore.' If anybody besides me approaches, paddle along the bank until you lose the overhang, then get the hell outa there. Head straight across the lake.

"Otherwise, wait for me until midnight. If I don't come, paddle across and beach to the right of the lights. Check into the Rabbit Hollow Motel under the names in your new passports and wait two days. If I don't contact you by then, you're on your own. Under no circumstances come back to the house."

He braked to a halt and turned to face Josh. "I'll miss you two."

Kate's face was pinched and white. "Uncle Dimitri . . ."

"No words necessary, child. You just take care of each other."

"I don't know how to thank you," Josh said.

"Don't yet," Oberman said. "We don't have you home free."

Oberman turned off the ignition and gave the keys to Josh. He left them in the clearing and disappeared in the woods.

Only then did it occur to Josh that Oberman was unarmed.

Jerry Russo had a murderer's hands and the imagination of an artist. He needed both.

Russo was used in those cases when a mark was suspicious and might resort to disguise. With his imagination he equated the basic features from a photograph with living faces, seeing through cosmetic changes, adding a mustache, subtracting a scar, all in his mind's eye. With his hands he killed.

He had excellent photographs of Kate Fleming. He had memorized them.

Russo had been stationed at Federal Plaza in Manhattan for three days, prowling the main entrance to the office building in which the FBI was located. His superiors considered the FBI the most likely contact for the mark to make. They had wanted their best man waiting for her. All in vain.

He did not like losing, especially to amateurs. He wanted Fleming.

Dressed in denims and a hiking boots, to blend into his surroundings, Russo had made his way quietly up to the house. Quietly after he had disabled the two dogs. He didn't like dogs, particularly large ones. He would have liked to kill them, but his orders were precise. They were to leave the neighborhood as untouched as possible. The neighbors would miss the Danes. He gassed them.

The house was a bachelor pad. He searched it for signs of visitors. The dishes were washed and put away; no indication of three for breakfast. The only clothes in the closet appeared to be Oberman's. They were all the same size. The guest room was empty, the bed neatly made. He began to wonder if the Viper was wrong.

Briefly he explored the farm buildings. No sign of the green Jag that had mysteriously disappeared from Garrett's garage, he mused. He radioed the information to Cochran. Then he went back to the house and he waited.

Cochran called back shortly after eight-thirty.

"He may have just passed here," he said.

"May have?" Russo demanded. They should have switched places. Cochran did not have his talent for recognition.

"Couldn't be sure. Car went by pretty fast."

"What was he driving?"

"A Mercury."

"Anyone with him?"

"No."

Russo paused. "Stay there. If I need help I'll call you."

He fingered the .38 automatic in his pocket. Oberman was to be taken alive and possibly left that way. His orders on Fleming were more explicit. Question her and kill her. He regretted only that he was not to be allowed to enjoy it.

His privacy had been violated. The absence of the dogs told him. Oberman crouched in the brush at the edge of the woods. The house and yard were quiet, but instinct told him that one of them would be there, in the house. He would come back for him.

Skirting the open spaces, Oberman made his way through the woods to the dark sedan. His leg began to throb. It could handle walking, but climbing up hills and over fallen logs and jumping gullies stressed it. It took him a long while to hike out to the edge of his property.

He remembered where the car was. It was empty.

The driver would follow the road in, he reasoned. He had probably not had time to study the approach through the woods. Besides, it was now quite dark. He glanced at his watch. The dial glowed faintly. After nine. He had time.

Out of habit most people walk on the left side of the road, against traffic. Oberman went up what would be the man's right, hoping the driver was not of British descent. He moved quickly, for he must intercept the man before he reached the house. He wanted to confront the intruders one at a time.

Oberman pulled a short throwing knife from a sheath strapped to his right shin. He had not killed in a long time, not killed in anonymity, ignorant of the identity of his victim, for even longer. Silent death was distasteful. It was also necessary, he reminded himself.

There was an erect shadow in the trees on the other side of the road. He froze and waited for the shadow to move. Too late. He had been seen. He did not see the gun until it was fired. A hot flash of pain brushed his arm.

Oberman ducked as a second bullet whined past his head. He didn't move. There was a road between them. The other man would have to show himself.

He could feel blood trickling down his arm, but his elbow bent and his fingers still flexed. He was lucky.

His opponent stood up, tempting fate. Oberman waited for curiosity to win out over caution, knowing it would.

And if he were lucky the man in the house hadn't heard the shots.

They squatted in the narrow canoe, grasping exposed roots of the tall pine above them to keep from drifting away from the sheltering bank. They spoke only in whispers.

A light breeze rustled the pine needles, filling the night with strange murmurings. The birds in the branches quieted, their chirping giving way to the hum of insects. Kate slapped at the mosquitoes and wished she were wearing long sleeves.

Gradually the moon came up, spilling a silver path across the smooth waters of the lake.

"What time is it?" she whispered.

"Going on ten," he replied.

"Is that all?"

Two sharp reports carried in the still night air. Kate stifled a gasp. "Was that from the house?"

"I can't tell. They were too far away."

"Where are the dogs? Why haven't they barked?" She remembered then that Misha was still in the house.

The canoe rocked as Josh made his way to her. He pushed the luggage aside and made a nest of flotation pillows for them in the middle of the craft.

"Come here," he said.

"But Uncle Dimitri said to be ready to move."

"I think it's going to be a while, Kate."

She settled against him, her body tense, straining to listen. But only the night sounds reached her ears.

Oberman searched the body carefully. No ID, of course, but the man did have a small two-way radio. He stuffed that and the gun in his waistband and dragged the body into the brush.

His house was a half mile deeper into the woods and the walk took him many minutes. He could see now that the difficulty in meeting the midnight deadline would be his own physical limitations.

He moved as quickly as he could, wishing he had the dogs to catch and hold at his command. It was ten-thirty by the time he reached the house.

Slowly he circled, keeping to the shadows at the edge of the woods. Behind the chicken coop he found the dogs and signs of their having been dragged there. They were asleep, their breathing deep and regular, not a mark on them. He sighed with relief. Thank God for small favors. He patted each of them and went on. He had to confirm he was dealing with only a two-man team.

The radio unit in his pocket beeped. He fumbled for the volume control, turned it down.

"Cochran? Cochran? Where are you, you son of a bitch?"

Oberman didn't reply. Much better to push this bastard out of the house than to have to assault his own home.

"Cochran, are you taking a pee or what?"

Oberman chose his spot carefully. Instinct told him the man would slink out the back. He could crouch in the shadow of the porch and not be seen, catch the intruder by surprise.

Hurry, hurry, not much time. Damn his leg.

As he made his way across the yard, a figure stumbled out the back door of the house, saw him, and began to run.

Damn, damn, damn. He had to have this one alive. He drew out the knife and threw. The blade sliced into the back of the other man's thigh. He yelped, but kept moving. At least the odds were now even, Oberman thought grimly.

The intruder was chattering frantically into his radio. The unit in Oberman's pocket beeped. He pulled it out. The man was babbling in grammatically unsound Russian, heavily accented.

Oberman's blood chilled. "If I were you I'd stop right where you are, comrade," he replied in the same language.

Stunned, Russo did. It was all the advantage Oberman needed. He launched himself at the other man, pulling him to the ground. But the fall knocked the wind from his own lungs, too. His opponent was younger, heavier. Oberman struggled to reach the knife, but the big man had a strangle hold on him. He felt the muzzle of a gun jammed in his ribs.

"Now we are going to have a little talk, comrade," the man said.

He yanked Oberman to his feet and pushed him ahead into the house. Oberman limped badly. He fought to catch his breath, his mind whirring as an abyss seemed to open at his feet.

Russo shoved him into one of the kitchen chairs and tied his hands behind him. "You must know that we don't want you," he said easily. He faced his captive, the gun trained on the middle button of Oberman's shirt. His leg was bleeding but he seemed not to notice.

"What do you want?" Oberman demanded.

"A friend of yours."

"Who?"

"Kate Fleming."

Oberman stared at him. "What would the KGB want with Kate Fleming?"

Russo's heavy eyebrows lifted. "You admit you know her?" he asked, neither admitting nor denying the affiliation.

"Would it do any good to deny it? Of course I know her."

"When did you last see her?"

"A couple of weeks ago when she was here on vacation."

"And since then?" Russo prompted.

"I haven't heard from her."

Oberman sized up his opponent. Brutish, not very intelligent, but certainly programmable. And cunning. Nationality? Slavic somewhere. It colored his English. Funny name for a Slav.

"I think you're lying."

"My word against yours. Where are my dogs?"

"In the woods, asleep." Russo glanced at his watch. "They'll be out a few more hours. Where's Cochran?"

"In the woods asleep," Oberman said evenly. Perhaps this game would be easier now that he knew who the other players were. "You know what a chance you're taking coming here, don't you? The Americans are just waiting for you people to contact me, so they can prove I'm a traitor."

"We know you have been discredited," Russo replied.

"I really don't appreciate your screwing up my life."

"I would be very happy to get out of your life. Just tell me where the girl is."

"I wouldn't know."

"Come now. Do you think I'm stupid? Do you know what I found in your bathroom? A brush, full of long blond hair."

"She left it behind on her vacation."

Russo smiled, an unfriendly grimace on his face. "Mr. Oberman, we can do this pleasantly, or we can do this unpleasantly. The choice is yours."

He had to stall for time, Oberman realized.

"Will you open the window, please. I need some air." He needed to be able to hear.

"I don't want anyone to hear you screaming," Russo said.

"I don't intend to scream."

They stared at each other across the table. At last the assassin got up and opened the window above the sink.

"Thank you," Oberman said. "Now, what's in this for me?"

Russo was taken aback. "I don't know what you mean."

"I've got information you want and you've got information I want."

"What information?" the other man demanded.

"Did your superiors tell you anything about me? No? I thought not. Well, let me tell you a little story." He told the hit man about Sonya and Sergei, pausing every so often to listen to what the breeze blew in, as if he were collecting his thoughts. "So," he concluded, "you call that into your boss. They tell me about my son, I tell you about Fleming. That's the deal."

Russo snorted. "Nice try. That would take days—supposing your tragic little tale is true. I don't have days."

"If they have my file they have the answers."

"You're in no position to make a deal," the Slav said.

"Quiet," Oberman commanded in a loud voice. "I thought I heard something."

He had.

Russo froze. "I don't hear anything. You shit. You're trying . . ."

But there was a scratch on the porch. They both heard it this time.

"Must be Cochran," said Oberman.

His captor got up and opened the door.

"Grab!" Oberman yelled.

Two hundred pounds of angry Dane threw themselves at Russo. One of them mangled the hand that held the gun. The second took him by the shoulder and slammed him to the floor. The man went down screeching.

"Guard, Goliath," Oberman commanded.

Both dogs withdrew. Goliath sat on his haunches inches from his prey.

"Come, David."

The other Dane trotted over. Oberman snapped his fingers. "Chew."

"They should have been out for hours," Russo whimpered.

"Too small a dosage," Oberman said. "It's one reason I have them." Hands free once again, he picked up the gun. "Now we're going to make that call," he said.

Just before midnight they heard a third shot. Kate jumped. It seemed closer. She realized now that Uncle Dimitri would never reach them by the deadline. For the first time she grappled with the possibility that he was dead. If so, they were lost.

"It's time," Josh said quietly.

"Can't we wait a little longer, please?"

"Five minutes," he said. He was already figuring what they would do if Oberman never showed. Their passports, the copies of the documents, all were in the hidden basement of the house. Despite the warning they would have to return to the farm, eventually.

"We never should have let him go alone," Kate said. "I think we should go back."

"Do you know how to use a gun?"

"No."

"Well, someone up there does." He hoped it was Oberman, but five minutes passed, then ten, and still there was no sign of him.

"Let's go," Josh said at last. He sat in the bow of the canoe.

With only one arm, he would be able to do little more than steer. Kate would have to provide the muscle.

Sadly, she nodded.

The moon had dipped behind a wooded hill at the far end of the lake. The water was dark, which suited their mission. Kate soon settled into a rhythm. The lights on the other side seemed distant.

"Shh," Josh said suddenly.

They heard it together, the strains of "Michael, Row the Boat Ashore," drifting across the water.

Kate sighed with relief. They made a circle and turned back. The return trip seemed longer. Her arms and shoulders ached.

As they approached, a new silhouette took shape under the pine tree, hauntingly human. At first Josh wondered if it was only his imagination, for the shadow didn't move. In a moment of panic he thought perhaps it wasn't Oberman, that they were paddling into disaster. But at last the figure stepped into the starlight and Josh recognized the retired agent's silver hair. He helped them land the canoe at the gentle sloping beach to the right of the overhang where they had hidden for so many hours.

"Uncle Dimitri, you're hurt!" Kate exclaimed.

It was true, Josh saw. Oberman's left sleeve was bloodied.

"A minor annoyance," he said. "Glad I caught you two."

"What happened?" Josh asked.

"There were two of them. They were after Kate. Didn't mention you. Come and sit with me on the grass. We have a lot to discuss and not a lot of time."

They followed him up the hill where the shadows of the trees came down to hide them and sat down in the grass. Oberman's face was grave.

"First of all you need to know that Kate was on the right track. We are dealing with Russians, but not the KGB. I don't think this is a sanctioned operation."

"A what?" Josh asked.

"Sanctioned. Government. Official," Oberman explained. "The gentlemen who were waiting for us really didn't know who they were working for."

"Who do you think it is?" Kate asked.

"Hard to say. The situation in the Soviet Union now is pretty murky. The economy is in a shambles. Not everyone is enamored of Gorbachev, 'specially the military. Frankly, this sort of smacks more of GRU than KGB—though I wouldn't bet the ranch on it at this point."

"GRU?"

"The Glavnoye Razvedyvatelnoye Upravleniye." The Slavic words rolled off his tongue like old friends. "Soviet military intelligence."

"They don't work together?"

"Not hardly. The KGB, the Komitet Gosudarstvennoy Bezopasnosti, the 'Sword and Shield of the Party,' is a political creature. And there's no love lost between 'em." Oberman's thoughts turned inward for a moment.

Suddenly the evening was chilly. Kate seemed to shrink against Josh. He put his arm around her, feeling tension expand in his own muscles, not knowing whether they reacted to cold or fear.

"Then they are after something bigger," he said. His own voice seemed distant somehow.

"I suspect so. Whoever they are they obviously have the money to hire manpower, experienced manpower. If I were to hazard a guess, I'd say that this business with LTS is just the tip of some iceberg."

"Does this change anything?"

"Not immediately." Oberman handed them a plastic garbage bag.

"Your passports, old and new, some extra cash, the rest of your clothes. And credit cards in your new names. Use them only if you have to and if you're sure the new names are clear. I think that's everything. Just don't tip over in the middle of the lake."

Josh swallowed. They were not going back to the house, but forward, against an enemy with vastly superior resources. Europe had seemed almost a haven to him when he'd conceived this plan. Now there were no havens.

"Do they know we've been here?" he asked, accepting the package.

"They have a pretty strong suspicion, which is why it's no longer safe for you to stay, but they can't confirm it. The two up there now won't do any talking."

Oberman spoke casually, but there was still nothing casual about death to Josh. At least it was the conspiracy's loss this time, he reflected grimly. He glanced at Kate. She didn't appear to have caught the insinuation. She probably couldn't imagine Oberman killing anyone in cold blood. Josh could. He found he could also applaud it.

"So where do we go?" Josh asked.

"Head for the far east end of the lake. There's a little stretch of beach there, very isolated. Hide the canoe in the brush and wait for morning. I tucked some crackers and cheese in the sack there. Best I could manage on short notice. If everything is clear, a gray-haired old coot in a vintage Chevy truck will wheeze in by the fire road and pick you up about noon. His name's Henry and he's harmless. Henry'll drive you into Augusta. From there you can catch a bus north. Don't use your passports, driver's licenses, anything with your ID on it until you cross the border into Canada. Don't call me until you get to Vienna."

"This sounds like the underground railroad," Josh said.

Oberman smiled. "That's precisely what it is. I do favors sometimes for old friends. Now then, I don't want you to fly direct to Austria. Fly into Milan and take a train north. Use your new passports at immigration, both countries. Stay in small hotels, no more than two nights in the same place. Keep a low profile."

Josh nodded slowly. He didn't have the instincts of a fugitive, he told himself. He'd have to rely on intellect to keep ahead of his pursuers. This, he knew, would put him at a strong disadvantage.

Oberman handed them a pad of thin, crisp notepaper in a little zippered case. Each sheet of paper was covered with odd groupings of letters, rows of them.

"This is a onetime pad," he said. "Each piece is a different encoding of the alphabet. When you call me, I don't want you to say anything in plain English except hello. Cut your message to the barest essentials and dictate it to me in code. Keep your transmission down to less than three minutes and use a public phone whenever you can. Call this number." He pointed at a number penciled in the corner of the first sheet of codes. "Memorize it."

"Harmless Henry's?" Josh guessed.

Oberman grinned. "Very astute."

"But how will you know what we're saying?" Kate puzzled.

"I have a matching pad. I'll communicate the same way. Now, when you get to Vienna you're going to have to work fast. Chances are the goods have already cleared customs and are on their way east. With some help, however, you may be able to stop them before they leave Austria. First day you're there, Kate, you go to customs. Josh, you find your friend Lee—but don't go through the embassy. Do you have an address, a phone number, anything?"

"I did," Josh said ruefully. "But I lost my address book in the fire."

"My address book!" Kate said. "That's how they found us."

"Could be," Oberman agreed.

"Uncle Dimitri, this leaves you in terrible danger."

He smiled. "I accepted that from the beginning. You made the assumption that they wouldn't trace you here. I made the assumption that they would—eventually."

"What happens now?" Josh asked.

"I'll just sit and wait. When those two goons don't come home somebody's gonna have to come looking. Who knows? Might even draw bigger fish into the net." He sounded pleased with himself.

"But what will you tell them when they come?" Kate asked.

"It depends on how they ask me," Oberman replied. "Look at it this way: at least I can divert their attention while you two disappear." He chuckled as he stood up. "Washington will find out, of course. 'Here's old Oberman, up to his tricks again.' "

Kate was not fooled by merriment. "Uncle, this leaves you in all kinds of trouble."

"My dear, a little excitement is just what I need. If you don't keep the juices flowing you age. Remember that, son," he said with a wink at Josh.

He ushered them toward the canoe. Kate put her arms around his neck. "I love you," she said.

Oberman returned the embrace awkwardly.

"Don't call me 'til you get to Vienna," he reiterated. "Good luck."

He stood there on the shore in the fading moonlight and watched them paddle away into obscurity.

Chapter
18

As the plane settled into its final landing pattern, Kate stared once again at the passport that identified her as Patricia Donovan. Mrs. Greg Donovan, complete with wedding band. The ring of brushed gold glittered on her finger. Oberman had thought of everything.

Below, clothed in summer haze and billowing industrial fumes, lay Milan. Surely no one would be watching for them to arrive in Italy from Montreal, she thought.

They had spent much of their flight spinning fantasies around their new personae, playing pretend like children. When they stepped off the plane their new names must fit comfortably; they must both voice the same legend, the details that made up a cover identity. Their lives depended on it. She must forget their escape across the lake and the anxious journey over the border to Canada, ignore the heavy money belt around her waist that concealed her true self and a small fortune in cash.

The plane touched down with a bump. The fuselage shuddered as the pilot applied the brakes. In French, English, and Italian the PA system welcomed them to Malpensa Airport and pleaded with the passengers to stay in their seats until the plane was parked. Few listened.

Kate and Josh hung back when the buses arrived, not willing to call attention to themselves. At last he took her arm and escorted her down the narrow aisle.

"Come along, Patricia." He grinned.

Immigration was perfunctory. The uniformed official glanced unsmilingly at them, at their passports, waved them through. Kate breathed a sigh of relief.

They had carried all their luggage with them on the plane, two hand pieces and a garment bag with most of their new clothes. That was all. Josh had little more left in the world. Casually they walked through the green doors marked "Nothing to Declare." No one stopped them.

Exhilarated with this first small victory, they burst into the noise and confusion of the waiting crowd. The air was thick and smelled faintly of jet fumes and garlic. Babies wailed, the public address system blared flight information, families screeched as homecoming members appeared from behind the frosted doors leading out of customs. The clamor was friendly, unorganized, frantic. It was Italy.

Josh followed the taxi stand signs. They stood in line with other travelers, mostly Italian. Kate felt more exposed not moving. At last it was their turn.

The driver accelerated as the last door closed.

"Dove?" he inquired.

"La stazione," Josh replied. "The train station."

Oberman had become accustomed to the surveillance. A car was parked near the main entrance to his property, sometimes blue, sometimes gray, always present. There had been a marked increase in the number of private planes overflying his farmyard.

The manager of the Rabbit Hollow Motel across the lake reported that a quiet couple with odd accents had moved in the week before and gave no indication of leaving. Each morning they rented an outboard motorboat and spent the day fishing—only they never caught anything. Oberman sent the dogs down to the water frequently to discourage landings.

The most isolated nest of observers he discovered by accident. He had been following one of the planes with high-powered binoculars to catch the call letters. His gaze had passed over the crest of the next hill and locked with that of another man with binoculars, a man staring down at him. Bulky the glasses were, probably with optional infrared lenses for night viewing.

None of them made any move to pay an uninvited visit. His security perimeter was never violated. He wondered why.

True, primary sources of information were always preferable. Only Josh and Kate could tell their pursuers what they knew and whom they had told. Were his keepers waiting for them to return, or guarding the secondary source of information? Did they hesitate to approach him because their leverage over him had now evaporated?

No longer could they dangle Sergei's safety before him as a

threat—or a promise. Sergei, his son, his last link with the idyllic years with Sonya, was dead four years, cannon fodder in Afghanistan as befitted the son of a capitalist spy.

No more did the Soviets or anyone else have a hold on him, he thought bitterly. His neutrality, his retirement, was over. Quietly, through friends, he moved to put support into the field for Kate and Josh.

For his observers he continued to play a different part. He went about his daily business, feeding the chickens and collecting eggs, romping with the dogs. He did not tempt fate by taking lone walks in the woods, but he remained visible.

And he watched the people who were watching him.

Thrasher had no files on the four letters of credit. Veronica Reese did have copies of Fleming's memos, however. Fleming was thorough, he had to admit that. Reference numbers, foreign banks, dollar amounts, they were all there.

He called the Hong Kong and Shanghai Banking Corporation and asked for Mr. Doppler. He had a good memory for names. Doppler was the man he'd spoken with before at Dominique's behest.

"I'm sorry, sir," said the switchboard operator. "We have no one by that name on our roster."

Thrasher stiffened. "Very well. May I have the export letter of credit department then."

"For which country, sir?"

"Uh . . . Switzerland."

"Yes, sir."

The crisp young woman at the Swiss desk could find no record of the reference number he gave her. He did not ask her to check the other three. He knew the truth now.

His legs quivered. He sat down.

Someone was bilking his company of seven million dollars. He suspected he knew who it was, but he also knew who was going to take the fall. He, Thrasher, had authorized the purchase of the components, compelled the speedy shipment of the orders.

Whatever had he done to Ken Bailey, he wondered, besides say no?

Now that he had accepted the reality of the situation, however, he would act. Bailey would not get what he wanted.

Thrasher punched his intercom button. "Dominique, get in here!"

"Yes, sir," her slightly metalized voice answered.

She glided into the room, ravishing in a pale apricot silk dress that caressed the curves of her body. She smiled.

"Sit down."

She did. The dress slid halfway up her thighs. In the past he had found that titillating.

He lowered his voice. "I am now going to call security. They will escort you from the building. You will be permitted to take only your pocketbook and your slutty body. But before you're thrown out I wanted you to know what happens to filthy young whores like you. They end up as filthy old whores, crones with painted faces and fetid, diseased cunts that no one will touch. I'll harbor that image of you."

The venom he saw on her face reinforced the mental image he had drawn of her. The carefully painted lips curled in a snarl and he sensed that without restraint she would leap across the desk and tear his throat out.

He picked up the phone and called security.

Zurich was run with typical Swiss precision. The train from Milan pulled into the Flughafen station at exactly 4:32. Travelers retrieved their luggage and off boarded in an orderly, unhurried sequence, like dominos falling into place.

Josh and Kate joined them. They climbed up the cement stairs out of the bowels of the station and into the bright, clean, tidy world that was Switzerland.

The terminus served both as train station and airport. Shops catered to a multilingual multitude, offering beer and books, duty-free liquor and cigarettes, banking services, and, of course, Swiss cheese, Swiss chocolate, and Swiss watches.

Josh guided Kate to an airy waiting room with white plastic seats. "It should take me no longer than an hour," he said. "We'll make the 5:45 train to Vienna." He smiled. "In Switzerland the trains always run on time."

Kate sat down with their luggage piled at her feet. She had tried to sleep on the train, but even the gentle rocking rhythm of the rails had failed to lull her. Every kilometer had taken her farther away from Kate Fleming and into the shadowy world of Patricia Donovan, farther from reality and deeper into oblivion.

Not even the Alps had diverted her thoughts. Soaring in barren, jagged magnificence from a diminished tree line of less than six thousand feet, they presented a forbidding landscape. The world was forbidding, she reflected. Deep inside those mountains, it was said, the Swiss had tunneled massive refuges in which to hide should the ultimate horror be unleashed.

Refuge. Did such a thing actually exist? she wondered. Would they ever be safe or would they always live like rabbits, alert to every sound, ready to run?

She huddled in her corner of the waiting room, avoiding the eyes of passersby. Perhaps they would find an answer in Vienna.

"That little prick! That randy, rutting little toad! He has the gall to call me a slut, to call me a whore? So what's he? He has to pay people to sleep with him.

"Men come in two types: the ones that force women to lie down and the ones that pay women to do it. And both of them suck!"

He let Dominique rave. It was her one failing. Tension built up in her until it exploded. Her saving grace was that she could bottle rage and frustration until the moment was right for release. Here, in the apartment, they were secure—as secure as possible in a precarious world.

"How much does he know?" he asked.

"He knows nothing! He doesn't have the brains to figure it out. All he's worried about is getting paid." She snorted. "That's the least of his problems."

She was still pacing, her platinum hair loose and flowing behind her, but her step was calmer now. Her hatred of men, bequeathed to her by her mother and reinforced by her own experience, was receding. Dominique had watched her mother let herself be used for years, buying her only daughter a future. Certain men, powerful men, could always buy women, just as they could buy cars and other capitalist toys.

Dominique had determined never to be owned. She had wisely sold instead the education for which her mother had paid so dearly and the twin passions she had inherited: love for the motherland and a hatred for men in power. Her devotion to the motherland gave her credibility. The hatred assured her loyalty to those who could use it effectively. She kept her soul, untempered with compassion, to herself.

He understood these things. He hated the KGB as well, for different reasons.

"It's not Thrasher we have to worry about," she said. At last the real source of her anxiety was surfacing. "I still say we should eliminate Oberman. Now."

He resisted shaking his head. Bringing Dominique back to reason required delicacy: the right words, the right timing, soothing body language.

"They'll come back to him," he said. "They have nowhere else to turn."

"And Oberman? He could be an even bigger threat. He may still have contacts in Moscow."

"And what if he does? What does he know, Dominique? What does he really know?" He let the question hang in the air for a moment, then answered it himself. "Nothing. Nothing.

"Russo didn't know who he was working for. He thinks— thought—it was the KGB. If Oberman thinks so, too, so much the better."

"And if he doesn't?"

"There are no links to us, Dominique. Russo called the answering service. They paged you. You called him back from a hotel room. The registration was false. The records at the answering service have been wiped clean. Dead end."

"Russo and Cochran both had records."

"So? They never met either of us. We've never used them before. Dead end. The accountant and the girl are chasing the shipment. Fine. Let them. Eventually they'll surface. We'll catch them. Tbilisi has feelers out. Maybe we'll get lucky."

She settled beside him on the couch, head back, eyes closed. He made no move to touch her.

"I just have the feeling that with this one snag the whole operation is beginning to unravel," she said. "There are too many loose ends, too many bodies lying around."

"No one that's going to be missed, except perhaps Muller. Men of his talent are hard to come by."

"Tbilisi wasn't happy about that," she admitted.

He smiled, not unkindly. "It's the control you regret losing, Dominique. The accountant and the girl are no longer under your control. Thrasher is no longer under your control. We will regain that control, I promise."

She looked up at him sharply. "How can you stay so calm?"

"It's in my genes, a trait inherited from generations of extended Siberian winters."

"And do you want to go back to that?"

He shook his head. It was safe to do so now. "No. And we won't. When Gorbachev is gone and order has been restored, we will go back in triumph. To Moscow, Leningrad, anywhere we choose."

"Or perhaps not." She smiled. "Once the motherland is safe from the corruption within, she will need us even more to protect her from enemies outside."

Chapter
19

The Vienna shipment was gone.

Politely the Austrian customs officials had glanced at the papers Kate had shown them, searched their records, and assured her that the goods had been cleared three days before.

"And then?" she had asked.

Why, a truck from her own firm, Tsholl Trading Company, had picked up the containers, of course. Surely there must be a mix-up in company communications, they suggested. Kate had strained to catch a glimpse of the delivery address.

The men had begun to regard her suspiciously. Supposedly a Swiss employee of a Vienna importer, she did not even speak German, only French. Odd. Copies of the documents, no originals. Odd.

Kate left.

This was to be expected, she reminded herself, the goods lost, Tsholl Trading a phony front with a phony address, unlisted by the chamber of commerce.

Look like a tourist, she chided herself. She stuffed the papers back into her pocketbook, strung the camera around her neck again.

"Don't take a direct route back to the hotel," Josh had warned her. He was beginning to sound like Uncle Dimitri.

Josh was off on errands of his own this afternoon. She did not want to return to the hotel alone. Somehow the streets seemed safer.

Vienna had a new subway system, clean and modern; but subways were confining, they frightened her. Kate stepped aboard a trolley, punched her ticket, and sat down. No one followed. She sighed with relief.

Three stops, she thought, then I'll get off and figure out how to get home. She leaned back.

As the train had passed through the silent, moonlit countryside the night before, it had been hard to imagine that Austria had for many centuries been a powerful state, a participant in wave after wave of wars that had raged across the continent. Only in Vienna, she reflected, with its palaces and boulevards, did one come face to face with the imperial past.

Vienna was a small Paris—without the Parisians. The city had a gracious personality, like a lovely lady dressed in a sweeping gown, timeless. Despite its elegance, however, Vienna was not cosmopolitan, not the melting pot of a London or Rome or New York. Perhaps, she thought, it is because the Austrians, landlocked as they were, had largely confined their empire to the continent, had never conquered and consumed other races. As a result the people who surrounded her were . . . well, not homogeneous, perhaps, but nondescript. You'd never notice one in a crowd, she thought.

They'd make good spies.

She wished she were invisible.

It had been surprisingly easy to find Elliott Lee, Josh mused. They'd exchanged hardly more than holiday greetings over the years. Elliott's address had never changed. Josh found him in the phone book. The shock in the diplomat's voice slowly warmed. Following Dimitri's admonitions, Josh had politely fended off questions about where he was staying. Elliott hadn't pressed. He had given instructions for a rendezvous.

So it was that Josh found himself on a U4 subway train bound for the suburb of Heiligenstadt. A gaggle of tourists with green Michelin guides filled the car, all babbling about Beethoven in one language or another. Austria, he remembered, took its music seriously. Little houses that had sheltered composers for brief periods became shrines, with plaques proclaiming the German equivalent of "Beethoven slept here." Josh thought it quaint.

The train slid into its berth and the tourists were herded off. Attired in jeans, a T-shirt, and dark glasses, Josh blended in with a tour group as they emerged from the station. A modern transport system was out of place in the little village. Save for the plastic and asphalt, Beethoven would still have recognized it, he mused.

To his right as he exited the station was the Austrian version of a fast-food joint, just as Elliott had said there would be. The kitchen whipped up almost anything rolled in bread crumbs and deep-fried. The locals sat on the green plastic chairs at little white metal tables in the open air and sipped beer. Josh ordered a glass and joined them.

When the beer was half drained, he saw Elliott alight from one of the buses continually pulling up in front of the terminal.

As Josh remembered, the man was short and slim, but most people overlooked his stature. Compact and self-contained, Lee created an authoritative presence.

"Josh." He smiled, clasping his friend's hand. "What a surprise. How are you?"

"Tamer, but basically happy," Josh replied, offering him a chair.

"We heard you were dead."

"Good. I'm safer that way."

Elliott eyed him oddly. "So what brings you to Vienna, business?"

"In a way," Josh said. "Would you like a beer?"

Elliott shook his head. "My waistline is expanding."

"Mine, too. How've you been?"

"Obviously leading a more boring life than you have."

Josh studied the foam coating his glass. "Elliott, I need a favor."

"So ask."

Josh had rehearsed the presentation in his mind a dozen times.

"Elliott," he said carefully, "you've been in the embassy here in Vienna a long time."

"True," his friend said.

"Which means you'd know just about everyone."

Elliott shrugged.

"I need access to some of those people," Josh said quietly.

"Who?"

"The CIA. And no, I'm not nuts. There's some funny business going on with the export of some of my company's equipment. I think our cartons are being used to ship somebody else's goods to . . . somewhere."

"Somewhere?"

"Let's say east of where the Wall used to be."

Elliott shook his head. "Since glasnost there's not a lot they can't get their hands on legally—along with the technicians to train them how to use it."

"Not everyone likes Gorby," Josh said obliquely.

Elliott let the comment slide. "And they're shipping through Vienna?"

"Among other places."

"Vienna's been a central staging point for pilfered technology for a long time," Elliott acknowledged. "Can you prove it?"

"I think so."

"Why don't you go to the authorities in the States?"

"It's a long story. The goods were already gone. I'm being hunted."

"By whom?"

"The other side."

Elliott raised his eyebrows. "And what do you want from me?"

"I need you to set up a meeting."

"I think I can manage that."

Josh smiled for the first time.

"This may take a day. Where can I reach you?" his friend asked.

"I keep moving."

"Wise, under the circumstances," Elliott agreed. "I take it you're not registered under your own name."

Josh shook his head.

"Mmm. Just as well. Call me tomorrow." He rose and offered his hand.

Josh didn't dally to finish his beer.

Thrasher eyed his ringing phone with distaste. The secretary on loan from sales couldn't seem to learn to screen his calls. It was enough for her to get his coffee order right. He never knew whom to expect on the other end, his wife, a regional manager—or a reporter.

"Hello. Thrasher here."

"Bob, this is Frank Silverman."

"Oh, hi Frank." At least it was a friendly voice. Silverman was part of his coalition on the board of directors.

"Listen, Bob, I just received a troubling call from Ken Bailey of Keiser Electronics. Is it true that we have outstanding receivables of two point one million dollars to Omer Electronics?"

Thrasher kept his voice level. "Yes. It's also true that it's not due until next week."

"Bailey said it was past due."

"Bailey doesn't know what he's talking about."

"Mmm. Last quarter's statement didn't look that good."

"And this quarter's will look worse," Thrasher replied. "The fire, the accident, the loss of production in Suffolk. Life's not rosy right now. But we'll keep our heads above water—and pay our bills on time."

Silverman paused. "Bob, what would you think about selling the home security division?"

"To Bailey?"

"To anyone."

"Frank, that's the business we know best, solid, profitable—and growing. Only a fool would sell."

"That's what I thought, but there are other board members who don't have your level of industrial knowledge. They see the bottom line and they feel a responsibility to protect the shareholders."

"Well, I happen to be one of those shareholders," Thrasher said, "a big one. How many other board members has our friend Bailey spoken with?"

"I don't know."

"Well, I'd like to find out. I don't appreciate Mr. Bailey making an end run around me. He approached me on this some time ago and I told him no." He tried to put some steam in his voice, though fear churned his innards more than anger.

"Settle down," Silverman advised. "We'll hash it out at the next meeting."

"I'm sure." Damn, Thrasher thought as he hung up. Now the cat was out of the bag. He'd have to explain the export affair, all of it. It had seemed so simple at the time: ship the goods and draw against the letters of credit.

Only there were no letters of credit.

Who would back him on this? Cosentino for one. But without the documents that had started all the trouble it would be difficult to justify what he had done. Nor did he have any hard evidence that Bailey was behind it.

"Shit," he said.

The hotel had overbooked a tour and so had given the "Donovans" a town house suite. The bottom floor had a sitting room furnished with oak antiques, a cloakroom, and a water closet. The top floor had two bedrooms, a large living area, a gigantic bathroom and skylights.

Kate found Josh in the middle of the living room dressed in

loose-fitting sweats. He had pushed the furniture to the walls; his back was to her.

In near silence he shadowboxed an opponent she could not see. But his movements were so precise, so controlled, that she could readily imagine the sequence of events: a swift advance across the floor in pursuit of the adversary, a defensive sweep of the other's feet, a spin to take himself out of danger. . . .

He froze when he saw her, then eased his crouched body into a natural stance.

"How long have you been standing there?" he asked with a grin.

"I don't know. A few minutes. What in the world are you doing?"

"Animal forms."

"What?"

"You asked me what I was doing. The answer is animal forms, conditioning exercises for kung fu. The ancients learned offensive and defensive techniques by observing the animals. Watch."

Knees bent and back straight, Josh made sharp, swooping upward movements with his arms, fingers curled stiffly skyward.

. "Eagle claw," he explained.

Shifting his feet to a solider stance, he battered an invisible enemy with forceful, direct punches, fists clenched, and swift, strong kicks.

"Tiger," he said.

The movements became crisper, faster. His footwork was more intricate, evasive.

"Panther?" she guessed.

"Right!"

"It looks like it's choreographed, like a dance," Kate said.

"It is."

"When did you learn to do that?"

"I studied when I was younger. Decided it was about time I got back into it. What did you find out?" He grabbed a towel from the arm of a chair and wiped his face.

"The shipment is gone," Kate replied. "It was picked up from customs three days ago and delivered to an address in the city."

"Where?"

"Right next to the Aeroflot office."

"How convenient. The embassy may already have the place under surveillance."

"So do the Viennese. There's a cop stationed on the block."

"That's as much to protect the Ruskies as to watch them," Josh observed.

She followed him into the bedroom. He began to strip. The scar across his ribs was still livid. His beard was now rich brown and full.

"Did you see Elliott?"

"Yep."

"Can he help us?"

"Yep."

Kate clapped her hands. "That's wonderful. At last we have someone on our side."

"Not yet they're not. We still have to sell them."

"We will," she smiled. "You can be very persuasive."

"I know." Josh reached for her. "I'll also negotiate for protection."

She sat on the bed beside him. He was warm and smelled of used gym clothes. His nose was slightly salty when she kissed him.

"I'm sorry I got you into this," he said.

"You didn't," Kate replied. "I'm here of my own accord. We got into this together and we'll get out the same way."

He put his arms around her and she felt the warmth of him, an island of sanity in a dangerous sea.

She'd never felt that way with Clint, she realized. Clint had offered a brash excitement but never security. He had given her moments of exhilarating joy and moments of intense anguish. He had rubbed her emotions raw and left her exhausted, but always craving more. But he had never given her peace.

Now, in the midst of a lethal madness, she was serene. She put her arms around Josh and squeezed.

"Thank you," she said.

He seemed surprised. "For what?"

"For being here."

Josh smiled and tightened his bear hug.

"I think we should check in with Oberman," he said.

Kate nodded and disengaged. "I'll get the code book."

They composed a simple message, giving their location and the results of the day's activities. Then Kate put the call through.

Her uncle was waiting at Henry's. The connection was so clear it was as if he were next door, but the conversation they held was strange and cryptic. Kate rattled off her groups of letters. After a pause he did the same, then silence. He must have had his response already drafted, she realized. She waited a moment, yearning to reach out with something other than antiseptic, nonsensical shorthand. But Oberman said nothing. She hung up.

"Warm greetings," Oberman's reply read when they had deciphered it. "All quiet here. Make tonight last in that hotel. Good luck."

"That's all?" Kate asked, tearing the first page from the one-time pad.

"Uh-huh." Josh put a match to the paper. It flared and disintegrated into nothing.

Chapter
20

Thursday, 8 August

Josh waited until noon to call Lee. He wanted to get Kate moved first. They left the suite reluctantly and checked into a small bed-and-breakfast place on the other side of the city.

Elliott sounded agitated. "I thought maybe you'd skipped town," he said.

"Nope. Just being cautious. You said it might take a day. Were you able to make contact?"

"Uh-huh. Do you know where the Spanish Riding School is?"

"Yes."

"Fine. Be there at one, the north entrance."

"Will you be there?"

"No."

"How will I know them?"

"You won't. They'll be looking for you."

Josh sighed. "Okay. Sounds easy enough."

"Do you have any documentary proof with you?" Lee asked.

"Yes."

"Good. Bring it."

"Anything else?"

"Yes. What names are you using?"

Josh hesitated.

"They need them," Elliott explained.

"Tell them who I really am," Josh said.

When he'd hung up he turned to Kate, puzzled.

"What's wrong?" she asked.

"I'm not sure."

"Did he set up the meeting?"

202

Josh nodded. "I don't want you to come."

"Why not?"

"Just a feeling. When I leave I want you to take one bag, just with necessities, slip out the back of the house, and check into the little hotel across the street—alone, under your own name."

"All right," she said slowly.

"Take only our real ID and don't check out of here. We may have to come back."

Kate swallowed.

"Give me two hours. If I'm not back or haven't phoned, call Oberman, then get the hell out of Vienna."

"But, Josh . . ."

He took her by the shoulders. "I just want you to be safe, Kate. Something about this just doesn't sit well with my gut."

"But I thought you trusted Elliott."

"We're not just dealing with Elliott anymore."

She nodded.

The morning air was full of the first breath of fall. The leaves had not yet begun to wither, nor the geese to fly, but Oberman felt a chill in the air. He pulled on a sweater before he left the house to feed the stock.

The farmyard seemed quiet somehow. Too quiet. It was then he realized that the chill was not in the morning but in his soul.

He hiked up toward the road. There was no car parked at the entrance to his driveway. He called the Rabbit Hollow Motel across the lake. The strange people who went fishing every day had checked out.

He scowled. For only one reason would the surveillance be pulled off him.

His heart sank. He had no way to reach them.

There was a clock ticking away his career, Thrasher thought. A board meeting had been called for the following Tuesday, just days before the Omer Electronics invoices were due. He had seven million dollars worth of receivables on his books that he knew he would never collect. Ken Bailey was maneuvering to take from him the division he had built and nurtured.

He slammed his fist on the desk. Well, damn it, Bailey wasn't going to have it.

Thrasher fished through his top drawer for the card Judson Rosen had given him. He had to go into the meeting with a solution, not just a problem. Rosen had the solution.

* * *

The Spanish Riding School, famed for its Lippizaner stallions, was part of the Imperial Palace complex.

Why the Riding School, Josh wondered as he joined the throngs of visitors pressing through the Heldenplatz, past the mounted statues of Archduke Karl and some prince of Savoy and row upon row of tour buses. Why not the embassy?

The crowd passed through the In der Berg, a smaller square with only one statue, and clamored beneath the rotunda, filling the space with a jabber of noise. Josh hung back against an age-grimed wall, his eyes roving the masses, trying to find watchful faces, faces watching for him.

Why did they need to know the name under which they were traveling?

Name.

No, he realized with a start. Elliott hadn't said "name." He had used the plural. In Heilgenstadt he had said, "I take it you're not registered under your own name." But today: "What names are you using."

He had never told Elliott about Kate. Someone else must have.

Josh turned and walked away, back to the Heldenplatz, head down. He jammed his hands in his pockets, counting trolley tickets. Three. He had to warn Kate. But first he must free himself from the prying eyes he felt on the back of his neck. How many of them were there? Two, four, a dozen? Lord, he felt helpless.

More buses were disgorging passengers. In even rows the gaily painted conveyances waited like quiet elephants. He stepped among them, between them. He pulled his shirttail out, rolled up his sleeves, donned his dark glasses, mussed his hair. The eyes would be expecting an accountant, neat and trim. He reemerged as a sloppy, bearded tourist and melted into the crowd.

Three-thirty. Kate paced the small room. She had already given Josh an extra half hour. She sighed and picked up the message she had coded earlier, just in case, when her head was clear and confident.

She picked up the phone and called Oberman. He answered on the second ring.

"Hello."

She began to dictate her message.

"Stop, Kate. Listen. They must have found you. They called off my surveillance sometime during the night. Run. Probably best to rent a car. But not at the airport. They'll be watching that."

"But, Uncle Dimitri, Josh isn't here."

"They may already have him."

Kate gasped.

"Get out of Vienna, Kate. Then call our mutual friend in New York and tell her where you are."

Kate heard footsteps in the hall, a key in the lock. She dropped the receiver and stifled a scream. There was nowhere to hide.

Josh stepped into the room. "Kate . . ."

"Josh, we have to get out," she cried, flinging herself at him. "Uncle Dimitri says . . ."

"I know. They know we're in Vienna. Grab the bag."

Josh stumbled forward suddenly, nearly knocking her to the floor. Three men shoved their way into the room. One of them wore a brown suit and had cold gray eyes. He had a gun.

"I don't think you're going anywhere except with us," he said.

The blindfolds that had been hastily tied around their heads were unnecessary. The body of the van was windowless.

Kate could see beneath the dirty rag wrapped around her head anyway. On occasion the reflection of oncoming headlights seeped through the darkness. The floor of the van was bare metal, with ridges, made for cargo, not passengers. It had not been swept in a long time. Grit had built up in the grooves, stained with dark splotches that may have been oil. The rank odor of grease permeated the small space, sickening her stomach. But perhaps fear alone was enough to do that.

She wore loafers. Her feet seemed indecently vulnerable toe to toe with the two pairs of laced black boots worn by the goons seated opposite them. Scuffed the boots were, and worn. Kate had seen little of the two men besides their boots. The man with the gun had consumed her attention. He now drove. She could see nothing of him, only hear his guttural exchanges with his cohorts.

They sat on what felt like slatted packing crates, none too sturdy. They swayed when the van cornered. She was grateful for the warmth of Josh beside her, even if he couldn't hold her. They were both cuffed behind the back.

A bump in the road jolted them against the metal side of the van, pinching her wrists. It hurt. At least the pain was real. Her toes moved in response to conscious command; they were real. All else was a bad dream.

Their captors spoke a jumble of languages, none of which she understood, one she couldn't even identify. She thought perhaps it was Arabic.

"Josh?" she whispered, but was instantly shushed. Strangely, the hiss to be quiet came from beside her, from Josh himself.

It was then that her wits began to come back. One of the languages their captors were speaking was German. She didn't understand it—but he did.

Chapter

21

"Let's go through this one more time, shall we?" said the
man Kate knew only as Franz. Heavyset, gray-eyed, beetle-
browed, he had assumed control from the first moment in the
Vienna hotel room the afternoon before. Now in this quiet house
in the countryside, somewhere, he controlled them still.

Franz dictated when they ate, when they slept, when they
relieved themselves. But mostly he conducted the interrogation.
He was relentless, redundant.

Not since they'd stumbled out of the VW van in the darkness
of the night, their hands still cuffed but blindfolds removed, had
Kate seen Josh. They had been driven for what seemed like
hours, but it may have been in circles. For all they knew they
might now be in Germany—or Hungary.

"Are you listening, Miss Fleming?"

"Yes," she said. She had learned that if she did not respond
he would slap her. A civil answer would do. If he did not like
the answer he berated, but he did not strike.

"Good. Under what name did you enter Austria?"

"Kate Fleming."

"Wrong! What other name did you use?"

"I didn't."

If he didn't know, she wasn't going to tell him. That meant
they had not found the cache of belongings in the hotel across
the street from where he had captured them. She squared her
shoulders defiantly against the hard back of the chair, longing
to stretch out on the bed again.

"But you did, Miss Fleming," Franz said. "Austrian immigration has no record of your entry."

"Austria doesn't keep such records," she told him. Not like your country, she wanted to say, where no one can take a leak without the government knowing. And what country would that be, she wondered. From his accent she could tell that for Franz English was an acquired language.

"When did you enter Austria?" he demanded.

"A few days ago."

"When!"

"Tuesday, Wednesday, I'm not sure."

"How?"

"By train."

"From where?"

"Germany." Let him try to verify that, she thought.

"Was Garrett with you?"

"Yes."

"Under what name was he traveling?"

"Garrett."

"Wrong!"

Kate sighed. Her head ached. Each question seemed to pound against her forehead. Tension had spasmed the muscles between her shoulder blades.

Franz sank down on the bed. The mattress sagged. He fingered the gun again. He never brandished it. The weapon was just there, as cold a menace as the man himself, but no more so.

"Why did you come to Vienna, Miss Fleming?" His tone was quieter as it always was when he opened a new line of questioning.

"To track a shipment of goods," Kate repeated.

"Why else?"

This query always confused her. There was no "why else." They had come to Vienna to find the illicit shipment.

"I don't know what you mean," she said wearily.

"Yes, you do. Who else knows?"

"Josh."

"And?"

"Phil Petersen."

"Dead."

"Webb."

"Dead. Do you want to die, too, Miss Fleming?"

He had never voiced the threat before. Kate shivered. He could have no other end in mind for them, she knew. But first they must discover how much she and Josh knew and whom they had told.

"Did you hear me?" Franz asked.

"Yes," she whispered.

"Do you want to die?"

"No."

"Do you want your friend to die?"

"No."

Franz snapped to his feet and marched to the door. He barked an order to the man standing outside in a language she neither recognized nor understood. She thought perhaps it was Russian.

Kate heard a jumble of footsteps in the hallway, muffled by the Persian runner. Unblindfolded she had never been permitted beyond the room and the bathroom across the hall. She did not know what lay beyond, if the house was large or small.

Two men, one a huge bouncer, the other small and dark with sharp features, shoved Josh into the bedroom. Like an athlete he regained his balance and glared at Franz. There was an ugly purple bruise on one cheek. His wrists were manacled together. His gaze fell on the gun, then on Kate.

Franz stepped between them.

"So, you see, you are both alive. And both uncooperative, I fear. Wrong answers, no answers. What should we do with you? Drugs? I think not." He whirled to face Josh. "In what room are you kept?"

"Next door." Josh's voice sounded raw, his eyes were edged with sleeplessness.

"Quite right. How many men are with you?"

"Two."

"And how do they keep you?"

"Handcuffed to a cot."

Franz nodded. "Take him back next door and beat him."

Kate gasped. Franz slapped her, then barked a command at his comrades, neither of whom had moved a muscle. Only the blond man understood even then. He interpreted for the other in German.

The last phrase Josh apparently understood. He stiffened. "Animals," he said flatly as they pushed him out the door.

Franz sat back down on the bed. His face was impassive as he listened to the ruckus in the next room. No sooner had the door closed than the beating began. Through the thick wall Kate could hear the muffled blows, grunts of pain. A body crashed against the wall so hard the painting that hung there jumped. Glass tinkled.

Kate fought back panic. Animals, animals. Not an epithet, she realized suddenly. A statement. Animals. Animal forms. Josh had many hidden talents of which their captors were ignorant. Now he had freedom of movement, probably for the first time since their arrival if they had indeed been keeping him secured to a cot. Her hopes soared, relief flooding her eyes.

Kate let her tears fall. Franz would misinterpret them. He sat with a pleased smile on his face. With a final thud the room next door was silenced.

"Shall we begin again?" Franz asked.

Josh did not wait for his tormentors to shove him into the room. He strode purposefully back into the small, informal salon where he had been held and questioned for the past twenty-four hours. He wanted to choose his own ground; he needed space.

The room was longer than it was wide, with a fireplace at the far end. In front of the cold hearth was a steel and canvas cot on which they had kept him shackled hand and foot. He relished this opportunity to stretch.

He waited until the door closed. The man with the gun on Kate must not see.

Josh turned to face the two men, his back to the fireplace, his wrists cuffed and crossed before him. He had only seconds to size up the situation. The dark-haired guard approached from his left. The blond brute who rarely spoke, the one who still carried the gun, was a pace behind and to the right.

Josh regulated his breathing, calming his mind so that his body could react instinctively. He was confident the adrenaline would come when he needed it.

Without warning Josh launched a crescent kick, a high, arcing dragon sweep of his left leg, to the side of the dark man's face. The blow knocked his startled opponent back and to the side, sending him crashing into the glass top of the ornate coffee table. Porcelain figurines flew in all directions as the glass disintegrated.

Josh spun with the momentum of the kick, bringing his hands up as he did so. The second man slashed downward with the butt of the pistol. Josh fended off the blow with his wrists, trapping the gun in the gap between his hands to disperse the potentially bone-shattering force. In the same movement he drew his left leg into his body and shoved. The man was too close to suffer the full brunt of the kick, but Josh was powerful enough to slam him into the opposite wall. The impact jarred the gun loose and bounced the goon right back into the middle of the room.

Clasping his hands together, Josh swung his arms as a single unit. He swept his body into the movement, like a batsman meeting a pitched ball. His foe had no time to duck. Josh saw his own hands crunch into the side of the man's face as if in slow motion, saw the harsh metal of the cuffs displace the cheekbone. His captor stumbled back against the wall and crumpled silently to the floor.

Chest heaving, Josh stood alone in the middle of the room, his ears straining for footsteps, for sounds from the adjoining room. There were none.

The struggle had demolished the salon. The dark-haired guard lay inert, covered with glass fragments from the shattered coffee table. The other, the dead one, was slumped against the wall. Josh could see his face, the eyes staring blankly outward. They were green. The left cheekbone was crushed, giving him a lopsided appearance. Blood still dripped from the nostrils.

Josh didn't even know his name. He knew him only as the one with the crew cut, the one most likely to strike with his fists if Josh did not reply to a question. Strangely, he felt no remorse. The man was dead. Josh Garrett was now a killer, playing the game of life by a new set of rules.

He had won.

"Stephan?" called the man from next door.

Which one was Stephan, Josh wondered. He did not answer.

"Stephan?" the call was repeated.

Josh tiptoed across the floor and posted himself beside the door.

No answer. Franz stood and gestured with the gun.

"Out," he ordered Kate.

Her knees wobbled. She grabbed the straight-back chair for support.

"Move," he snapped.

Unsteadily Kate made her way out of the room and into the hallway, the gun at her back. Franz opened the door to the salon and pushed her in ahead of him. From out of nowhere a foot flashed, kicking the weapon to the ceiling. Josh brought his clenched fists down on Franz's head. The man crumpled to the floor.

It had all happened so fast that Kate was dazed. Josh's warm arms around her, the scent of his body, brought her back to the moment.

"It's over," he said quietly. "Are you all right?"

"Yes, yes. Are you?" She hugged him tightly to still the trembling in her limbs.

"I'm fine."

They clung to each other for a moment. If she closed her eyes and imagined they were alone in that room perhaps her pulse would begin to slow. But they weren't and it didn't. Her heart still beat like that of a frightened rabbit.

"One of them has to have the keys," Josh said at last as he released her.

She stared down at his hands, still cuffed together.

"You beat them . . . with those on?"

"Even caged tigers are dangerous," he said.

Kate glanced around her for the first time. Franz sprawled at her feet. The other two bodies lay still.

"Come on, help me," he said.

She could not bring herself to touch Franz and approached the man against the wall instead.

"Not him," Josh said. "I'll pat him down."

Kate was just as glad. The man was bloody. She rifled the pockets of the man resting in shards of glass. Behind his right hip she found a chain of keys.

"Success!" she said. Right now this odd assortment of keys was more precious than diamonds. One of them was for a VW vehicle of some kind, perhaps the van in which they'd been transported. A couple were larger, like house keys. The remaining two were small, as if to unlock luggage.

Besides the cuffs on Josh's wrists there was another pair locked around the base of the upturned iron cot. They must have used it on his ankles, she realized. The little keys fit both.

"Have you seen or heard anyone besides these three?" Josh asked.

"No."

"Good. Neither have I. Maybe we'll be lucky."

"What do we do now?"

"Handcuff them together and get the hell out of here."

He grabbed the man in the glass by the heels and dragged him to the middle of the floor beside Franz. Kate turned to the other man. He hadn't moved, but seemed to be staring at them. Kate realized he was dead. She froze.

"I had no choice," Josh said quietly behind her.

Three weeks ago she had met him over a cup of coffee in his office, before anyone had died as a result of the lethal letters of credit, when life had been bland and ordinary. It no longer was.

"No, you didn't," she whispered, but a chill shook her.

Josh finished locking the three men together, the dead body in the middle. He pocketed the fallen gun and emptied their wallets.

The rest of the house was deserted. They found themselves on the ground floor. Elegantly furnished, it must have been the summer home of a wealthy family, Kate surmised. The kitchen and pantry were bare, signs of infrequent occupancy. Josh searched the house for telephones, ripping the connections from the walls. She followed, afraid to be alone.

Outside the night was still and the sky exploded with stars. Woods surrounded the house, shrouding it from prying neighbors—if there were any. Not even a dog barked. The van was a dark shadow in the driveway.

Josh scrambled into the driver's seat and started the motor. The roar shattered the silence. With only parking lights lit, the van crawled up the driveway to a road, unpaved.

"We must be out in the boonies," Josh said under his breath. "Left or right?"

"Right," Kate said.

They putted along the rutted track for fifteen, maybe twenty minutes before intersecting a paved road.

"Civilization," Josh said triumphantly.

The forest was still dense on either side, theirs the only vehicle about, but at least Kate felt they were headed somewhere.

Thirty minutes later they came upon a sign reading WIEN, 53K.

"Hot damn! We're even in Austria," Josh said. Dawn grayed the horizon. She could make out his face now. He was grinning. "Would have been a little awkward to get this crate across a border," he reflected. "We don't even have passports."

He was right, Kate realized with a start. Franz had taken them. Now the only documents left to them were in their new identities—if they could retrieve them from the hotel.

Kate felt as if they had lost a lifeline. They were no longer Kate Fleming and Josh Garrett. They were the Donovans, they were adrift.

And Josh was a killer.

Chapter
22

For the Austrians the price of a militant past was an impotent present. Only the stern occupation of Allied troops at the end of World War II had prevented the Iron Curtain from clanging shut on them as it had on the Hungarians next door. Neutrality was their penance for having been on the losing side twice in a century. But not the vibrant, esteemed neutrality of the self-righteous Swiss, who fought with no one and chided those who did, all the while hoarding the riches of despots of the right and left alike. Rather, as a defeated power the Austrians had re-treated into a quiet retirement from the world stage, pretending their Nazi past did not exist. Village life went on as it had for generations; many rural and mountain people even clung to tra-ditional costumes. Austria never disappointed tourists. Kate had always found it the most charming country in Europe.

She tried to concentrate on that as she watched a maid in a loden cape wave her walking stick at a small herd of milk cows, shooing them off the road in front of the kaffeehause. The bells around the animals' necks clanked and tinkled in a discordant canticle, in harmony with the meadows and mountains beyond.

Kate had lingered at the café most of the day, waiting for Josh to return. It was dangerous for the two of them to enter Vienna together, he had insisted. So she waited, trying not to be con-spicuous.

She longed for a bed, but one could not rent a room in Austria without presenting identification. She spoke only French and the smattering of German she knew to the waitress. Their pur-suers would be looking for Americans.

Vienna was fifty kilometers away. How long would it take

Josh, she wondered, to discard the van, hitch a ride into the city, retrieve their belongings and passports from the hotel (if he could), rent a car as Greg Donovan, and come back for her? What if they were waiting for him in Vienna? Surely Franz could not have escaped yet.

And what kind of man would come back for her? Try as she might she could not banish from her mind the picture of the man with the dead green eyes, his face warped out of shape, blood still warm enough to flow but life gone. Josh had killed him.

At the moment there hadn't been time to worry over it. The chance for freedom had been too precious, her relief had been too great. But now she thought about it and remembered how matter-of-fact Josh had been. That he had had no choice she did not doubt. That he had found the strength and courage to prevail against the odds she admired. That he could so coolly dismiss the episode bewildered her.

Circumstance had thrown them into close association almost since their first meeting. She longed for time to pull back and evaluate him, their relationship, and her own feelings. After all, what did she really know about him, about what he'd been and done before they met? Not a lot. They had so little shared history. And most of that was violent.

But she did know what he was capable of and that frightened her.

Left untended her mind wandered into ugly daydreams. She wrestled with her own stream of consciousness and brought her thoughts back to the present. Sitting in her corner of the café, she sipped coffee and pretended to read the book she'd found on the floor of the van.

Few people knew of Bob Thrasher's condominium in Northport, not even his wife. He kept women there occasionally, never steadily. He didn't like demands. No one he knew kept a weekend home in the old whaling village on Long Island's North Shore. His peers preferred the Hamptons or Connecticut. So he felt free to stroll the one main street with its diagonal parking and antique shops and watch the boats in the harbor. Northport was one of the Island's sailing meccas, but Thrasher did not come there for water sports.

He was stunned to discover that Judson Rosen knew of his hideaway. Fortunately he was not keeping anyone in the condo at the time. (Or had Rosen known that, too, he mused.) The last to entertain him there had been Dominique and Thrasher would just as soon forget it.

Rosen arrived at noon with a bottle of white wine, chilled. Thrasher had never before seen him without a suit and tie, but as he observed the consultant, seated now on the black leather sofa, glass in hand, there was a familiar air of formality in the man, formality and command. The short-sleeve blue shirt had a button-down collar, his slacks were neatly creased, his shoes shined. Thrasher felt almost unkempt in his safari shirt.

"So Bailey's putting the screws to you," Rosen said.

"He's gone behind my back to the board," Thrasher confirmed.

"How much support do you have there?"

"In fair weather a majority. Now? I don't know. I do know I have to go into that meeting with more than a pep talk. I have to have an alternative. Bailey's proposal would lead to the downfall of the company."

"But a merger with Omer . . ."

"A merger with Omer would not only help resolve our immediate difficulties but improve our future marketing position." Not to say his chances for survival, Thrasher thought privately.

Rosen sipped his wine. "How many shares of LTS stock do you own personally?"

"About seven percent."

"And control?"

"Maybe another five."

"What about the other members of the board?"

"Individually I can outvote them—unless Virginia Petersen throws in her lot with one of them. Collectively, no."

"But some of them are in your corner?"

"Some." Thrasher was cautious. What with the recent disasters and Bailey's meddling, he wasn't sure how much of his support might have eroded.

"How does Bailey know so much about your position?" Rosen asked.

"He had an inside source," Thrasher responded, tight lipped.

"Had?"

The LTS president sighed. "It was my secretary. I fired her."

Rosen raised his eyebrows. "Ah, so." He seemed to sense Thrasher's embarrassment and dropped the subject.

"I think perhaps we can do business, Bob," he said. Only the tips of his straight white teeth showed when he smiled.

* * *

The Fiat was dusty, its white paint dulled with grime; two clear arcs sliced into the windshield where the wipers had scrubbed them clean. Kate recognized Josh behind the wheel before he opened the door. She grabbed the book and hurried to meet him. Never had a hug been more welcome.

His eyes were as tired as hers must be, his clothes two days worn, but he was safe. And she wasn't alone any longer.

"Are you all right?" she asked, pushing the uncombed hair off his forehead. There was a bruise underneath she hadn't seen before.

"Yeah. You?"

"Now I'm fine. Did you have any trouble?"

Josh shook his head. "For the time being I think we've lost them."

"Where now?" she queried as he opened the door for her.

"Away, by back roads, to find a place to sleep." He grinned crookedly. "You never dreamed life with a number cruncher could be so exciting, did you?"

His conscience didn't seem to trouble him at all.

"Frankly no," she said wearily, sinking against her own door and fastening the seat belt tightly around her. "But then I'll bet you never thought that exporting could be such risky business."

"Financially, yes. Physically, no," he admitted.

As he drove she could see the welts and bruises around his wrists where the cruel cuffs had been. Her own wrists were not so damaged. It must have been the fight, she thought, reminding herself that Josh would indeed have been killed if he hadn't . . . If he hadn't.

"They were speaking Russian, weren't they?" she asked. They'd scarcely spoken in the van the night before, both too stunned, too shaken to debrief.

"Two of them did," Josh confirmed. "I don't think the three of them shared a language in common."

"I couldn't understand any of them—except Franz when he spoke English."

"That may or may not have been his name, but I think he was Russian," Josh said as he lowered the gear for a steep descent. "He didn't speak German. The other two did. The blond one was German, judging from his accent. The other one was an Arab."

"From where?"

"Iraq. If I understood their conversations correctly—and sometimes it was hard to follow—Dimitri was right on target.

These guys aren't KGB and Mr. Gorbachev definitely hasn't sanctioned this little caper.''

"Who are they?"

"Soviet military, GRU, with the Iraqis thrown in for good measure. I think we've stumbled onto something a lot bigger than just pilfered technology. That's why they're so worried about us. I don't think the Soviet government knows about this at all—but apparently Baghdad does."

Kate was too tired to contemplate the implications. "We've got to reach Uncle Dimitri," she said. "He'll know what to do."

"I sure as hell hope so," Josh said.

They shook hands at the door. The sun hung over the harbor and summer sleepiness lulled the afternoon, but Thrasher felt alive, exhilarated.

"Keep this under your hat until Tuesday," Rosen advised. "Lord only knows what other spies Bailey might have lurking around."

"I wouldn't want to spoil the surprise," Thrasher agreed, pumping the man's hand with enthusiasm. Rosen hadn't even driven for an unreasonable fee.

"By the way," the consultant said, pausing at the top of the long stairway down to the parking lot. "I might be able to suggest a replacement for your secretary. I think I know exactly what you're looking for."

"Send her around."

"I will. She'll be there Monday morning."

Thrasher closed the door with a great sense of both relief and satisfaction. It was done. He would save LTS, he would save his career—and he would stick it to Ken Bailey.

He finished the excellent bottle of chardonnay himself.

"They can't simply disappear," Dominique said.

"They have. And they've had at least twelve hours to do so," he replied.

"Twelve hours!"

"Garrett left the interrogators in an isolated safe house, without transportation, without communication, handcuffed to a dead comrade. They had to chop off the man's hands to escape."

Dominique puffed nervously on a cigarette as she paced. "Our friends in Tbilisi and Baghdad will be furious."

"They are."

His seeming serenity seemed to enrage her. "So what do you intend to do about it? Just pack up our bags and head for Brazil?"

"On the contrary, my dear. We'll continue with our takeover plans. As far as we know, my placement is still safe and the project's not under suspicion. However, the takeover plans don't even have to come to fruition in order for us to get what we need, if it comes down to that. A week, I think, two at most, and we're out if need be."

"You don't think Thrasher will change his mind, take the easy way out and accept the other offer?"

He shook his head. "It wouldn't be a good business decision and he knows it."

She glanced at him dubiously. "You forget Oberman."

"No. He's being taken care of—permanently."

"So we cut our losses and run."

"Precisely, if we have to." He sighed. "It would not be the ideal solution. Actually it would be rather messy. It would be highly preferable to keep our coup a secret, not let Washington—or Moscow—know how much the pendulum has swung in our favor. And I have potential access to so much in my current placement. It would be . . . a great shame to sacrifice it." He looked up at her, a firm set to his jaw. "But as long as we gain our main objective we still win the war and we can retire to Moscow in triumph—and we are very close to winning."

"What about Garrett and the girl?"

He shrugged. "Eventually they will surface—and when they do we'll be waiting. We won't leave any loose ends. Besides, it will be far too late."

Chapter
23

"Greg Donovan" even had a telephone credit card, courtesy of Dimitri Oberman. Josh wondered where the referenced number was actually installed. Perhaps it belonged to Henry, the old geezer in Maine who had picked them up at the lake.

No matter. It could not be traced to Kate or himself.

He had trouble explaining to the Swiss operator what he wanted to do until Kate tried in French.

It was very early in New York. Veronica Reese was still in bed.

"Where are you, girl?" she demanded. "It's been over a week and I've been worried to death. Are you all right?"

"Yes," Kate said. "We're safe."

"You in Europe?"

Kate paused. "What makes you say that?"

"Person-to-person call from a French operator and I can't imagine why you'd be in Tahiti. Now listen up. Man named Dimitri called and left a message for you. Seemed to know you were on the run. Dimitri sounds like Russian to me."

"What did he say?"

"Hold on a minute. I have it written down. He made me repeat it back to 'im and all." She dropped the phone with a clank.

Kate covered the mouthpiece with her hand. "Uncle Dimitri called her," she whispered. There was no need to speak softly. They were alone in the spare hotel room they had rented the night before. Both too exhausted to continue beyond the fall of darkness, they had chosen the smallest place they could find that still had phones. But Kate still feared the walls had ears.

"Terrific," Josh said. "Let's hope he didn't leave it in code."

Franz had found and burned their one-time pad.

"Here it is." Veronica's voice was back, calm, matter-of-fact. "You still there?"

"Yes."

"Good. Now listen up: Dimitri says, 'Go out the same way you came in. Meet a friend at the consulate.' You got that?"

"Go out the same way we came in. Meet a friend at the consulate," Kate repeated.

"Right. I sure hope you know what it means, 'cause it sounds like gibberish to me. You catch up with that shipment in Vienna?"

The question caught Kate by surprise.

"Come on, girl," Veronica prompted. "You've worked with me long enough to know I'm no fool. Why else would you be in Europe?"

"We missed it," Kate admitted, relieved.

"Mmm. Too bad, 'cause rumor has it all hell's gonna break loose at good old LTS next week at the board of directors meeting."

"What kind of hell?" Kate asked.

"Well, those invoices from Omer Electronics come due next Thursday, I don't think we have the cash to pay 'em, ain't nobody gonna loan us the money just now, and my money says the shit's gonna hit the fan."

"You're probably right," Kate agreed, her mind racing. Thursday. They were running out of time.

"You ask me and I think Thrasher's startin' to panic," her assistant continued.

"How so?"

"He fired Dominique the Ice Cube last week and word has it she was spying for Ken Bailey."

Kate knew better.

He had studied the old man and his habits for two days, covertly, from the peak of a neighboring hill. The rest of the surveillance team had been called off three days before when the young couple was traced to Austria. They wouldn't be coming back.

Now, only he was left to watch the old man—and finish the job. Discretion had been discarded by those higher up.

Spanovich was a minor commercial functionary with the Soviet mission to the UN. He was also one of the best-trained marksmen in the Soviet Army. So good, in fact, that he had been recruited for special services by the GRU. Rarely used, he enjoyed the privileges of a pampered expert in his field. This was one of those times he paid his dues.

He glanced at his watch. Six-thirty. The old man usually fed the chickens at quarter to seven. Once more Spanovich scanned the farmyard. All was still. He had a clear line of fire to the chicken coop. The battered pickup truck was parked in front of the house, the green Mercury behind the barn, both out of the way. There was nothing to obstruct the path of the missile save perhaps the dogs. He would only have one shot. He would aim high, for the brain.

Spanovich turned his attention to his weapon. It was a Remington Model 700 "Varmint Special," 7.62 NATO calibre, favored by U.S. SWAT teams for just this sort of work. Sniperscoped in the hands of a man of his talent it was lethal at five hundred yards. It was not automatic. It did not have to be.

Spanovich sat quietly on his haunches like the hunter he was and waited.

"He wants us to go back to Milan," Josh reasoned as he downshifted to meet the next grade.

"To meet someone," Kate agreed. "But who?"

The alpine air was fresh and scented with evergreen, the late morning cool. Spirits revived by a solid night's sleep and a hearty breakfast, she embraced the long day's drive ahead. No one in the world knew where they were, even who they were, she thought wryly. She wished they could drive forever.

"I have a feeling this is one of those 'don't find us, we'll find you' situations," Josh said. The bruise on his cheek was purple, but fading, the one on his forehead still livid. "Why did he call in reinforcements now when he didn't before?"

"I don't know." Kate's face was troubled. "He didn't give us away," she added in a whisper.

"No. That was Elliott," Josh said grimly.

He maneuvered gently around a narrow hairpin curve. The mountain rose steeply on their right and plummeted just as precipitously to their left, jagged and rocky, punctuated with tufts of sturdy grass and little yellow flowers. It was a wonder the tour buses ever navigated the passes.

When the road straightened he sighed. "If they'd known where we were before I kept that rendezvous at the Spanish Riding School they would have picked us up. But they didn't.

They had to follow me back to the hotel and I wasn't clever enough to elude them. No. It was a set up. Elliott turned me in." There was bitterness in his tone.

"Did you tell him anything?"

"No, nothing. I'm sure of it." Something, some sixth sense, had cautioned him to keep his own counsel.

"Josh, it may not have been Elliott. It may have been someone Elliott told, someone he trusted and thought would help us."

He turned to her, abashed. "You're right. I guess I've gotten to the point where I suspect everybody." It was an observation he did not like making about himself.

She touched his arm. It was the first physical contact she had made with him all day, he realized.

"I understand that," she said, "but don't you think you should give Elliott the benefit of the doubt and warn him?"

He nodded, promising himself he would. The immensity of the conspiracy they faced overwhelmed him. "I still can't figure out what they're after," he said. "LTS doesn't make anything worth killing for. They destroyed Webb themselves, so the outlet for whatever they were stealing couldn't have been that important. They weren't trying to protect that. What are they trying to protect? Why do they want LTS?"

"Maybe it's not what we make but what we might make," Kate ventured.

"Like what?"

She shrugged. "I don't know. Something out of research and development."

"It couldn't be anything commercial. It would have to be military."

They'd reached the bottom of the grade. The road flattened out and Josh accelerated. Kate rolled up the window.

"LTS doesn't have any defense contracts. What about BATT?" Josh asked.

"There's a lab someplace on Long Island," she said. "Nobody ever talks about it much."

"What do they do?"

"They have a contract with the government to work on something called EMP."

Josh pulled the car off the road and braked to a halt on the grassy shoulder. Kate was grateful for her seat belt.

"EMP?"

"Yes."

"Do you know what that means?"

"No," she admitted.

"It stands for electromagnetic pulse."

"Which is?"

"Electrical fields created as a byproduct of a nuclear explosion. I did a paper on them in college when I was thinking about being a physicist. They can destroy computer chips, which means that in the event of a nuclear attack everything from home computers to defensive missiles to all communication systems could be rendered useless instantaneously."

Kate was aghast. "Isn't there any way to protect them?"

"Sure. The design of shielding for electrical circuits is part of all avionics and communications research," Josh acknowledged. "The problem is that the development of more sophisticated—and smaller—chips is running ahead of our capability to harden them against EMP. And the smaller the chips the less energy it takes to knock them out. In a very real sense our survival may one day depend on our ability to protect computer chips instead of people from nuclear blasts."

"And because our computerization is way ahead of what the Russians have they're after our EMP research?"

"They used to be. I gather from the conversations I overheard that the Soviet military still is."

"Unknown to their own government?"

"Uh-huh. And whatever they get they're sharing with the Iraqis."

"That's an odd alliance."

"Maybe. I don't know. Maybe you take your friends wherever you can find them."

"And they didn't say anything about why they wanted control of LTS?"

"No. But access to the EMP research is the only logical explanation we have so far."

"But we're not the only ones doing the research," Kate said. "Motorola, Hughes, GE are working on similar projects, or so I've been told."

"Maybe so," Josh said. "But their security may also be a lot tighter because they're all big contractors for the Department of Defense. Besides, EMP shielding is system specific, which means if these guys tap into a particular project they also get the goods on whatever weapons or communications system is being developed at the same time. Do you have any idea what system is involved at LTS?"

Kate shook her head.

He put the Fiat into first and climbed back onto the road. "I think Veronica's right. I think the shit's gonna hit the fan. If so, our friends don't have to actually take over LTS. They just have to have control of it long enough to gain unquestioned access to that lab."

Kate struggled to grasp the import of his conclusions. "What if we're right?" she asked.

"What do you think it would mean if someone could fly bombers and missiles with impunity and we couldn't get ours off the ground?" he asked.

The old man was late. It was nearly seven o'clock. Spanovich lay prone and watched the back door of the farmhouse below him. The rifle rested on the bipod legs extending down from the heavy twenty-four-inch barrel. He had hollowed out depressions for his pelvic bones. Every few minutes he rearranged the position of his arms. It wouldn't do to have them fall asleep. The dogs were out so the man was up. The assassin had assumed this most stable of firing stances as soon as the beasts had appeared. A breeze wafted up his back and down the mountain. He shivered, though it was not cold.

At last he heard the faint slap of the distant screen door as it slammed shut. He raised the Remington into position and squinted through the scope.

The old man had a dusty fishing cap on his head, studded with lures and flies. It made an easy mark. Spanovich aimed about sixteen inches high, calculating the flight path and natural drop of the bullet over four hundred yards. Gently he squeezed the trigger.

The cap flew into the air as the cranium beneath it exploded. The old man crumpled to the farmyard ground. The pan of scraps for the chickens fell, scattering the contents. The dogs appeared from nowhere, barking, agitated, sniffing the body for signs of life. Spanovich was satisfied there were none.

He stood, retrieving the ejected shell casing as he did so. Leaning the rifle against a tree, he set about obliterating all signs of his presence. From the way the man had fallen, it would be difficult if not impossible for the local authorities to guess from which direction the fatal shot had come, but he wasn't taking any chances.

No one lived within two miles of Oberman. The shot had probably gone unnoticed. Still, he had a quarter-mile hike ahead of him back to the Jeep. He slipped the gun strap over his shoulder.

It was then he heard the dogs. Barking and baying they crashed through the undergrowth at the base of the hill.

They couldn't have seen him, he thought. He was too far away, too well hidden. But a gust of wind struck him in the face and suddenly he knew. They had smelled him.

He ran, knowing they would hear him, not caring. He had a lead on them and he intended to keep it.

The woods were virgin, untouched. The forest floor was littered with generations of fallen branches and a cushion of pine needles that hid the ridges and dips cut by spring rains. He stumbled unwittingly over a half-submerged log and sprawled headlong. The heavy rifle barrel clunked against his head. Spanovich swore profusely in Russian and scrambled to his feet. The barking behind him rose in pitch.

He plunged forward but his knee screamed in protest. Something in the back of the joint had given way and the leg wobbled when it had to bear his weight. He limped on, taking the weapon off his back, slipping a fresh cartridge into the chamber, wishing for an Uzi.

He glimpsed the dusty black Jeep through the trees. But the dogs had eaten up the distance with astonishing speed. He had no choice. He turned to face them.

Accustomed to hunting as a team, they came at him from two sides. The one shot Spanovich was able to fire went wild. The last thing he knew was the fetid odor of a breath of stale liver.

Chapter
24

Thrasher arrived at the office early. It was going to be a good day. He could feel it. He actually smiled at the receptionist.

"Good morning, Linda. How are you?"

"F-fine, sir," she stammered, dumbfounded that he even knew her name.

"Any calls?"

"Not yet, sir."

"Well, I'm expecting a young lady this morning, a candidate for my secretary. When she comes send her straight back to me, will you?"

"Yes, sir."

He strode jauntily down the corridor to his suite, leaving Linda gaping in his wake. Confidence, he thought, that's what this place needed. Phil Petersen had always filled the halls with confidence.

There were letters on his desk to be signed and two calls to be returned from anxious board members. He hadn't wanted to face them last Friday. Today he would. And tomorrow he would face them all—and win.

He picked up the phone and dialed Frank Silverman first.

"Bob, I'm glad you called," his ally on the board said. "I tried reaching you this weekend but your wife said you were out of town."

"I was. What can I do for you?"

"Bob, as near as I can make out Ken Bailey has spoken personally with every member of the board. Hollingsworth is going to make a motion to let Bailey pitch his proposal to the entire board himself tomorrow morning."

"Let him."

"What?" Silverman was clearly astounded.

"I said let him. What that little weasel wants to propose won't solve our cash flow problems, won't help us grow in the future. What I have to propose will."

"You mean you have an alternative?"

"Yep. A humdinger. Frank, my boy, take my word for it: Bailey will never know what hit him."

Silverman started to stammer a question, but the intercom light on Thrasher's phone was blinking.

"Oops, gotta go, Frank. But believe me, Bailey's coming out of that room with his hands empty." He clicked over to the waiting line. "Yes?"

The temp answered. "Mr. Thrasher, there's a lady here to see you."

He smiled. Rosen had kept his promise. "Send her in."

The door opened and a tall, slender woman stepped in. "Hello, Mr. Thrasher," she introduced herself in a husky voice. "My name is Juana López."

At first glance she wasn't much to look at, Thrasher had to admit. But though Juana's face was pockmarked, her body was long and lithe, her breasts displayed nicely by the light-blue V-neck top she wore. The pearls at her throat rested on smooth, clear olive skin, and when she crossed her legs he could see that her thighs were shapely.

"So, Miss López, Judson Rosen tells me you're just what I'm looking for."

"I think so, Mr. Thrasher." She leaned forward to place a résumé on his desk, bending just enough to let her pendulous breasts droop to complete fullness. He licked his lips. "I have twelve years experience as an executive secretary and assistant. I type eighty-five and take steno at one-thirty. My references are excellent."

"I'm sure they are," he said, pulling the résumé to him but not glancing at it. "And . . . uh . . . how does it happen that you are unemployed at this fortuitous moment?"

She lowered her large black eyes and said softly, "My last employer met with a boating accident and there was no one to carry on the business."

"How tragic. You do realize that this position requires some-one of unimpeachable discretion?"

"Yes, sir." She looked up at him again and her smile was almost sweet. "Mr. Rosen explained the circumstances under which your last secretary was . . . uh . . . left."

"I see. Did he also tell you that there would be overtime involved?"

"I always expect to work overtime." Her voice, husky as it was, seemed to drop to new registers. She stood and leaned toward him once again, her hard nipples rippling against the silk blouse. "I think I have all the credentials you're looking for, Mr. Thrasher."

He was mesmerized. He felt his cock stiffening, unbidden. She stood at least six inches taller than he did, he realized, but horizontally that wouldn't matter.

The sudden buzz of the intercom broke the spell.

"Mr. Thrasher, you have a 9:30 meeting with the insurance adjusters," the loaner secretary reminded him.

He cleared his throat before he answered. "Quite right. Tell them I'll be down directly."

Thrasher straightened his tie. "You're hired," he told the woman. "I'll be back about eleven."

Elliott Lee was a nervous man. Josh Garrett's call the night before had thrown him into a maelstrom. In that instant the world had become an alien place, the familiar faces at the embassy sinister. One of them was evil, a mole, but which?

Lee was a marked man and he knew it. He had one alternative and that was to disappear.

He stuffed a last pair of socks in a pocket of the garment bag and adjusted his shoulder holster. Lots of American diplomatic personnel wore them now, even minor ones. It made their European hosts edgy. It made him feel safer. At least it had when all that had threatened him were faceless Arab terrorists.

It was nine P.M. He left the lights on in his apartment, the thin draperies drawn, and tiptoed down the back stairs of the building.

"Leaving again?" called a cheery voice.

It was Fräulein Stoop, the widow who lived at the end of the hall. She always used the back staircase, he remembered.

"Good evening, Fräulein," he said. "You know how bureaucracies are: no rhyme or reason, just 'do this, do that.'"

She bobbed her gray head sympathetically. "So where are you off to this time?"

"Just to Munich overnight."

"Ach, Munich. Lovely town—if you like Bavarians."

She didn't, he knew, and could discourse forever on the subject. He brushed past her.

"A thousand pardons, Fräulein, but I shall miss my train."

He left her muttering to herself on the steps.

The back door led to a quiet alley. Partway down, before the narrow passageway emptied onto the Webergasse, was a door on the opposite side that led into a neighboring apartment building, a building that had a garage in the basement. Lee kept a car there. Did anyone at the embassy know about that car? Probably not. He only used it on weekends. No, of course not. Who kept track of such things? People owned cars, they didn't own cars. It was no one else's business. He would drive to Switzerland, approach a U.S. consulate there, or perhaps in Holland. Someplace where they wouldn't be watching, where he could trust.

But first he would lie low for a while. He'd like to help Josh, but right now he feared for his own life.

Lee glanced up and down the alley. Nothing. He adjusted his grip on the heavy garment bag and headed for the door to the garage.

It was just past three in the afternoon in New York. Thrasher was ready to leave when his phone rang. He eyed it warily. Rosen had warned him not to let the cat out of the bag, and all that long, exhilarating day he had fielded inquiries from angry, concerned, curious, and even frightened members of the board. Had he revealed anything to them? He thought not. He was leaving now so as not to take any more chances. He waited for Juana to pick up the call.

She did. The intercom buzzed. "Mr. Thrasher, it's a Mr. Zim from Omer Electronics. He says it's urgent."

He didn't want to speak with Omer's president, but he supposed he did owe the man the courtesy.

"Hello, Mel," he said.

"Bob, I want to wish you luck tomorrow," Zim told him.

"Oh?"

"I just want you to know that if you can sell your board on the idea of merging with us I'll go along. And we'll extend the payment period on those receivables."

Thrasher beamed. "That's very considerate of you, Mel."

"Not at all. Both of our futures are riding on this. Give me a call and let me know what happens."

"Will do." The acting president of LTS hung up with a sense of elation. His plan really was going to work, he thought. Rosen was right. All the pieces were falling into place. Not only was he going to save LTS, but he was going to take over Omer

Electronics, one of his biggest suppliers, vertically integrate his company—and be a very powerful man.

"There's no answer," Kate said.

They'd been trying to reach Henry's ever since they'd checked into the hotel. A hard day's drive had gotten them to Bergamo, an old provincial town about fifty kilometers northeast of Milan.

Milan never had enough rooms, no matter what the season, and in August all of Europe was on the move. They hadn't even tried. Space in Bergamo was scarce as it was. They had found a room in a lovely inn in the old city.

Like many of the old medieval Italian towns that had survived, thrived, into the twentieth century, Bergamo was really two cities, an ancient walled past up on a hill and a modern, mechanized present spread out on the plain below. The old city, or Citta Alta, was a maze of narrow, cobblestoned streets, weathered stone and tiny shops.

And churches. Kate had counted at least five, each identifiable by its distinctive bell at the tolling of the hour, every hour, but never together. As the afternoon lengthened the chronologic symphony went on longer and longer, first the deep rich bongs of the steeple nearest them, then the playful pings from behind the inn, and then the other belfries, one by one.

Kate estimated that they had been harmonizing with one another for centuries. One would have thought the parish priests would have gotten together to synchronize them. But this was Italy. The chorus chimed ten as she once again replaced the receiver.

"He might be out," Josh said.

"I suppose. Do you think we should call Uncle Dimitri?" She wanted desperately to speak with her uncle. When they were out on the road she had felt relatively safe, but now as they were poised to make contact with the world again she was frightened.

"I don't know. Can you trace an international call?"

Kate ran her fingers through her hair. "I don't know. What would I say to him anyway? We don't have the codebook."

"He must know that," Josh said, slipping his arms around her. "That's why the message through Veronica was in plain English. Too bad he didn't leave another number with her. Go ahead; give his place a try."

She did, long into the night. She called Dimitri's and Henry's and Veronica's. The hotel operator grew impatient with the repeated demands on her time. But no one ever answered.

Chapter

25

Milan was not a city made for modern vehicles. The streets were narrow and oddly angled, sometimes cobblestoned. Parking was a nightmare and the Milanese were totally uninhibited about leaving their *macchinas* wherever they fancied: on sidewalks, in crosswalks, double-parked. Many cars in Italy were small, light, and near portable. Some drivers proved it by lifting the tiny conveyances into spaces into which they could not have wedged them otherwise.

Josh and Kate took the train in from Bergamo.

"I want you to hang back," Josh said quietly as they rolled and pitched along. "I'll go in first."

"Do you think it's another trap?" Kate asked. She was tired of running. They both were. Worry lines creased the corners of Josh's eyes, but the sense of purpose that had propelled them into this shadowy existence had not dissipated. She could see it in the grim set of his jaw.

"I don't know. I don't think so. Oberman's the only person we've been able to trust and I don't think they've gotten to him."

Kate sighed, wondering what would happen to them when this was all over—if it ever ended. Would Josh go back to number crunching? Would he welcome the routine of monthly closings of the books and profit and loss statements? Would she want to find herself a stable new position with upward mobility and good insurance benefits and two weeks vacation a year? Or would they both be too unsettled for all that?

"What are you going to do?" she asked.

"I'm going to march up to the front desk, plop my fancy fake passport down, and demand to see the commercial attaché, the CIA station chief, and the consul general, in that order."

And that is precisely what he intended to do as he approached the U.S. consulate at the Piazza della Repubblica an hour later.

Only he never had the chance.

He felt a subtle, solid pressure in the middle of his back. A voice said, "Mr. Garrett, it may not be safe for you in there. I think you'd better come with me."

Kate joined them, escorted by two burly gentlemen in jeans.

"Our car is around the corner," said the man with the gun.

This time they were not separated. Bundled into an official-looking black Peugeot, Josh and Kate were taken to a villa outside the city and shown into a comfortable sitting room. They never saw a weapon.

The owner of the house was obviously wealthy. The foyer was floored in varigated patterns of polished hardwoods. The salon was furnished with black velvet sectionals spaced around a gigantic table of white Italian marble, inlaid with a mosaic of various hues of gray. The fireplace was made of the same white marble and the carpet appeared to have been dyed to match. On the mantle and in niches set into the textured black walls was a magnificent collection of crystal.

"Would you like a cup of coffee or a glass of sherry?" asked the man they had come to know merely as Martin. He was sixtyish and rotund. The circle of his belt tilted, dipping in front to accommodate his protruding paunch. Kate surmised that it probably dipped lower every year.

"No, thank you," she said. She clutched the brown envelope full of documents they had hoped to share with the consulate. No attempt had been made to seize the envelope or either of them.

"Suit yourself," Martin said. He poured himself a glass of sherry from an ornate decanter. "I apologize for this rather abrupt treatment, but as you already know we have a mole in the Vienna embassy and Dimitri didn't want to take any chances." He sat down across the broad coffee table from them. His partners had disappeared. "All our embassies and consulates are probably being watched."

He was right, Kate realized. Embassies, consulates, airports. Any place to which they might naturally turn. Dimitri would have known that, too. "How do you know Uncle Dimitri?" she asked.

Martin smiled. "That's a long story."

"Can you help us get out of Europe?" Josh demanded.

"Maybe. But Dimitri said it might be safer just to take you out of circulation for a while and let us do the hunting. He said you're on to some high-class industrial espionage. Is that true?"

"It might be," Josh said. "What else did Dimitri tell you?"

"That you're traveling under assumed names, identities that he arranged, and there are people who would rather have you dead. That's quite an accomplishment for a deceased soccer player. How did you manage?"

Martin eyed them both through small round lenses. Kate thought he looked like Santa Claus, only bald and beardless. But Josh didn't trust the man. She kept silent.

"It's a long story," Josh said.

"Do you have proof about the smuggling of technology?"

"We don't know what they're smuggling out of the U.S., but we have documents that prove something extra's being shipped out, enough for you to launch an investigation."

"Why didn't you go to the authorities in New York?"

"We wanted to, but at the time the other side thought I was dead and was attempting to implicate Kate in that crime, among others."

Martin's interest sharpened. "I see. Do you have the documents with you?"

Josh nodded.

"Let's see what you've got."

Josh took the brown envelope from Kate and spread the contents on the marble table. They could not avoid divulging them now, she realized. Either Martin was legit or he wasn't. If he were, he could help them. If he weren't, they were dead anyway.

"Tell him all about it, Kate," Josh said. "You understand this better than I do."

Kate sat forward. "These are the packing lists delineating what our company shipped against four purchase orders we received from four separate customers in June and early July of this year for delivery to Switzerland, Hong Kong, Panama, and Mexico. None of these items requires a validated export license. In total they filled two twenty-foot shipping containers."

"And all were sent to the same forwarder," Martin added.

She nodded. Martin understood documents. That would make the explanation easier. She continued.

"All four of these orders were shipped against letters of credit we subsequently found to be nonexistent. None of them ended up where they were supposed to. As you can see from these packing lists and the ocean bills of lading prepared by Webb Overseas, only two shipments were ever made, one to Vienna and the other to Hong Kong. And each of them had magically doubled in size. Webb sent two full twenty-foot containers worth of goods to each destination. According to his packing lists they were full of the same goods we shipped to him in less than half the space. Now what would you think?''

''I think Mr. Webb shipped out something else, something he didn't want customs to know about.''

''So do we,'' Kate said. ''Just before these shipments left the country there was a fire at one of our factories, and the only items that turned up missing afterward were some of our export shipping cartons.''

''And we saw some of those unused crates at Webb's warehouse,'' Josh added.

''Only we can't prove it because Webb's dead and his place was burned to the ground,'' Kate said.

Martin's eyes twinkled. ''Sounds like you two have done your homework.''

''You've heard this story before?'' Josh asked.

The agent sat back and sipped his sherry. ''Not often. U.S. companies usually don't figure it out. Americans are generally so naive when it comes to this sort of thing that they spend more time figuring out how to subvert restrictions on technology exports than they do in helping the government prevent sensitive material from falling into the hands of unfriendly powers. And most of the time it's not greed either; it's stupidity. Remember the helicopter gunships that Hughes sold to West Germany a few years ago—only they ended up in North Korea?'' Martin shook his head. ''We're a very naive people.

''So,'' he continued cheerfully, ''for whom were these mysterious, unknown goods intended?''

Josh and Kate exchanged glances.

''It's important, you know,'' Martin told them solemnly.

''We're not sure,'' Josh said. ''And that's the truth. The group that grabbed us in Vienna was an odd assortment. The leader was Russian, I think. He spoke English and Arabic. One of the others was German, from Leipzig. The other was an Arab. I gathered he was Iraqi.''

''They told you this?''

''No. The German and the Arab communicated in German— there was no one language they could all speak together. I guess they figured an American wouldn't understand anything besides English. I do. I lived in Germany for quite a while.''

The agent smiled. "Good show.''

"A Russian and an Iraqi. Aren't they rather strange bedfellows?" Josh asked.

"Not necessarily. There are a lot of Moslems in the Soviet army, conscripted out of the republics in the south.''

"And the Soviet military's not overly fond of Gorbachev.''

"No," Martin confirmed.

"Dimitri thought this might be a GRU operation," Josh said. "Is the Soviet military that disaffected?''

"They're not happy." Martin carefully placed his empty sherry glass on the marble table and settled back in his chair. "There's never been any love lost between the GRU and the KGB," he explained. "And Gorbachev is strictly a KGB man. Western journalists conveniently tend to forget that. Meanwhile, the Soviet military's fallen on hard times. They lost a lot of face—and lives—in Afghanistan. Perestroika has brought the army's abuses of minority recruits to the front page of *Pravda*. Glasnost threatens to diminish the power and prestige of the military even further.

"Yes, I'd say that it's entirely possible that there are elements in the armed forces that would sign a pact with Satan himself if they thought it would restore their power and privileges.''

Kate swallowed.

"Jesus," Josh breathed.

"From what you tell me, I suspect this is an operation the GRU has had ongoing for quite some time. They've just diverted its intentions. I wish we knew what they were stealing.''

Kate glanced at Josh. He shook his head.

"Can you stop the shipment in Hong Kong?" she asked. "There may still be time.''

"We can try," Martin said. "With Webb dead you can be sure they'll be setting up another conduit. We'll be on the lookout for it. Maybe we can plug the drain at the source.''

"What about us?" Josh asked.

"I'd like to offer you our protection until this is over.''

"If you don't mind I'd rather not sit this one out. I have a score to settle.''

Martin stared at them for a long time. Was he real, Kate wondered. Would he let them go if they asked? Or would he rather not have amateurs interfere? And if he wasn't real, would he rather have them dead?

* * *

The formal conference room buzzed. No one spoke in tones that carried beyond their own little conversation group, but everyone was talking. The overall effect was that of a beehive.

Coffee in silver urns was set up in the corner on white linen tablecloths. A glass on a doily, a pad of paper, and a monogrammed pen were set at each place on the long mahogany table. Pitchers of water were evenly spaced the length of it. Preparations had been completed in advance, for not even the secretary who usually took the minutes was to be allowed inside.

All conversation ceased when Thrasher made his entrance. He enjoyed the impact he made.

Maury Leiberman, the chairman of the board, cleared his throat. "Now that we're all here I think we can get started, gentlemen."

They all took their places at the table, Leiberman at the head, Thrasher at the foot, the other twelve members arranged informally according to their alliances. By his count, Thrasher figured that maybe three were still solidly in his corner—for now.

"By mutual consent we will dispense with the reading of the minutes and discussion of old business," the chairman announced. "The first item on the agenda is an update from Bob Thrasher on the current state of affairs of LTS in the wake of a number of unfortunate occurrences of which I am sure you are all aware. Bob, the floor is yours."

Thrasher rose. Usually he didn't. His short stature was not quite so evident in a meeting like this when he was sitting down. But today it didn't matter. He began slowly, not wanting to reveal his hand until he was ready to pounce.

"The fire and the accident on the bridge have left us in a vulnerable position," he acknowledged. "The loss from the fire will top ten million. Though insurance will cover most of that, we are without crucial production capacity at a time when market demand is increasing. In a competitive marketplace such as ours this could have long-term effects, because it will not be easy to reclaim market share once we've lost it." His candor surprised them, he noticed. Good.

Halfway down the table to his left a hand went up. It was Joe Hollingsworth, Bailey's strongest proponent on the board. What had Bailey promised him, Thrasher wondered.

"Won't the insurance company order an investigation?" he asked, a knowing smile on his face.

"They already have."

"I mean a further investigation," Hollingsworth said.

"And why would they do that?" Thrasher asked.

"Because they may suspect the fire was deliberately set, just as the police now do."

"Do you really think Phil Petersen would arrange for such a thing?" Thrasher asked.

Hollingsworth was momentarily taken aback. He was stepping on a respected man's grave. "Well, perhaps not on that scale, but . . ."

"But what?"

"LTS is very short of cash."

Now the card was on the table.

"That's true," Thrasher said matter-of-factly. "We have seven million dollars worth of receivables we'll probably never collect and two point one million of it is due to a key supplier, Omer Electronics, in two day's time."

A collective gasp filled the room. Oh, yes, they'd known about the payables to Omer and they knew the drafts drawn on the L/C's had not yet been paid, but he was betting they didn't know that LTS never would see that seven million dollars. He'd stolen Hollingsworth's thunder.

Everyone began to bark questions at once. He held up his hand for silence. Leiberman banged an oaken stand with his gavel.

"Then how in good conscience can you refuse Ken Bailey's offer?" Hollingsworth demanded over the murmuring of the others. "Our immediate problem is to save this corporation from bankruptcy, a responsibility you may take lightly but which many of us do not."

"Our immediate problem is not to avoid bankruptcy but to assure the survival of this corporation," Thrasher said coldly.

"How did you manage to ship seven million dollars worth of goods without getting paid?" demanded another voice.

"Very poor judgment on the part of an employee who has since been fired."

"Water under the bridge," Hollingsworth snapped. "I think we ought to hear Ken Bailey out."

Heads nodded around the table.

"Fools!" Thrasher slammed his fist down on the table. "If you sell the home security division to Bailey what do you have left? I'll tell you—nothing. Yes, Bailey's come to me too. He even offered me a job. And why? Because he thinks LTS is finished. And it will be if you take him up on his offer." He had their attention now. He held center stage and felt ten feet tall as he paced the room. "Home security is our bread and butter, it's the business we know best, it's what built this company into a force to be reckoned with. What were we before that market segment exploded? A little parts supplier like Omer Electronics. And now we dominate one of the fastest growth markets in the electronics industry. And you want to give that up for a few lousy pieces of silver to a slick salesman?"

They were chastened into silence, even Joe Hollingsworth.

"There's a better way, gentlemen," he said quietly. "A way to ease the drain on our cash flow and increase valuable production capacity at the same time, a way to vertically integrate our operations and strengthen our market position. Gentlemen, I propose a merger with Omer Electronics."

He didn't tell them about the investor who would cement the two companies together in a joint acquisition. That could come later. One step at a time.

The man known as Martin let them go. He had given them new documents of identification and two tickets to Montreal, which Kate suspected he had had all along. Then he had driven them back to the station to catch the train for Bergamo. As he'd dropped them off, he'd wished them good luck and disappeared. He'd asked no more questions, answered none. He hadn't even probed for their real identities.

When they returned to the little hotel in the Città Alta the evening bells were ringing nine o'clock in their merry, uncoordinated rhythm.

Josh found that it was easier to play hide-and-seek with an enemy you knew to be after you than with an opponent who might or might not be. He never saw signs of surveillance and that made him more nervous.

"Why did Martin seem content with the documents?" Kate asked as she gathered up their few belongings.

"I don't know," he replied. "I guess because industrial espionage and factional intrigue in the Soviet Union are their concerns, not the fate of LTS."

"They would seem to be one and the same. Why didn't you tell him about the research project?"

"Because right now that's only a theory. Besides, if Martin's on our side he wouldn't let us go back and possibly screw things up in New York. And if Martin's on the other side I don't want them to know we've uncovered the truth. Let them think the main operation is still secure. It's the only way we'll have a chance at them.''

"If he weren't on our side it wouldn't matter,'' Kate said. "He never would have let us go.''

Kate picked up the phone.

"Who are you calling?'' he asked in a harsher tone than he intended.

She looked surprised. "Uncle Dimitri, of course, to let him know we're safely on our way home.''

Neither Henry's nor Oberman's phone was answered. Josh was beginning to suspect that they had nothing to go back to. And if they did go back, what could he and Kate hope to do by themselves?

"Come make love to me,'' he said, holding out his hand. Life seemed very short just now and he wanted the comfort of her body.

She submitted to him, the first time they'd made love since their escape from Austria. But there was no passion in the act. When it was finished she rolled away from him.

"Kate, what is it?'' He reached for her hand.

"I'm tired, Josh. That's all. I'm just tired.''

But that wasn't all, he knew. He could date her emotional distance from the moment she'd realized what he'd done in that house in the woods.

And there was nothing he could do about it.

Chapter
26

The trip down from Montreal had been tedious and tense. They'd taken turns driving but neither had slept. Flying would have been faster, but airports were public places and probably monitored. The conspirators would expect them to try to return and Kate could feel the net tightening around them as they drove south.

Dimitri Oberman's would be no safer. That was probably being watched, too, but they felt compelled to stop there. He was still not answering either phone.

Josh parked the rented car in the brush at the far end of the lake where Henry had picked them up on that long-ago morning. Had it really been less than two weeks before?

The canoe was still there, untouched. They slid it into the water and set out for the big pine trees that overhung the lake at the edge of Oberman's property, going in the same way they'd come out. This time, with Josh paddling, too, they made much better time. The skies clouded and the water darkened as they crossed the lake. Thunder rumbled in the distance, lending a greater sense of urgency to their mission.

The moment they stepped ashore they should have set off sensors, brought the dogs running, but the woods were quiet. Josh took Kate by the hand and led her up the hill.

Not until they were well in sight of the barn did the dogs detect them. They came bounding through the woods, baying a warning. When they saw Kate they stopped short and whined before coming forward in greeting. Their behavior was oddly anxious, not the usual enthusiastic ritual of tail-wagging and body-wriggling to which Kate was accustomed.

241

She scratched their heads and called them by name. Goliath seemed eager to lead them down the hill. They followed. David raced ahead. The first heavy raindrops spattered the pine needles.

In the farmyard lay the body, untouched, with David standing guard.

Josh took Kate by the shoulders and sat her gently on the woodpile beside the chicken coop. "I'll go," he said.

The dogs sat still as statues as he approached the crumpled form. The torso and legs were curled up as if the man were asleep. Only his arms, flung out at disparate angles, indicated alarm. A pool of blood had soaked the earth around his head and dried. There was no face. The maggots had begun their work. The tableau told a stark story. The stench of death hung over the barnyard.

Josh knelt beside the corpse and studied the clothes, the boots. He was about to call to Kate when she appeared beside him, a fishing cap with its collection of lures and hand-tied flies in her hand.

"It's Henry," she said.

The heavens opened and the cleansing rains began.

Chapter
27

Veronica wished she had quit. Her original two-weeks' notice would have been up two days before and she could have left LTS behind. She wished she had.

Thrasher was strutting about like a peacock, basking in his triumph. The glow of his success reflected off of Paul Cosentino, the man who was supposedly her boss but who still knew next to nothing about exporting. Veronica found herself implicated in the guilt that was supposedly Kate's for having shipped the orders they would never be paid for.

And it was all a damned fraud.

Thrasher was the one responsible for the seven-million-dollar bad debt, Cosentino still didn't know the difference between Saudi Arabia and South Dakota, and Veronica was strongly suspicious of Thrasher's new secretary. She matched Kate's description of Webb's assistant down to the pockmarks on her face. The woman's presence frightened her. She began to think that Thrasher really had been behind the conspiracy after all. But he wasn't that smart.

So Veronica kept her mouth shut and waited. The last thing she expected was a call at the office.

"International," she answered. "Veronica Reese speaking."

"Hi there. This is Glynnis. You gonna be home tonight?"

She hadn't planned to be. Now she would. The name was wrong but the voice was Kate's. Her pulse quickened. "Yes, ma'am," she said emphatically.

"Terrific. I'll pick you up at seven."

Veronica cradled the receiver gently. She was surprised to

find herself shaking. Whatever the game was, it wasn't over yet and she was smack dab in the middle of it.

At seven she was poised on her couch, the phone beside her and a notepad in hand. Instinct told her Kate would call, not come by, that her friend could not afford to be seen.

She'd had one false alarm already and jumped when the phone rang again. Steady girl, she told herself.

"Hello?"

"Veronica?"

"Yes. Lordy, am I happy to hear you. Where are you?"

"Close by," Kate replied.

"How close?"

"This is not a long distance call."

"Thank heavens. Listen, girl, I don't know what's goin' on around here, but the shit hit the fan Tuesday and Thrasher came out smellin' like a rose."

"What about the payments due to Omer on Thursday?"

"That's all part of it. There's gonna be a merger between Omer and LTS and they graciously extended the receivables thirty days. It's some sort of deal Thrasher put together."

"Thrasher and who else?" Kate wanted to know.

"Ahh. There you have it. You know and I know that man isn't bright enough to do something truly creative, 'cept maybe lie," Veronica agreed.

"Bailey?" Kate suggested.

"Not on your life. Thrasher all but kicked him in the butt. No. It's some consultant named Rosen, least that's what the rumor mill says. I haven't been able to pick up any details. There is one other development that may be significant though."

"Oh?"

"Thrasher has a new secretary. Her name is Juana López and I swear she has the same voice over the phone as that witch who used to work for . . ."

"Webb," Kate finished. "My God."

"I don't mind tellin' you, Kate I don't like what's goin' on around here."

"With reason. Veronica, for Christ's sake don't approach her. Don't give Juana any excuse to let her know you suspect."

"You can count on that, girl. What are you goin' to do?"

"I don't know," Kate said honestly.

"Well, don't go just yet," Veronica told her. "I have one more message for you. This guy Dimitri's been callin'."

Kate caught her breath. "Did he leave a number?"

"Nope. But he said if you was to call that I was to tell you to go to New Jersey, said you'd know where, and he'd meet you there."

There was a pause at the other end of the line. Then Kate said, "Thanks, Veronica. I think everything will be all right now." She hung up without saying good-bye.

They had spent the night at Oberman's, careful not to turn on any lights. Misha and the dogs had been starving. It was evident that Oberman had left them in Henry's care and departed voluntarily, perhaps as much as a week before. Josh had buried Henry's body in the woods. There was nothing more they could do now. Knowing that Oberman was still alive had filled them with new hope and they had tackled the drive south with revived enthusiasm. The message relayed through Veronica had made them feel almost triumphant.

They drove to the motel in which Kate and Oberman had stayed the night before she was to have made the aborted attempt to contact the FBI. He was waiting for them, seated in the small lobby, reading a newspaper.

"I'm sorry, no vacancy," said the frumpy clerk behind the bullet-proof glass shield of the registration desk.

"They're just here to meet me for dinner," Oberman said. He rose stiffly and straightened his game leg. "Glad you could meet me, daughter," he told Kate, and embraced her. He shook Josh's hand warmly. "Rough trip?"

"It had its moments," Josh said.

Oberman led them to his room. There were two double beds, a cheap bureau, and one chair. The smell of soy sauce permeated the place.

"I called our mutual friend and she said you were in town, so I ordered out. I hope you like Chinese food," he told them. "Quarters are a little cramped, but we'll move our base of operations to the city tomorrow. Would you like a glass of wine?"

He reminded Josh of an old soccer coach he'd known in Germany, all business on the surface yet trying to reach out and care for each of his players as individuals, unsure just how to do so.

"Chinese is fine," Josh said with a smile.

Oberman seemed to relax. He sat in the chair and observed them both. "Why don't you start by telling me what happened over there." He pulled the cork on a bottle of burgundy and poured into three plastic glasses.

While Kate ate, occasionally pausing to embellish details for him, Josh did. He told Oberman about their trip to Austria, their futile attempt to recover the goods, their betrayal, and their isolation from American authorities. "When we got to Italy we couldn't even prove who we were," he said.

"No wonder you were suspicious of poor old Martin," Oberman observed.

"We couldn't afford to trust anyone," Kate said. "We just wanted to get out of Europe alive."

"Then suddenly Martin was there and we were out," Josh concluded. "Thank you," he added. "How did you manage it?"

Oberman smiled and reached for a fried wonton. "I still have some connections. My friend Martin says you gave him a copy of the documents."

Josh nodded. "We didn't want them on us anymore. Besides, they're not as important as we thought."

"What's the end of the story?" Oberman asked.

Josh met the man's gaze squarely. "Apparently you were right about this not being a sanctioned operation. The thugs who snatched us didn't realize we spoke something other than English. I eavesdropped on some interesting conversations in German."

"And?"

"Whoever these characters work for they don't like Gorbachev. They're taking orders from someone in Tbilisi. At least two of them were."

"Southern Soviet military command," mused Oberman.

"That's not all," Kate added. "The other one reports to Baghdad."

The older man raised his eyebrows.

"What's really frightening," concluded Josh, "is that this isn't some half-baked coup plot. These people are well into a long-term operation aimed at getting their hands on some high-class technology. No matter whom they decide to use it against their intentions can't be benign."

"What are they after?"

"Part of what they want is a research project being carried out by a very quiet little division of BATT, so quiet and so little we hardly noticed it when LTS acquired the company. We think that's what the conspirators have been after all the time."

"BATT has a lab out on Long Island," Kate explained. "In

Suffolk County, which you said used to be off limits to anyone with a Soviet passport."

"What's in that lab?"

"A government-funded project on electromagnetic pulse research."

Oberman whistled. "No wonder they want to get their grimy fingers on it. But isn't driving LTS into bankruptcy a bit of an awkward way to do it?"

"Not into bankruptcy, into acquisition," Josh said. "They don't want to destroy the company and they don't want to disturb the ongoing research. They just want to have access to it."

"Which we think they did have until LTS acquired BATT," Kate chimed in. "The acquisition led to a big management turnover. We think the GRU had someone inside the lab until LTS took over and when he was fired they lost access to the research project. They want back inside, and because of the sensitive nature of the research security is tight."

"I see," Oberman said. "So everything that's happened to LTS the past few months—the fire, the accident, the dead L/C's—is all part of an elaborate scheme to put the company in a vulnerable position, to set management up for rescue by some knight on a white horse."

"Uh-huh," said Josh. "And Thrasher's the perfect patsy. His ass is in the sling and he'd do anything to save it."

"And we think we know who the white knight is, too," Kate added.

"Who?"

"A man named Rosen. There was a Judson Rosen fired from the lab not long after the acquisition."

Oberman cocked his head to one side. "Is this guy about six feet tall, slender, gray eyes, brown hair?"

"Yes," Kate said slowly. "Why?"

"Because in that case I think we have all the pieces. Mr. Rosen frequents Dominique Attinger's bed. One of them." He folded his hands and rested his chin on the outstretched index fingers. "Now all we have to do is flush the bastards out."

Kate and Josh exchanged glances. So that's what Oberman had been up to the past week.

"My God, we were right," she breathed, and seemed to shrink against the headboard. "Couldn't we call in reinforcements now?" Her voice was plaintive.

"Like who?" Josh said.

"Like Martin and whoever he works for."

"Martin is retired, like I am," Oberman said, "though he does have better credibility than I do. He'll track down that errant shipment. He'd even buy my story about stolen goods, but I'm afraid my stock with the Company isn't good enough for them to move quickly enough on Mr. Rosen.

"Besides, it would take time to convince them, time to brief them on the personalities involved. We may not have that much time. No, I was always a lone wolf and preferred to run my own operations. This is no exception. I don't want anyone else screwing it up. We'll blow the lid off this thing and then hand the feds—and the Ruskies—a gift-wrapped package."

This was Oberman's chance to reclaim his honor, Josh realized.

"I have a score to settle, too," the former agent added softly as an afterthought.

"Two," Kate told them with regret. "They killed Henry."

Lines of sorrow creased Oberman's face. "I didn't think they'd go that far."

"You're as wanted as we are," Josh said. "And I want ten minutes alone with Rosen."

Chapter
28

Juana had exceeded Thrasher's expectations. He'd never dreamed how titillating it could be to watch a woman pleasure herself—or let him do it for her. He had debated whether to share his newfound knowledge with his wife. In the end he decided against it, for she would only wonder where he had learned such tricks after nearly thirty years of marriage.

Gretta was in the Hamptons where he would join her on Sunday. But Saturday he claimed for himself, to savor his victories and daydream of the glories to come. Robert Thrasher, visionary, savior of LTS. He could see the headlines in *Business Week* and the *Wall Street Journal* now.

He retreated to Northport, to the condominium overlooking the harbor, and spent a lovely morning watching the sailboats dance in the breeze.

He'd almost invited Juana to join him, but had learned that women, if pampered too soon in a relationship, came to expect much more than he was willing to give.

At noon, as the sun dangled just above the treetops, he decided to go down to the village for lunch. He strolled leisurely along the cracked sidewalk of Bayview Avenue, lined with some of the oldest homes in Northport, gingerbread houses with terraced yards and widow's walks where the wives of the whalers used to watch for their men to come back from the sea.

The street was quaintly narrow, barely able to accommodate parallel parking on one side and leave enough room for one car to squeeze through on the other. When there was two-way traffic one driver had to duck into an empty parking space to let the other pass. It kept speed down.

A car with Canadian plates passed him. He didn't notice the occupants.

Suddenly a figure fell in step beside him.

"I think it's time we had a little talk, Mr. Thrasher," a woman's voice said. He turned, astounded, to find Kate Fleming staring at him.

"Wh-what . . . ?"

"We'll be safer and more comfortable if we go back to your condo." She was so matter-of-fact, so brazen.

"H-how do you know . . ."

"You're not the most discreet adulterer in the world," she said.

Thrasher stood like a bear at bay in his narrow kitchen and gulped a whiskey and soda.

"Listen, lady," he said between crunches on ice cubes, "I don't know who the hell you think you are but nobody accosts me in my own home and accuses me of being a fucking spy!"

"I didn't say you were," Kate said, amazed at how calm her voice sounded when she was churning so inside. She strode to the sliding glass door that led out to the patio and cracked it open. A sea breeze ruffled the drapes. "I said you were being used by one."

"Bullshit. You just want back at me because I fired you."

"And you're grabbing at straws to save your career because you've nearly mismanaged LTS into bankruptcy and you know it. And so does the GRU." She spoke softly, but the impact of her words made him sputter. Before he could retort she went on. "They maneuvered you right into giving away the store, Thrasher. Who do you think Dominique Attinger was really working for?"

His mouth fell open. "How do you know about her?"

"I know about a lot of things, like the fact that she was your so-called expert on international finance who kept assuring you that the L/C's were good."

"She was working for Bailey," he insisted.

"She was working for Soviet military intelligence. So does Juana whatever-her-name-is-now. And so does Rosen."

"Don't be ridiculous. The arms race is over."

"Don't be a fool. Do you believe everything you read in the papers? People with power and privileges don't meekly lay down their weapons and go home. Apparently the Soviet military saw troop withdrawals and budget contractions coming a long time ago and decided to do something about it. Rosen—or whatever his name is—is part of it.''

''Don't be silly.''

''I'm not. We've been watching them. Rosen and Dominique are very chummy. She has a second apartment, just for meetings with him. These are very dangerous people you've crawled in bed with, Thrasher. Look what's happened to everyone who got in their way: Ralph Payton, the night guard out in Suffolk; the driver of the truck; Chun, the banker; Webb, the forwarder; Phil Petersen; and other people you don't even know. They're all dead, Thrasher. I've been lucky so far, but don't try to tell me this isn't happening. I have the scars to prove it.''

She was nearly shouting now, wishing she could cram the truth down his throat, force him to share the terror she'd lived with these past weeks. She'd wanted to be tough in this confrontation, to tell him what a prick she thought he was, but Thrasher was key to their plan to foil Rosen.

Thrasher was rattled now, speechless. Kate calmed her breathing. She was in charge.

''Now, are you going to sit down and listen to me?''

He hesitated.

''If I have to,'' Kate continued, ''I'll resort to crude forms of blackmail, like telling your wife about this little love nest or calling the chairman of the board. But I don't want to have to do that, so why don't you pour yourself a refill and sit down.''

He complied.

Kate helped herself to a glass of soda.

''It's really very simple,'' she told him, leaning against the bar. She wanted to stand to maintain her height advantage over the little man. ''Just over that hill on the other side of the harbor is Centerport, and in Centerport BATT has a research lab. The conspirators want access to that lab.''

''Rosen used to work there,'' Thrasher said, almost in a whisper.

''You got it. And as long as he did the GRU could monitor progress on the EMP research project. When Petersen fired him the Russians were left scurrying around like ants when you stomp on the entrance to their hole in the ground.''

''They want it back.''

''Mm-hmm. And they've used you to get it.'' And your ambition and your libido and your stupidity, she thought, but she didn't say so.

''Why don't they just try to steal it?''

"Think, Thrasher. The research isn't finished yet and because of the security at that place no outsider could ever get in and out without being noticed. They want the research to continue; they want a finished product and they don't want the U.S. government—or the Soviet government—to know they have it."

"So if you know all this why don't you go to the police?" Thrasher asked smugly.

"Because we don't have proof that would stand up in a court of law." She finally sat down. "Besides, Mr. Thrasher, I've learned something in the last few weeks. I've learned that these people don't play by the rules and that you can't play by the rules to stop them."

Thrasher sat idly turning the glass in his hands. Finally he looked up. "Miss Fleming, I think you're trying to sell me a fairy tale and if you don't get out of here I'm going to call the police. There's still a warrant out for you."

Kate gasped.

"I wouldn't do that if I were you," said a voice from the patio door. Josh pushed the opening wider and stepped into the room.

Thrasher dropped his drink.

Oberman knew Dominique's habits well now. He knew where she bought her fingernail polish and which bars she frequented. She did not own a car and disdained rural life. She had her hair done twice a week and never ate dinner in. She blended well with her cover as a spoiled, moneyed East Sider.

She also kept a second apartment at which she received no mail, at least not under the name Attinger. There she received only Judson Rosen.

It was Rosen they needed to know more about. He was a shadow.

Oberman would have liked to see the man's personnel records at LTS, but it was Saturday. The phone and residence of the Russian (if that were indeed what he was) were unlisted, of course. Attinger's second apartment was the only possible point of intercept. Rosen had slept there three times in the days the retired agent had been watching. So he staked it out.

Sure enough, about ten A.M., Rosen emerged from the brownstone on Seventy-first Street and strolled down to the Lexington Avenue subway outlet at Sixty-eighth. Oberman followed, wishing that his bad leg did not make him stand out. Staking out a place was one thing. Actually tailing someone was another. Anonymity was crucial.

Rosen rode south to Grand Central Station, caught the shuttle across town to Forty-second Street, and transferred to the IRT for the one-stop ride to Penn Station. There he bought a ticket for the Long Island Railroad and a paper to read on the train.

Oberman purchased a *National Inquirer.* It suited his disheveled dungarees better than the *Times.* While he waited he phoned Veronica. Kate and Josh had somehow tracked Thrasher to Northport out on the island and were on their way there. He thanked her and hung up.

Rosen was moving. He descended to track level and boarded a train bound for Huntington, a major population center on the North Shore of Long Island. At the last moment Oberman stepped aboard.

The car was mostly empty. Rosen sat forward of the double electric doors, his back to them. Oberman placed himself aft in the smaller of the seating compartments, from which point he could watch Rosen and reach the door quickly when his quarry got off. He settled in behind the tabloid.

The conductor charged him an extra dollar for not having purchased his ticket in advance. No matter. It caused less of a stir than if he had bought a ticket for the wrong train. He paid passage to the end of the line.

The ride to Huntington lasted over an hour. Rosen never budged as the commuter made stops along the way. In Huntington everyone got off, for it was as far as the electric engines went. Anyone going farther east would have to switch to a diesel train. Rosen headed for the parking lot.

Oberman fished a fifty-dollar bill from his wallet and stopped at the taxi stand. He chose a young driver in blue jeans.

"Where to, mister?"

"You see that man in the tan sport coat over there walking through the parking lot?"

"Yeah."

"We're going to follow him—very discreetly." He handed the boy the fifty dollars.

"Golly. Are you the police or something?"

"Or something. All right. He's in that gray Thunderbird. You got 'im?"

"Yes, sir!" The driver put the cab in gear.

"Stay about two blocks behind him and keep at least one car between us if you can," Oberman cautioned.

Rosen turned right out of the parking lot and headed east.

"Where does it look like he's going?" Oberman asked, wishing he had a map of Long Island in his head.

"Not into Huntington. Centerport maybe, or Greenlawn or Northport."

Centerport. The lab. Logical. Rosen had worked there for three years, had hoped to work there for possibly several more. It would make sense for him to live nearby, to have left his car at the station and taken the train into the city for the night.

He realized with a start that Northport was also a stone's throw away, that Rosen may also have arranged a rendezvous with Thrasher that day.

And there was no way to warn Kate and Josh.

"What do you want me to do?" Thrasher asked weakly. His shoulders slumped and his bravado was gone. His world, the world in which he was a hero and a tycoon, had crumbled.

"Very little really," Josh said. "The hardest part will be keeping your cool, knowing what you know now."

"You won't be in any danger if you do," Kate assured him. "You'll never have to leave your office."

Josh sat down beside the quaking executive. "We want three things from you, Thrasher, three things and maybe you can keep your job. We want copies of the personnel files on Juana López, a.k.a. Medrona, Dominique Attinger, and Judson Rosen. Second, we want the plans for the security systems at the Centerport lab, all of them. You're to deliver those to Kate tomorrow before noon."

"But how . . ."

"She'll come by for them. Where do you keep those plans?"

"My copies are locked in the safe in my office."

"Does your secretary have the combination?"

"No!" Thrasher exploded, taking umbrage.

"Relax," Josh told him. "What we want you to do is ask Juana to make copies for you."

"But she'll probably make copies for herself."

"That's the whole idea. We want to make it very tempting for them to break into the lab."

Thrasher was growing paler by the minute. "But isn't that taking an awful chance?"

"Not when we'll be waiting," Josh said. "It's the only way we can get the goods on them that will stand up in court." He didn't intend for Rosen to live that long, but there was no reason to share that with Thrasher. The man was terrified enough already.

"There's one more thing you have to do," Kate told the tottering president of LTS. "You have to tell Rosen that the lab won't be part of the acquisition."

"Yep, he's headin' into Centerport all right," the cabbie said.

They had just come through the one-street village of Greenlawn, a strip of small bank branches and independent businesses from pharmacies to a florist. They followed the Thunderbird down a winding hill through a pleasant wooded neighborhood. Oberman leaned forward as they crossed 25A, the major east-west route along the North Shore of Long Island, and headed north into the peninsula that was part of Centerport. Ahead of them Rosen proceeded confidently about ten miles an hour above the speed limit.

"Is there any other entrance into this section of Centerport?" Oberman asked. He had not been able to find another on the maps he had acquired. If Rosen were making a run at the lab Oberman found himself ill-prepared to stop him.

"Nope," the driver confirmed. "This is it."

Oberman sat back and studied the area intently as they passed, correlating geographic reality with the abstract map his mind had photographed.

As far as security was concerned, he mused, the BATT lab was well situated. The tiny peninsula was less than two miles long, extending into Northport Harbor on Long Island Sound. The houses were spaced on large, forested lots. Dogs roamed unleashed and children played baseball in the streets. Little Neck Road, the narrow, meandering, two-lane affair on which they drove, was the only land access route. It could be easily blockaded.

The lab was hidden in the woods on land purchased from the old Vanderbilt estate, one of many the family had acquired on the East Coast. Oberman doubted that many of the neighbors even knew the research facility was there. They probably thought it was just another of the estate buildings, like the planetarium or the coach house. Gates barred the entrance to the BATT property. Rosen drove past without pausing. The cab followed.

The Soviet agent turned right into Gina Lane on the east side of the little peninsula. Oberman cautioned the driver to slow. Ahead of them the trees thinned as all the homes fronted on the water, very exclusive real estate. Across the harbor loomed the giant red and white smokestacks of the Northport power plant of the Long Island Lighting Company, a crassly industrial backdrop to an otherwise idyllic setting.

Rosen pulled into a driveway in front of a subdued gray ranch with white shutters. Oberman could see water glinting in the neighbors' backyards.

He had the cabbie drive past and stop around a curve in the road. Gina Lane was circular, he noted, feeding right back into Little Neck Road. Ordering the boy to stay put, he doubled back to the house.

The name on the mailbox said Rosen, the yard was carefully manicured. The aerials on the roof were not for television reception. This, then, was the front for the man's cover identity as a respected and successful technical consultant, a man who was probably known and admired in the executive offices of half a dozen defense contractors on Long Island—Grumman, Hazeltine, Unisys, Fairchild. Here he was, living comfortably right in the middle of rural Suffolk County—in which no Soviet citizen was permitted to set foot due to national security considerations. Mr. Rosen probably had his fingers in more than one technologically restricted pie, Oberman mused.

The grounds of the house would be wired for security, he knew. He crept down a neighbor's property line instead. He had to see the backyard.

Along the edge of the water everyone had docks, mostly empty now, for the wind was brisk and the sailing would be excellent, a rarity for Long Island Sound in August.

At Rosen's dock were two small outboards. Offshore floated a forty-foot Lancer Motorsailer, large enough to handle the open waters of the ocean as well as the relatively quiet waves of the sound. Judging from the hardware bristling above the cabin, it was rigged with sonar in addition to sophisticated communications equipment. It occurred to Oberman that the Soviet compound in Glen Cove, Nassau County, was only a few miles away. Astern the ship bobbed a huge outboard motor, two hundred horsepower he gauged from this distance. Across the white hull was emblazoned her name, *Natasha*. The halyards slapped against the masts as the craft rocked lazily back and forth.

Oberman clenched his jaw. Suddenly the scenario was complicated, but he would need his car to determine just how much. That bit of reconnaissance would have to wait for cover of night.

Chapter
29

Oberman reminded Josh of his German soccer coach again, psyching up the team for the big game. Individual dreams and fears were shunted aside in favor of the common objective, winning. The time for reaching out to the players with fatherly concern was past. The coach approached the coming confrontation with single-minded concentration.

Josh watched him press his fingers together with studied intensity. Oberman did not pace as he briefed his troops. He did not waste his energy on aimless movement, but poured it all into his words and the avalanche of ideas behind them.

Josh and Kate sat very still together on the drab beige bedspread and listened. Josh found himself caught up in a surge of pregame excitement, felt the rush of fervor and determination that had gripped him in his playing days. Only this time much more was at stake.

He could not fathom what was in Kate's mind as Oberman outlined her role in the plan. Detached, she sat staring at her hands in her lap.

She was resigned to the futility of calling in law officials, he knew, convinced that even if the authorities were to believe their story they would insist upon picking up Rosen and Attinger for questioning. Without hard evidence, the conspirators would slip through their legal fingers. Rosen would know how to use U.S. civil liberties as a shield. Kate had abandoned her faith in the ultimate triumph of constitutional justice with reluctance. What ethos she now believed in he did not know. Perhaps she didn't either.

"Time is what we must manipulate in our favor," Oberman

was saying. "We mustn't give them enough to counterplan. We want Rosen to have to think on his feet, to realize his cover has probably been turned, to act. He mustn't have time to trust subordinates to do the job. We have to nab him with his hands in the cookie jar—and hope he doesn't find a hole in the net."

"Could he?" Kate asked.

"Rosen isn't stupid," Oberman replied. "He'll realize he's being set up. That should come to him as a shock. He'll only have two alternatives—abandon the mission entirely or try to get into the lab to salvage what he can. I'm banking on his making the mistake of thinking that he's only up against a couple of amateurs, which means he'll make that run at the research project."

"And we'll be waiting," Josh affirmed.

Oberman nodded.

"He'll be armed," Kate said flatly.

"So will we," her uncle said.

Kate's eyes widened. "How . . . ?"

"It's very simple if you know where to look. Josh and I'll have the guns. With any luck, this caper will go down quietly before the momentum carries it back to you."

Kate was silent. Her lips pressed together in a thin, hard line.

Josh had to admit he didn't like the odds. They knew from experience that Rosen had reserves to call on.

"Rosen may still not make the move himself," he said. "He probably has a contingency plan."

"I'm sure he does," Oberman agreed. "I think that's why he has that boat—which means one of us has to baby-sit it."

Josh started to open his mouth but the older man held up his hand. He smiled. "I can't run, but I can swim. Besides, given Rosen's inside knowledge of the research facility I don't think he'd send someone else in." He shook his head. "Nope, Rosen'll have to act and he'll do it himself. I just wonder how many other fish we'll catch." There was no reservation in his tone. "And now I think we should go to bed. Tomorrow is going to be a very long day."

Even with the limp he made no noise as he moved. He paused at the door, his gray hair shimmering in the fluorescent light of the street lamp in the parking lot. "Good night."

"Good night," Josh replied.

Kate sighed.

"Are you ready to sleep?" he asked her.

"No."

"Let's take a walk."

The night before they had moved their base of operations from New Jersey to Long Island, to a motel on the North Shore, convenient to highways that would take them either west into Manhattan or further east to Centerport. It was not far from Josh's demolished house.

He'd thought he was accustomed to pretending to be someone else until he'd come home. Fighting back the awkwardness, he told himself that the false names that flowed so easily off his tongue and the beard that greeted him whenever he glanced in a mirror were now reality. Still he shunned appearing in the daylight. It was dark outside now.

Kate slipped on a pair of sandals. She was not smiling. Josh sat beside her and cupped her face in his hands. She received his kiss without emotion.

"It'll all be over tomorrow," he whispered.

"Will it? What if the GRU or the Iraqis send someone to get even with us? What if Rosen shows up with an army? What if Thrasher tips him off? You don't know. Nobody knows." She caught her breath. For only the second time in all the weeks he had known her, in all the weeks they had run together, tears trickled down her cheeks. This time they weren't for John.

He tried to put his arms around her, but she pulled away.

"Kate, don't turn your back on me now. I may die tomorrow. You may die tomorrow. All we have for sure is tonight."

She faced him, furious, tears smearing brown mascara down her cheeks like rain on a dusty window. "I saw your face when Uncle Dimitri said you'd have a gun. You're going to kill tomorrow. Again."

The words stung him into silence. Finally it was out in the open, the ugly fear that had wedged them apart since Austria.

"You're a killer," she whispered.

He wasn't surprised she thought so. He was only surprised how much it hurt to hear her say it.

He swallowed. "I'm not." He stood and backed away from her from her rage, from her fear of him.

"You killed!" she countered. "Twice. And you'll kill again tomorrow."

"Twice?" He was bewildered.

"The man in Austria and the man they found in your house."

"He was alive when I left him, for Christ's sake."

"And the man in Austria?"

"I killed him," he admitted. "But that doesn't make me a

killer. It was a lucky blow—and he would have killed me if I
hadn't hit it lucky.''

"And you never regretted it.''

"No! No, I didn't. And neither did Dimitri,'' he lashed back.
She stared at him.

"You think he invited those two goons up at his place to tea?''
More silent tears spilled down her cheeks.

He closed his eyes. He was having trouble putting it all together. He'd found something in himself these past few weeks
that he'd barely known existed, a blood lust he'd felt only rarely
in his youth, always on a soccer field when there were teammates
to restrain him, never in life. And now Kate had seen it, too.

He sank down on the bed beside her.

"Kate, I'm scared too. I'm afraid we're going to lose. I'm
afraid we're going to die. I don't know who I am anymore, I
don't know what I've become, I don't know what I'll be when
this is over. But I love you, Kate. And I need you to love me,
because the only decent thing that's happened to me since this
all began is you.''

He was tired. God, he was tired. His side ached and his head
ached, the tension inside him pounding to get out. He closed
his eyes, as if that would somehow quiet his system.

Kate's fingers gently brushed his cheek. A chill shook his
body. He caught her hand and held it. Kate put her arms around
him and kissed his face. Her lips were soft. He rocked her back
and forth in the silence until his heartbeat slowed and the tension
eased.

"Promise me when this is over you'll go away with me," he
whispered, "someplace safe, someplace quiet.''

Kate sighed. "Is there such a place, Josh?''

He had no answer.

She pulled away from him. "Josh, I'm not sure what's real
anymore. I don't even know if I trust my own feelings.'' Her
eyes searched his face, as if seeking there a clue to her own
confusion. "It's almost as if everything's happened to us in isolation, without reference to people and places familiar to either
one of us. Do you know what I mean? Do you know what I'm
trying to say?''

She rose and walked over to the window, arms folded across
her chest. The curtains were closed against the outside world.

"I think so,'' he said. "Kate, I've never lived as intensely
with anyone as I've lived with you. The simplest, most ordinary

thing we've ever done together was have lunch in the park, but I think I started falling in love with you even then."

The expression on her face softened. He held out his hand and she came to him, shyly. He wanted to hug her tightly, to somehow fill her with the sense of confidence he suddenly felt. But he contented himself with holding her hands, and he remembered how he'd noticed them that first day, practical fingers with trim nails, an artist's hands. He caressed them as he spoke.

"Loving someone day to day, Kate, when you're surrounded by other support systems, by your job or your family or your home, that's easy. We've never had that security. What we have must be something very special."

Her tears splashed on his fingers. He put his arms around her and let her cry, wishing he could, too.

"We'll win, Kate," he assured her. "We'll win and then we'll go away together and forget the whole bloody mess."

"How can you be s-so sure?" she hiccuped.

"Because we know more about them than they know about us," he told her.

"Yes," Kate sniffed against his shoulder. "But they have an advantage too. They're outside the law and they know it. They'll be ruthless. They don't have consciences."

Their greatest mistake might be in believing that we do, Josh reflected. But he didn't share that thought with Kate. He found it disturbing enough himself.

"They're not outside the law," he said. "They just think they are."

That assertion seemed to calm her. He searched her face for signs of the joy of spirit he was used to seeing there. "It ends tomorrow, Kate. We'll make it happen, you and me and Dimitri." He chuckled, a forced sound for her benefit. "Can you imagine how frustrated they must be? Based on his personnel records with BATT, Rosen's been working on this project for at least three years. God only knows how long it took to work him into place to get that position. Never a murmur of scandal. Then he runs into a couple of amateurs who don't like the way he does his paperwork. And try as he might he can't seem to get rid of us. I'd love to see the look on Juana's face when you walk into that office tomorrow morning."

Kate tried to smile, but the tears had left her drained.

"I do have a major decision to make," he said.

"What?"

"Do I keep my beard or shave it off?"

Half a laugh escaped her. "What?"

"My beard. Do you think I should keep it?" He scratched his bewhiskered chin speculatively.

She turned his head first one way then the other.

"To be honest, the contrast with your pearly whites is a little dazzling," she said with a familiar twinkle in her eye.

"Is that good or bad?"

"I think I'd like Josh Garrett back, clean shaven. Greg Donovan has a beard."

That was too close to the truth. He kissed her. This time she responded, not with passion but with a tenderness that surprised him. The gentleness of her fingers on his body reminded him of the simple man he had once been, a civilized man, weaving his life into recognizable patterns. The kind of man he wanted to be again.

After tomorrow.

Chapter
30

Kate's spine tingled as she stepped off the elevator. It had been four weeks since she had been fired, four weeks since Thrasher had summoned her to his suite and berated her, since Dominique Attinger had stood guard while she cleaned out her office. The events of that day seemed insignificant now.

She didn't want to see what Paul Cosentino had done to the office he had inherited. It would remind her too much of the way the world used to be. But one purpose of her visit was to be seen. Briefly. The warrant was still out.

Familiar faces called greetings as she passed. Kate responded with a wave and a cheery smile.

Veronica feigned surprise at her visit. She was in the wrong business; she should have been an actress.

"Lordy, girl. It's nice to see you. What you been doin' with yourself?" She could turn on the dialect when she wanted to.

"A little traveling," Kate replied. "How's things?"

"Quiet. You know how August always is. The rest of the civilized world is on vacation."

Kate laughed, tempted to ask for the late news from key markets, if the new distributor in France was working out, but it was no longer her concern. Still, after having built up the department it was hard to cut the ties.

"Is Paul in?" she asked.

"Nope. He's at lunch with Arthur Barnes of Australia."

Kate felt a stab of envy. Arthur was one of her favorite distributors. Lucky Paul. For some people on the fringes of disaster life was still ordinary.

"Well, no use for me to stick around here then, I guess."

She stepped close to Veronica's desk. "If I were you I'd report in sick right now and disappear for a couple of days," she said under her breath.

The other woman's eyes widened. "That dangerous?"

Kate nodded solemnly. "I'll explain, promise. You've been more help than you know." She held out her hand and said full voice, "Good to see you again, Veronica. Hold down the fort."

Arms swinging jauntily, Kate returned to the elevator and rode up to the executive floor. Faces there seemed a bit more surprised to see her. Josh's office was still empty, she noted. She went straight to the presidential suite to find that Thrasher had not yet moved in. There were workmen pounding together a platform in the middle of the main office, however. Shaking her head, she went on to the vice-presidential corner of the floor.

In Dominique's accustomed place sat the woman she recognized immediately as the same person who had left Webb's offices that long ago Thursday afternoon when she and Josh had paid the forwarder a visit. She thought she saw a fleeting glimmer of alarmed recognition in Juana's eyes.

"May I help you?" the woman said stonily.

"I'd like to see Mr. Thrasher, please."

"He's busy."

"I don't think he'll be too busy to see me." Kate kept her voice low, confident. She met the woman's gaze without blinking, without smiling.

At last Juana buzzed the intercom. "There's a Miss Fleming here to see you."

Contact, Kate thought.

Thrasher's response was long in coming. For a moment Kate feared he'd lost his nerve. She almost sighed with relief when he asked her to come in. She closed the door behind her.

Thrasher was standing behind his desk, not nearly as imposing as he had imagined himself the last time she had stood before him.

"I was afraid . . ." he began.

Kate held a warning finger to her lips.

"You will be hearing from my lawyer, of course," she said, "but I wanted the pleasure of telling you myself that I'm suing LTS."

Surprise registered on Thrasher's face. Kate made a rolling motion with her hand. Talk, talk, she mouthed.

"Then your coming here gives me the opportunity to kick

you out of my office again," Thrasher said. His voice was unsteady, but he spoke without hesitation.

Kate gave him a "thumbs up" sign and approached the desk.

"Then you'll be further delighted to know that you're named personally in the suit," she said.

Kate opened her ample handbag. Thrasher tried to stuff a thick file folder in it. No room. He took the papers out of the folder and crammed them into the bag. The task so preoccupied him that he forgot to answer. Kate stood back.

"Well, at last I've rendered you speechless, I see. You certainly weren't the last time I saw you. No matter. Since then I've collected lots of interesting information about you and about LTS." She pointed to her purse and raised her fingers in a victory sign. "I'll be seeing you in court." She winked at him. He managed a smile in return.

Before leaving she dropped a small folded note on his desk, Oberman's idea. It said, "Job well done. Now bait the trap. Burn this immediately."

"Get out of here," Thrasher snapped, grabbing the note.

Kate did just that, slamming the door behind her. She caught Juana with her desk drawer open. Taping perhaps? Swinging the bag over her shoulder she quick-timed it to the elevator. Juana was coming down the corridor after her. Kate jabbed the elevator button.

Hurry, hurry, she prayed. She did not want to share an elevator with Juana López Medrona. The dial over the door crept upward, nine, ten, eleven. When the door opened she jumped inside and held down the "close" button.

"Wait!" she heard a woman call, but she kept her finger on the "close" control and it won out over Juana's frantic fingertips.

She exited at the rear of the building. Josh was waiting for her in the gypsy cab, motor running. She scrambled into the backseat.

"How'd it go?" Josh asked as she leaned back and tried to catch her breath.

She handed him her pocketbook and closed her eyes. Papers rustled in the breeze from the driver's open window as Josh examined what Thrasher had given her.

"It's all here," he said. Josh leaned over and kissed her. "How's my favorite spy?"

Kate glanced up at his clean-shaven countenance. His smooth cheek felt strange to her now. "Shaken," she admitted. "I've never come face to face with one of them before. Somehow it's different when they're flesh and blood beings instead of abstracts.''

''Different how?''

''Josh, I swear that woman would have strangled me if she could have.''

Thrasher barely had the adrenaline under control when his watch beeped twelve-thirty. Rosen was due in his office momentarily. Sinking into his chair, he tried to compose himself by taking deep, slow breaths, concentrating on counting them through rather than on the upcoming confrontation. It was a familiar technique, often successful, but when the intercom buzzed he noticed that both fists were still clenched.

''Mr. Rosen's here, sir,'' Juana said.

It was twelve thirty-nine. Had Rosen arrived late or had Juana delayed to advise him of Kate's visit?

''Send him in.'' Thrasher glanced nervously at the residue in his ashtray. Dust, he noted with relief. He reminded himself to smile.

Rosen was back in uniform, three-piece suit, shined shoes and all.

''Good to see you,'' Thrasher said. Shading the truth was not new to him. How often had he told his wife he was going fishing? She thought it was his favorite hobby and always put lures in his Christmas stocking.

''Equally so,'' Rosen replied. ''Is everything going as planned?''

''Yes. Mel Zim kept his promise and it's as if we have a new lease on life around here, thanks to you.''

Rosen distained the short-legged chairs in front of the platformed desk. He headed for the sofa. Reluctantly Thrasher followed. He would have felt safer behind his desk. He chose the highest chair.

''I understand you had an interesting visitor this morning,'' the spy said.

''Oh? How did you hear about that?'' Thrasher tried to sound casual. Rosen was unnerving to talk with at the best of times. He always seemed in such perfect control. He never distracted himself or anyone else with nervous twitches of his fingers or a rhythmic jiggle of the knee. He sat perfectly still and his concentration was absolute.

''People in the halls were talking.''

People like Juana, Thrasher thought bitterly. He shrugged. "No big deal. She says she's going to sue, though I can't imagine on what grounds. The woman is irrational. That's why I fired her in the first place."

"Mmm," was Rosen's only comment.

"The important thing is that the board is entirely receptive to our plan and I see no reason why we can't proceed immediately."

"Are you authorized to negotiate for LTS?"

"Naturally. I haven't contacted Zim personally about this, of course, as you will want to be a part of those discussions too, you and . . . uh . . . your principal."

"Yes."

"There is one small change," Thrasher hurried on. He had to remain in charge, drive the conversation his way. "There is a small, nonmanufacturing division that won't be a part of the deal."

Rosen's eyes became animated for the first time. "What's that?"

"The research project. It's self-supporting, government funded, and all that, but it doesn't actually make any money for us."

"I find that hard to believe," the other man said dryly. "Since when doesn't business make a buck off a government research project?"

Thrasher chuckled halfheartedly. "Believe me, Judson, we'll make more money selling it off to some outfit that's heavier into defense research than we ever would holding onto it."

"You already have an offer?"

"Not firm."

"From whom?"

Thrasher cleared his throat. "Well, I'm not really at liberty to say. I'm not handling the negotiations."

"Who is?"

"Well, Phil Petersen was . . ."

"Which leaves it in your hands," Rosen insisted.

Thrasher squirmed inwardly. "Judson, believe me, LTS makes a better package without the research project. I know you may have a soft spot in your heart for it because you worked on it, but it makes no noticeable contribution to profitability and it will bring in a healthy supply of cash." He tried to put a note of authority in his voice.

"I think I should have been consulted."

With effort Thrasher smiled again. "I think I know what I'm doing with my own business."

At least he hoped he did. Lord, how he wished he had taken Ken Bailey up on his offer.

"The little toad," Dominique spit. "He knows his business like he knows his wife."

"Agreed, but that's not our problem now," Rosen told her. "We're being set up."

The woman was silent as she pondered that pronouncement. "So what do you propose to do?" she said at last.

"Call in reinforcements and move. We'll have to implement our worst-case scenario."

"When?"

"Now."

"I'll arrange to clean up all the loose ends," Dominique said.

Thrasher was just about to call Paul Cosentino and invite him for a long, late lunch in celebration of how well the morning had gone when Juana entered his office and closed the door behind her. A week ago he had found her desirable. Now she reminded him of a black widow spider, nasty and venomous. He was about to learn how venomous.

"I'm leaving for lunch," he said.

"Yes, you are," she said calmly. "Only you're not coming back."

She lowered the file folder she was carrying. Behind it was a shiny, black revolver, pointed straight at him.

"The game's over, Mr. Thrasher."

He was a loose end.

Oberman had the taxi drop him off at the entrance to the Vanderbilt property.

"It's closed today. They ain't gonna let you in," the cabbie said. He had an odd accent for Long Island, unfiltered with Brooklynese. He had a full twenty-six letters in his alphabet and pronounced his r's like a Californian, as if he meant them.

"A friend is waiting for me," Oberman told him. He paid the man off and watched him go. Then he skirted the estate and turned up Gina Lane, the little circular drive that ran past the water—and Rosen's house. At one corner of the abbreviated street was a padlocked cyclone gate that marked the rear of the Vanderbilt land. From that vantage point he could see the length of the neighborhood waterfront. For a closer view he had a pair of binoculars.

A battered Chevy was parked in front of the Rosen place. It tweaked his memory, but he couldn't connect it just then.

The breeze was quiet. The boats at the private docks drifted at anchor in the ripples, leftover waves from the sound. Further out Rosen's big Lancer Motorsailer waited. She was not uninhabited, however.

Only one of the dinghies remained at Rosen's dock. The other was tied beside the sailboat. As he watched, Oberman could see two burly figures making an inspection of the craft. One was squat and blond, his Slavic features topped with a crew cut that had allowed the sun to redden his scalp. The other was slightly taller, with dark hair sprouting from both his head and forearms. From their manner he gathered that they were familiar with the boat, for their actions had a sense of purpose.

They made Oberman uneasy. Had he known that Thrasher and Juana Medrona were also already aboard he would have been even more alarmed.

Kate dropped him off at the deli on the corner of Route 25A and Little Neck Road. She did not get out of the car. Dressed in a trim red and white skirt suit, hair piled on her head in a bun, she looked the part of a professional security consultant. The adventure of the morning had emboldened her. She also looked confident.

"I love you," Josh said.

She blew him a kiss. "I'll see you," she said. "When it's over."

She stayed to watch him set out. Had he turned, he might have seen the longing in her eyes as she allowed herself a fleeting moment to wonder if she would ever see him again.

Josh hiked into Centerport. He carried a stout walking stick and hoped he looked like a friendly tourist. The contents of his knapsack were anything but friendly.

According to the wiring diagrams provided by Thrasher, the northeast corner of the BATT property was penetrable, as long as he didn't touch the cyclone fence.

He had two alternatives: over or under. The thick stand of oaks and undergrowth of mountain laurel would shield him from the prying cameras. Oberman had marked a zigzag path on the schematic that would take him within yards of the building, there to wait until Kate appeared with the lab's director—or until the

Russian made his move. Josh was the first line of defense in case Rosen beat them to the lab. He could not afford to be seen waiting on the public-access road.

Wearing green fatigues and a sturdy pair of rubber-soled shoes, he felt awkward in the role of suburban guerrilla. On his back he carried a pack containing a twenty-foot rope, a collapsible spade, the walkie-talkie with which he could communicate with Oberman, and a store of munchies in case he was marooned all night in the lab. To his distaste he also carried a .45 calibre automatic pistol. The weapon was not unfamiliar to him, just alien.

A tall oak spread branches on either side of the fence, an easier access than grubbing in the hard ground with his tiny shovel. He swung the rope around an overhanging limb, looped it, and pulled himself up. His shoulder muscles performed but objected, another reminder that an accountant's life was softening him. He stuffed the rope back into the pack and pulled out the walkie-talkie. He had been amazed how quickly Oberman had been able to equip them for this little escapade.

"Number Cruncher here. Do you read, Farmer?"

"I have you," Oberman's voice came back. "Where are you? Over."

"I'm in. No sign of anybody yet. Will advise. Over." The jargon did not come to him naturally.

"Quiet on the beach, too. Stay in touch. Over and out."

Josh clipped the communicator to his belt and slithered down the tree trunk. Following the route Oberman had mapped out, he crept his way to the edge of the woods nearest the front entrance where he could monitor the comings and goings. For a full five minutes he barely breathed, but his approach had apparently gone undetected. He began to relax.

The plan was for the director to let him in the rear of the building, which was least likely to be watched. Then he and the security guard would prepare for the Russians. If everything went according to plan Rosen would not escape the premises. Josh would disarm him, the guard would call the police, Oberman would secure the Natasha and wait for reinforcements.

He settled in to wait.

Nathan Davenport lived in Fort Salonga, a dot on the map not far from the BATT research lab in Centerport. Few other blacks lived in his very white, upper-middle-class neighborhood, but Dr. Davenport was no stranger to tokenism. He had been the only black in his class at MIT; he was still the only black scientist at BATT.

Davenport was proud of the research project he headed. Like a single parent raising a child, he oversaw every aspect of the operation, from the hiring of personnel to security arrangements. It was the latter that Kate Fleming had come to discuss with him. He thought it odd that she had asked to meet him here, at home, and not at the office.

"Thrasher told me you were coming, but I must admit you don't look like a security expert," Davenport said. His voice was low and melodic.

Kate smiled as she followed him into his paneled study. It was a man's room, smelling of leather and tobacco, unlike the bright, modern rooms through which they had just passed. The house was silent; no one else was home.

She waited until he was seated. He was a tidy man, she noted, not what she expected from a scientist. The top of his desk was clear.

"I'm not here to discuss general security arrangements, Doctor," she explained. "I'm here to avoid a specific attempt to steal your work. Are you busy tonight?"

He stopped midway in the act of loading his pipe. "I beg your pardon."

"We have reason to believe that an attempt will be made tonight or tomorrow by agents of Soviet military intelligence to break into the lab in Centerport."

"That's absurd."

"Is it? You're very close to a breakthrough regarding the protection of the new circuits of the Stealth fighter communications system from electromagnetic pulse, are you not? Technology that may very well be applicable to other defense and weapons systems?"

"How would you know that? That's classified!"

"I have a copy of your last report to the Department of Defense." She did not give him time to absorb that revelation. She wanted him thoroughly rattled, unarmed. "You also had a man in your employ by the name of Judson Rosen."

"Yes, but . . ."

"Judson Rosen is a spy for the GRU who regularly reported on your work to Soviet military authorities in Tbilisi in Soviet Georgia. You didn't know it, Dr. Davenport, but you were serving two masters."

Davenport had forgotten his pipe. He stared at her blankly.

"As Mr. Thrasher told you, we're going to need your help."

"What do you want me to do?" he whispered.

"I want you to come with me to the lab and introduce one of our people as a security consultant to the guards. We need your authority to get him inside. We intend to be waiting when the GRU makes their move."

Davenport swallowed. "And how do I know you're not . . . them?"

"Because I am," said a voice from the doorway.

Kate whirled. It was Dominique. She was armed. She was smiling.

Afternoons lingered in August. The sun still promised at least an hour of daylight when an Audi sedan was waved through the gates of the lab, followed by Kate driving the rented Skylark with Quebec plates. The place was nearly deserted. Only one other car remained in the lot. Josh stretched his legs to uncramp them.

So far so good, he thought. Kate would make the introductions, then drive back to a curve in Little Neck Road just before the Vanderbilt estate, there to wait until she received instructions to close the one access road to the peninsula if need be. They all hoped the operation would never go that far.

The man in the Audi parked and got out. He was tall and black, with gray at the temples. Davenport. Suddenly another figure emerged from the backseat. He carried a large, expandable briefcase. The second man waited for Kate. Even at this distance Josh could see that she was frightened. Her hands were empty. No walkie-talkie. This was wrong, all wrong.

Josh raised the antenna and quietly hailed Oberman.

"Farmer, are you there?"

"Yes."

"We have a problem here. Davenport's not alone. Kate hasn't saluted me yet." A salute was to have been her signal that everything was going as planned, that he could circle around to the back of the building and wait to be let in. The hairs on the back of his neck began to prickle.

The man beside Davenport stepped forward to the edge of the woods. "You can come out, Garrett. You're outnumbered."

Josh froze. Kate would not have given him away. It had to have been Davenport.

"Come out, Garrett, or we shoot the girl now." He moved

aside. Standing behind Kate was Dominique, a gun at his friend's head.

"Josh, he means it," Kate called in an unsteady voice. "They know you're here." She emphasized the "you're." Did that mean they didn't know about Oberman?

"Farmer, are you still there?" Josh whispered.

"Yes, but I can barely read you."

"Rosen's here, with Dominique. They have Kate. It's up to you now."

Leaving his pack and walkie-talkie in the woods, Josh raised his hands and stood up, his eyes on Rosen's gun.

A cruel smile twisted Rosen's lips. "Fine. Now we have the whole little band of heroes. Just come along quietly and nobody gets hurt."

Dominique opened the driver's door of the rental car. "Get in," she ordered Kate.

"Where are you taking her?" Josh demanded.

Rosen waved him back. "Not too close. I understand your hands are lethal weapons. Your girlfriend's being taken to a safe place. As long as you cooperate, she stays alive. Is that clear?"

Josh nodded. He exchanged a brief glance with Kate, hoping she could read in his eyes what he would tell her if he could, words of encouragement, of defiant hope.

Dominique got in the passenger side of the car and the two women drove off.

"Whose car is that?" Rosen demanded. He never took his gun off Josh.

"It belongs to the guard," Davenport stammered.

"No one else is in the building?"

"I don't think so."

"Fine. Let's go inside, shall we?" Rosen said. He herded Josh and Davenport before him.

A uniformed guard rose to meet them in the lobby. Without a word of warning Rosen shot him in the face. Josh didn't even have time to register the man's features before they were gone in a mist of blood and brain. His stomach turned. The scientist retched.

"Sorry, Doctor, but I can't afford distractions," Rosen said. "We have work to do. Down the hall to the utility room. Now!" He knew precisely where they were going. He had worked here.

Josh steadied Davenport as they stepped over the body. He tried not to look at the spreading red stains in the military-gray carpet.

The utility closet was at the end of the hall.

"Open the door," Rosen said.

Josh did so.

"You stand out of the way. You, Doctor, inside. Find some duct tape. I know they have some. They used it on a broken window last spring."

Davenport crept into the closet and rummaged along the shelves.

"I've got it," he said at last.

"Fine. Bring it along to your office."

They retraced their steps, passing the body once again. The stains were still spreading.

Davenport's office was near the front of the building, large and airy, with tall windows. Rosen set the briefcase on the over-sized oak desk.

"I want everything you have on the EMP project. Now."

Davenport glanced nervously at Josh, then opened a safe built into the wall. He began emptying computer tapes and printouts into the briefcase.

"It won't all fit," he wavered.

"So fill that box over there."

"It . . . it isn't finished."

"That's all right. I'm taking you along to finish it for me."

Davenport hesitated.

Rosen turned the gun on him. "Hurry it up. We only have ten more minutes before my associate shoots the girl."

Josh nodded at the scientist.

When Davenport was finished Rosen ordered Josh to lie down on the floor with his arms on either side of one leg of the huge desk. Josh did as he was told, expecting to hear a gunshot at his ear.

"Tape his wrists together," Rosen snapped. "Don't be stingy. Make sure there are plenty of layers."

Davenport knelt to comply. His hands were shaking.

"You may be wondering why tape, why not handcuffs—or perhaps why I don't just shoot you," the Russian said. He sounded as if he were enjoying himself. "Well, this time I intend to make sure you get blown up with the building. I have enough plastique to obliterate this place. It won't be long, but I want you to know it's coming. You can take comfort in the fact that the Fleming woman will outlive you by at least several hours. We won't shoot her until we're well out to sea—and my friends and I have had time to enjoy ourselves."

Josh twisted his body and kicked upward at Rosen's crotch.
But his hands were now secure and he could not reach far
enough.

"Don't tempt me, Garrett. Take off your watch, Doctor, and
your wedding band. Put them on our friend here. When the
police find his body there won't be much left. I don't want them
to find the remains of handcuffs. I do want them to find your
jewelry. Everyone will think you're dead—just like they already
think he is." He turned a last time to salute Josh. "Few men
get to die twice, you know, Garrett."

With Davenport lugging the box and briefcase full of top-
secret files and computer tapes they left Josh on the floor. He
could hear them pause in the foyer, probably to set the bomb,
he thought in desperation. Rosen wouldn't lie about that. The
explosion and fire would mask his crimes. Then the front door
closed and he was left alone with the dead.

Josh wedged his shoulder under the desk and heaved. It
wouldn't budge. He twisted and tugged at his wrists, but the
tape was two inches wide and gummy. Josh examined his bind-
ings more closely. On the outer edge of the visible layer, that
closest to his fingers, was a small tear. Davenport was not as
terrified as he had appeared. He'd kept his wits about him. One
of the properties of duct tape is that under the adhesive it is
woven. Once split it would tear in neat straight lines. He grabbed
the first layer with his teeth and pulled. It ripped all the way
across. The layer beneath was also notched. Exultant, he ripped
it open. The pattern continued. God bless Davenport, he
thought.

Finally the last layer gave. He pulled his right wrist out of the
strangle of tape. He was free!

Josh raced for the front door. It was locked. Rosen wasn't
taking any chances. He saw the timer on the guard's desk. He
had seconds. He fled back to Davenport's office and hurled the
heavy chair through the window. An alarm went off, a loud
ringing in his ears.

Josh hurtled himself through the window, landing neatly on
his shoulder and rolling to absorb the fall. Instinct told him to
run. He did, pausing only for the knapsack and the gun, ignoring
the cameras he had avoided on the way in. They didn't matter
now.

As he ran he tried to raise Oberman.

"Farmer, Farmer, coming your way. They have Kate and
Davenport and the project."

There was no answer.

Suddenly behind him a tremendous explosion shattered the dying afternoon. He dove under a laurel bush, reliving the nightmare of the evening his house was destroyed, as debris rained around him.

Minutes after Josh's whispered transmission about Kate's abduction the rented Skylark parked in Rosen's driveway. Two women got out. Oberman was too far away to see faces, but he recognized Kate's red and white suit and Dominique's platinum hair. The two went directly to the dock behind the house and hailed the sailboat. One of the men aboard skittered down the rope ladder into the dinghy and headed toward shore to pick them up. Good, Oberman thought. That meant they were leaving the second dinghy for Rosen. At least something was going their way.

With no hesitation he tucked a sealed plastic bag containing a pistol and two extra clips into his belt, shed his shoes, and slipped into the water. The men aboard the *Natasha* were watching the dinghy. Oberman gulped air and went under. Even in August the waters of Long Island Sound were too chilly for him. He must be getting old.

He swam powerfully, smoothly, unimpeded by his leg as he was on land. In the water the muscles did not have to bear his weight. He did not surface until he was certain he was on the seaward side of the vessel. He came up about ten yards beyond it and fifteen yards off the bow. He dove a second time and approached the sailboat on the port side, bobbing quietly to the surface once more.

Peering around the stern he saw that Rosen and Davenport had now arrived. Where was Josh? he wondered. But there was no time to worry about that now.

He waited, silently treading water. He wanted Rosen aboard. He wanted them all aboard, confined. Pray God Kate was out of the way.

"Did you get it?" Dominique demanded as the second dinghy approached.

"Everything," Rosen assured her. "What about Juana and Thrasher?"

"Already aboard."

A Latin woman appeared beside Dominique. "Mission accomplished," she said. "What about Garrett?"

"This time he's gone for good," Rosen replied.

Oberman heard a gasp that must have come from Kate and the slap of flesh on flesh.

The dinghy clunked against the side of the sailboat.

"Get the doctor and the files below," Rosen commanded in a low voice. "And for Christ's sake get those guns out of sight. We're home free if we just keep our cool and ease this baby out to sea for the rendezvous tonight."

Other voices floated across the water, indistinguishable. Two boys had emerged from the yellow house next door and were clambering into the speedboat.

Oberman paddled to the anchor chain and shinnied up. All attention was still focused on those arriving. He slithered over the gunwale and flattened himself against the cabin.

"Weigh anchor and let's get out of here," Rosen told the crew.

The impact of the explosion startled them. The first shock wave rocked the boat wildly.

"Kate, jump!" Oberman shouted, leaping into the clear. He opened fire, dropping the two stunned crewmen where they stood. Rosen's bullet slammed him in the side as he dove for cover. At first there was no pain, but the impact knocked the wind out of him. In a vague way he knew that he was badly hurt, but he felt no fear, no regret. With failing strength he saved himself for one last act, and he nodded with satisfaction as he heard two bodies hit the water.

Out of the chaos Kate's mind seized Oberman's words. She kicked the gun out of Juana's hand. It sailed over the side. Grabbing Davenport by the sleeve she yanked him over the railing with her, fearing shots in their wake. The water was cold and the skirt she wore hampered her kicking. Davenport was beside her, sputtering.

"Swim," he gasped. Short of air as he was she still sensed that he was calm.

Bullets pinged around them. They dove. Terror gripped Kate for the first time as the murky water closed over their heads. How deep would they have to go to be safe? How long could they stay down? Josh, oh Josh, please don't be dead.

Davenport was tugging her back toward the *Natasha*. No! she thought frantically, but she realized he was right. Rosen would expect them to swim for shore. They would never make it on one breath. In the shadow of the boat they might be able to come up for air safely.

Her hand touched the slimy hull. Lungs bursting, she sur-

faced. She tried to take deep breaths without gasping. Davenport bobbed up beside her. As the water drained from her ears
she heard more gunfire from above. Uncle Dimitri!

Rosen's voice floated down to them. "Forget it. The bastard's
done for. Juana'll live. Start the engines."

Dominique replied, the icy calm in her tone for once absent.
"But what about . . ."

"I'll find them. Just get ready to get us out of here!"

A sudden swell dunked them. Kate came up coughing. They
dove, but it was too late. From the shouting above Kate knew
they had been spotted. They had no choice now. They struck
out for shore. It seemed so far away, a blur she could see only
through a film of salt water.

The rumble of the *Natasha*'s engines reached them, drowning
out other noise. Then she heard the reverberation of a smaller
motor bearing down on them.

The *Natasha* still hadn't moved, Josh could see as he pounded
up to the dock. Dominique was at the rail, firing at something,
someone in the water.

"Stop, you fool," Rosen yelled. "We need him alive!" He
dove neatly into the water and came up beside the dinghies.
"Cast me off."

Josh saw two heads in the water then, one black, one blond.
Kate!

"Jesus, man, get down. Those bastards have guns," hissed
a voice.

Huddled in the speedboat were two frightened adolescent
faces. Josh ran to them, crouching low.

"Police," he said. "I'm taking your boat."

One of the boys handed over a key, his hand shaking. They
both crawled out and took cover behind the dock.

"Call the cops, call the Coast Guard," Josh ordered. "Now!"

They scampered up the sloping lawn and into the yellow
house, slamming the door behind them.

The speedboat was as well tuned as its gleaming paint job
indicated. The motor sprang to life, growling like a wild thing
eager to be off. He pushed the throttle forward and the beast
leaped ahead with a jolt.

As he swung the craft around he saw Rosen closing on Kate
and Davenport. The man stared at him in amazement. Both
boats accelerated. Dominique had spied Josh, too. She fired.

The bullet struck him in the left shoulder, knocking him backward. He turned and squeezed off an answering shot. A woman screamed. He thought it was Dominique, but the boat veered away from the *Natasha*. He couldn't see. He righted his course, gunned the motor, and headed straight for the dinghy, crouched low.

Rosen had no time to jump. Josh slammed into him broadside at close to fifty miles an hour. The dinghy disintegrated. Josh maneuvered a sharp turn and cut the motor to a soft purr. He searched the water anxiously for Kate. For some reason she was heading back to the *Natasha*, back to danger. Then he saw why. Oberman was there, sagged over the railing, gesturing her to return. Dominique's body floated facedown in the water, her hair spread out on the surface like an ivory fan. He felt no regrets.

A great weariness overcame him. His shoulder throbbed and he realized he was bleeding. His ears still rang, but he was suddenly aware of extraneous sounds, water lapping, sirens, gulls crying.

The ragged splashing of Rosen as he surfaced riveted Josh's attention. He was calm enough now to feel hate. The other man's stroke was feeble. One hand was crushed and bloody. Whatever other damage he might have suffered was under water.

"Help," he gurgled. "I'll drown."

Josh circled him slowly, like a shark.

"For God's sake, man, you can't let me drown."

"Why not?" Josh's tone was cold.

"You'll be no better than a murderer," Rosen gasped.

Did he think that was a threat to his decency, to his humanity, Josh wondered. Then Rosen knew very little about what he had become, about what Rosen and his kind had forced him to become.

"Tell me who tried to kill me—and my brother."

The Soviet agent sputtered and bobbed in the wake. "That was a mistake, I swear it. They weren't supposed to kill him."

"But they nearly did. On whose orders?"

"But it was a mistake!" Rosen was starting to panic now.

"On whose orders did they break into my brother's house!"

"Mine, mine. But I didn't order them to kill him. Now for God's sake let me aboard."

Slowly, slowly, Josh circled. There were shouts from shore, answering cries from the *Natasha*. He glanced up to see Kate waving frantically, one arm around Oberman, his around her. Tears streaked her cheeks. They were safe, he realized. He reached for some trace of emotion. There was none. He was cold, empty. It was all over except for him and Rosen.

The police had arrived. They wouldn't let Rosen drown. They would put him in jail, read him his rights, get him a lawyer, all nice and civil and civilized. Maybe one day they would exchange him. Along with the fear he now saw triumph on the Russian's face. Triumph and murder. He moved in.

Painfully Rosen hauled himself into the boat and lay gasping like a beached flounder.

Josh killed the motor. He realized then that in the collision he had lost the pistol.

"Take me to shore," Rosen said.

"The game's over," Josh said softly. "You lost."

He was ready when the knife came. He had known Rosen would try something. He had seen it in the man's ferret eyes.

Josh ducked and caught Rosen's one good hand with his one good hand. Locked in the struggle they thrashed for position in the bottom of the boat, their blood mingling.

Josh's grip was a vise, fastening Rosen's hand to the hilt of the knife. The long blade glinted in the failing sunlight. Slowly, slowly Josh forced the point toward the Russian's chest.

The determination on Rosen's face turned to fear, then terror, a terror that pumped adrenaline into Josh's system. Kate was watching, he realized. He could push harder. He could kill the son of a bitch. He could be one of them.

Rosen screamed as the cold steel pierced his flesh, but pain and loss of blood had weakened Josh.

Suddenly he heard a shot and Rosen went limp.

Josh fell back against the side of the boat, expecting the Russian to leap after him, pressing his advantage.

There was only stillness.

Josh struggled upright. Rosen lay against the opposite side of the craft. His eyes were blank. Josh and the boat and the body were covered with red. The dead man's face was a mask of disbelief.

"You didn't know I could play by your rules, did you?" Josh said.

He looked back at the *Natasha*. Oberman was lowering a pistol. Josh glanced at the knife in his hand. The blade was still shiny. Now we'll never know, he thought.

He felt consciousness ebbing and he welcomed the darkness.

Epilogue

Fall, afterward

When she sought tranquility Kate went to the mountains.

She had considered Maine, but it held too many memories. Besides, Uncle Dimitri needed solitude too, to mend and to receive old friends, now that his good name was restored.

The press still prowled her parents' ranch in Wyoming. She had had enough of the press, enough of the police and the FBI and a dozen other acronymic organizations.

So they fled to Colorado, to Steamboat Springs.

Kate gazed out over the hazy little valley from the balcony of their condominium. Fall touched the mountains. Here and there amid the evergreens was a patch of orange or yellow. But the wind that blew across her face was still warm, still fragrant. She was home.

Josh came up behind her and put his arms around her. "You got a letter from Veronica, pretty lady," he told her.

Kate rested against him. New York seemed so far away. "What did it say?"

"The board ousted Thrasher."

"Really?" She was hardly surprised.

"Mm-hmm. Publicly they said it was for health reasons. His nerves were shot."

Kate could not help but feel some sympathy for Thrasher. He was inept and under investigation by a federal grand jury, but in the final moments he had held fast.

"They want me to come back," Josh added. "They want both of us."

"Will you go?"

"I don't know. Veronica also says we got a message from our

281

old friend Martin. He's in Hong Kong and he nabbed that second shipment.''

Kate turned to face him. "No kidding! What was it?''

"Computer components for a cruise missile guidance system and a very advanced IBM mainframe originally designed for NASA.''

"Webb wasn't dealing in small change, was he?''

"Nope. Though I wonder if he ever knew what he was really handling for them.''

"Any news on Juana yet?''

"Yep. She pleaded guilty last week and was sentenced to twenty-five years. As she was the only conspirator left to go to trial, I guess the Soviets figured it was not in their best interests to have it drawn out. They want to play down their internal instability.''

Iraq had suddenly found itself bereft of aid from both the USSR and the U.S., and the effects of the GRU plot were still reverberating around the fragmenting Soviet Union. Only bits and pieces made the papers, whispers of purges in the Soviet military, of a tightening of the stranglehold the KGB had always had on Soviet society. She remembered what her Uncle Dimitri had said on that August day not so long ago: "Humanity has no place in the scramble for power.''

With a soft wind rustling through the pines and Josh's arms safe around her, the scramble for power seemed so distant now, Kate thought.

"Do you care?'' she asked.

He paused. "No,'' he said at last.

"Josh, tell me the truth: Would you have killed Rosen if Uncle Dimitri hadn't?''

He stared at her silently for a moment with eyes as blue as a clear mountain day. "I don't know, Kate. At that moment in time I wanted to kill him. I didn't have the strength left. If you're asking me if there will ever come a time when I'll kill again, I can't say. But I'm not a violent man, Kate.''

"No,'' she smiled. "You're a kind, decent, capable man who was backed into a corner.'' She sensed he needed confirmation of that and held him close. He hugged her in return.

"What are you going to do now?'' she asked.

He sighed and pulled back so he could look at her as he spoke. "I don't know. I kind of like it here, being out of the headlines. The papers in New York are still milking the story. Veronica sent clippings. But this morning's *Denver Post* had us